A KILLER COFFEE CC

BOOKS 7-9

HOLIDAY ROAST MORTEM

DEAD TO THE LAST DROP

FROTHY FOUL PLAY

BY

TONYA KAPPES

TONYA KAPPES

WEEKLY NEWSLETTER

Want a behind-the-scenes journey of me as a writer?
The ups and downs, new deals, book sales, giveaways and more? I share it all! Join the exclusive Southern Sleuths private group today! Go to www.patreon.-com/Tonyakappesbooks

As a special thank you for joining, you'll get an exclusive copy of my cross-over short story, *A CHARMING BLEND.* Go to Tonyakappes.com and click on subscribe at the top of the home page.

HOLIDAY ROAST MORTEM

A Killer Coffee Mystery

Book Seven

BY
TONYA KAPPES

ACKNOWLEDGMENTS

Thank you to the amazing readers who send in recipes to be included in the Killer Coffee Series.

Burnt Sugar Cake was submitted by Jeannie Daniel, Twinkie Cake was submitted by Robin Kyle, and Rich Potato Chowder was submitted by Chris Mayer. I've made all of them, and they are amazing! I hope you try them too. Be sure to let me know if you do!

I'd also like to thank Mariah Sinclair for the adorable covers for the Killer Coffee Mystery Series. They are so fun and Pepper makes the cover.

Thank you to Red Adept Editing for the wonderful editing job you do to make my words make sense.

And a huge thank you to my husband Eddy. He does all the things that would normally take me away from writing. Without him by my side, I'd not be able to be a full-time writer and fulfill my dream.

CHAPTER ONE

The twinkling Christmas lights that wrapped around the wooded deck of the Watershed Restaurant added a shimmer atop Lake Honey Springs. A nice romantic evening with Patrick was exactly what I needed to get into the spirit of the season.

Since I'd been working so many long holiday hours at the Bean Hive, my coffee shop, I'd been busy getting all the holiday coffee blends and special-ordered baked sweet treats ready for my customers, so I'd not taken much time for my relationship with my husband or our fur babies, Pepper and Sassy.

"You look beautiful." Patrick Cane reached over and laid his hand on mine.

Patrick's big brown eyes, tender smile, and sensitive heart drew me into him when we were just teenagers and I came to Honey Springs during the summers to visit my aunt. "I'm glad we made time for me and you."

"Me too." I put my other hand on top of his and rubbed it. I couldn't stop blushing. My heart skipped a beat.

Patrick owned Cane Construction, and the economy had been booming around our small town of Honey Springs, Kentucky, so he was just as busy as I had been at the coffee shop.

Neither of us were complaining because we certainly had seasons of dry spells in which the money just trickled in.

"Geez, buddy!" A man sitting next to us jumped up when the busboy accidentally knocked his table and spilled the man's water in his lap. "Watch what you're doing."

"Calm down, Ryan." The woman across from him had turned red, though she was trying to hide her face behind her blonde hair. She looked around the restaurant to see if anyone was watching.

Of course everyone could hear them. They were louder than the jazz band playing Christmas carols in the corner of the restaurant.

"Are you joking?" Ryan glared over at her and he quickly replaced the man's glass with another glass of water and apologized before hurrying away.

"No, I'm not joking," she spat. "You can be such a jerk. Things happen."

The man grabbed the glass and took a drink, glaring at the woman across from him before he went back to finishing his meal.

"That looks delicious." Patrick and I pulled back our hands so Fiona Rosone, our waitress, could put our plates on the table, taking the attention off the couple next to us.

Patrick's loving gaze had turned from me to the honey-glazed salmon on his plate.

I had ordered the panko-encrusted chicken, one of the Watershed's specials, along with a plain sweet potato and asparagus. I would definitely take some of the sweet potato home with me to give to Sassy and Pepper. Not only did they love it, but sweet potato was good for their digestion and their coats.

On most days, the dogs came to work with me, and I tried to keep an eye on them so customers wouldn't slip them something they'd ordered from the counter, but it was hard to police that. Plus, Pepper was a wonderful vacuum and sniffed out any little morsel of food.

"The babies?" Patrick's smile lit up his face when he noticed I was saving some of my food.

"Of course." I shrugged, knowing how much I treated them like real human babies. Having children was something Patrick and I did want, but it wasn't in the foreseeable future.

We'd only been married a year after many years apart, during which time I'd gone to college, attended law school, started a law firm with my now-ex-husband, and then moved here to open the Bean Hive. It took all that time to find the life I considered to be... well... perfect.

"It's so pretty here tonight." I looked out the window of the floating restaurant.

Logsdon Landscaping had done a fantastic job decorating. The Christmas tree on the outside deck glowed with colored lights and fun lake-themed ornaments. The Christmas trees inside the Watershed were decorated a little more elegantly, with white lights and fancy ornaments with glitter, large ribbons, and bows. Beside the tree outside sat a sign on a fancy gold stand declaring Logsdon Landscaping Co. the decorator.

Amy Logsdon had taken over the dying family landscaping business. When she did, she saw a need for people's help in decorating for all the seasons because we celebrated and decorated every holiday on the calendar. We'd even had our annual Christmas festival in the town square last weekend.

The Pawrade was still my favorite event of the entire festival. In the Pawrade, we dressed up our fur babies and raised money for the local Pet Palace, Honey Springs's local SPCA.

But what Amy did to turn the company around was amazing. She took the landscaping business to a whole other level. She took clients, like the Watershed, and completely decorated the exteriors and interiors of the buildings in addition to storing the decorations all year long instead of having the business try to find a place to store them. This part of Logsdon Landscaping focused primarily on the outside decorations. Some people had hired the company to come to their homes and put up their lights, their large yard displays, and more.

It really did help cut back on all the work the Beautification Committee had to do, freeing up their time to focus more on the business side of the festivals.

Focusing on that was a very nice option to have, but I loved to decorate and had made it part of my life, which helped me get so excited for the holidays.

"It is pretty." Patrick looked over the candlelight at me. "You make it prettier."

"We are already married. You can stop laying it on thick." I couldn't stop smiling.

Fiona knew us so well, she'd already brought a to-go box over to the table. She knew I needed the box so I could take home the dogs' portion.

"That was so good." Patrick pulled his wallet out of his pocket, took out the cash for the bill, and leaned back in his chair. "Now we can go home, snuggle with the kids by the fire for a few minutes before we decorate our tree."

"Heaven." Sometimes I couldn't believe I'd hit the jackpot in my thirties. In my twenties, it was a bumpy ride but worth every up and down it took to get to this moment right here. Plus, Patrick was such a romantic. He loved cutting down a live tree and decorating it. He had a full night planned, and I would definitely go along with it.

We smiled at each other before the couple next to us interrupted with their loud argument.

"I told you that I've had it." The woman pointed at the man with her steak knife. "I won't put up with this behavior anymore."

"Keep your voice down," the man shushed her. "When we got married, you knew exactly what you were getting into."

"I've had enough." She picked her napkin up from her lap and wiped her mouth. "After Christmas, I'm filing for divorce."

"Over my dead body." He threw his napkin on his plate.

"So be it." She slammed her napkin on the table, and water splashed out of her glass.

The scooting sounds of their chairs did cause others to look around, but since they were next to me and Patrick, I think we were the only ones who heard them arguing.

Patrick and I watched the couple rush out of the restaurant.

"I hope we don't ever get like that when we reach their age." Their sadness gnawed in my gut, and I couldn't help but wonder if they were once all goo-goo eyed like Patrick and I were.

"Never. Ever." He shook his head. "Unless Penny and Maxi stop getting along… then we might have a problem," he said, joking about the sudden friendship between my mom and aunt.

"I wouldn't be joking about them because they've already had a falling out this week about who was going to bring the fruitcake on Christmas." I let out a long sigh.

"You decide." Patrick thought it was as easy as that when it clearly wasn't.

You see, my mom, Penny Bloom, and my aunt Maxine Bloom had never gotten along in my entire life, until recently. My mom had been really jealous of my relationship with my aunt Maxi. And well… let's just say that I've always had a connection with my Aunt Maxi I'd never had with my mom, and when I got divorced, it was of course Aunt Maxi I'd run to. Here I was a few years later with some history under my belt, and my mom had moved to Honey Springs. She and Aunt Maxi were the reason Patrick and I were married by the justice of the peace.

"I've got enough people to coordinate without refereeing them." I was now rethinking my decision to host a big Christmas Day supper for my friends and family at the Bean Hive Coffee Shop.

My friends had become family in our small community, and I wanted them to surround me during the holidays. Everyone had something special to bring to the occasion, which would be a joyous one even if Mom and Aunt Maxi decided not to get along.

"Will that be all?" Fiona asked and picked up the check with the cash.

"Yes. Very good." Patrick leaned back and patted his stomach. "Keep the change."

"Delicious as always." It was a treat to come to the Watershed, and it took some effort to actually get dressed, put on makeup, and look presentable. Not like when I went to work at the coffee shop with my hair pulled up and my baking clothes on underneath my Bean Hive apron.

Patrick, being the southern gentleman he was, got up from his chair and walked over to help me out of mine.

"Let's get home and decorate our own tree." Patrick reached his hand out to me.

"Fire, snuggles, decorating." I took his hand in mine. "Patrick Cane, you are something else."

"I just want to keep you happy during this Christmas get-together." We walked toward the back of the restaurant so we could go outside to look at the decorations. "I know how stressed you can get, and if I can help out, I'm going to. So you"—he opened the door to the outside and had me walk past him—"my dear, will be pampered by me."

He pulled me to him once the door shut behind us and shielded me from the winter night wind, which whipped across the lake and over us, sending chills along my body.

Patrick stood behind me with his arms wrapped around me, and we looked across the lake to the Bee Farm, where Kayla and Andrew Noro had put up a big display of wood cutouts of bees wearing Santa hats. The display was all lit up so the people on the land side of the lake could see and enjoy it.

The Bee Farm was a small island in the middle of the lake. It was amazing to visit and see exactly how the bee farm worked. I got all my honey from Kayla. It was so fresh and tasty, not only in the coffees and teas I served at The Bean Hive but also in the baked goods.

"Everyone seems to be really ready for this season compared to last year." Patrick's warm breath tickled my ear. He rested his chin on my shoulder.

"Why did you mention that?" I jerked around and looked at him. "You are giving us bad juju."

Last year, a murder took place during the Pawrade at the annual Christmas tree lighting in Central Park, located in downtown Honey Springs. I wanted to forget that forever.

"It's not bad juju." He laughed and grabbed my hand. "Let's get home to the kids."

We were walking along the Watershed's pier toward the parking lot when we heard the same couple from inside the restaurant arguing outside near their truck.

"I'm telling you that I'm not going to stand for this. Do you understand?" Ryan yelled at the woman, who I assumed was his wife since he'd said something about how she knew before they got married this was how it was.

"You know what?" The woman jerked the door open. "I'm going to call a lawyer!"

The couple both slammed their doors. The tires squealed as their truck took off.

Patrick's grip tightened on my hand.

"I think that's Ryan Moore's truck." Patrick seemed to recognize people's vehicles more than their faces. "He owns the butcher shop where I pick up those steaks and chops you like so much."

"They seem very unhappy." I frowned.

"I don't think they are going to have a good Christmas." He opened the passenger-side door for me.

"Don't worry." I kissed him before I got in. "It took me a divorce to find you. I'm for sure not going to let you go."

I hooked my seatbelt while he got inside the truck.

The Watershed was on one far left side of the boardwalk, which held many specialty shops along with the Bean Hive.

My coffee shop had a perfect location right in the middle of all the shops. Directly in front of the coffee shop was a long pier that jutted out and was perfect for people who liked to fish deeper out into the water.

"I love how they put the lighted garland around all the carriage posts," Patrick said about all the lights along the boardwalk. "It's prettier than just the wreaths the committee has put up in past years."

"Yes, but the Beautification Committee did the best they could with what they had." I still had to give Loretta Bebe credit. She did work hard on trying to make Honey Springs gorgeous during the festive times of the year.

Our cabin was located about a seven-minute drive from the boardwalk, which was a very windy road running along the lake. I usually rode my bike with Pepper nestled in the front basket while Sassy went to work with Patrick at the construction sites for most of the day until he stopped in for a cup of coffee. That was when she liked to stay at the coffee shop with Pepper and me.

Lately, it was either too cold or there was too much ice on the road to ride the bike.

"Be careful," I warned Patrick when he took one of the sharper curves. "The weather report said there could be some black ice on the road."

The taillights of Ryan Moore's truck showed the vehicle had started to cross over the center line of the small road.

"There must be some up there." Patrick pointed at the car. We watched as the driver jerked the truck back over. "Whoa!"

"Oh no!" I yelled as we watched the truck cross over again, this time going through the trees and down the embankment toward the lake.

I eased up in the seat of Patrick's truck and looked down to see if the people in the truck were okay when we got to the place they'd gone off the road.

"Call 911!" Patrick yelled at me. He put his truck in park when we saw the other truck had actually gone into Lake Honey Springs, with the front end heading underwater.

I fumbled for my phone and dialed while trying to see Patrick through the pitch dark of night. The headlights of the sunken truck were fading fast into the depths of the water.

I rattled off the information to the dispatch operator and jumped out of the car when I saw Patrick had jumped into the lake. I grabbed the blankets and his work flashlight out from behind the seat and headed down to the lake.

"Patrick!" I screamed when I didn't see him come back up. "Patrick!" I frantically screamed, dropping the blankets on the beach and shining the flashlight in the water. "Patrick!"

I ran up and down where the truck had gone in, but I was not sure where it was because I could no longer see the headlights. When I heard some splashing a few yards out in the lake, I moved the flashlight and saw Patrick.

"I've got the woman!" Patrick swam toward the bank with the woman in the crock of his arm. She was coughing and wheezing. "She's alive!"

In the distance, I could hear the sirens. They echoed off the lake. I ran to meet Patrick and the woman, holding one of the blankets to wrap around her.

"I've got to go and get Mr. Moore." He laid her gently on her side on the ground before he went right back into the water.

"Here," I told her, picking up more blankets and then wrapping them around her. "Are you okay?" I asked.

She looked up at me.

"My husband," she tried to say but was shivering. "My husband!" She jumped up as the shock of it all started to set in. "Ryan!" she screamed.

"Please, put this around you until the ambulance gets here." I tried to put the blanket back on her shoulders, but she attempted to run back into the water. "Stop! Don't go back in there!"

"Ryan!" It was all she seemed to say while I jerked her back and literally held her back.

The ambulance and police showed up, taking over just as Patrick came back up from the depths of Lake Honey Springs with the limp man over his shoulder.

After Patrick got him to shore, we let the emergency crew take over.

"What happened?" Sheriff Spencer Shepard asked when he got there.

"I think they hit black ice because we saw them swerve, then correct, then swerve again, ending up in the lake," Patrick told Spencer while we stood to the side and watched the EMTs give Ryan CPR. "We saw them having supper at the Watershed. It's Ryan and Yvonne Moore. He owns the butcher shop in town."

"Yeah." Spencer's brows furrowed as he nodded.

The bright yellow lights of the tow truck circled, lighting up the darkness.

The people in the tow truck were working on retrieving the Moores' truck from the depths of the lake while the emergency workers continued to attend to Ryan.

"No!" Yvonne fell to the ground, lying on Ryan and grabbing our attention.

Spencer excused himself and hurried over to see what was going on. We watched as the emergency workers looked at Spencer and shook their heads.

"Oh no." I gasped, bringing my hand up to my mouth, knowing Ryan Moore was dead.

CHAPTER TWO

I sprang into action and headed straight over to Yvonne Moore. Though I didn't know her, I knew this was not what was expected. Of course I'd heard them arguing, but who didn't argue? We said things all the time that we really didn't mean, and I was sure this was what'd happened between this couple.

Yvonne had refused medical treatment, and I sat with her, letting her talk to me. Mostly she just rambled. I was sure she was still in shock. Since owning the Bean Hive, I'd learned how to be a really great listener. People loved to talk over a nice big cup of joe. The liquid was better than truth serum.

"What am I going to do?" Yvonne's eyes frantically searched my face like I had her answer.

"We are going to call someone for you. But first, we are going to go sit in Patrick's truck. It's too cold out here." I guided her to the truck and tried to watch out for anything she could step on so it didn't hurt her bare feet. "We can use my phone. Who would you like to call?" Once I got her in the passenger side of the truck, I held out my phone.

She pushed it away.

"I have no one." She looked out the windshield, nervously picking at her fingernails. "My mom lives with us. But she's elderly. She doesn't drive, so she can't come..."

"I'm so sorry." I rubbed her back, hoping to give her at least a little comfort. I just couldn't imagine if I didn't have anyone, and that was what her case seemed to be. I remembered the small bag of clothes Patrick kept behind his seat for the times when he was working in the rain or snow. "Your feet must be freezing."

I reached around the back of the seat and pulled the duffle bag over. I flipped on the interior light and unzipped the bag to take out the socks.

"Here, put these on," I told her, and she took them from me.

"Thank you. I slipped off my heels in the truck after we got in and..." She shook her head. The tears continued to pour. "Ryan always made fun of me because I never wore anything but heels. I don't even own a pair of tennis shoes, and here we are in a lake town with some hiking and outdoor things."

I listened to her ramble. It must've felt good to get it out.

"I can't stand gardening or any sort of outside work, so when I'm in the house, I like to go barefooted." She smiled, but then her expression faded to a frown, and more tears fell down her cheeks. "Ryan said he loved that about me, how I always kept myself always pristine. He had no problem hiring landscapers."

"Do you have any children?" I asked, hoping to figure out who I could call for her, though she said she had no one.

"No." She shook her head. "Just my mom."

We sat there in the dark, silent truck as we watched the workers take Ryan's body and put it into the hearse.

Spencer walked over and knocked on my window.

"Ma'am, I'm sorry about your husband." He was good at comforting people during times of loss. "I'm going to need to ask you a few questions if that's okay."

"Yes. Sure. Anything." Yvonne nodded.

"Can you tell me if you'd been drinking?" Spencer asked.

"No. We had left the Watershed and were driving home." She continued to shake her head and blink as though she were trying to remember something. "We had water, but while he was driving, I noticed he'd begun to slur his speech. He'd started shaking and gone over the line in the road when I asked him if he was okay. That's when it went from bad to worse. The truck veered off the road, and the next thing I remember is being pulled out of the water by that man." She pointed out the window at Patrick.

"Did your husband have any sort of medical condition?" Spencer was taking notes on his little notepad.

"No. He had his yearly physical back in October, and from what I recall, all the blood work came back normal and no other tests were scheduled." Yvonne wiped off a dripping tear. I reached over and patted her.

"What about drug use? Did your husband use recreational drugs?" His questioning made Yvonne jerk up. He'd definitely offended her.

"Absolutely not, and I will not let you say anything like that," she said immediately.

"I'm afraid there was a reason your husband drove off the road. If he was in good health, not drinking or doing any sort of recreational drugs, I'm going to have an autopsy done just so you'll know exactly what caused his death." Through Spencer's sly sheriff ways, I could tell he was trying to get her to agree to an autopsy. In the state of Kentucky, the law didn't ask for an autopsy unless they suspected foul play.

"Oh, okay." Yvonne shrugged. "Sure." She readily agreed.

If I was her lawyer, I'd tell her to take the night to think about the situation, but I wasn't, so I kept my lips sealed.

Not that I was still a practicing lawyer. I wasn't, but I did keep my credentials up and could practice if I wanted to. Still, although I never thought Yvonne did anything to her husband while they were in the car, I couldn't stop mentally replaying her and Ryan fighting not only in the Watershed but also in the parking lot. If I remembered correctly, there were a few "over my dead body" comments, and now he was dead. That was a red flag to me. Coincidence? Maybe.

Then it dawned on me. I bet Patrick told Spencer about the Moores' fight.

"Is there anyone we can call for you?" he asked, ending his questions because he was satisfied with her agreeing to the autopsy, which would answer any questions he might have.

"No one I can think of." She shivered.

"Patrick and I can take her home," I told Spencer. "She said her mother lives with her, so she won't be alone tonight."

"Is that all right, Mrs. Moore?" He looked through the truck at her.

"Yes. Of course." She eagerly nodded then looked at me with a pinched smile and grateful gleam in her eye before the sadness drew back over her.

Yvonne and I sat in silence as we waited for Patrick to finish talking to Spencer and the tow-truck driver. They'd yet to pull the truck out, but I really did think they were waiting until we took Yvonne home. It was something she probably shouldn't see.

"Mrs. Moore, I'm Patrick Cane. I guess you met my wife, Roxanne." He was so good about introductions when I'd never even told her my name.

"Roxy. You can call me Roxy," I told her, leaving out my usual, "my friends call me Roxy." I think this situation already called for us to be friends.

"I normally would say it's nice to meet you, but right now I really can't wrap my head around what's happened." She continued to stare out the window from the passenger side. I sat in between her and Patrick.

"You don't need to say anything." I continued to pat her. It was the only thing I knew to do to comfort her. Not that petting her like I did Pepper was any comfort, but I was at a loss here.

"If there's anything we can do for you, you just reach out to us." Again, Patrick always seemed to know the right things to say.

"Thank you. I guess they will let me know when they will release him so I can make arrangements." She started to sob all over again.

I just continued to pat her but glanced over at Patrick. The lights on the dashboard created enough light to see his eyes. They held sadness for Yvonne. We both felt it for her.

"I know where you live." Patrick took the winding road past our cabin and headed deeper into the wooded part of Honey Springs, where one found big farms and farmland. He was heading toward the Hill Orchard.

"Thank you," Yvonne whispered. She was trying to pull herself together. She shifted, sniffed, and tried to fix her hair, which had dried and left strands stuck to her face. "I just don't know what happened. One minute we were..." She stopped herself from talking, but I bet she was going to say "fussing." "It was like he just fell asleep. I bet it was a heart attack. Don't those take you pretty fast?"

"I have no medical knowledge." I wasn't going to say one thing or another. Fast or not fast, something happened to her husband. "The autopsy will bring the closure you need."

I wanted to say something about God's timing or things happening for a reason, but I didn't. I didn't think those words would make her feel any better, and getting her home to her mom was probably the best thing.

When Patrick pulled into the asphalt driveway that I'd driven by so many times and came up to the gate, I was a bit excited. While passing by this gate and driveway, I'd often wondered who lived there or what was back there.

"Can I help you?" A woman's voice came from the box on the post after Patrick pushed the button.

"Daryl, it's Yvonne. Please let us in." Before Yvonne got the entire sentence out, the gate started to open. "Please ignore the half Christmas lights. The company we hired won't have everything completed until the end of the week. Ryan loved Christmas and all the fanfare."

"Logsdon Landscaping?" I asked, though I already knew the answer because I'd seen their trucks pulling into the driveway when I'd driven past.

"Yes. I believe that's them. You use them?" she asked. "Ryan loves them. They do all our landscaping too."

"I don't use them, but I own a little coffee shop on the boardwalk, and they've done all the Christmas decorations for the Beautification Committee this year," I said and looked both ways going up the driveway.

I could see why Ryan had him do their landscaping. They had a lot of land. The massive red brick home was all lit up with spotlights, and the fountain in the circle drive didn't show any signs of freezing in the cold temperature as the carven swans spewed water.

"The Bean Hive?" Yvonne turned slightly and asked.

"Yes. You've been there?" I questioned.

"I have. Mostly at night when Ryan and I finish having dinner out..." Her voice trailed off again as if she'd just remembered what happened.

The house's door opened. Two women, one older and one younger, stood there.

Yvonne opened the door and got out. I slid over and followed her up to the door while Patrick stayed in the truck.

"Mom, Ryan..." Yvonne couldn't even finish her words before she collapsed.

"Yvonne!" The younger woman knelt and tried to help Yvonne.

Without even having to look, I heard Patrick's door slam and his footsteps racing up to help out.

"What is going on?" the old woman asked, tugging the shawl around her shoulders. Her hair was pulled up in a tight grey bun on the top of her head. "Who are you? Daryl, call the police."

Daryl was too busy trying to wake Yvonne up to so much as think about calling the police.

"Ma'am, I'm Patrick Cane, and this is my wife Roxanne. We saw your daughter and her husband's truck run off the road. Unfortunately, your son-in-law didn't make it. I did pull them both out of the water."

"Water? What do you mean didn't make it?" The older woman sounded as though she were searching for answers.

"If I can get Mrs. Moore inside, we will explain it all." He handed her a business card. "This is Sheriff Spencer Shepard's information. He asked me to give this to you since Mrs. Moore is not in any shape at this time to really comprehend what has happened to her and Mr. Moore."

"Get them in the house," Yvonne's mother said. Patrick picked up Yvonne, who regained consciousness, and Yvonne's mother gestured for Daryl to appear.

I'd like to say I was looking around at the house since this was my one chance, but I was so focused on poor Yvonne that I didn't even notice anything but the suede couch Patrick had laid her down on.

Daryl had come back with a tray of waters, giving Yvonne her own personal straw. We all sat down and watched Yvonne become increasingly aware. Patrick told her mom what had happened. He did leave out the part of us overhearing them argue, which was going to be our little secret.

Or so I thought.

CHAPTER THREE

Patrick and I stayed only about another half hour at the Moores' home. Yvonne had started recalling all the details, and we knew it was our time to leave. Both of us remained silent until we got home. I wasn't sure what Patrick was thinking, but I was thinking, *What if that was me?* and feeling really sad for Yvonne.

We had very little time for our previous plans of making a fire, doing a little decorating, and snuggling with the dogs after we got home. Instead we snuggled with the dogs in our bed. Patrick had no problem, as usual, going to sleep. I wasn't sure how he did it, but as soon as the covers were pulled up to his chin, he was out for the night, even after all the excitement we'd had.

I was a totally different story. So was Pepper. Pepper couldn't get situated. I couldn't get settled. Both of us just tossed and turned, taking a few sideways glances over at Sassy and Patrick, who were both out like lights.

"Okay," was all I had to whisper before Pepper jumped off the bed and I followed closely behind him.

Our home was a neat little cabin that I'd purchased when I moved to Honey Springs. Long story short, Patrick had ended up buying my Aunt Maxi's gorgeous home overlooking Lake Honey Springs. When we got married, one of the hardest decisions we had to make was where we were going to call home.

Of course, we both wanted to stay in our respective houses, and ultimately I won. The nice cozy feel of my cabin was perfect for the four of us. The cabin had a family-room-and-kitchen combo as you entered off the covered front porch, which, by the way, was across the street from the lake and had the most gorgeous view. Plus, the back side of the cabin was surrounded by the woods, making it very private. This time of the year, the leaves were already off the trees, and snow would arrive any day now, making the environment a beautiful winter wonderland.

The small kitchen was perfect for the cooking we did. So for this season of our life, the cabin was perfect. Plus, it was just a few minutes to get to the boardwalk.

There was no sense in waking up Patrick. He would know exactly where Pepper and I had gone when he woke up—the Bean Hive.

Since it was bitterly cold out and the morning sun had not even thought about waking up, I quickly got my things together, put Pepper's coat on him, put my own coat on, and headed out the door.

"It's gonna be a chilly one," I told Pepper on our way out. I fumbled with the keys to unlock the car door. Pepper eagerly jumped in the front seat. "We will have to keep the fire going all day."

Pepper wiggled around like he knew he was about to spend the day either on one of the coffee shop's couches or on his dog bed. Both were located in front of the fireplace. He was spoiled.

I couldn't help but slow way down when I passed the Moores' crash site. The torn-up ground where the tow truck had pulled Ryan Moore's truck out of the lake was still fresh.

Goosebumps crawled along my arm just thinking about what had taken place a few short hours ago. I gripped the wheel and made sure I took the curves super slow. Black ice was exactly that—ice on the road that was hard to detect because of the black asphalt. When your tires came into contact with black ice, you barely knew what hit you. I still couldn't help but wonder if the Moores had continued to argue in the truck and Ryan hadn't been paying full attention to the road when they slid. But I also remembered Yvonne saying Ryan had started to shake. Was it from anger? Then again, she was in shock, so I wasn't sure she knew what she was even talking about.

I pulled my car into the closest parking spot near the boat dock. Not many people would be here to take their boats out today in this frigid weather. As soon as I turned the car off, Pepper was already in my lap and waiting for me to open the door. He bolted out of the car, not waiting for me, as he did every day. Then he darted up the ramp of the boardwalk, where I'd meet him at the front door of the Bean Hive.

The boardwalk was safe, and I was already armed with pepper spray. Patrick had given it to me after I was subjected to an arson a year ago at my cabin. Someone had lit my Christmas tree on fire. But I tried to put those past situations in the back of my mind because I was moving forward and not living in the past.

Briefly, I stopped and looked at the display window of the first shop on the boardwalk. The store was Wild and Whimsy, the local antique shop owned by Beverly and Dan Teagarden. My eyes feasted on the Christmas display in the window. It was an antique table set for the holiday feast with festive wear and adorable mini light-up Christmas trees lined up in a row, along with wreaths tied on the back of each chair.

"I shouldn't've stopped," I said to myself and filled my head with ideas for the Christmas dinner I was hosting for family and friends at the Bean Hive.

The next shop was the Honey-Comb Salon, which reminded me I was in desperate need of a holiday trim. The Buzz In-and-Out Diner was next, and the small light on in the back of the diner told me they were getting ready to open in about an hour, so I hustled on down the boardwalk because I, too, had early customers and the coffee had to be turned on.

"Hey, buddy," I greeted Pepper at the door of the coffee shop. He jumped up, resting his front paws on the door like he was helping me with the key and turning the knob.

I ran my hand along the inside of the wall beside the door and flipped the light on while releasing a long sigh. It was my happy place, and coffee was my love language.

I peeled off my coat and hung it on the coat rack in the back of the shop where the counter was located. Then I picked up and donned my Bean Hive apron. I moved down the counter and flipped all the coffee and tea pots on to let them brew while I walked to the fireplace. Along the way I stopped at each table to make sure the afternoon high-school staff had fully stocked the condiments there. Your basics: sugars, creamer packets, honey, and various other things. I liked to use those little antique cow cream pourers with real cream from the Hill's dairy farm for each table, but I made sure it was fresh every morning.

With a little bit of kindling and some newspaper, I lit the fire on the first try. On my way back to the counter, I checked the self-serve coffee and tea bars to ensure they were ready to go for those customers who didn't want to wait in line and instead used the honor system by putting their payment in the jar. One aspect of my lawyer days had helped me open the shop—I believed in the honesty and innocence of people until proven guilty. No one seemed to cheat the honor system.

The coffee shop was perfect, and I was beyond thrilled with the exposed brick walls, wooden ceiling beams, and shiplap wall. I'd created the last myself out of plywood painted white to make it look like real shiplap.

Instead of investing in a fancy menu or even menu boards that attached to the wall, I'd bought four large chalkboards that hung down from the ceiling over the L-shaped glass countertop.

The first chalkboard menu hung over the pie counter and listed the pies and cookies with their prices. The second menu hung over the tortes and quiches. The third menu that appeared before the L-shaped counter listed the breakfast casseroles and drinks. Above the other counter, the chalkboard listed lunch options, including soups, and catering information.

Pepper sat next to his bowl, waiting eagerly for his morning scoop of kibble. After I filled his bowl, I pushed through the swinging door to the kitchen area of the coffee shop, where I liked to prepare weekly lunch items and bakery goods, even though there was now a bakery a couple of shops down where the tattoo parlor used to be.

With the oven turned on to preheat, I walked over to the freezer, where I pulled out the already prepared usual fare, like the various quiches, donuts, muffins and cookies. Today called for a comfort day since the death of Ryan Moore made me feel a little off.

"I'll make the burnt sugar cake." I smacked my hands together.

The burnt sugar cake was a long-time family recipe that included a lot of sugar, flour, butter, and cream, all the things that screamed comfort in a delicious piece of cake. I got out a few cake pans, since I would be making plenty for the entire week, and sat them down on the preparation station in the middle of the kitchen. I proceeded to the dry ingredient shelf first and then retrieved the wet ingredients from the refrigerator.

By the time I got all those items, the ovens had reached the desired temperature and I was able to get some of the frozen items in the oven to start baking.

"Good morning," I heard Bunny Bowoski call out from the coffee shop.

"I see you, Pepper," Mae Belle Donovan echoed.

Their interactions put a smile on my face. I loved how Mae Belle was such a best friend to Bunny. She was also in her eighties but wasn't employed by me. Still, Mae Belle came to the coffee shop with Bunny in the early hours when Bunny was the one to open, which was today.

Even though I wasn't due to come in until a little bit later, when I couldn't sleep, I usually got up and came on in.

Bunny was probably closer to eighty than not, but she was a regular with nothing to do. She made herself at home and ended up helping people while she was here. She was a great baker and loved to gossip, two things this coffee shop thrived on, so I hired her.

"What's wrong?" Bunny pushed through the swinging door with her heavy coat still on, her brown pocketbook in the crook of her elbow, and a hat parked on top of her grey chin-length hair. Mae Belle followed her.

They were always dressed similarly. Always had on some sort of coat and hat, but not just any hat. Today's choice was one of those little discs with netting around it. Something Bunny would've worn to woo men back in the day... after all, they were older.

"What do you mean, what's wrong?" I asked and sifted all the dry ingredients together.

"All my morning chores are done, and the coffee is already brewed. Plus, you weren't supposed to get here until eight. It's five-thirty." She looked past my shoulder and at the clock on the wall. "I'm opening."

Mae Belle gave me a quick hug before she waddled over to the small coffee pot we kept in the kitchen.

"There was bit of an emergency last night, and I couldn't sleep from thinking about it." Not that I was giving up some big secret. I was sure it'd be all over the news.

"Emergency?" She looked shocked.

"I heard something over the scanner last night about that wreck, but they were very vague." Mae Bell carefully sipped the hot coffee.

As I beat in the eggs, butter, and vanilla, I recapped to them what happened.

"Oh dear." Bunny's brows drew together, and she took her own cup of coffee and sat on one of the stools butted up to the counter next to Mae Belle. "I've been getting my meat from them for years. It's a shame he and Jo Beth haven't had a relationship since he married Yvonne."

"Jo Beth didn't care for none of his wives." Mae Belle's face squished like she smelled a skunk.

"Jo Beth?" I questioned.

"His daughter." Bunny took the bobby pins out of her hair and the hat off her head. "That's right, you didn't live here back then. Jo Beth was so mad when Yvonne came around. Said she was a gold digger." Mae Bell nodded. "But she still came around until Yvonne moved the mother in. From what I hear, that lady is my age and in real bad health."

"Bad health?" I questioned because I didn't think Yvonne's mom looked sickly, just a little slower than Bunny. They might have been the same age, if I recalled correctly.

"That's a shame." Bunny pushed off the counter and stood. "I sure hate to see anyone go to the grave and have disagreements left behind."

"He has a daughter?" I clearly remembered asking Yvonne if there were any children to call. She said no—just her.

"Jo Beth Moore." Bunny waddled back through the swinging door. "Ain't you listening? Come on Mae Belle."

I hurried and got the ingredients into a few of the pans. Then I stuck those in the oven so I could question Bunny and Mae Belle some more.

"I figured you'd be out here." Bunny had already gotten herself, Mae Belle, and me another cup of coffee. I followed them to the couches and sat down to warm up by the fire.

"I asked Yvonne if I could call someone. She said they had no one, and when I asked about kids, she said they didn't have any." I brought the cup of up my lips and took a nice drink.

Everything was better with coffee. Conversation. Friends. Food. And now figuring out the truth out about Yvonne.

"You know..." I hesitated to tell them but figured what the hell. "Patrick and

I actually saw them at the Watershed having dinner next to us. They were in a big fight. There were some not-so-nice things said."

I took a drink.

"Do tell." Bunny leaned in closer to me and drank some of her own coffee. Mae Belle nodded encouragement for me to continue.

"He mentioned something about how she knew this when they got married, and she said how she didn't like it, then he said something about over his dead body." I looked up over the rim at Bunny when I took another sip. "I completely forgot she mentioned something about not putting up with his behavior."

"You don't think..." Bunny hesitated this time, like she wanted me to finish her sentence.

"Somehow she made him crash? Or he drove into the lake on purpose?" I asked.

"Nah," we said at the same time and shook our heads right before the bell of the door dinged.

"Sheriff," Bunny looked over her shoulder. "You're not Looooowretta Bebe."

Bunny was referring to one of our most regular and early-bird clients, Loretta Bebe... "Low-retta," as Loretta would say in her big southern drawl.

"Let me grab you a coffee." Bunny got off the couch and headed over to the counter. "We was just talking about the big goings-on last night."

"That's why I'm here." Spencer threw a look at me. "Can I talk to you in private?"

Mae Belle's eyes shifted between Spencer and me.

As if on cue, the timers on the stove went off, signaling the first batch of frozen items was ready to be taken out of the oven, plated, and put into the glass displays for the customers.

"Here's your coffee." Bunny lifted the cup in the air and set it on the counter next to the cash register. "I'm going to get those out so you two can talk."

Spencer was all sorts of serious. I'd never seen him wait until someone left the room before he questioned me on anything.

"This seems very official." I got up from the couch and walked over to the coffee bar, where Spencer was doctoring up his coffee.

"I'm afraid the preliminary autopsy report on Ryan Moore came back." He slowly stirred the full creamer into his coffee.

"Oh, good. I bet Yvonne will be so happy to be able to make plans for the funeral." I tried to relieve the tension a little, but he was definitely tense.

"I'm afraid that won't be happening anytime soon." He slid his glance over to me. "I'm afraid the toxicology report came back with hemlock in his system."

"Hemlock?" My eyes narrowed. "Isn't it a bit cold and snowy for hemlock to grow?" I asked and looked out at the window as the snow, which was predicted, started to fall.

"That's what is so unusual and why I need to investigate a little more." Spencer took a sip of the hot coffee. "I'm afraid this was a homicide."

"Last night after I cleared the scene and got back to the department, I got a disturbing phone call from Jo Beth Moore." Spencer was giving me details that made me pause.

"His daughter?" I asked, trying to clarify what Bunny and Mae Belle had told me.

"Yes. One of the emergency responders is a close friend of hers, and they told her about her dad. I talked to her for a few minutes, and she told me how Yvonne and her dad had been fighting. She asked me to bring Yvonne in for questioning." He let out a long sigh, like he was gearing himself up to tell me something big. "I didn't think two things about it until I got the hemlock report."

"Wow." I blinked a few times. Suddenly my mind felt foggy. "I'm still trying to process the fact he was murdered."

"Who was murdered?" My aunt Maxi Bloom had used her landlord key to let herself in. She flipped the sign. "You're gonna be killed by the regulars if you don't get this place opened."

A few customers had apparently been waiting outside. I'd not realized it was already six a.m.

"Hold on," I told Spencer and hurried over to the swinging door. When I noticed the shoe shadow coming from underneath the door, I knew Bunny and Mae Belle had been listening to every word Spencer and I had said. "You can stop listening and fill the display counters," I told her through the door. "We've got customers."

Spencer took a seat at one of the tables while I ran up to a few people and some of the others took advantage of the self-serve bars, which was exactly what they were meant for.

"What is going on? What are those two hens listening in on?" Aunt Maxi glared at Bunny and Mae Belle. The three of them were the worst and best of friends. I just had to take them with a grain of salt.

"We was just talking about you frequenting the Moose." Mae Bell Donovan had a glint in her eye like she wanted to know what darn business Aunt Maxi had up her sleeve.

"What? Y'all the Moose police?" Aunt Maxi looked Bunny and Mae Bell up and down with an appraising eye. "Or are y'all trying to be my mother?"

"That's enough, ladies." I let out a dramatic sigh and gave Aunt Maxi the stink eye.

Aunt Maxi pulled off her sock cap and pushed the tips in her hair, making it stand to high heaven. Her hair was bright red, in contrast to the blonde color she was sporting a week ago. I'd like to think the cold weather had given her the rosy checks, but it hadn't. She'd put on a little too much makeup for my taste. She took her hobo bag off from across her body and dug deep in it before she pulled out a can of aerosol hairspray. "What's he talking 'bout? What murder?"

"Last night..." I told her about the accident, leaving out the part about the big fight Patrick and I'd seen the Moores have. "Now, Spencer said he was murdered."

"I bet it was that Jo Beth." Aunt Maxi shook the hairspray.

"You can't spray that in there." I'd told her a million times.

"My place. I can do what I want," she grumbled and pushed the button, letting the heavy hairspray keep her now-bright-red head of hair in place.

"If the health department came in here, you'd get me shut down," I warned her.

"I don't see no one." She looked around to prove the point and kept spraying.

I let out a long sigh.

"I told her the same thing," Bunny whispered on her way past us with some quiche hot out of the oven.

"Of course you did," Aunt Maxi said to Bunny in a sarcastic tone.

"I did, Maxine Bloom." Bunny nudged Mae Bell on her way past. "Didn't I?"

"Mae Belle is your best friend. Of course she's gonna take up for whatever it is your saying." Aunt Maxi rolled her eyes.

"*Ahem.*" Spencer cleared his throat and motioned me over.

"Here." I untied my apron and gave it to Aunt Maxi to put it on. "Wash your hands too."

She shrugged and went about waiting on customers, but not without giving them her two cents on what they were ordering. Aunt Maxi was her own woman, and she was proud of it.

"Why are you here to see me?" I asked Spencer the question I wanted to know most since he'd delivered the bombshell.

"Patrick had mentioned how the two of you overheard a fight between the Moores that was in the Watershed and carried over to the parking lot. Then you saw Ryan Moore swerve a few times before he careened off the road and into the lake. I wanted to get your account of it." He took out the small notepad from the inside pocket of his brown sheriff's jacket and set it down on the table in front of him.

"Roxanne!" Aunt Maxi called my name. When I looked up, she waved me over. "Hurry up!"

"Can she wait until you answer my question?" He shook his head, apparently somewhat fed up with the chaos going on in the coffee shop.

"You've come at a bad time. Is there any way I can come to the station?" I asked. "When it's not so busy?"

I was sure by the crowd already gathering at the coffee shop that word of Ryan's murder had gotten around. Every time a crime was committed in Honey Springs, the town folk loved to gather over coffee and gossip about it. And in the few mumblings I overheard, I'd heard Ryan's name mentioned.

"Fine. But I'm very serious, Roxy. I need your exact account of what happened or what you heard." He put his notepad back in his pocket and grabbed his coffee cup before he stood up.

"Promise. Today." I crisscrossed my heart with my finger and headed over to see what Aunt Maxi wanted.

"Hey, do you mind running over to All About the Details and making sure Babette remembers Christmas Day supper?" I wouldn't have time to remind everyone we'd invited, and Aunt Maxi loved making her rounds to all the shops on the boardwalk, so giving her this job to do was perfect.

"Roxy," a woman gushed from underneath a heavy scarf around her head and large sunglasses, taking my attention away from Aunt Maxi. "I'm so thankful for you."

"Oh. That's exactly why I opened the Bean Hive." I smiled at the woman, figuring she was complimenting me on the coffee shop. "I love coffee so much, and I wanted others to feel the same way."

"No." Aunt Maxi smacked my arm. "This is Yvonne Moore under that get-up."

Yvonne took her glasses off her face, and I recognized the eyes but not the dried version of herself.

"I'm so sorry. I didn't recognize you without wet clothes and it being dark, since it was nighttime." My brows made a V shape. "How are you this morning?"

"Well, it's why I'm here. Can we talk?" she asked, putting her glasses back on her face.

"Of course you two can—in the back." Aunt Maxi took the liberty of answering for me. "Bunny, you and Mae Belle stay out of the kitchen." She wagged a finger at them.

"Sure." I nodded. "Let's go back where we can talk." I motioned for Yvonne to follow me. "How can I help you?" I asked once we were away from the prying ears of the elderly gossip queens.

"It appears my husband was poisoned." She pulled the scarf off her head and the glasses off her face, exposing a beautiful complexion and not one wrinkle. Her hair was much blonder than I'd remembered and styled straight, free of bangs and parted down the middle. She definitely didn't look like the woman from last night.

"I heard it was hemlock poisoning." I didn't wait for her to tell me.

"Is that what the sheriff told you?" she asked. "I couldn't help but see he was here when I came in to see you."

"I'm sorry." I glanced over at the timer just as it went off and walked over to get the items out to place them on the cooling racks. I listened to her while I did my chores.

"I'm afraid the sheriff came over early this morning, and he mentioned how the couple who had found us overheard me and Ryan fussing all night."

"Yes. I didn't mention it last night because it didn't seem relevant." Then I looked over at her, and my jaw dropped.

"Yes. I can see by the look on your face that you must know the sheriff thinks I killed Ryan." She tugged off her gloves. "Ridiculous." She placed them on the workstation along with the scarf and sunglasses.

"I'm sorry." It was all I could say. Then I offered her a piece of the burnt sugar cake, hot out of the oven. "There's no need to thank me."

It wasn't very clear why she was here.

"If you'll excuse me, I need to get these out there and help out." I tried to make my own getaway, but she put her hand out to stop me. "The morning rush can be brutal."

"I heard you were a lawyer, and I want to hire you. It appears as though they want me to come in for formal questioning, and I need someone on my side. You were so helpful last night…" Her voice cracked. Tears gathered in her eyes. "I just don't have anyone to turn to. The company lawyers are his family's lawyers, and well…" She hesitated. "They don't care for me too much. Said I was a gold digger just because I'm fifteen years younger than Ryan."

"I… I'd love to." I had no idea why I agreed. The words just came right out of my mouth.

"Thank you!" She gasped and clapped her hands over her mouth, and then she threw them around my neck. "You were a lifesaver last night and now."

CHAPTER FOUR

"A lifesaver?" Leslie Roarke, the owner of Crooked Cat Book Store a few shops down from me, asked after I'd inquired about any hemlock-related books she might be carrying. She looked up at me and pushed her kinky copper hair out of the way. She opened the jar next to the computer, took out a dog treat, and gave it to Pepper.

"Yeah." I flipped through another book on deadly poisons, scanning the pages for anything involving hemlock. I was careful not to spill the coffee cup I'd brought with me. I'd also brought one for Leslie.

"Have you told Spencer you're going to represent her?" Leslie asked and clicked away on the reference computer that stored the shop's book inventory.

"No. I haven't." I took a deep breath. I loved the smell of bound books almost as much as I loved the smell of freshly brewed coffee.

The Crooked Cat Bookstore just so happened to be my very favorite bookstore on the boardwalk. It was one of the shops at which I had the fondest summer memories. Aunt Maxi would drop me off first thing in the morning, and I was so excited to hang out with Alexis Roarke for the day. She did her work while I sat in the beanbag chair in the display window.

Alexis was Leslie's mother. Unfortunately, Alexis had succumbed to an early death, leaving Leslie the bookshop. Not everyone was a "Leslie fan," but she was kind to me and Pepper.

Crooked Cat was still just as I remembered. The beanbags had been replaced by newer ones. The brick fireplace in the middle was still the focal point, surrounded by comfy chairs and big rugs. The dark shelves seemed to go on for miles and miles with beautiful books lined up. The children's section had small furniture and a puppet stage with a big sign that listed the times of the next puppet shows.

In the back of the store was my favorite section of all, the banned books. Aunt Maxi always said that Alexis liked to cause problems when it came to banned books and loved to let everyone know to buy the banned books first. I remember Alexis had a big stamp that read Banned, and she stamped each book on the inside along with a smiley face.

"I think I have some other books in the back," she called out as she walked to the back of the store, where the office and some storage were located.

Pepper and I made our way back through the bookstore. I took my time.

The bell over the bookstore dinged.

"There you are. Bunny said you'd be down here." Louise Carlton walked in with an animal carrier. "I wanted to drop off this gorgeous angora rabbit we got in over the weekend. She's going to make someone's Christmas very happy. She's the only animal that didn't get adopted during the Pawrade."

"Oh no." I sighed deeply and looked at my friend.

Louise was the owner of Pet Palace. After I'd gotten Pepper, I knew I wanted to help in some sort of way, and volunteering on Sunday nights just wasn't enough. It took a lot of paperwork, but somehow, I got my wish. I'd like to say it happened because I was a great lawyer, but honestly, I think Aunt Maxi could sweet-talk the lips off a hog, so the health department allowed me to have animals in the shop portion of the coffee shop. It was a big secret that I let Pepper in the kitchen with me.

Pepper immediately ran up to the front of the bookshop because he loved Louise just as much as I did.

"How much longer are you going to be?" she asked and slid her eyes to the back of the bookstore when Leslie came back out.

The two women looked at each other, giving what I called the Baptist nod. The courteous smile and slight nod were just a polite southern way of acknowledging someone who wasn't quite your favorite person.

These two women didn't see eye to eye. Their grievance was in the past, and I wished they'd left it there, but they hadn't.

"I'll be down there in a few minutes, but Aunt Maxi is there." I took the book Leslie handed me. "If you want to let her do the intake, that'd be great."

The deal Louise and I had was pretty cool. I was able to feature one animal from the Pet Palace each week. It was great because people who might be potential forever-homes for our furry friends could interact with the animals and see how they'd get along. Coffee and animals, perfect in my eyes.

There was some paperwork that had to be completed along with the animals' records and cute photos we liked to put next to the register. We also kept a donation jar for the Pet Palace there, since the Pet Palace did run on donations.

"Fine." Louise's silver bob swung, and the bangled bracelets underneath her coat sleeve could be heard. Louise loved to wear all sorts of jewelry. "Call me when you get a chance."

"I will." I peeked in at the bunny, who was happily munching on some food. "Awww. How gorgeous."

I could see Leslie rocking back and forth as though she were trying to see the bunny.

"Would you like a peek?" I asked her.

"No." She shook her head and went back to busying herself at the computer.

After Louise left, I headed over to register to pay for my stack of books on hemlock.

"You know, a bunny would be amazing for the bookstore." I saw the total come up on the register, and I shrugged and took my money out of my pocket. "Just think how cute the Santa photos would be with a bunny in there too. Or even the Easter Bunny photos."

"Don't you have some reading to do, Roxy Bloom?" She held the bag of books over the counter. I took them. "If you find another book online you'd like to have, let me know."

"I will." I patted my leg. "Let's go, Pepper."

I stopped at the door and zipped up my coat, giving Pepper one last opportunity to get some good patting in from some of the customers in the bookshop. "Don't forget Christmas Day dinner at the coffee shop," I reminded her before Pepper and I headed back down the boardwalk. We went not only to drop off the books but to meet Yvonne Moore at the station.

At least, I'd planned to do that until I walked into the Bean Hive. There, in the very place I'd escaped my previous life, did my previous life stand in front of me with a cup of coffee in his hand.

"Kirk?" I nearly flung the bag of books at him. Just the sheer sight of my ex-husband made my stomach sour, and no amount of coffee would help that.

"You look fantastic." He hurried over to me and took the book bag.

I let him take the bag, and I unzipped my coat, unraveling the scarf from around my neck, really restraining myself from wrapping it around his neck and choking the life out of him.

"Hemlock." He'd opened the bag and read the title of one of the books. "Does this have to do with Ryan Moore? Are you representing his wife?"

I simply pressed my lips together. My past with Kirk seemed like another life.

"I thought I told you a couple of years ago that I didn't want to see you again." I held up my ring finger. "I'm a married woman now."

"To him?" Kirk asked with a tone of disgust.

"Yeah. Him." I pushed past him and grabbed my bag back while Aunt Maxi glared at him. "I've forgiven you for the crappy marriage we had where you cheated on me with our client."

The images of him giving a lawyer consult, which wasn't the type of consult I thought he was giving the night he phoned to tell me he was going to come home late, were still stuck in my head after I'd decided to take him supper after I got his call. The consulting he was doing was an altogether different type of consulting from what we even offered... if y'all know what I mean.

"But I still haven't forgiven you for what you did to Patrick when he came to visit me in college." I hung the bag of books and my jacket on the coat rack and took the apron from Aunt Maxi.

"I tried to kick him out." Aunt Maxi couldn't stand the sight of him either.

"It all seems to have worked out now." Kirk drew his hands out in front of him. "You've got the coffee shop you've always wanted and your sassy aunt."

"I've had it." Aunt Maxi pushed up her sleeves like she was going to do some sort of boxing.

"Settle down." I put my hand out to her. "We do have to thank him for me being here."

Granted, it was Kirk I had to thank for pushing me over the edge with his affair and running off to Honey Springs, where Aunt Maxi had encouraged me to open the Bean Hive. I still couldn't help but wonder what would've happened if he'd not run into Patrick on our college campus when Patrick had come to see me and professed his undying love… maybe not undying, but it made for a good story. Still, on that day, Patrick had written me off forever after Kirk told him I wanted nothing to do with him and Kirk was my man. Patrick, being the southern gentleman he was, left campus, and I didn't see him until the day I came back to Honey Springs… broken.

"What do you want?" I put my hands on the counter and leaned over.

"I was going to ask you a few questions about Ryan Moore, but in light of the books you've purchased, I now have a lot of questions." He held up the black briefcase I'd given him with his name embossed on the front. The briefcase was so expensive, and I gave it to him when we were graduating from law school. I was drowning in debt but used what little credit was left on my American Express card to buy it for him as a graduation gift.

"Like what?" I wondered how he knew about Ryan Moore. "Are you some ambulance chaser now?"

"Don't be ridiculous, Roxanne." Kirk loved to call me Roxanne when he thought I was being a child. "I'm in town to talk to the witnesses of my clients' sudden death, which we now know was murder."

"Client?" He had my attention.

"Clients," he corrected me. "Ryan and Jo Beth Moore."

"By reason of deduction, I'm thinking Yvonne Moore has called you for legal advice." Kirk might've been a big jerk, but he was a good lawyer.

"Coffee?" I asked, using the "you can get more with honey than vinegar" approach my Aunt Maxi always chirped about.

The right side of his mouth rose in a little grin. He knew all too well how to get my attention when it came to court cases. We might not have made a great couple, but we did make a great partnership in the courtroom.

"You know how I like it." He pointed with the briefcase to a two-top café table near the fireplace. "I'll meet you right over there."

Turning around, I grabbed two white ceramic mugs off the open shelf and stuck them under the industrial carafes. I filled mine to the top and his halfway.

"What is this about?" Aunt Maxi sidled up next to me with the stink eye.

"Jo Beth Moore called him." That was odd, since he didn't even live in our area. "He knows something about Ryan Moore, and he's willing to give it to me."

"There's a catch." Aunt Maxi wagged a finger. "You know it, and I know it."

"Yep." I grabbed both cups by the handles. "I'm going to find out over coffee."

CHAPTER FIVE

It took a lot of deep breathing and slow steps across the coffee shop even to bring myself to look at Kirk as if he had something I wanted to hear. I just wanted to fling the hot coffee all over him, which would bring me a lot of satisfaction.

Able to control myself, I sat the cup in front of him and pushed the condiments toward him. Then I eased down in the chair across from him while I watched him ruin the perfectly good cup of coffee by adding the sugar, creamer, and honey. Didn't he know he could buy a latte with all that in it?

"That was a long sigh." He slowly stirred his coffee and smiled from across the table. "You just really hate me. So you really aren't over me."

"Don't be ridiculous." Honestly, I had no idea he could even hear the internal groans coming from me. "I'm still mad about the lies you told Patrick before you and I were even engaged."

"Listen, I'm not here to rehash old times. Trust me." He picked up the cup and took a sip. "Man, you do make a good roast."

"Stop beating around the bush. What do you want, Kirk?" I asked, not needing the chitchat. I had to get to the station. "I'm busy."

"Busy trying to defend a client that is one hundred percent guilty of killing her husband?" He was using his manipulative ways with me as he carefully crafted his words and slowly took out some file from his briefcase.

"Don't be all professional on me." I glared at him and opened the file he'd pushed across the table. "I know all your little manipulative tricks."

With evident great satisfaction, he sat back in the chair, crossed an ankle on the opposite knee, and picked up his coffee.

"Go on. Read it." He gave that smile I wanted to smack off his face. I'd seen him do it when he knew he had the opposing lawyers in a chokehold they couldn't get out of.

I opened the file and quickly scanned down through it.

"You did Ryan Moore's will?" I asked. "How on earth did he get hooked up with you?"

"More importantly, did you see where all of his money goes to Jo Beth?" he questioned.

"It's not even signed." I shut the file and stuck it back on the table.

"He was signing it today. Convenient for your client to have killed him." He dragged the file back and stuck it in his briefcase. "And we are pursuing murder charges."

"Ridiculous." I scoffed. "She was devastated last night."

So I might've left out that she'd come in to see me this morning.

"Is it?" He leaned up and drummed his fingers on the table. "From what I've read in the police report, you heard them arguing twice, and you saw them go off the road."

"That doesn't make her a killer." I was confident in my statement.

"No, but when you think about it, what did Ryan Moore mean when he said how Yvonne knew this was how it was going to be when she married him?" Kirk grinned. "I have several recorded phone conversations and a videotaped conversation with Ryan Moore on why he wanted to change his will."

"Why did he want to change his will to a daughter who never spoke to him and hadn't in years?" I was willing to play his game. It was still early in the investigation, and I wanted to see his hand.

"Simple. Grandchild. Jo Beth Moore is pregnant, and after she revealed it to her father and Yvonne Moore, he contacted me and told me all about it." Kirk ran his finger around the rim of the cup. "That's when I had him come into the office and tape his wishes. Then I drew up the will and had it ready for our appointment today."

I gulped. Kirk did have a sudden case against Yvonne, and it would take some of my amateur sleuthing skills to help figure out why Ryan would even do such a thing. Part of his estate, maybe, but the whole thing going to a daughter who didn't care for his wife—that was fishy.

The bell over the coffee shop dinged. To buy some time to let what Kirk had said sink in, I looked up to see who it was and caught Patrick's stare. His eyes lowered when he saw I was sitting with Kirk. It didn't take two seconds for Sassy to sniff me out. She came running over and stood next to me.

"Whoa!" Kirk put his hands in the air when the big standard poodle turned around and snarled at him in a way that showed a little teeth.

"No, Sassy." I put my hand on her head. "Be a good girl," I snapped. She sat down.

"Here you go, Patrick. A piece of burnt sugar cake for my favorite nephew." Aunt Maxi showed her love for Patrick in an over-the-top way just to make Kirk uncomfortable. She must've seen Patrick coming in from the outside and had a nice big Red Velvet Crunchie for him. "They are so good today. I think Roxy did an excellent job. She loves you so much."

"What are you doing here?" Patrick took the plate from Aunt Maxi but quickly set it down on a table. He kept his eye on Kirk. "I thought I made it perfectly clear a couple of years ago that you weren't welcome in Honey Springs or the Bean Hive."

"I'm here to help your wife and you about my client's untimely death since you were witnesses." Kirk stood up, and memories of the last time these two stood toe-to-toe flooded back like a nightmare.

"You're nuts if you think I'm going to talk to you." Patrick's shoulders drew back, and his chest popped out.

"Stop it." I jumped up and planted myself between them. "We will talk to you after we are subpoenaed to do so."

"Don't say I didn't try to warn you, Roxy." Kirk didn't bother looking at me. He kept his eye on Patrick.

"Roxanne," I corrected him. "Only my friends call me Roxy."

As Kirk made his way to the entrance, Patrick hollered, "Cane! Roxanne Cane!"

Kirk turned around and gave me one last look before he bolted out of the door into the frigid air. A cold chill swept across the floor and crept along my skin, forming goosebumps. These goosebumps went clear to the bone, giving me pause.

I'd love to say that Patrick was happy with me taking Yvonne Moore on as a client, but he wasn't. After Kirk had left the Bean Hive, Patrick asked me a million questions about why I needed to do that. "Let the law take care of it" was his take.

"I am part of the law," I told him and took the apron off so I could go to the station. "I might be crazy, but I told her I would come down there with her."

"Does Spencer know?" Patrick asked.

"No." I zipped up my coat and looked over at the dogs' bowls to make sure they had water. Sassy and Pepper had gotten in their beds and were asleep right next to the bunny's cage Louise had left.

"He's going to tell you it's a conflict of interest. And look what happened last time you put your nose into a murder." Patrick didn't need to remind me.

"It's fine. I'm looking into it for her and making sure the police do a thorough job." I made it sound so professional and avoided going all in, but now that Kirk was here, I wanted to go up against him, even though I knew I had a tough road ahead of me.

"It's fine that she never mentioned the daughter?" He looked at me with furrowed brows.

"Did you know about Jo Beth?" It suddenly hit me that Patrick probably knew all about the Moore family.

"Of course I did, and she was shocked. I never figured she'd leave out the stepdaughter." Patrick shook his head. "There's something really bad that makes this whole thing stink."

"I'm not disagreeing with that, so I'm just looking into it after I go give my statement." I tried to bring his worried face to ease. "You told Spencer about the fight at the restaurant and how Ryan mentioned 'you knew this before we got married,' didn't you?"

I wanted to be armed because I was certain that was how Kirk had read the reports.

"Yeah. I told them everything. Now the guy was poisoned. Be careful with Yvonne," he warned. "There was a lot of stuff going on about her. Gold digger stuff."

I didn't even ask him what it was because I knew if the public already thought that about her *and* the will was being switched to the future grandbaby, then it certainly didn't look good that Ryan had shown up poisoned. It definitely made Yvonne look guilty, and it was my job to find other suspects.

"I'll be fine." I looked over my shoulder at Bunny. She was making more coffee and cleaning down the counter since the breakfast rush was over. "Will you be okay until lunch?"

"I'll be fine, honey." She winked and shooed me out along with Aunt Maxi and Patrick.

CHAPTER SIX

"You're honestly going to take her on as a client?" Patrick asked me.

Patrick and I weaved in and out of the crowd as we made our way to the parking lot. Sassy and Pepper ran ahead of us.

The boardwalk was filled with holiday shoppers and people taking photos next to the photo booth the Beautification Committee had rented. A photo with the backdrop of Lake Honey Springs was a fun souvenir for tourists to take home along with all the decorations from the Logsdon Landscaping Company.

"I'm going to see what she has to say." There was not a definitive yes or no for me. "In light of her lying to us about children and the fact Ryan changed his will… well… let's just say I will need her to clarify a lot of things before I commit to representing her if it does go to trial."

"Right here at Christmas?" Patrick asked.

"It's not going to take any time away from Christmas," I assured him. "Look!" I pointed at the air. "Snowflakes."

"We still need to decorate our tree." Patrick walked me to my car. "Can we please do it tonight?"

My mind shifted from murder to Christmas. Instantly, I felt much lighter.

"Be sure to remind any of our friends about Christmas Day dinner," I told him.

"I will." He put his arm around me when we stopped at my car. "I know you have that curiosity button on about Ryan and Yvonne, but please don't be late coming home tonight."

Curiosity was my greatest vice.

"Right now I'm going to go to the sheriff's department to give Spencer my account of things and see Yvonne, finish up at the Bean Hive, and then come right home." When I went to give him a kiss, he had a strange look on his face. "What?"

"I don't know. I guess I'm all flustered about Kirk showing up." Patrick played with a couple of my curls. "I saw you two, and it just threw me for a loop."

"Patrick Cane." I held my ring finger in the air. "I'm all yours, whether you like it or not."

I threw my arms around his neck and gave him the biggest kiss, one that must have left him with no doubts about who my man was and always would be... outside of Pepper of course.

I waited until he had the dogs in his truck before I pulled out of the parking lot and headed to downtown Honey Springs.

The boardwalk was only about a three-minute drive to town, seven if it were any other season and I could ride my bike. The cozy town was so charming, and with the revitalization of the boardwalk, Honey Springs had flourished into a great community.

The first building when you drove into the downtown area was the Honey Springs Church, where you could pretty much find every single citizen of Honey Springs on Sunday morning. Next to the church were the firehouse and police station, where I was going. Across the street from that was the Moose Lodge, which stood before the big circle in the middle of town. This circle was known as Central Park.

Along Main Street were the Brandt's Fill 'er Up, Klessinger Realty, the courthouse and its adjoining city hall, Donald's Barber Shop, and the local community college. Other shops around Central Park twinkled with Christmas lights and window displays of all things holiday.

When I pulled up to the front of the sheriff's department, Yvonne Moore was already standing next to the door, waiting for me. This time I wasn't fooled by the big sunglasses.

"I was afraid you changed your mind," Yvonne eagerly greeted me.

"Why would I do that?" I looked at her. "Maybe because my ex-husband is going to represent Jo Beth Moore with the new will your husband had him make up along with video footage of Ryan telling Kirk what he intended. Or the fact that there is a daughter when you clearly told me last night you had no children." I sucked in a deep breath. I could see the information all hit her at once. "Let's get one thing straight." I held up a finger. "I expect any potential client to be one hundred percent truthful with me. There are no excuses. No little lies here and there. I maintain that a lie, no matter how big or small, is a lie."

"I didn't lie to you. I don't have children. You asked if I had any children you could call. Why would I tell you to call Jo Beth when she's not been around and she knew once she was pregnant that Ryan would change his will? So she got pregnant by a disgruntled employee who knew that Ryan wanted to pass the company down and decided to conspire with Jo Beth to make our life a living hell."

Her words fell over me like a weighted blanket.

"I'm sorry," I quickly apologized and realized Kirk showing up out of the blue had a greater impact than I'd thought it had. "I haven't even gotten to hear your side of things. Why don't we walk over to the gazebo in Central Park and talk before we go in there?"

She nodded, tightening the scarf around her neck.

"Let's start from the beginning. Give me a brief history on your relationship with Ryan and the Moore family." The span of time was very broad but would give me a good sense of how they lived their lives.

"It's no secret I was a kitchen utensil company rep that had Honey Springs for my territory. I sold directly to Ryan. Things like butcher knives, meat slicers, more industrial-type equipment butchers use. He made me laugh. He was charming." Yvonne smiled. It was the first time I'd seen her do it, and it was refreshing.

We crossed Main Street and walked over to Central Park. The stroll over there was actually nice, with the snowflakes fluttering around, the lights strung along the fence around the park, and the gazebo decorated with the town Christmas tree.

She continued, "He didn't want children. I didn't want children. I moved in with him. I thought Jo Beth and I would be great friends. From what Ryan had told me, she was amazing. Girly thing. I had no idea she wasn't going to accept me until I met her, and when Ryan left the room after he'd introduced us, she let me know just how much she'd make my life a living you-know-what."

"Why would she do that?" I asked and took the lead to sit on one of the benches in the park.

"I asked Ryan the exact same question. He immediately called her up and asked her. He never told me what she said. The only thing he told me was if Jo ever had children, he'd leave his fortune to them." She sat down, her knees toward me. "I was fine with that. I had no idea he was even worth that much when I was selling to him."

"He married you anyway? Even though his daughter was against it?" I had to question this because I knew Kirk would be all over the relationship between his client and mine.

"Ryan thought she'd come around." She shook her head. "She never did. It's a shame too. He loved her, but as soon as she got pregnant, she showed up at the door."

"Tell me about it." I wanted all the details about Jo Beth and how she sounded so vindictive, which could be a clear motive to have killed her father. "And the father of the baby."

"Gio Porto is his name. He was Ryan's best butcher. Ryan claimed Gio was buying low-quality meat, and Gio said he wasn't. People got sick. Ryan fired him. Ryan came home one night and said that he found Gio and Jo Beth in his office, rummaging through his desk." Yvonne gnawed on her bottom lip and watched the tourists walk by the tree, stopping for selfies. "They had words. Ryan came home with a black eye. I told him to call the police. He was about to, but Jo Beth showed up at the door. That's when Jo told us she and Gio were an item and she was pregnant."

"So she's a few months pregnant?" I asked.

"Apparently. Ryan told me at dinner at the Watershed how he'd gone to see a lawyer outside of Honey Springs. Kirk something." She snapped her fingers as if trying to remember. "He's bound and determined to keep his promise to Jo after all of these years."

"What promise was that?" I asked for clarification.

"He wasn't there for her as a father, and before me he'd really tried hard to make amends with her. He promised her he'd leave the company to her and her children, signing over the company when she was pregnant."

"Go on." Yvonne's story only made me think Gio and Jo Beth had a great motive to have killed Ryan.

I had found a case of revenge *and* murder at once.

"Ryan said he was going to go the next morning, today, and sign off on the will to change the company. That was the argument you overheard us having. It wasn't that I didn't want him to keep his promise, just put something in place to guarantee the child got the company when the child was of age and maybe went to business college. Something that kept the kid accountable. Ryan wouldn't hear of it." She picked at her gloves. "He said he'd be the child's mentor." She closed her eyes and brought her hand to her head. "Now he's dead. I don't understand."

"I know this is hard for you to even consider, but do you think Jo got pregnant by Gio on purpose? Not only because she knew the agreement but also to sock it to him that the baby's father is someone Ryan fired and got beat up by?" I looked over and put a hand on her.

"I..." She gulped. "I guess it's possible. But..." She blinked. Tears rolled down her face. She looked like she just couldn't believe Jo could be this vindictive.

"I'm sorry, but I have to ask." It was a question I'd hated to ask my other defense clients when I was a full-time lawyer. "Did you kill Ryan?"

"No!" she blurted.

"Do you have any access to hemlock?" I knew this was an odd question considering hemlock didn't grow in the winter.

"I don't even know what hemlock looks like, much less know anything about how to poison someone with it."

But where did I start? Who would know about flowers?

All About the Details!

Babette Cliff, the owner of All About the Details, would know everything about flowers, since she was the only event planner in Honey Springs and did every single event. Surely, she'd come across hemlock before.

"I'm going to call Spencer Shepard and tell him that I will represent you on any sort of interrogation." She looked slightly relieved when I said it.

"What if they charge me with murder?" she asked.

"Let's take it day by day." I didn't want to make a full commitment. I wasn't sure Yvonne was what Aunt Maxi would call, and I quote, "playing with a full deck of cards." I'd yet to get a good reading on her and was still somewhat leery about some of the vague answers she'd given me.

"I'm going to tell him that we will be in tomorrow morning to give your statement. You go home and don't talk to anyone. Understand?"

"Yes." She nodded.

"Do not answer the door or the phone. No one." I made myself very clear. "In the meantime, do you recall anything strange the night of the murder? Where he'd gotten hemlock in his food or drink? Or on his skin?"

I'd not been able to figure out this hemlock poisoning part and how it could happen. Nor had I had any time to read the books I'd gotten from Crooked Cat, but I planned on keeping my head in those books until I understood everything I could absorb about the plant.

"Ryan said he was starving and couldn't wait to eat at the Watershed. He didn't even have his before-dinner cocktail," she recalled.

"I can go over to the Watershed and question them. I do know your waitress, Fiona." I was trying to fit all of this in my schedule for today. The better prepared I was to see Spencer with her in the morning, the better her chances of getting off that suspect list.

"We also had a guy. He was terrible. He even spilled Ryan's water all over him." She laughed.

"Wait." I smacked my hands together. They stung from being cold. "I remember him. I remember that happening. I can question him too. I'd like to get a list of your house staff, and if you have an employee list for the butcher shop, I'd like that too."

I stood up.

"Sure. You can have full access to Ryan's home office." She stood up. "You can have anything I have access to."

"That'd be great." I hugged her, knowing it was probably not a client-appropriate thing to do, but she needed one. "I'll be in touch later today."

"Okay." She hurried across the street. I watched her get into her car and drive off.

"What was that?" Spencer walked out of the station. "I have been sitting in here watching you two have a powwow and expecting you to come in, and she takes off."

"I can't give you a statement from me." I knew he was going to flip.

"Why not?" He asked.

"I'm not stupid. I know you suspect Yvonne did it, but I'm not so sure. That's why I agreed to represent her during her interrogation. We will be here in the morning." I had to get my P's and Q's ready with this hemlock discovery and didn't know enough to have brought her in for questioning today.

"Geez, Roxy." He ran his hands through his hair before he wiped them down his face. "You've got to be kidding me." His hot breath mixed with the cold temperature, letting steam roll out.

"I'll see you in the morning with my client." I wasn't going to divulge anything.

Nor would I wait for Spencer to process what I'd told him, and I certainly knew this wasn't the last time I'd hear from him.

Now I was determined, and All About the Details was my first stop.

CHAPTER SEVEN

The Christmas Carolers were strolling around and singing some festive carols in harmony when I got back to the boardwalk. Even though we were a destination lake town, many families and couples had come to love Honey Springs for the year-around cabins that were available to rent. Today those tourists were out and about, going in and out of the shops on the boardwalk, which were great for those last-minute gifts they needed for Christmas.

The snowflakes were still batting about with a few peeks of sun here and there appearing through the small cracks in the grey winter clouds. It was getting colder, making the snow stick and creating the cozy Christmas feeling I loved.

I'd stopped into the Bean Hive to get a little treat and coffee for Babette.

"Any news?" Aunt Maxi asked after I walked into the kitchen, where she had taken the liberty to make more burnt sugar cake using my recipe.

Bunny was at the front helping customers.

"I'm going to help Yvonne out during her interrogation. She sure does appear to be the number-one suspect, though I might have a couple more to add to my list." I grabbed a to-go box and cut a couple of slices of one of the cakes on the cooling rack.

"I want you to stick it to Kirk." Aunt Maxi stopped the mixer and walked over to the counter, where she pulled out one of the dry-erase boards we sometimes used for daily specials.

I watched her write "victim," "suspects," and "motive" like she'd done before when we stuck our noses in different investigations.

"Who are they?" She was referring to my comment that I had a few more names to add to the list besides Yvonne.

I laughed and shook my head as I closed the to-go box. I loved how we pretended to be mini-sleuths.

"Gio, the disgruntled employee who Ryan had fired and just so happens to be the father of Jo Beth's baby."

Aunt Maxi jerked her head up.

"Good." She wrote everything down and circled "baby."

"We also have Jo Beth."

"His own daughter? I know they didn't get along, but his own daughter?" she asked again with disbelief.

"Oh yeah. If she got pregnant on purpose with Gio's baby, she'd obviously stop at nothing to get back at her father." I held up two fingers. "Revenge and money."

I could see Aunt Maxi's wheels turning and her eyes shifting over all the things she'd written on the wipe-off board.

"Where are you going?" she asked.

"To find out more about hemlock." I grabbed the box and two cups of coffee to go in a carrier.

"I'll keep figuring on this." She tapped the board with her finger.

Now that we had a couple of other people to look into, I needed to know more about hemlock. Babette Cliff was my go-to gal.

"It looks like I'm in time for a little morning snack," I said to Babette when I walked into All About the Details with a couple of slices of burnt sugar cake and two coffee cups.

"You're a lifesaver." She was sitting on one of the white couches in the large open entryway of the event planning store.

When you walked in her store, it was like literally walking into a cozy home. Even though there were gray concrete floors, the store had a big cream shag carpet under a coffee table and folded-up quilts on the edge of the other white couch. There was even a large kitchen-style table with table settings at each chair like you'd have in your home.

Beyond the sitting area and homey feel was a large event area with several tables and a stage in the front. Many events were hosted here. In fact, Babette was going to host a big party called After the New Year for the entire community.

The concept was to have a big party after the holidays and the turnover of the new year during which time, as a community, we could start the year off right. She looked like she was knee-deep into planning it.

"It's good and hot too. I just picked it up on my way over." I set the coffee and treat on the coffee table.

"Thank you." She uncurled her leg from underneath her and reached over to grab the cup. "Planning my own event is more stressful than anything I've ever done."

"I'm sure it's going to be perfect." I couldn't help but notice some of the drawings she'd sketched out. "But I totally understand, which reminds me—you are coming for Christmas Day supper, right?"

I pinched off a piece of the burnt sugar cake and popped it into my mouth.

"Yes. I'm looking forward to it. I can't wait to spend the day with my friends." She sank her teeth into the sweet treat. "Delicious." She picked up the coffee and took a sip. "Oh dear. A little caramel?"

"My Jingle Bell Blend." I always loved coming up with new coffee blends for the holidays. Christmas was so much fun because there were so many flavors to play off and use. "I wanted to pick your brain about something."

"Oh yeah?" She eased back into the couch cushions and held the cup in both hands.

"Hemlock. What do you know about it?" I asked.

"You know the little white flowers along the Lake Honey Springs going past your cabin? Kinda looks like Queen Ann's Lace or maybe baby's breath?" she asked, and I nodded. "That's actually hemlock. It's all over Kentucky, but I know the city really tries to make sure the transportation department mows it down or at least tries to destroy it. But it's hard, so making the public aware of the difference is a life-or-death situation."

"Is it still poisonous if it's dried or dead?" I asked since it was winter and everything on the banks looked to be dead and brown or covered in snow.

"Sure. It's poisonous no matter what form." She narrowed her eyes. "Does this have to do with Ryan Moore? I heard someone saying he was thought to have been poisoned."

"Yes." I gave her a quick rundown on how Patrick and I had found the Moores in the lake. I included a little background on why I was asking about the hemlock, leaving out any details that were within client confidentiality. "Somehow Ryan got something with hemlock in it."

"The plant itself produces over one thousand seeds, and someone can keep those seeds. Most of the farms around here check almost daily for any signs of hemlock because the seeds get mixed into the grass and cause a lot of animal deaths." She took a drink. "It's a pretty horrific death, from what I've heard. People who have been poisoned go into convulsions. They have a lot of saliva."

"I need to check the Moore property for hemlock," I said and noticed the look on Babette's face. "What?"

"I know you're not from here, but from what I remember, Yvonne was not welcome into the family, and I heard he'd changed his will, giving her nothing. I can see her doing it," she said.

"Aunt Maxi?" I asked with a cocked brow.

Babette smiled from behind her coffee cup.

"Thank you for answering my questions about hemlock. I have a stack of books to look through, but I knew you'd give me a good start." I got up from the couch. Sassy and Pepper popped up from the shag rug. "I'll see you on Christmas Day. Let's go," I told the fur babies.

There were a few people on my list to see, and that included Jo Beth, who would wait until after lunch.

Since the Bean Hive was truly a coffee shop and food paired well with coffee, I did offer a light lunch, but those who wanted something bigger could go to the diner on the boardwalk. I only offered simple things like soups, hashes, and casseroles that were easy to make. Whatever I made was the only lunch item the entire week.

I had about fifteen minutes until the lunchtime crowd started to come in for about a two-hour period, and I was happy to see Bunny had already changed the chalkboard to reflect the weekly lunch special, which was potato chowder. Just thinking about it made my mouth water.

"How's it going?" I asked Bunny, who was holding the cute rabbit Louise had dropped off.

"This cutie has gotten a lot of attention. I don't think she's used to it." Bunny pulled a carrot out of the pocket of her apron.

"Maybe someone will take her quickly." I used two fingers to rub down the bunny's head. She jerked her head up, sniffing my fingers.

"Any news on the murder?" Bunny asked. She put the rabbit back in the cage before she followed me through the swinging door to the kitchen. She picked up a book from the counter and handed it to me.

Inside was a Post-it Note from Lesley at the Crooked Cat. The book, which she'd found in the back, was all about the effects of hemlock poisoning and how much was needed to get into the body's system until it killed.

"I think Lesley really likes the rabbit." Bunny smiled. "So tell me what you found out about the murder." She looked over at the whiteboard Aunt Maxi had started.

I glanced over her shoulder at it.

"There's only one person who can really clarify a lot of this," I told her.

"Jo Beth?" She questioned.

"Mmmhmmm," I hummed. "I think I'll just go see Jo Beth myself." The ding over the coffee shop door signaled a customer. "You grab the bread for the soup special, and I'll go see who it is," I told Bunny. She looked comfortable sitting in the chair, and sometimes I worried about her age and if she was working too much.

I rubbed my hands clean on my apron and pushed through the door. Aunt Maxi was helping herself to a piece of quiche.

"It's just you." I walked over, and on my way I grabbed a plate and handed it to her. "Use a plate and enjoy."

"I'm good." She tried to push the plate out of the way, but I insisted. "I wanted to tell you that I heard something about a girlfriend while I was snooping around," she said.

"Girlfriend? What are you talking about?" I asked and poured us a couple of cups of coffee. I had a few minutes before the lunch rush would start. "Let's go watch the snowflakes."

We walked up to the long bar that was the length of the front of the coffee shop. There were stools all lined up so customers could sit there and look out the window at the gorgeous lake or just get some natural light while they read.

"Ryan's girlfriend." Aunt Maxi's words hit me like a lead pipe. "He's been fooling around, and I heard Yvonne had threatened to leave him. Just found out about it a couple nights ago."

"Really?" I asked. "I met with Yvonne a couple hours ago, and she never mentioned a word about it. She made it seem like the entire thing pointed to his daughter getting pregnant by a disgruntled employee—though she did comment to him that she wasn't going to put up with his behavior anymore."

"Yvonne Moore has been pretty proactive in trying to clear her name instead of being a grieving widow." Aunt Maxi was right. "Think about it. She has this public argument with him. They have a car crash because he was poisoned by hemlock."

I needed to find out exactly how long that had to be in your system before you died. It was on the list.

"She showed up here immediately after the sheriff told her Ryan was poisoned, not accusing her of it. She's trying to get a leg up, and maybe she did do it." Aunt Maxi just had to put that in my head.

"That's why I have to find Jo Beth. I think she has a lot of answers to my questions," I said, confirming my next step.

"I know Jo Beth pretty well. When I taught Sunday school, she was in my class." Aunt Maxi finished off the last bit of the quiche and put the fork down on the plate. "Plus, she's cleaning a rental for me today."

She grinned at me. We both looked over our shoulders when we heard Bunny come in from the kitchen. She held the ceramic bowl that fit inside one of the many Crock-Pots I had already lined up behind the counter. My idea was to put the potato chowder in those pots so we didn't have to keep going back into the kitchen whenever someone ordered it.

"I called her a few hours ago, figuring you were going to need to talk to her if you wanted to represent Yvonne but more importantly to stick it to Kirk." Aunt Maxi picked at the edges of her hair, getting it to stand up even higher. She pushed her plate for me to take.

"Your legs broke?" I teased.

"You sassin' me?" She wagged a finger.

"Of course not." I laughed and stood up to take her plate to be washed. "You're going to take me to see her?"

"Nope." She shook her head. "I'll help Bunny out here."

"I don't need your help," Bunny called out. "Whenever you offer to help me, you get me in more trouble than is worth it."

Bunny and Aunt Maxi had never been the best of friends, but at least they weren't at each other's throats like they had been when I moved to Honey Springs.

"I'm still staying." Aunt Maxi winked.

"Don't you dare make my employee mad." As I kissed Aunt Maxi on the head, a few customers came in. "Good afternoon," I greeted them. "Take a seat anywhere. I'll put this plate away and grab a couple of menus."

"Sit by the fire with a bowl of Roxy's potato chowder," Aunt Maxi suggested to the couple. "It'll warm your bones right up."

CHAPTER EIGHT

Jo Beth just so happened to be cleaning a house in the downtown neighborhood. Since the boardwalk was on the way home, I left the dogs at the coffee shop and planned to pick them up on my way home.

"Hello!" I hollered into the house when I opened the door. I heard a vacuum running. "Jo Beth?" I called out louder.

I stood there for a few seconds and realized she couldn't hear me. I took my boots off and stepped into the hallway.

"Jo Beth?" I called toward the noise of the sweeper. When she didn't answer, I walked back into the bedroom, where Jo Beth was bebopping to some music through her headphones while she vacuumed.

"Ah!" She screamed and dropped the handle when she saw me. "Who are you?" She reached down and grabbed the vacuum handle again.

"I'm sorry I scared you. I did call out," I quickly tried to explain as I watched her pick up the vacuum like she was going to use it as a weapon. "I'm Maxine Bloom's niece."

"You got my money?" she asked. Her long black hair was covered with a handkerchief neatly tied around her head. She wore a pair of overalls and Converse tennis shoes.

"Money?" I questioned.

"She owes me for cleaning today." She put the vacuum handle down and her hands in her pockets, making the jean material taut over her pregnant belly.

"Yeah. How much does she owe you?" I could get out some cash from my car if it would break the ice.

"One hundred for today. Don't stiff me. I've got to pay my lawyer. So I'll be done in a few minutes. I vacuum last." She went to flip the vacuum back on.

"I'm not here to pay you, but I've got the money. I'm actually here to talk to you about your dad." Her eyes questioned me. "In full disclosure, I'm looking into things for Yvonne."

"Kirk told me you might come see me." Her eyes narrowed. "Get out."

"Listen, either you can answer my questions now, or I can dig up all sorts of dirt and drag it through the court. I simply want a few questions answered." I had no idea what kind of dirt she had, but I was pretty good at reading people, and she looked like she had a full past she kept swept under the rug. "Is Kirk representing you?"

"He's representing my father." She effectively opened the door for me to ask some questions. "No matter what Yvonne told you, she only married my dad for his money."

"I know you say that, but your father told her your children would inherit the company. What I think they questioned was the father of the baby." She glared at me. "I'm not saying you and Gio don't love each other, but I do think it's possible you got pregnant by him not only for you to get back at your father for marrying Yvonne but for Gio to get back at your father for firing him."

"You have some nerve." I couldn't miss the flare in her temper. "You have no idea how much I helped my father with his company—and for him to discard me when he got married, not to mention Gio. My dad claimed Gio was buying low-quality meat because Yvonne's mother got sick after eating some beef Dad had brought home."

She picked up a few of the cleaning supplies that were on the floor and put them in the bucket.

"If anything, I thought this baby was going to bring me and my father closer after Yvonne had taken him from me." She looked at me. "I love my dad, even though he could never be faithful to my mom or Yvonne."

"Are you saying your father was having an affair?" I asked, since Aunt Maxi had mentioned the idea and now so was Jo Beth.

"Of course he was. That's why he really fired Gio." She shook her head. "Gio caught Dad and his mistress in his office one late night. The meat-truck driver had called and told Gio he was running late. It was Gio's job to check the inventory. He was a manager and had his own key. He said he went to put the invoice in Dad's office, and that's when he found Dad and Abigail."

"Abigail?" I asked.

"Abigail Porter." Jo Beth's brow rose.

I gulped. I still couldn't help but get a gut check when it came to Yvonne and the possibility that she wasn't disclosing the truth.

"Did Yvonne know about the affair?" I asked.

"I don't know. Gio and I didn't tell her. But from that point on, Dad kept close tabs on Gio and made sure to document any little thing Gio did wrong or not the way Dad liked it." She unplugged the vacuum and rolled up the cord.

"Let me help you." I picked up the vacuum when I noticed she was starting to clean up her things.

"Thanks. I'm going to put them in the car." She seemed like a nice girl to me. A little lost and rightfully so, since she'd just lost her dad. "But you know, even though Sheriff Spencer Shepard cleared me and Gio, I still think he thinks I did it."

"You talked to Sheriff Shepard?" I asked.

"Yvonne didn't even call me about my dad. A friend of mine did from the squad." Her voice cracked. "She didn't even have the decency to call me."

That was another gut punch I was trying to get over. Though Yvonne had told me why she didn't tell me about Jo Beth because she wasn't her daughter, she still should've called her.

"My dad and I met for lunch the other day. He gave me the name of the lawyer and his phone number so when the lawyer called, I'd take the phone call. I knew Dad was working it out so my baby and I had a future. Yvonne had no clue what Dad was coming up with. She actually gave him the idea to be my mentor and my baby's. Now I think she's screwed it up by killing him." Jo Beth's eyes filled with tears. "Granted, there were a lot of things I didn't do right when I was growing up and people I wasn't the nicest to, but my dad always helped me see better in people. He might've been upset with Gio and rightfully fired him if Gio had ordered the low-grade meat, but Dad was willing to give him another chance because I love Gio."

I knew it was an awkward time to even bring up the subject, but we were limited in our time together.

"You don't think Gio killed your father?"

"What benefit would that have?" she asked with furrowed brows as a tear rolled down her face. "Dad was going to give Gio another chance, and Gio knew it. Besides, Gio knows that if I ever found out anyone did anything to my father, they'd be cut from my life as well. Gio was very excited about the baby and our future before my father's murder. We were together on the night of my dad's death."

"Your dad was poisoned, so it could've happened over a period of time." Then it hit me. Who on earth did Ryan Moore hang around with the day of his murder?

I had no idea, but I had seen with my own eyes Ryan Moore eating at the Watershed.

Suddenly, I had the urge to grab an afternoon cocktail at the Watershed bar.

CHAPTER NINE

"Uh-oh." Fiona's reaction was pretty priceless when she saw me walk into the bar of the Watershed. Her black hair was down from the normal low ponytail she wore when she was waitressing. "There must be something wrong if you're coming in here in the afternoon."

"What?" I winked and pushed back a strand of my curly hair. "Can't a gal get a drink when she wants one?"

"Coffee?" Fiona laughed.

"I'm afraid you know me all too well." I sat down in front of her and watched as she carefully twirled one of the glasses around the dish towel to dry it.

"I know of a great little coffee shop just down the boardwalk that serves one hundred times better coffee than that old coffee pot back there." She nodded behind her and picked up a beer mug from the dishwasher caddy to dry. "You might've heard about it. The Bean Hive."

"Yeah." I played along. "I went there once. Meh." I shrugged, laughing. "Actually, I wanted to ask you a few questions about the other night when Patrick and I were eating supper."

"The same night the Moores were here?" She put the glass and the towel down and leaned her hip on the bar. "Spencer Shepard was in here earlier asking the same thing. What gives?"

"I'm sure he told you Ryan Moore's death has been ruled a homicide." I waited for her to confirm with her head gesture. "He was poisoned."

"Really?" Her jaw dropped, and her eyes flew open. "No wonder Spencer asked for the receipts when I couldn't remember what they ordered. And he was insistent on making sure I recalled if they'd had cocktails. The Moores never drink. Only water." Her chin slowly turned, and she twisted her head away from me, her eyes narrowed. "What's it to you?" she asked.

"I'm going to be looking into things for Yvonne Moore." I waited for her to respond. Exercising this kind of patience was a trait taught in law school. Actually, it was very important for lawyers to be able to sit, listen, watch, and see how people responded. Now that I'd told Fiona what I had to do with the situation, I hoped she'd start talking.

"I told Shepard they didn't order anything off menu or that had to be made special. No drinks. Just water." She looked over when a customer walked in the bar. "Hey, Jimmy. Your usual?"

The customer, Jimmy, who she obviously knew, gave her a quick yep.

"What about the waitstaff that night?" I asked and watched her grab a small cocktail glass and pour in a four-finger bourbon, no ice.

"Usual." She walked the drink down to Jimmy and came right back.

"No one new?" I asked.

"Nope. I'm the manager for the waitstaff and bussers. I haven't hired anyone new in months." She pulled out a binder from behind the counter and thumbed through it. "Here is the staff a couple of nights ago."

She flipped the binder around. I scanned down the page and noticed the waitstaff's phone numbers were next to their names.

"Can I get a copy of this?" I asked after I noticed the only guy on the page was Pat Frisk. He had to be the busser who'd spilled the water all over Ryan Moore. Bussers were great at listening, and I couldn't help but wonder if Pat had overheard some of the low-whispering fighting the Moores were doing that night.

"Why?" she asked, as she should have.

"I would like to talk to all of them to see if they heard or saw anything. Every little detail is important." It was true. I'd found in past cases how the smallest of clues gave way to the biggest cracks in cases.

"Sure." She took the binder. "I'll be right back."

While she went to make me a copy, I grabbed one of the hemlock books out of my crossbody and flipped to the index in the back. I drew my finger down until I came to the poisoning section, then flipped directly to that chapter.

"What'cha reading?" Fiona asked and slid the copy of the binder next to me.

"Hemlock. Ryan was poisoned from hemlock." My words made her shudder.

"This time of the year?" she asked in a troubled voice. "Hemlock doesn't grow in the winter, especially with snow on the ground."

I turned to look out the window. The snowflakes that had been dancing about in the wind had turned to much larger ones that were sticking to the ground.

"Someone has access to hemlock, and I've got to find out who," I told her and read out loud. "According to this book, hemlock poisoning can take place over days. Or, if in a large dose, it can take six hours."

"I grew up on a farm outside of the lake and hemlock grew all over. My daddy spent half the summer trying to get rid of it before our cows ate it and died." She let out a long sigh. "My brother ate some once, and I'll never forget it."

"What happened?" I asked.

"My parents had rushed him to the hospital and had his stomach pumped out. He was sick for days after that." She frowned as the memory came back to her. "That's the year my mama made my daddy sell the farm. And the beginning of the end of their marriage."

"Gosh. I'm so sorry." I was saddened to see the somber look in her eyes.

"It's all good." She grabbed the bourbon bottle by the neck and a shot glass on her way back down to fill Jimmy's glass.

Fiona must've had a deep hurt that she felt the need to cover up. She filled up Jimmy's glass, the shot glass, and they clinked them in the air before sucking down the brown liquid.

I picked up the piece of paper, stuck it in the hemlock book, and then stuck both in my crossbody. I got off the stool.

"Thanks, Fiona," I called when I passed her and Jimmy.

"No problem. I hope I helped." She offered a smile.

I took my time walking over the metal bridge between the water and land that led to the Watershed. Since it was a floating restaurant, the bridge or a boat was the only way to get to it. I pulled up the edges of my coat around my neck before I grabbed on to the rails. The temperature was below freezing, making the wet snow turn into patches of ice.

Once I got to my car in the parking lot, I decided not to go back to the Bean Hive. Bunny would already be gone and the afternoon help would be there. I'd assess the roads from here to my cabin to make the call if we needed to close down. The staff was my number-one concern, and I certainly didn't want them to drive on icy and dangerous roads.

It was nice to pass a few salt trucks, though I did take it really slow. The roads weren't covered in ice like I'd anticipated them to be. Plus, I'd flipped on the radio station just in time for a weather update. The roads would be icy overnight once the temperatures dropped even more.

After I pulled into my driveway, I grabbed my cell phone and texted one of the afternoon employees to let her know to close early if we only had stragglers coming in. Since there were no planned activities on the boardwalk tonight, I figured the tourists would be nestled in their rented cabins or the Cocoon.

There was nothing better than the smell of a real fire. When I got out of the car, I could not only see the smoke coming from the cabin chimney but smell it. I couldn't help but smile. The freshly fallen snow lay perfect on the roof of the cabin, and the lights from inside glowed.

"I'm home," I sang when I opened the door. Pepper and Sassy ran over to me. Before even taking my coat off, I bent down to let them smother me with kisses.

"Why am I always the last one and get the leftover smooches?" Patrick asked. He was standing in the kitchen with one of my aprons on. He did not care that it was one with lipsticks and lips printed all over it. "Supper is almost ready."

"You're amazing." I unzipped my coat and hung it on the coatrack. I took off my shoes and headed straight over to kiss my husband. "Looks delicious."

"I thought I'd go by Moore's Butchery and get us some chops so I could pan-fry them." They were sizzling in the pan, and the crust Patrick had dragged them in was starting to brown. "Go warm up by the fire and tell me what you found out today."

Patrick's attitude had really changed from a year ago. The first time I'd stuck my nose into one of the sheriff's investigations, Patrick had practically forbidden it. Now he was good at accepting me for me and knew he had to come to love that part of me. It was a part that I'd grown into when we were apart those ten years.

"I'm not even sure how to start." I walked over to the potbelly stove. The window in the door where you put the wood glowed red from the fire inside. On the counter was a bowl of freshly made popcorn that Patrick had already popped for us to make garland.

I sat on the hearth and picked up the needle, thread, and bowl. I carefully strung the needle as I told him about how I'd gotten the list of employees working at the Watershed from Fiona.

Not only had Patrick finished cooking supper, he'd set the café-style table and lit the candle in the middle. Sassy and Pepper had snuggled up on the couch while we ate.

"It was so sad to see her recall how her own brother being poisoned by eating hemlock had led to her parents' divorce." I told him about Fiona's situation. "Very sad."

"Well, I did find out some things." Patrick picked up the wine glass and took a sip, making me wait.

"Some... *things*?" I emphasized the plural.

"Mm-hmm." He took another sip and enjoyed the pain of my waiting. "Gio was there."

"Getting meat?" I asked.

"Nope, cutting it. In fact, he's now head butcher again." Patrick picked up his knife and cut another piece of his pork chop. "Don't you think it's a bit soon?"

"Yeah." My mind was so jumbled with this case. The cause of Ryan's death kept everything from fitting. If it was a clear case of being shot, stabbed, or strangled, it was easier to catch someone without an airtight alibi, but poisoning... it was an altogether different beast.

"What?" Patrick put his utensils down and stared at me. "You've got that look."

"I need to find out who has hemlock stored somewhere. That means I have to go to everyone who had motive enough to kill him and trace their footsteps back for a few days." I knew I also needed to talk to the staff of the Watershed.

"I'm going to also go see and talk to all the people who worked at the Watershed."

"How are you going to do that?" Patrick asked.

"I'm going to call them or go see them." Doing that sounded way simpler than it was really going to be. From past cases when I was a full-time lawyer, this type of activity took weeks, and *that* was when I had a paralegal.

I didn't have weeks. Nor did I have a paralegal to help. Thank God, Aunt Maxi was into the case. She'd surely hunt some of these people down. Especially Pat. He was someone I really wanted to talk to since he'd been the Moores' busser.

"Not tonight." Patrick got up and walked over to the box of decorations he'd put next to the tree. "Tonight you're all ours."

"There's no other place I'd rather be." I grabbed my wine glass and walked up to the nice fir we'd picked out, admiring it. It had the perfect stiff needles for the ornaments we'd collected from over the past year in celebration of the life we'd begun.

"I did get something for us today." He pulled out one of those clay ornaments with a man and woman along with two dogs. The ornament was personalized with our names.

"I'm so lucky." I took the ornament and ran a finger over it. "I love it, Patrick Cane."

CHAPTER TEN

There was nothing better than a full belly and the love of your life next to you to help you get a great night's sleep. Or maybe it was that I hadn't slept a wink the night before, but I'll say the warmth of the bed with Patrick, Sassy, and Pepper making it all cozy got me the shut-eye needed to ensure I was wide awake and raring to go when the alarm went off.

"Good morning." I looked up and saw Patrick standing over me with a cup of coffee. "I didn't even hear you get out of bed."

"You were out." He smiled and gave me the coffee once I pushed myself up in the bed.

Sassy jumped off. Pepper stayed tucked in the covers next to me.

"I got a service call from Camey." He had done all the remodeling for Cocoon Hotel, and Camey was great about calling Patrick if something needed to be repaired. "One of their ovens isn't working in the kitchen."

He sat on the edge of the bed and put on his work boots.

"Tell her I'll be down to bring her coffee this morning." I pulled the covers off. Pepper stuck his head out from underneath. "I'm sure Bunny has it all ready. Ask Camey if she needs me to bring anything for her guests to eat."

Not that I had a lot, but I certainly had enough in the Bean Hive freezer to take down to her guests while Patrick fixed the oven.

"I will." He got up, turned, and kissed me goodbye. "You keep your nose out of anything that'll get you in trouble."

I gave him a smile and wink. We both knew I wasn't going to commit to anything that I couldn't guarantee.

"Love you!" I hollered out to him. I pulled the covers back over me when my legs got a chill. "Just a few more minutes," I told Pepper.

He immediately put his head under the cover, apparently thinking it was a great idea.

The coffee warmed me and got my brain in somewhat of a working order. Items on the to-do list I needed to accomplish today started to drift in one at a time.

"We need to go to the Bean Hive and get Camey her coffee for the hospitality room." I was talking to Pepper like he was truly listening, but the light snoring from underneath the covers told me he was fast asleep. Sassy had gone to work with Patrick. "We also need to meet Yvonne at the sheriff's department, which means I need to dress a little better than my regular Bean Hive clothing just in case Kirk shows up."

It wasn't unusual for Kirk to request to be present during a police interview of a potential suspect in a case he'd taken on. In this instance, I was sure he would enjoy having to deal with me.

"He has no idea what he's in for." I drank the last sip of coffee in my mug and put it down on the table. "Let's get moving, Pepper." I threw back the covers and got out of bed, ready to face what the day was going to bring.

It didn't take long for me to take a shower and put on a pair of black slacks with black boots, a white button-down shirt, and a black blazer to match. The long-sleeved Bean Hive shirt would go fine with the pants once I was back to work at the coffee shop.

Patrick had filled Pepper's bowl with kibble before he left, so Pepper ate and waited patiently by the door.

With my overcoat zipped up, I bent down and put Pepper's sweater on him. He loved his sweater. He danced around, his little grey stump tail wiggling as fast as it could go. I gave him a good scratch under his chin and used my fingers to comb down his beard.

"Are you ready?" I asked in an excited voice. I opened the door, grabbed my crossbody, and with my keys in hand, went out the door.

Pepper ran around and did his business while I opened the trunk and got out a blanket for him to sit on since the snowfall was still on the ground. I was happy to see the roads weren't covered, which meant the road crew had done a great job. I grabbed the old briefcase I kept in the trunk I'd used in my lawyer days. Truthfully, there was nothing in it, but I was going to look the part.

Honestly, I'd totally given up on being a lawyer when I moved to Honey Springs, but once people started to find out I was once a lawyer, they did ask me for various services. Unfortunately, this wasn't the first murder I'd come across, though I wished it would be the last.

"You ready?" I asked Pepper again when he got back to the car. I opened the door and fixed his blanket before he jumped in. I used the edges of the blanket to clean off the snow from his fur. If I didn't, it'd clump and hang on the fur.

I slowed the car down when we went around the curve where the Moores had wrecked. The tire marks in the grass were covered with snow, but I knew they were under there.

"We have to figure out where the hemlock came from," I said out loud. Pepper had planted his front paws on the door handle and was looking out the window. "And I need to talk to Abigail Porter."

I didn't want to ask Yvonne about Abigail, her supposed best friend who Jo Beth claimed her father was having an affair with, but if it would take her off the suspect list and put Abigail on as a replacement, I had to do what Patrick asked me not to do... be nosy.

"Something smells good in here." The smell of cinnamon, nutmeg, and sugar filled the air and swept over me when Pepper and I walked in the Bean Hive.

"Good morning!" Bunny called from behind the counter. "You can flip the sign."

I did exactly what she told me to do. We had a few minutes before opening time, and I was glad to see she'd already gotten the display cases filled and the coffee pots all brewed.

"How did you sleep?" she asked and handed me a cup of the Jingle Bell Blend.

"Like a log." I took a sip before I even took off my coat. "It's so cold out. This is so good. Thank you."

"You're welcome, dear." Bunny was buttering me up for something.

"What?" I asked.

"Well..." she hesitated and wrung her hands, looking worried. "I've lost the bunny rabbit."

"What?" I jumped up and put the mug on the counter, then headed straight over to the cage to see for myself.

The rabbit was not in there. I moved the cage. I moved the free-standing coffee station. Nothing. Frantically, I ran around the shop moving things, looking for rabbit poop and anything that looked like it might be chewed on, but nothing.

"I'm sorry. I have no idea what happened." She stood there with the most pitiful look on her face.

"Let's trace your steps." The situation was like a mystery, and I always found in cases that retracing steps was a great way to find... "Bunny! You're brilliant! I have to retrace Ryan Moore's steps for the day."

I ran back to the kitchen and brought out the wipe-off board with the suspects Aunt Maxi and I had listed.

"You're not mad?" Bunny asked with some caution in her voice.

"We need to find the rabbit. Where could've it gone?" It wasn't like we were open, and it also wasn't like the rabbit could open the cage door and walk out. "Tell me exactly what you did this morning."

"My alarm went off, and my arthritis was aching from the cold." She rubbed her elbow.

"No. I'm sorry your arthritis is acting up, but start from when you opened that door." I pointed at the front door of the Bean Hive.

"I opened the door with my key and stuck it right back in my pocketbook." She seemed to be into this sort of questioning. Her voice picked up with excitement as she recalled the facts of how she'd locked the door, hung up her coat, put up her pocketbook, put on the apron, and headed directly to the coffee pots to flip them on. "Then I went back to the kitchen and turned on the ovens."

She had the same routine each of us did when we opened. In fact, I had a checklist posted not only next to the register but on the refrigerator in the kitchen.

She'd done everything on the list, including getting the food ready for the display cases.

"I even put a few logs on the fire." Though she tried to recall what happened to the rabbit, she did have a little pride in that fire. "That's when Lesley Roarke knocked."

"Lesley?" I asked and felt a sense of relief. "You didn't say she came by."

"It's not unusual for the owners of shops to come and grab a cup on their way to their own stores." She was right. Many of the shop owners knew we were there getting ready for our early-morning customers well before their doors even opened.

"I know, but I was just at Crooked Cat yesterday when Louise came down there looking for me to drop the bunny off. I told Lesley a rabbit would be great for the bookstore and especially the children's story time." I smiled. "If I recall correctly, I do believe story time is today." I walked behind the counter and started to look around. "Are you sure she didn't say anything or leave a note?" I asked.

"Not that I remember." Bunny's worried look came back.

A few customers came into the coffee shop. A gust of cold air swept along the floor and circled around me, sending goosebumps all over my body. I smiled at the customers while they looked down the display counter.

"I'll call her." I dug deep into my crossbody and grabbed my phone, only to find a text from Lesley. "Here. She left a text." I read out loud, "Roxy, I decided to give the rabbit a try at story time. Your idea really sounds good. I went to get a coffee from Bunny this morning and told her I was going to borrow the rabbit for the day. Bunny said okay, but she seemed to be occupied with something else, so I'm not sure if she heard me. TTYL."

"TTYL?" Bunny jerked back.

"Talk to you later." Was that really all Bunny had heard from the text? "She said you seemed to be occupied with something else. Are you okay?"

"I'm fine." Bunny shuffled around me. "I'm glad the rabbit is okay."

"Yeah. Me too." Now that Lesley brought it to my attention and I'd asked Bunny, I could clearly see she was hiding or very nervous about something.

That was yet another mystery to solve, but I didn't have time to explore it.

"I'm going to take the carafes down to Cocoon Hotel." I took two of the industrial carafes from the coffee pot and replaced them to fill up. "You okay for a few minutes?"

"Of course I am. I reckon you're gonna be on me now that Lesley said my mind was occupied." Bunny didn't like to have tabs kept on her. She was very proud of her independence. "I won't have none of that. You hear me, Roxanne Bloom?" She shook her crooked finger at me.

"It's nothing I don't ask every time I leave." That was the truth. I always made sure I asked whoever was working with me if they'd be okay when I had to run errands. Only this time, Bunny's reaction did make me think she was hiding something. But what?

CHAPTER ELEVEN

"Good morning." I was caught off guard when Aunt Maxi and I ran into each other as I was leaving the coffee shop. "Want to walk down to Cocoon with me so I can drop off the coffee?"

"I was gonna warm up by the fire." She hemmed and hawed and looked into the window of the Bean Hive. Pepper did look very snug in the dog bed next to the fireplace. "I guess I can." She tugged the stocking hat she had pulled on her head down a little more, covering her ears. She also wore a bright red velvet coat and matching red gloves.

"You'll be fine. Besides, you've got so much red on, you look like you're on fire." I laughed and handed her one of the carafes.

"I can't help it if I'm full of style and glamour." She definitely always dressed eccentrically but in a fashionable way, something I could never pull off.

"What are you doing today?" I asked on our way down the boardwalk to Cocoon. I was glad the snow had melted off the boardwalk. The effect made for a really nice, crisp walk as the dawn started to pop up over the trees. The Christmas lights wrapped around the carriage poles gave off a warm glow. The sights filled my soul with joy, though if I took a second to think about Yvonne, the joy was somewhat dampened.

"What did you hear?" She jerked.

"Are you hiding something?" I questioned her, since her reaction was not like her.

"You rarely ask me that this early." Aunt Maxi shrugged and returned to her normal self.

"I've got to meet Yvonne Moore at the sheriff's department, but I need someone to look into something for me at the Watershed." I'd actually left the copy of who was working at the Watershed that Fiona had given me. "I also need to retrace Ryan Moore's steps for the entire day."

"What's at the Watershed?" Aunt Maxi did seem interested now that she knew it was part of the investigation.

"It can take six to nine hours for hemlock poisoning to go into effect, and if I can trace back Ryan's steps and who he interacted with from that day, I might get a clue to more suspects." It wasn't like I doubted we had a good list now, but Jo Beth, Gio and Yvonne seemed so obvious, and each one had their own reasons.

Though I'd not talked to Gio, Jo Beth was right. Why would he bother getting blood on his hands when he was going to flourish by just being the dad to Ryan's grandchild?

"The last place he was alive was the Watershed. Fiona was his waitress, but there was a Pat working there that night too. He was the busboy. He spilled water all over Ryan, and I just wanted to know if Pat overheard Ryan and Yvonne saying anything. Or really any leads." I knew the event was memorable, so maybe Pat did hear something. Anything.

"According to the schedule, Pat is working the lunch shift today. If you had time, I thought you might be able to stop in before you come to lunch." Aunt Maxi never missed a lunch with me at the Bean Hive.

"I can do that." She gave a hard nod. "But I won't be eating lunch with you today."

"You won't?" I was looking forward to enjoying the scenery of the walkway between the boardwalk and the Cocoon Hotel, but Aunt Maxi shocked me by telling me she wasn't coming for lunch. That ruined it.

"Nope. I've got me a date. Why do you think I've got a little hitch in my giddy-up?" She was awfully giddy for this early in the morning.

"I… I…" I stammered.

"Close your mouth. You'll catch cold." Aunt Maxi picked up her step and hurried in front of me.

I'd not realized how hard I'd gripped the carafe's handle until I made it inside of the Cocoon Hotel and put the coffee down in the hospitality room.

"Are you all right?" Camey Montgomery asked. She wore a festive green sweater with a little white faux fur around the cuffs of the sleeves. The green made her scarlet hair pop. Her thick bangs hung perfectly across her brows.

"Yeah." I worked my hand open and closed. "Aunt Maxi just shocked me by telling me she has a lunch date."

"Really?" Camey had picked up a copy of one of the southern Christmas magazines she had stacked on the table beside a chair near the hospitality room's fireplace and fanned herself.

We both looked at Aunt Maxi. She was helping a guest figure out the coffee carafe to get a cup.

"I'm burning up," Camey panted.

"You havin' your own personal summer over there?" Aunt Maxi asked with a laugh.

"Yes. I think I'm going through the change." Camey shook her head. "You'd think at my age it'd already happened."

"I'm sorry. Maybe it's the stress of the ovens." The suggestion was supposed to make her feel better.

"Patrick is a lifesaver. He has three of his electricians here, and he's back there elbow deep too." Camey turned when Newton Oakley, her handyman for the hotel, walked in and waved her over. "Excuse me. I've got a final meeting this early morning with the Logsdon Landscaping to pay for the decoration near the lake. Have you seen them?" she asked me from over her shoulder on the way out of the room. "Go look!"

Camey disappeared, but someone bigger than life walked right through that door.

"I thought I heard you in here, yapping." Loretta Bebe was dressed to the nines. She had on a houndstooth wool skirt suit. Her black purse dangled over her elbow. She wore pearls the size of baseballs in her ears and around her neck. Her short black hair stood out against her tan skin, something she said was because of her Native American heritage, but we all knew it was from the tanning bed over at Lisa Stalh's house and that tanning bed she kept in her garage.

"Hello, Low-retta," Aunt Maxi's said in her southern "bless your heart" voice. "What are you doing up at this time of the day?" Aunt Maxi leaned over and whispered to me, "She had to get up two hours ago to get into that get-up."

"Oh, Maxine, what's this I hear about you and Floyd? I mean, come on? The thought of Bunny Bowoski's leftovers. Shock-ing." Loretta was poking the bear... Aunt Maxi.

I really wanted to say something, but the shock of Aunt Maxi and Floyd was something I couldn't process. In fact, it left me dumbfounded.

"Don't be jealous." Aunt Maxi winked and watched as Loretta traipsed past us and helped herself to a cup of coffee and pastry. "Besides, that high horse you seem to be on this morning makes your ass look big."

"Aunt Maxi," I gasped and grabbed her by the elbow. "It was so good seeing you, Loretta." I jerked Aunt Maxi. "Let's go."

"What?" Aunt Maxi jerked her arm from me. "I can say as I please and do what I want."

As much as she tried to get away from me, I clung on to her and gripped her tighter.

"What is wrong with you?" I asked once we made it outside on the hotel's porch. "No wonder Bunny is in a weird mood. You stole Floyd from her."

"I didn't *steeeal* anyone." Aunt Maxi drew out her word trying to convince me.

"If I recall correctly, the first time I ever saw you and Bunny interact, she stated you'd been down at the Moose trying to steal Floyd." Aunt Maxi tried to interrupt me. "And," I said too loudly for her to even think she could say something until I was finished, "You told her not to flatter herself because you wanted a man who could walk without stopping every two feet so he could get his footing up under him so he didn't fall."

"Did I?" She puckered her lips like she didn't remember. Aunt Maxi wasn't fooling me any. She had the mind of an elephant, which supposedly remembered everything... or maybe that was just another one of our southern sayings.

"Yes, you did, and you need to let Floyd go this instant," I demanded.

"I will do no such thing. You need to go back to the coffee shop and simmer down." She was trying to scold me into thinking what she and Floyd had done to poor Bunny was all right. "Now let me tell you something. I sure hope you don't find yourself in my situation." I was sure she was referring to my uncle's passing, leaving her a widow. "But when pickins are slim, you take what you can."

"I'm sure there's more men at the Moose than Floyd." I wasn't going to let her bully me into thinking she was right about him.

"Fine. I won't go back into the Bean Hive." She stomped off once we reached the ramp to the boardwalk. "I'll let you know about Pat."

I shook my head. No matter how she and I clashed about Floyd and her morality, she was too dang nosy to stay away from the little bit of investigation I needed her to do.

CHAPTER TWELVE

Bunny and I got through the morning crowd without talking about what was bothering her, and now that I knew what it was, I decided to let her tell me when she was ready.

The breakfast rush had ended just in time for me to head down to the department to meet Yvonne Moore.

The grey clouds hung low over our small town. They were thick snow clouds, and I was hoping, unlike most of the other residents in Honey Spring, it would be snowy for Christmas. I couldn't see all of Central Park from the parking lot of the department, but the twinkling lights were on, and the Christmas tree stand had people mingling in and out of the firs.

Steam puffed out of one of the vendor tents, which I knew had to be from the freshly popped kettle corn I was smelling. Though I was going into the department to try to defend someone in a murder case, my heart still had the joy of the season.

I was very thankful for Honey Springs and how it'd embraced me. Unfortunately, that joy quickly faded when I jerked around to see who was knocking on my car window.

Kirk.

With a huge smile on his face, he waved. In fear my eyes would get stuck, I refrained from the big eye roll I felt like I was on the verge of giving him.

I opened the door and grabbed the empty briefcase. "Kirk," I said stiffly. "I thought I'd see you here."

"Yes. You do know me." He laughed. "I take no pleasure in taking down your client."

"We will see." I turned and watched Yvonne pull into the parking lot.

When she got out of the car, she smoothed out her black pressed suit coat and the hint of a cream shirt underneath, as if her drive over had sullied them. She gave a quick shake of her hair, but not a strand shifted. She dropped her hands to her side, and with her head lifted, she drew back her shoulders and focused on the door of the station.

"Oh man." Kirk smiled so big. "This is going to be good. See you in there, Roxanne Cane."

I threw him a tight smile before I turned to greet Yvonne.

"So, let me do all the talking. Understand?" I wanted confirmation. She nodded.

I led the way into the department, where Spencer Shepard, Kirk, and Jo Beth were already standing.

It was as if the time had stopped between the two women. Both of them were hurting, and I couldn't help but feel as though the one wanted to reach out to the other and vice versa. But it was Jo Beth who took the deep breath and whispered something into Kirk's ear, at which point he led Yvonne off in a different direction.

"Mrs. Moore. Roxy." Spencer walked over, placing the file up under his arm. "If you two don't mind following me into a room, we'll get started."

"Will Kirk be joining us?" I asked.

"If you'd like, but it's not necessary. I can give him a report of the statement." Spencer had always been fair to me.

"I don't oppose it if Yvonne doesn't." I looked at her.

"I'm fine with it. I have nothing to hide." Yvonne shrugged with the utmost confidence that I loved.

"Bring him in." I stopped at the door of the room and told Spencer, "You sit right here."

I'd assessed the room because I knew exactly where Kirk had always preferred to be when he was involved in client statements. If we occupied his space, he'd be unable to think clearly. It was one of his weirdo techniques he claimed was a key to his success.

Yvonne took her seat, and I plopped the briefcase up on the table.

Spencer and Kirk came in directly. Kirk looked frantically about the room. He grabbed a chair with his hand and began to shift it right then left. He appeared to be in a pickle. He fussed with the chair a few more seconds before giving in and sitting down.

My soul felt a bit of a satisfaction as I watched him squirm.

Spencer sat down in the chair right across the table from Yvonne and pushed the button on the microphone before he pushed it into the middle of the table.

He rambled off the date, time, and case number before he started to ask the usual questions—"state your name, birthdate, address, occupation. How did you know the victim?"

"I understand you and your husband were fighting on the night of the wreck. I also understand you'd told him you were filing for divorce. Is that correct?" Spencer asked.

Kirk shifted in his seat.

"Yes. I did say that." She looked at me, and I gestured okay.

"Why did you say that?" Spencer asked.

"He was having an affair." She lifted her chin. Though she was trying not to cry, I could see the puddles forming in her eyes.

"Do you have any access to hemlock?" Spencer asked Yvonne.

"No," she stated matter-of-factly. "I don't even know what it looks like."

"In these photos we found on your house computer"—Spencer opened the file and took out some photos. He slid them across the table for Yvonne to look at. "The small white flowers are hemlock. And according to Daryl, your housekeeper, she said you pick those all the time around your property."

"I had no idea they were hemlock." She looked at the photos and then eased back into the chair.

"Just because my client picks flowers off her own property doesn't mean she's a botanist. She only likes to make her home pretty. And you know it's hemlock?" I asked Spencer.

"We had some of the dead weeds tested around the property, and according to Logsdon Landscaping, who does all of the Moores' landscaping, they have hemlock on the property." Spencer's words put a huge smile on Kirk's face that I wanted to smack right off.

"That might be the case, but Yvonne has no access to any sort of hemlock that's alive." I shook my head. "If you haven't noticed, it's winter."

"That's where you're wrong." Spencer opened the file again and took out more photos. "Here is a photo of some hemlock in a small greenhouse we seized during the search of the property."

This piece of evidence was hard to swallow. Not only did they have my client fighting with the victim, who'd been caught cheating on her, but they also had the live murder weapon.

"My client Jo Beth Moore would like to bring murder charges against Yvonne Moore for the murder of Ryan Moore." Kirk jumped up and smacked the table.

"That's ridiculous. I didn't kill him!" Yvonne screamed out.

"Yvonne." I tried to calm her, but it didn't help.

Spencer put his hand out to her and Kirk.

"Mrs. Moore, I understand how terrible it is to find out your husband had cheated on you. Trust me, if you just tell us the truth that you did kill Ryan Moore from the hemlock of your greenhouse, we can lessen the charges." Spencer was trying to wrangle a confession from her.

"No way." I shook my head. "My client..."

"I did it. I killed Ryan." Yvonne Moore buried her head in her hands.

A feeling of dread crawled through me.

CHAPTER THIRTEEN

"That was easier than I thought." Kirk took pride in watching Spencer haul Yvonne off to the booking part of the station. "I'm sorry, Roxy. Really. You always tried to see the good in people."

"Yeah. That's why I stuck around married to you too long." I gripped the handle of the briefcase and headed out of the interview room.

The tension began to rise in me from just the sheer knowledge that Kirk was walking behind me. The only bright side to this situation was that Kirk would be getting out of Honey Springs.

"Excuse me. I need to tell my client the good news." He hurried around me, brushing up against me, practically making me sick to my stomach.

I couldn't get out of there fast enough. Once in my car, I grabbed my phone to follow up on what Yvonne had asked me to do when they were handcuffing her.

She wanted me to call her mom and let her know that Yvonne had confessed to murdering Ryan and that the raid had found her hemlock in her greenhouse. "Promise me you'll call her," she'd said.

"Forget it." I threw the phone down in the passenger seat and pulled the back of the bag of Gingerbread Softies.

I took a bite and looked at it. It was the treat I had planned on sharing with Yvonne after we answered Spencer's questions in celebration of the interrogation being over, but the bad taste of seeing Kirk and Jo Beth walking out of the station left a sour feeling in my stomach.

"Forget it." I put the cookie down and threw the car in gear.

There was no better time to eat a cookie than while telling Yvonne's mom what'd happened in person. Besides, if she was as fragile as I'd heard, I wanted to make sure Daryl was with her and she didn't pass out at the news, so doing it in person was a much better idea.

The snow was falling in big flakes, which made me take the roads a lot slower than normal, but it also gave me some time to think.

For someone to be so adamant about not killing her husband, she sure did an about-face, which made me wonder what she was hiding. Really hiding. I had no time to question her, since they were going to take her straight to booking. That would take a few hours. I'd be sure to call and set up a time with the station secretary for talking privately with Yvonne and getting the real scoop.

The Logsdon Landscaping Company must've been finished with the outside decorating because there were lights strung along the fence, along the gate, and around all the oak trees that lined the Moores' driveway.

I rolled down the window and pushed the button on the gate speaker box.

"How can I help you?" Daryl asked.

"It's Roxanne Bloom. I'm here to talk to Yvonne's mom about Yvonne." Immediately the gate buzzed open.

Slowly I drove up the driveway and noticed in the rearview mirror that my tires were leaving tracks. The water fountain was turned off. A big blow-up snow globe feature was in the middle, which wasn't there the other day. Then I thought about Yvonne leaving here this morning. Did she look at the decorations and think of how Ryan loved Christmas? Did she even know she wouldn't be coming back today? Had she planned on confessing this entire time?

Daryl had the door open when I got out. She waved me inside in a hurried fashion.

"Where's Mrs. Moore?" Daryl looked out the door when I stepped into the foyer.

Wow. A huge tree spanned from the floor to the ceiling of the mansion foyer. Clearly it wasn't there when Patrick and I had brought Yvonne home the night of the wreck... or murder.

"Yvonne, honey," I heard Yvonne's mom say before she entered. "I packed up all your warm fuzzy blankets. I need to know—what do you want me to do with all these heels?"

A pair of red snakeskin stilettoes dangled from her fingers, and a towel hung over her shoulder.

"I'm sorry." She looked between Daryl and me. "Did Yvonne go upstairs?"

"Can I talk to you?" I asked.

"Sure. I don't think we were introduced properly the other night. I'm Belinda." She turned to go back to where she'd come from. "We can talk in here while we pack. Daryl, please tell Yvonne the first round of Goodwill will be here soon."

Daryl knew something was up because she followed us into the room where Yvonne had lain down on a couch, but there was no couch now. In fact, there were piles upon piles of boxes.

"I'm sure Yvonne told you that I'm Roxy Bloom. I'm a part time"—I started to say "very part-time but didn't—"attorney. And when she was asked to come to the station to give her statement, she asked me to come along." My head tilted to the right and left. "Just to make sure she was represented."

It was so strange of her to suddenly confess. Why would she bother disguising herself to come to the Bean Hive the next morning and ask me to help her? Something wasn't right, and if Yvonne thought I was going to accept this type of sudden change in plea, she didn't know this lawyer very well. Now I was confident something was wrong.

"Yes." Belinda nodded eagerly. "Excuse the mess. We are moving to a much smaller place. Yvonne can't live without her blankets because, you know, she hates to be cold." I didn't know, but I let Belinda tell me about her daughter, knowing in a few minutes she'd be devastated at the news about Yvonne confessing to Ryan's murder.

Belinda put the shoes down and walked over to the built-in glass shelves that I didn't remember from the other night either. She took down a trophy and pulled the towel off her shoulder to dust off the trophy. She looked at it and smiled. "And she loved her trophies. Those were the days."

She held the trophy in my direction. I walked over and looked at it.

"Championship State in breaststroke," I read off the gold-plated plaque glued on the front.

"Yvonne held the state record for years before anyone beat her." Her mom put the trophy down in the box.

I just so happened to look in and saw many more trophies that must've been displayed on the shelves. Yvonne knew how to swim. My mind curled back to how Patrick pulled her from the water. Wouldn't her keen sense of swimming kick in to help get her own self out of the truck? Did she know Patrick and I were behind them? Did she see us in the rearview mirror, and when Ryan drove off the road, did she figure we'd jump in, and if not, she would save herself, making sure Ryan was underwater for a good period of time and would drown for good measure?

All the reasons why I believed Yvonne Moore didn't kill her husband just flew out of my mind and made me start to think she did kill him.

"Ryan loved looking at her trophies, even though she'd gotten them way before they knew each other." She let out a long sigh and picked up another trophy. "Where is that daughter of mine?" She tilted her head around me. "You know, she's not slept a wink since Ryan. She loved him so much."

"I'm not sure if you knew Yvonne had me meet her at the station to talk to Sheriff Shepard, but she did confess to killing Ryan."

Belinda dropped the trophy, shattering the angel statue right off the pedestal and sending it across the room.

"There is no way Yvonne would do such a thing." Belinda grabbed her chest with one hand and put the other hand on the wall to steady herself.

Daryl hurried over and took her by the arm, guiding Belinda to the only seat in the room, an old armchair stuck in the corner.

"Get my medication." Belinda's chest heaved up and down. Daryl scurried off.

"I'm so sorry. Are you ill?" I asked, wanting to get down to what Bunny had told me about Belinda. I pulled the cookies from my crossbody, not really sure if this was a good time to offer them to her, but I knew in most cases, cookies were a good medication for calming the nerves.

She took one of the cookies and held it in her palm.

"I've had heart problems for a long time. When Ryan and Yvonne got married, they moved me in so I could be taken care of by Daryl." Slowly she shook her head. Her eyes were closed.

"I know what I told you is a shock, but she wanted you to know the hemlock she keeps in the greenhouse was confiscated for evidence." I'd made good on what Yvonne had asked me to promise to tell her mom.

She was definitely not taking the news well. Her cheeks flushed white, and her chest still heaved up and down at a rapid pace.

"Do I need to call your doctor?" I asked and knelt beside her.

"No." She opened her eyes and looked at me with a fear so deep that I could feel it. "I know she didn't do it. She doesn't have it in her. What about Jo Beth? She's the one who had the most motive to kill him for the company."

She took a bite, and her face relaxed.

"Not really. The company was already signed over to her, and Yvonne didn't disagree. She only wanted Ryan to mentor the child until he was educated or well trained. Ryan had no issue with that." I really wanted Jo Beth to have done it. "And Gio, the father, really had no reason to either."

Daryl, who came in with the medication, chimed in on the conversation. "He was bitter and angry over Ryan firing him. Gio said the accusations Ryan was making about buying the cheap meat would ruin his butcher career."

"That's true and looks like a great motive, only he got a much better deal than jail. Now his child will be heir to the company, and he didn't have to get his hands dirty at all. It's probably the ultimate revenge without killing anyone," I told them.

"I just can't believe it." Belinda looked at Daryl as if Daryl had some sort of answer. She ate the rest of the cookie. "You are really a good baker. I know Ryan and Yvonne enjoyed your coffee."

That wasn't the praise I was looking for when I offered my coffee and baked goods to people. What I wanted was the look on their faces and to see that coffee and cookies were a nice common denominator in any situation.

"Can you tell me about the greenhouse?" I asked Belinda when I noticed she was a little more calmed down.

"I don't know anything about it other than Yvonne complaining Ryan would rather be out there more than in here." Sadness and a worried look mixed on her face as the lines around her eyes and mouth deepened. "There's no way I could get out there, and I never saw Yvonne go either."

"Hello?" a woman's voice called from the front of the mansion. "Yvonne?"

"What is she doing here?" Daryl's head jerked up. "What are you doing here?" Daryl turned her question to the lady who walked into the room.

"Yvonne called me to meet her." The woman snarled at Daryl and took a moment to look at Belinda and me. "Hi, I'm Abigail Porter."

My eyes grew. *So, you're the best friend. The other woman.*

Why on earth would Yvonne ask Abigail to come see her if she knew she was going to confess?

CHAPTER FOURTEEN

"Where is Yvonne?" Abigail asked. By the annoying tone in her voice, she must have felt the same way Belinda felt about her.

"You have the nerve to waltz in this house after you've been dying to get in here as Ryan's wife, booting my sweet Yvonne out, and now you've driven her crazy to the point where she confessed to poisoning Ryan." The words seethed out of Belinda's mouth.

With shaky arms, she pushed herself up to stand out of the armchair. Slowly, with Daryl's help, she walked right over to Abigail and stood up to the mistress.

"Get out." Belinda pointed at the door. "You've ruined everyone's life, including a sweet innocent child that has yet to be born."

I stood there watching as the women seemed to remain still for a few seconds. Abigail's eyes were drawn down her nose as she glared at Belinda. Belinda lifted her chin with a pride on her face as she looked up at Abigail.

"Fine. I don't want to harm an old lady and make you die from a heart attack," Abigail said with a deceptive calm that unnerved me.

"I'll be right back," I told Daryl and Belinda, hurrying out of the room after Abigail.

Although Yvonne was now in the process of being locked up in jail, I still had unanswered questions that I needed to be answered for me to really accept that Yvonne had made that sudden confession.

"Abigail!" I called once I opened the front door. She was already getting in her SUV.

Her head jerked up, and her eyes slid over the roof of the vehicle and focused on me.

"I wanted to know if I could ask you a few questions." I walked down the front steps, taking care not to slip and fall.

The snow had now covered the ground. It was the type of soft snow good for making snowmen, and underneath that was the thin layer of ice that made it more treacherous than it looked.

"Who are you?" she asked. The fur coat she had on wasn't fake as I'd thought. I wondered if Ryan had given it to her, but I kept my mouth shut.

"I'm Roxanne Bloom. I own the Bean Hive Coffee Shop on the boardwalk." It was an automatic response I'd been giving people when I introduced myself. "Gosh. I'm sorry. I'm also a lawyer, and Yvonne had asked me to go with her for her questioning this morning—only I think she's confessed but didn't actually kill Ryan."

Abigail's shoulders fell. She appeared to have relaxed a little.

"I don't know what you want with me." She touched the handle of the door and jerked it open.

There were two men wearing green Carhart overhauls and green baseball caps with the Logsdon Landscaping logo on them. The men drove around on a golf cart. They both looked at us when they drove past and out into the field, stopping to check on some of the lights wrapped around one of the many light-up trees.

"Ryan loved Christmas." Abigail pinched her lips together like she let a confession slip.

"I know you're feeling a loss too." I let her know in a subtle way that I knew who exactly she was to Ryan. "I don't believe Yvonne killed Ryan. I think she's covering up for someone."

"You think I killed him?" Her eyes popped wide open, and her mouth dropped open a little.

"I didn't say that, but I know you were close with him, and I'd like to ask a few questions to just ease my mind and put my case to rest." I had nothing to hide, but I sure was going to go see Amy Logsdon so I could get a list of people from her company who'd worked at the Moores' mansion. Ears were everywhere, and I had to talk to everyone.

"Get in." She opened her car door and got in.

I opened the passenger side. The car was so warm and cozy inside with the big leather seats.

"You know, when Yvonne called me this morning, I thought she was going to forgive me." Abigail fiddled with the temperature controls. "Seat warmer?" she asked me.

"Yeah, that'd be great." I instantly felt a little warmth on my hiney when she pushed the button. This was a luxury I wasn't used to. "Forgive you?"

"Oh yeah. Ryan and I have been over for at least a year. It was a one-night stand thing. Not a big fling like all the people in Honey Springs made it seem like. We never made it to the bedroom either." I guess she noticed the confused look on my face because she continued speaking. "Like I said, Ryan loves—loved"—her voice cracked when she corrected herself—"Christmas. I have a ten-year-old son from a previous marriage, and Ryan and Yvonne throw these big Christmas parties. You know, the kind with Santa, gifts, food, cookies, and he even had reindeer flown in just for the occasion."

I'd never been invited. Those parties must've only been for the elite society of Honey Springs. *Loretta Bebe,* I thought and made a mental note to check with her when she came into the Bean Hive tomorrow morning since I was opening.

"A couple of years ago, both of us had a little too much to drink. We were standing in the kitchen talking, then all of a sudden, we kissed. Yvonne walked in, and she kicked me and my son out." Yvonne moved her gaze to look out of the windshield. "I've been trying to make up for it since. She blocked me from her phone, social media, parties. Even when my father died, I tried to contact her, but she never reached out. This morning was the first time I'd heard from her in two years."

"How did you hear about Ryan's death?" I asked.

"On the news. I was shocked and wondered if I'd heard right. Then I got on the computer and found an article about it. I wasn't in love with Ryan. It was a fluke kiss with drinking involved. That's all." She shook her head and looked over at me. "He died of hemlock poisoning?"

"Honestly, I'm not completely sure if it was that or drowning on top of it. But there was hemlock in his system. Enough to have made him have all the symptoms before he passed out and drove the truck into the lake." I left out the part about how I felt it was odd that Yvonne was an excellent swimmer and didn't even get herself out of the water, which made me think she did have a hand in the murder. Then my reasonable lawyer side replayed her sudden confession.

"I guess I just found it very odd how she had asked me to be present, and then she suddenly confessed after the sheriff told her it was hemlock poisoning and had photos from her social media of flower arrangements she had in her home, where she used hemlock as baby's breath." I honestly needed to get on social media. But more pressing things in my life took up my time, so I certainly didn't need another thing to add to it.

"Social?" Abigail laughed. "Yvonne is all about appearances. Even after Ryan and I begged her and pleaded with her, telling her the truth behind the kiss, she still didn't believe us. Saying how it made her look bad. Her social media was the same. Ryan is the one who would put the flower arrangements together. Yvonne never set foot in his greenhouse. He loved it out there. Yvonne would say that he had an obsession disorder. Once he got fixated on something, he did it until he got it or perfected it." She laughed. "It's how he got Yvonne. He chased her all over and wouldn't give her one moment's peace. Every time we were somewhere, he'd show up. After they got married, she'd say how he was obsessed with the butcher shop and spend his time there. When he got home, she said he was obsessed with the greenhouse and coming up with all sorts of hybrid plants like he did with meats at the butcher shop."

"So you're not surprised he had hemlock in the greenhouse?" I asked.

"Not at all. He grows things year around in that thing. Have you seen it? Top-of-the-line cooling and heating system." She looked past me and out the window. My eyes followed hers. "I'd say I'd show you, but I think they want me off the property."

Daryl and Belinda were standing at the front door of the house. Both women glared at the SUV.

"Would you like to stop by the coffee shop to continue our conversation? I have coffee and cookies." When I saw the smile cross her lips, I knew she'd be there.

"I can later today. Will you be there?" she asked when I was getting out of the car.

"Yes. I can." I shut the door and walked back up to say goodbye to Belinda. "I want you to know that I don't think Yvonne killed Ryan, and I'm going to get to the bottom of this."

"Thank you so much. But I don't want that woman anywhere near this house, even if we have to get a restraining order." Belinda gestured to the back of the SUV.

"I understand that." Then I went in for the kill. "But if she's the key to getting Yvonne off the hook for murder, then…" I shrugged.

"Daryl," Belinda gasped. "I bet you're right."

"Right about what?" I asked about the gasping and very shocked looks on their faces.

"Daryl said Abigail probably killed Ryan and made it look like Yvonne had done it." Belinda nudged Daryl, then waved us into the house as she vigorously ran her hands up and down her arms as though to ward off the chill.

"I just think that Abigail has tried to get her hands on Mr. Moore for a lot of these years. I see things, ya know." Daryl tapped her temples. "I'm 'sposed to be here takin' care of Miss Belinda, and I am, but it's like I blend in and no one even notices me."

"You overheard something?" I asked.

"Overheard nothing." Belinda gestured for Daryl to keep talking.

"Well, let's just say Mr. Moore and Abigail were seeing each other when they were telling Yvonne they weren't." What she just said meant that Abigail had flat-out lied to me. "This fall I was going out to find Mr. Moore in that greenhouse of his when it was late for Yvonne because we had to get Miss Belinda to the emergency room. I walked all the way to the greenhouse in the dark to tell Mr. Moore we had to go, and through the window, I saw something I shouldn't."

"Go on, tell her. She's going to help get Yvonne out of jail." Belinda nodded.

"Abigail and Mr. Moore were in the biggest lip-lock I'd ever seen, even in the movies." Daryl's eyes grew as a big sigh escaped her. "Yvonne came out lookin' for me. And that's when she saw it too."

"Well, you two let me handle this. I'm going to talk to her again, and I'm going to go see Yvonne." I heard my phone chirp the announcement of a text from inside the crossbody bag. "Yvonne needs to tell me why she confessed to a murder the three of us know she didn't do."

CHAPTER FIFTEEN

The text was from Aunt Maxi. She said she was going to stop by the Bean Hive before her lunch date to give me an update about what she'd found out from Pat, the busboy who'd spilled water all over Ryan the night of the wreck.

I wasn't sure I continued to think of the *wreck* as what had killed him, but calling it the night of his murder continued to put a sadness in my heart during what should be a joyous time of the year.

Speaking of joy, I still had so much I needed to do for the Christmas Day supper, but all the plans I'd made for that had been put on the back burner so I could focus on Yvonne.

"Bee's Knees Bakery and Wild and Whimsy to get those Christmas dishes I saw in the display window are probably two things I can do today," I rattled off a couple of the shops by thinking out loud the things on my to-do list. "Amy Logsdon."

I stopped at the end of the Moores' driveaway to make the call.

"Call Logsdon Landscaping," I said into my phone. "Is Amy Logsdon there?" I asked the person who answered and gave her my name when she asked for it.

"Hi, Roxy." Amy picked up with a cheerful voice. "Merry Christmas."

"Merry Christmas." This was one thing I did love about Honey Springs.

Every time you saw someone you'd not seen in a while, it was like no time had passed. "I have to say how magical you've made Honey Springs this year."

"You know, when the Moores asked us to decorate for them a couple of years ago and we ended up using one of our empty storage units, I knew this could be a very big business. Who has the space to store their decorations anymore? Plus, it seems like everyone is so busy, it's perfect we can do it." She laughed. "They go to work and come home to instant holiday fun without all the hassle."

"The Moores." I was glad she brought the subject up.

"Yeah. Tough, right?" She sighed. "I heard you and Patrick came upon the wreck and just can't believe Yvonne was arrested for his murder. I knew they had some pretty big fights, but from what my guys said, the making up was well worth the fight."

"I'm not so sure Yvonne killed him, and I'm representing her." I didn't tell the full truth, but that was okay. I was still curious about why Yvonne had taken the fall when I was almost sure she didn't poison Ryan. "I called because I wanted to see if I could talk to your employees who have been putting up the Moores' decorations. I'm trying to find out if they'd seen anything unusual or off outside of their fighting."

"Yeah. I have no problem. In fact, most of them are over at the nursing home putting the final touches on the banks before the big snowstorm comes. I think I've got two at the Moores' winterizing some things Ryan had put on the list." She told me something I'd not yet heard.

Those two employees must've been the two I'd seen on the golf cart.

"Did you say snowstorm?" I asked then put the car in drive. I surely didn't want to get stuck out here since I had to be at the coffee shop before Patrick got off work.

"You know how the weather reports around here go." She laughed again. "I'm sure they are probably wrong. Say, I'll get those names over to you, and you're more than welcome to head down to the lake and ask around."

"Thanks so much, Amy. Have a wonderful Christmas if I don't talk to you before." I hung up the phone. Then I reached over, flipped on the radio, and hummed to the smooth sounds of Bing Crosby's "White Christmas" along with a few other Christmas tunes while I drove my little car very slowly on the snow-covered roads all the way back to the boardwalk.

The snow didn't stop any of the tourists from getting to their holiday shopping. The carolers had found a nice spot under the awning at the Buzz In-and-Out diner.

"Happy holidays, Roxy!" James Farley, the owner of the diner, waved. "Santa Claus is coming to town!"

"You better keep the fact you're a great singer a secret because here comes Low-retta Bebe, and she just might recruit you for the town theater." I couldn't stop smiling because he made even more of a dramatic attempt to be louder when Low-retta walked up.

"Roxy, just the person I wanted to see. I was heading down to the coffee shop." Loretta's southern drawl turned "wanted" into "wouunted." She curled her leather-gloved hand in the bend of my elbow and waved at James over her shoulder, dragging me down the boardwalk.

"James, don't forget about the Christmas Day supper," I reminded him. He lifted his chin in the air for acknowledgement.

"I wouunted to let you know I'll be bringing my Twinkie cake to the supper." She squeezed my arm, but it was more of a painful pinch. "I can't tell you my recipe, so I wouuunted to let you know before you take a bite and get a hankering for any such idea about getting my secret family recipe."

"Oh, Loretta," I gasped and opened the door to the Bean Hive, letting her go first. "I'd *never* ask for such a prized possession," I assured her, though I could probably dissect the thing and figure out exactly what was in it, in which case I'd be sending her over the edge. Aunt Maxi would love that.

"Well. Well." Loretta tugged off the gloves in a dramatic one-finger way when she saw Aunt Maxi sitting at the bar at the front of the coffee shop. "I hear you've been making your rounds at the Moose."

"I hear they've got an opening just for you down at the crazy house." Aunt Maxi glared.

"Oh, Maxine." Loretta flung a glove Aunt Maxi's way. "What on earth do you wouunt with old Floyd? He can't barely walk, and he clearly has issues with eating. Every time I see the man down at the diner, he's always got something spilled on his shirt. And not to mention, you'd be stuck taking care of him."

"It's none of your business whose company I keep, Loretta." Aunt Maxi picked at the edges of her hair. "Besides, we are only having lunch."

"I have lunch with men all the time, but I don't get the rumors you're getting." Loretta pulled her phone from her purse. She jabbed at it a few times until she finally showed Aunt Maxi the screen. "You need to get on Compassion Companions."

"Compassion Companions?" Aunt Maxi and I asked in unison. Only, my voice was more of a "no she won't" and Aunt Maxi's voice was more of a "what is that?"

"It's a dating app that doesn't include men from the Moose. These are men who are well classed, if you know what I mean." Loretta gave a theatrical wink and a little grin. "They've got money. Not like Floyd and the ten-cent wing night at the Moose."

"Loretta." I took the attention off the app because I could see Aunt Maxi's wheels turning, which was never a good thing. "I appreciate you letting me know what you're bringing." I used my fingers to zip my lips. "I'll never ask for the recipe."

"Oh my Lord." Aunt Maxi returned to her regular self. "Are you bringing that Twinkie dessert?"

"It's cake," Loretta corrected her.

"It'd be much cheaper to head on down to the grocery store, grab a box of Twinkies, line them up, and frost the top." Aunt Maxi did all the hand gestures to convey the actions in her words.

"Forget I ever told you about Compassion Companions." Loretta shook a finger with a big diamond ring on it at Aunt Maxi. "You don't have enough class in your bones to even think about any men on there."

"Good gravy, Low-retta, who ever heard of someone getting all bent out of shape over a Twinkie?" Aunt Maxi only fueled Loretta even more. She stormed off and went over to grab a coffee from the coffee bar.

"Aunt Maxi, I'd be ashamed." I *tsk*ed and headed over to Loretta. "Coffee on me." I put my hand on her back. "And I can't wait to taste your famous cake."

"You must take after your mama's side." Loretta smiled and helped herself to two cups of coffee.

Bunny was too busy bringing out the chowder and breads for the soon-to-be lunch crowd to even care that Aunt Maxi was there, but when it was all put out and I'd cleaned off all the café tables and restocked the coffee and tea bar, I told her she could leave for the day. Her mood really took a dive when she saw Aunt Maxi in the coffee shop.

Aunt Maxi was still there, needing to talk to me, and waited patiently on the sofa stroking Pepper. They both sat there, enjoying the warmth of the fire.

I stopped briefly to look out the window. The snow was still falling. Honey Springs Lake looked like a glassy mirror with all the images of the snowy trees. The view was gorgeous, and I gave a little prayer for everyone to be safe while driving on the roads, even though the radio station mentioned on my drive back from the Moores' that the roads weren't slick. Amy had mentioned a snowstorm was coming, and from the looks of the flakes, I thought that just might be happening.

"Okay, what did you find out?" I asked Aunt Maxi and sat down next to Pepper.

"You were all wrong about Pat." Aunt Maxi took out her phone from her pocketbook. "This is Pat."

She handed me her phone, which showed a photo of Aunt Maxi and a woman with blond hair and big boobs spilling out of her white Watershed button-down.

"Are you having a shot?" I asked about the two small shot glasses they were holding up with big grins on their faces.

"Turns out Pat is a bartender who did work the night of the murder." Aunt Maxi took the phone and smiled. "I just so happened to be bellied up at the bar. What is it about bartenders that make you talk?"

"You mean liquor?" I knew it took Aunt Maxi only one small glass of wine to get a little tipsy. No wonder she was so mean to Loretta.

"I was a grown woman about to go on a lunch date. I needed a little relaxation." Aunt Maxi was sitting so close to me that I could smell her breath.

"Just how much relaxation did you drink?" I asked.

"That's not important." She grinned. The closer I looked at her, the more I realized Aunt Maxi was drunk. "What's important is that Pat is a woman and you were wrong, Roxanne Bloom." She jabbed me in the chest with her finger.

"I'm getting you a cup of coffee." I stood up and walked over to the coffee bar, where I got a big cup of black coffee. I set it down on the coffee table in front of the couch. "You drink that, and I'll be right back."

"Did you hear what I said?" She tried to make eye contact with me, but the liquor she'd been drinking had to be settling in because she was slurring her words. "They didn't have a busboy that night who was a boy."

"Okay." I shook my head at her and grabbed one of the blankets from the wooden ladder that was leaned up against the wall next to the fireplace, which was really there for decoration. She looked as if she were about to pass out. Clearly, she had no idea what she was saying.

"Let me know when Floyd gets here," she said and slinked down a little more into the cushions. She pulled the blanket up to her chin. Pepper wiggled his way underneath it, ready to take his nap too. "I told him to get me here."

"Mmmkay." I shook my head and made it back to the counter. "Aunt Maxi is drunk," I said to Bunny. "I asked her to do one thing: find out if Pat from the Watershed knew anything about the Moores when they were there the night of his death. And she goes, gets a photo with some bartender, and drinks."

"The bartender is Pat." Bunny untied her apron and shuffled over to the coat rack in exchange for her coat. "Pat is a woman. She sometimes fills in for Floyd at the Moose." Her voice drifted off as she pinned her little hat back on her head.

"Pat is a blond, very voluptuous woman?" I asked, realizing Aunt Maxi had been telling the truth in her drunken stupor.

"Very blond and very voluptuous." Bunny retrieved her black pocketbook from underneath the counter and hooked it on her arm. "Floyd said she was very good for business."

I could only imagine how that woman in Aunt Maxi's photo sweet-talked those older men into having more, just like she'd done to poor old Aunt Maxi, who was now sawing logs with her mouth wide open.

"So, there was no busboy in the night we were there?" I clearly remembered the busboy with the Watershed black shirt on, the logo on the right side of his chest. "Then who was that?"

I blinked a few times. The scene played in my head. Ryan and Yvonne were fighting. The busboy, or whoever he was, bumped into the table and spilled Ryan's water glass into Ryan's lap.

"Bunny," I gasped. "The guy at the Watershed. He gave Ryan a full glass of water to replace the one he purposely knocked over."

"Okay." She buttoned up her coat.

"No. Don't you know what this means?" I asked her.

"That Mr. Moore got soaked?" she questioned.

"No. The water was poisoned with the hemlock." It made perfect sense to me. "This guy doesn't work for the Watershed. I didn't notice him at any table but the Moores', and he didn't give anyone water but Ryan. Ryan drank it. There was enough time for it to get into his system before he started to feel the effects of it, which caused him to drive off the road and into the lake, where his lungs quickly filled up and he actually died from drowning."

I went to grab my phone to call Spencer Shepard, but when I heard Bunny gasp, I moved my attention back to her.

Floyd had walked into the coffee shop, and he was standing over an unconscious Aunt Maxi, who now had a wee bit of drool running out of the corner of her mouth.

CHAPTER SIXTEEN

"Let me get this straight." Crissy Lane had made herself comfortable in one of the café table chairs with all her fingernail polish laid out. She had her sun-washed blond hair pulled up into a ponytail, exposing the natural red roots below. Her red freckles were a dead giveaway she was a real redhead, but she didn't like her hair color for some reason. She blinked her big, long fake lashes as she tried to get clarity from me. "Maxine was passed out when Floyd came to pick her up for their lunch date, then he left with Bunny. Now they are back together?"

"Yep." I left out how I'd told Floyd that Aunt Maxi was a closet drunk and Bunny was a much better companion. Bunny didn't even correct me. She was so happy when Floyd apologized and asked her to go to lunch that she even made up more drunk stories about Aunt Maxi. I was sure Aunt Maxi would get wind of those tales and let Bunny have it.

"Maxine and Floyd have been all the gossip at the Honey Comb." Crissy Lane was probably my closest thing to a best friend, and she did hair and nails at the Honey Comb, the boardwalk's salon.

Like Patrick and I had, Crissy and I had hung out together during the summers I spent here and kept in touch like pen pals.

"They were starting to say they were either on Team Maxine or Team Bunny." Crissy laughed and looked around at the polish on the table, then she finally picked one. She shook it up, beat it on her palm, and shook it some more. "I'm so glad it's over. What did Maxi say when she woke up?"

"Patrick had stopped by for lunch, and I had him take her home." I walked over to the coffee bar and opened the cabinet on the bottom to refill the creamers, sugars, and stir sticks. "She was still pretty out of it."

The industrial coffee pots were brewing and ready for the afternoon employees, a couple of girls from the local high school who were in the business and home economics classes. I'd already mentored Emily Rich, who ended up becoming a pastry chef and opened the Bee's Knees Bakery, the bakery here on the boardwalk. Emily had gotten so busy now that she was baking all the cakes for the events for All About the Details, not to mention the special orders for all the holiday parties. I reminded myself to stop by there on my way home when the afternoon girls came because I did want to check on the fancy cookies I'd gotten for the Christmas Day supper.

My nephew, Timmy—Patrick's sister's little boy—loved Emily's sugar cookies. They had the right amount of icing, and her Christmas designs would make a perfect addition to the dessert table.

"I was thinking red with some candy canes painted for your nails." She showed me the very red polish. "And we can make your ring fingernail white."

Crissy was going to paint my nails for the festive occasion. Wearing nail polish was rare for me, since I was always keeping my hands in hot or soapy water. But I was willing to make her happy. After all, when she offered to do my nails, I had said no, but she ended up begging, saying it was my Christmas gift to her, which guilted me into it.

"One finger white?" I asked and looked over my shoulder when the bell over the door dinged.

"It's all the rage." Did Crissy really think I cared about popular things?

"Abigail," I greeted Abigail Porter when she walked in with her fancy fur. She'd changed her shoes from the boots I'd seen her in earlier to a pair of snow boots trimmed in fur. "Can I get you a coffee while we talk?"

"No. I'm fine." Her words were like daggers to my heart.

Who refused coffee? And how was I going to get her to open up about everything with nothing to keep our minds wondering… like coffee?

"I'll be done in a minute," I told Crissy.

Then when Abigail shooed Pepper away, I nearly wanted to kill her. I didn't trust anyone who didn't like all furry animals enough not to wear them.

"We can chat over here if you'd like." I suggested near the fireplace on the sofa where everyone loved.

"No. We can stand." She wasn't going to budge a bit. "Did you talk to Yvonne?"

"Not yet. I plan on going there after I get off work." I picked Pepper up, gave him a few kisses on his head, and then put him back down. That would hold him for a while, since he was bothering Abigail for a pat.

"Come here, Pepper." Crissy patted her leg. "Let's go get one of your treats," she told him and got up from the table, taking a nail polish with her and leaving Abigail and me alone in the coffee shop with only a few customers talking over scones and coffee.

"I do have something I need to ask you about since we spoke at the Moores'." I wasn't going to ease into it. I intended to rip it right off like a Band-Aid. "I understand that you'd been here recently to see Ryan in his greenhouse."

"Who told you that?" A look of horror crossed her face.

"It really doesn't matter, but from what I understand, you and Ryan were in a pretty big lip-lock." I didn't want to tell her too much.

She shifted from hip to hip and rolled her eyes with her jaw slightly open, and I could see her tongue playing with her teeth as if she were annoyed.

"Ryan called me a week ago." She sucked in a deep breath and shook her hair out, then flipped it so hard it landed over her shoulder. "He told me he wanted to tell me something in person. I was thinking he was going to tell me he and Yvonne had made amends about the truth between what had happened. He said he was in his greenhouse. I went there."

"How did no one see you park in the driveway? Or even get through the gated entrance?"

"There's another way onto the Moores' property down the road past the Hill Orchard."

"Really? No gate or anything?" I tried to think of exactly where the entrance would be, but nothing came to mind.

"Nope. There's a gravel drive that looks like it leads to nowhere a little past the Hill Orchard on the left." When she said gravel drive, I knew exactly the gravel drive she was talking about.

"I thought that was just a piece of gravel the transportation department had made for tourists who'd gone too far and needed to turn around." The winding roads were narrow, and I could barely turn my small car around for a U-turn, much less these bigger vehicles.

"No. It leads right to the greenhouse. Anyways, I went, and he told me how he and Yvonne had been having some issues. He even told me about Jo Beth and the baby. He also told me how he missed our friendship and my son." She brought her hand up to cough. She was shaking.

"I know it's hard to tell." I wanted her to relax and not be so nervous. "Let me get you a water."

I hurried through the coffee shop and around the counter to grab her a bottle of water. She took a few sips and then continued.

"Thank you. I guess I'm a little more upset about Ryan's death than I thought." She was a little paler than I'd remembered her from earlier. "I hate to say it, but it felt good hearing he missed us, and I kissed him."

"You did?" I wasn't sure I heard her right.

"Yes. He rejected me. He said that he didn't call me there to rehash what happened the year before but to tell me we weren't invited to the party and he didn't want me to hear it from anyone else." She swallowed hard and brought her hand up to her brow. "Anyways, Yvonne—she loved him. The only reason I agreed to come here, though I'm feeling a little ill, is that I want to help in any way I can. I'm not sure why she'd be covering for someone, but now that you know what happened in the greenhouse, I can't help but wonder if he told her about the kiss, and she figured he'd been cheating on her like all the rumors out there said."

"Can you think of anyone who would want to kill him outside of the family?" I asked.

"He did take a phone call when I was there from Logsdon Landscaping." That got my attention.

"Logsdon?" I asked.

"They were in some sort of argument about the nursing home. He wanted something one way, and they did something different. He was mad." She shivered, pulling the edges of the fur coat up around her neck. "I really need to get going."

"Why would he care about the nursing home?" I asked her before she walked out.

"He owns it." Her words lingered along with the fancy perfume she wore as she darted out of the door.

"What was that about?" Crissy walked out of the swinging kitchen door.

"I'm not really sure, but I believe Yvonne Moore is covering up for someone. I can bet it's not Abigail Porter." I gnawed on Abigail's last words. "Did you know Ryan Moore owns the nursing home?"

"That's who Amy Logsdon was talking about when I was doing her nails last week. Something about how she'd given him a big break on their landscaping and the decorating over the past two years to help start the business, and he thanked them by starting his own landscape company in the spring. She was so mad and was trying to convince all the ladies under the dryer that they needed to stay with Logsdon Landscaping for all of their landscaping needs."

I could feel the shock contort on my face.

"What?" Crissy asked with a sideway glance.

"Did you hear her call him by name?" I needed to know.

"No, but I can find out." She pulled her phone out of her back pocket and started to type away. "I was busy running back and forth while she was talking, so I missed that part."

"You just gave me a perfect motive for Amy Logsdon to have killed Ryan Moore." I couldn't believe it.

"What?" Crissy's brows furrowed, and she looked at the phone when it beeped. "Yep. Ryan Moore." Whoever she'd asked had texted his name back.

"Jo Beth and Gio have been cleared!" I hollered over my shoulder on my way through the swinging kitchen door. I grabbed the whiteboard Aunt Maxi had started our little investigation on. I set it on the counter, and Crissy came behind it to look at the board.

"Last time we did this, you solved the murder." Crissy had once been involved in my nosiness, and we had all piled into her small VW to look for clues.

"And we are going to do it again." I pointed to the only three suspects we had. "Yvonne has now confessed, but I'm thinking she's covering for someone. Amy Logsdon has the most to lose. If she lost all her business to Ryan, she'd have nothing. When I asked her about him today, she was cool as a cucumber."

I could hear Amy laughing on the phone and in the next breath talk about Ryan's death, then laugh at something else.

"Taking away someone's livelihood is a pretty big motive." I wrote Amy's name on the whiteboard and put the dollar sign next to it for the motive. "And..." Slowly, I shifted my gaze to Crissy's face. "Amy would know all about hemlock."

Her jaw dropped open. We both turned to look at the door when the bell dinged. It was my afternoon employees. Pepper ran over to greet them.

"Oh my goodness, Pepper, you sure are festive with your red toenails." One of the girls squealed so loud she practically cut the air.

"What?" I jerked around to look at Crissy.

"I knew you weren't going to let me do yours, so while we were in the kitchen, I did his." Crissy shrugged and smiled.

"Oh, Pepper, I'm so sorry," I told him when we walked out of the door of the Bean Hive after I'd gotten the afternoon staff settled and sent Crissy on her way. "But you do look adorable with your matching red sweater on."

Pepper didn't care. He darted off down the pier instead of heading down the boardwalk.

"Pepper!" I yelled after him, knowing the pier and the Bait and Tackle Shop in the middle of it were closed. There was only one other set of footsteps in the snow, followed by Pepper's paw prints. "Where on earth is he going?"

The snow was falling, and I wanted to hurry up and stop by the Honey Springs Lake banks where Amy had told me the crew from the Moore house had been working. I knew I couldn't call Amy back and ask her about her little issue with Ryan, but I sure could play dumb and ask her workers if the rumor I'd heard was true.

Then I wanted to get home and out of the weather just in case it did turn into a snowstorm.

Luckily, Pepper had stopped right before the Bait and Tackle. He was digging in the snow drift that had gathered along the pier from the lake winds, which wasn't unusual when we did get snow.

"Pepper, stop that." I tried not to smile when I noticed his little red nails digging in the white fluffy snow. "It's probably a dead racoon," I told him when I saw some fur.

My mood faltered quickly when I saw him uncover what appeared to be boots trimmed in fur. He moved away. I bent down and uncovered what appeared to be a body.

"Abigail?" I gasped.

CHAPTER SEVENTEEN

At least I wasn't alone for what seemed like forever as I waited for Spencer Shepard to get there, because I wasn't sure what kind of shape I'd have been in if people hadn't heard me screaming.

Granted, it probably wasn't good for the community's businesses, since most of the people who had gathered around Abigail's body and me were more than likely tourists. I was sure a few of them had even called 911 because I could see them using their cell phones.

Spencer had moved Pepper and me back a few feet, where I joined the rest of the gathered crowd behind the police tape the deputies had put up.

"Why don't we all go to the Bean Hive?" I suggested to the crowd. "I own the coffee shop and can give free coffee and a sweet treat to warm everyone up."

The crowd started to disperse and walk down the pier towards the coffee shop.

"Please tell Spencer that he can find me at the Bean Hive," I told one of the deputies because I knew Spencer would be looking for me to answer some questions.

The Bean Hive was packed, and the afternoon employees were a little unsure of how to handle so many people, so I let the employees go home for the night. It was probably better since the snow was getting worse, and in no way did I want to put them in danger.

I had all the coffee pots going. I got all the burnt sugar cakes and ginger softies I'd made ahead of time out of the freezer and into the oven. If I'd not known better, I'd have thought I was having a little Christmas gathering with all the chatter and the smell of sugar, cinnamon, nutmeg, and freshly brewed coffee drifting all around us.

Pepper had retreated back into the kitchen, where he was safe and away from getting under people's feet, which he tended to do sometimes.

I grabbed a couple of logs from the big basket on the hearth and placed them in the fireplace, where I stoked them a couple of times to get a nice warm flame going. When my cell phone buzzed and I saw it was Patrick, I grabbed it to answer.

"What is going on down there?" he asked.

"I was leaving. I promise," I told him in a little preparation for what was about to come out of my mouth. "Pepper and I were leaving. Pepper ran down the boardwalk and uncovered a snow-covered and dead Abigail Porter."

"Abigail who?" Patrick didn't know who she was since I'd yet to tell him.

"Abigail was believed to be the woman having an affair with Ryan Moore, only she told me she wasn't. She's also best friends—*was* best friends," I corrected myself and pushed through the kitchen door when I heard the oven timers going off, "With Yvonne Moore until about a year ago."

"I want to say that I'm shocked you know all of this, but I'm not." The tone in Patrick's voice surprised me. He didn't seem all that upset. "I've got bigger issues here. Poor Maxi is sick to her stomach. I had to bring her here. The roads are getting bad."

As he told me about Aunt Maxi, I couldn't help but find it very entertaining, since Aunt Maxi never drank. I couldn't wait to get the real scoop but wasn't looking forward to telling her about Bunny and Floyd's reveal of their relationship either. Aunt Maxi's actions made it apparent she was somewhat lonely, or she'd not have been seeking Floyd.

I quickly got out the four sheets of treats I'd put in the oven and placed them on the cooling rack. Instead of plating them, I'd decided to push the cooling racks next to the coffee and tea stands so the guests could just help themselves.

I tucked my phone between my ear and shoulder while I maneuvered the contraption toward the door. Just as I was about to push through, Shepard stuck his head in.

"Hey, Patrick." I stopped and put the phone back up to my ear using my hand. "I've got to go. Spencer is here."

"I'm coming to get you in my truck, so don't leave. It's too dangerous." Patrick was always thinking of me, and no matter where he was in this crazy world, I knew he had my back and best interest at heart.

Spencer pushed the door open and pulled the cooling rack towards him.

"Just put it out on the shop floor near the coffee stand," I told him when I noticed everyone was getting coffee and not getting tea.

"What's going on?" Lesley Roarke was standing near the cash register with the bunny in her arms.

"Long story," I told her and took the bunny from her when she extended the animal my way. "Dead body on the pier, so I invited all the tourists who saw it in here for some hospitality so we didn't scare them away."

"Gosh." Lesley reached over and scratched the bunny on the head. "Jingle was a hit today. You were right about the kids loving her."

"Her?" I questioned. "Jingle?"

"The kids asked me her name, and I had no idea, so we came up with a name after we read the books chosen for story time. *Jingle the Festive Cat,* but we changed the name of the book to *Jingle the Festive Bunny* and adlibbed most of the book." Lesley smiled.

"You know, I love seeing you so happy." I ran a warm hand down her arm and tucked Jingle in my other one like a football. "Not that Jingle makes you happy, but you've embraced the Crooked Cat since your mom's passing."

"I really hated that bookstore growing up because it took mom away a lot. Book conferences, book sales, business conferences, and not to mention all the times she dragged me there." She shook her head. "Those were the events that I remembered when I was so bitter towards her. When I truly take the time to think back, it's the conversations she'd have with me during those long days in the bookstore that I didn't realize had shaped me into who I was until after she was gone..." Her voice trailed off.

"That's so amazing you have those memories and have let go of the hurt. Your mom would be so proud of you." I squeezed her arm before I let go.

"You think?" she asked as we stepped aside for someone to grab a ginger softie.

"I know." I ran my hand down Jingle. Her little nose twitched a couple of times, making Lesley and me giggle despite everything going on around us.

"You know..." Lesley grabbed Jingle back from me. "It's going to be so cold tonight. Why don't I get Jingle's cage and take her home with me for the night?"

"I think that's a great idea. Let me get her stuff." Since I'd yet to unpack anything Louise had left for her, I walked behind the counter and grabbed the bag with the adoption papers, food, hay, and treats, in hopes I wouldn't get those back.

"I grabbed a couple of cookies." Lesley shrugged, and I was happy to see she couldn't help herself.

"Can I talk to you now?" Spencer stepped in between us. "Lesley." He nodded.

"Spencer." She blushed and turned as if she didn't want me to notice.

Oh, I noticed.

"Sure. Can you help Lesley to her car with this stuff while I make sure everyone is good here?" Lesley didn't need help with a little bag and a cage, but her love life with Spencer needed a little push.

Though I knew Spencer wanted to protest because he was investigating and on the job, he was too much of a southern gentleman not to take up the challenge.

"Lesley, don't forget the Christmas Day dinner here. And I'm sure Spencer is coming too." I threw it in for good measure, not making eye contact with his searing stare before I pushed them out into the cold.

"Can I get you anything else?" I made my way around the coffee shop asking the various tourists but was happy to see they'd all helped themselves. A few of them had even placed some to-go orders. I quickly boxed those up and checked them out before Spencer made it back.

The coffee shop was clearing out, and I got Spencer a cup of cappuccino, his favorite, ready so we could talk about Abigail.

"There's a lot I need to tell you about this." I grabbed the whiteboard from behind the counter only to be met with a serious eyeroll from him. "You make fun of me, but this has been great." I didn't give him time to protest.

Conveniently, the last person left the coffee shop, leaving us alone. I took the opportunity to turn the sign around to Closed since it looked as if a big snowstorm would soon come down on Honey Springs, and the only people I saw on the boardwalk were the deputies still processing the scene.

"Y'all come in and warm up with some coffee and the fire when you need to!" I yelled out to them. They waved their hands and nodded.

"That's mighty nice of you, Roxy." Spencer pulled out his notebook. "You know the drill. Start from the beginning."

"First off, I have to say that if Abigail's preliminary autopsy report comes back with hemlock poisoning, I expect you to let Yvonne Moore go, because there's no way she poisoned Abigail from jail." I lifted a brow.

"Let's just take one thing at a time. We aren't sure how Abigail died, so we are treating it as such. Yes. We will do an autopsy." He somewhat agreed in his own way.

"Anyways..." I quickly recapped that Abigail had been Yvonne's best friend and that Yvonne caught her and Mr. Moore in a lip-lock at the Moores' annual big Christmas party. I also told him how Abigail had gone to see Ryan in the greenhouse and kissed him. That might lead one to think Yvonne killed Ryan because of his philandering ways, but in reality, she could've done that a year ago, and now that Abigail was dead, there was no way she could've struck twice. "There's this busboy, but not a busboy from the night of Ryan's death."

"Now you have me all confused." Spencer had been writing so fast as I talked that he barely had time to take sips of his drink.

"The night of the murder, I noticed this busboy spilled Ryan's water glass all over him." I began to tell the story about this busboy who wasn't really a busboy. "So who was that guy?"

"I can get the security footage of the boardwalk from that night as well as the Watershed." Spencer plucked his phone off his utility belt and made a quick call while I helped a few of the deputies with some coffee when they walked in.

Patrick and Sassy had also come in, making Pepper so happy to see them. I was happy too.

"I'm almost done here." I kissed him when I noticed Spencer had gotten off the phone. "You can grab my stuff from behind the counter. I can come in early tomorrow to clean up and get ready for the half day."

Since it was Christmas Eve tomorrow, I would be open only a half day like the rest of the shops on the boardwalk. It was actually a day I looked forward to. Last year it'd been a quiet day, so the shop owners got together for a little festive cheer on the boardwalk. Big Bib brought up his portable firepit, and we had a great time around it.

He was the owner of the boat dock. It was still open during the winter months, which were actually his busiest, since he worked on people's boats and fixed any problems so they'd be ready to put in when boating season started back up.

"I can't help but think you need to question Amy Logsdon." It was something I knew would throw Spencer off. And I was right. The look on his face contorted into so many different forms of confusion that I had to force myself not to smile. "Apparently, Ryan Moore is starting a new business venture into landscaping."

I told him everything I'd heard and what Crissy Lane told me she overheard.

"You know they twist tales like the hair is twisted in that place," he said, reminding me how the gossip spread through the salon, but I didn't need reminding.

"Like my Aunt Maxi says, there's some truth to the tales. You just gotta weed it out." I shrugged. "Amy would have motive. This landscaping and now decorating is her life. She's put all her money in it. The Moores and the nursing home were her biggest customers."

"Nursing home?" Spencer looked up from his notebook.

"Ryan Moore bought the nursing home." I threw my hands up in the air as if to say, "Who knew?" I got up and grabbed my coat off the coat rack. "You let me know about Abigail's autopsy. I'd like Yvonne to go home before Christmas."

"Why would Yvonne confess if she didn't do it?" Spencer asked me a very good question that I'd been pondering.

"It's a very good question that I can't answer other than she's covering up for someone." I sucked in a deep breath and zipped up. "But who?"

CHAPTER EIGHTEEN

I'd like to say it was all festive and happy after Patrick took us home, but Aunt Maxi had passed out on the couch, leaving Patrick and me to retreat to the bedroom, where we brought a big bowl of popcorn with M&Ms in it. There, we watched a couple of Christmas movies we found on TV. So the night wasn't a total loss.

Even though I was the one who was going to open the Bean Hive, Bunny had texted me to let me know she wasn't coming in for the half day. She and Floyd weren't going to waste any more time. They were going to spend the day together, and she was sorry she wasn't going to make it on Christmas Day in light of what had happened. That meant she didn't want to be around Aunt Maxi, and I didn't blame her, though I did make sure she knew she and Floyd were more than welcome to come.

I got up before my alarm sounded and knew Patrick was fast asleep. Sassy snored between us with her big legs in the air. Pepper had found his way to the couch and snuggled up in the crease of Aunt Maxi's legs. He could stay home with them today while I worked.

Instead of risking waking them up, I pulled my hair into a ponytail and grabbed jeans and my Bean Hive sweatshirt. It would be a fine outfit for a half day. Besides, I had a lot of baking to do to get ready for tomorrow's big Christmas Day at the Bean Hive.

Patrick was off for the next week, so it was just fine that I took the truck to get me to the boardwalk through the snowstorm, which did hit overnight. Even though I could see the work crews had been plowing all night, they still barely made a dent.

With the truck in four-wheel drive, I was pulling into the parking lot in no time. The lights of Wild and Whimsy were on when I walked past. With my nose up to the glass window, I knocked on it with my gloved hand, getting Beverly "Bev" Teagarden's attention.

"Get in here." Bev rushed me into my favorite little shop.

I stepped inside. My eyes immediately looked at the set Christmas table Bev had decorated in such a lovely way, the one I'd been ogling from the outside for a couple of weeks now.

"I was wondering if you were going to be in today after all the big ruckus on the news."

"You mean the body?" I asked and ran my hand along the Christmas china on the display table I'd been eyeing.

"No, I mean Yvonne Moore being set free. She even complimented you, saying you gave her the best Christmas present ever—getting her free." She pointed at the small TV she kept on the counter that she watched during the day. "They just released her."

"What?" I couldn't believe it. "I had no idea she got out. That means Abigail was poisoned."

"What?" Now it was Bev's turn to be confused.

"Nothing. I need to go see Yvonne Moore." I turned my attention to the display window and gestured to the table. "Can you package these up for me? I want to buy the entire set. I think they are going to look great for tomorrow's lunch." I had to get over to the Moores' and see Yvonne before I opened. "Can Dan bring them down later?"

Dan was Bev's husband and business partner.

"We can make that happen." She winked.

"I've got to go, but I'll see you later today." I put my gloves back on. "Be sure to tell Melissa and Savannah to come too."

Melissa and Savannah were the Teagardens' daughters. They were very sweet young women.

I was never more thankful to have Patrick's truck and the ability to drive behind a snowplow than on my way to the Moores' house. The plow truck was taking a little too long. I wanted to go see Yvonne, get the details, and talk to her about Abigail and what her next move should be now that the sheriff seemed to have new leads.

I eased around the plow in the oncoming lane and kept my hands steady on the wheel even though I was using four-wheel drive. The big truck could just as easily slip on the road as any car. It was a few miles down the road, when I passed Hill Orchard, that I realized I'd gone too far. Luckily, the gravel turn-around wasn't too far, which I now knew was the drive to the back of the Moores' property where the greenhouse was located. I'd turn around and head back, certain not to miss the Moores' gated entrance.

The truck's headlights shined down the gravel path just as my curiosity kicked in. Like a force I couldn't control, an itch I had to scratch, I punched the gas, sending the truck right on down the gravel path until I stopped just shy of the greenhouse.

"Do I?" I asked myself and my conscience, not sure who was going to answer first. "Yes, you do."

I threw the truck in park and kept the headlights on for light since it was still too early for the sun to show itself. I closed my eyes and sucked in a deep breath.

"What are you doing?" I asked myself before I jumped out of the truck. "I've got to see for myself."

I was only doing something I would do anyway if I were trying the case in a court of law. But somehow someone was getting hemlock, and it was either coming from this greenhouse or Amy Logsdon's landscaping company, for which I was sure Spencer had gotten a warrant by now.

My legs pushed down deep into the snow, which practically came up to my knees. I trudged through, picking my legs up high in the air before letting them down, each step carefully maneuvered so I wouldn't fall and hurt myself. Especially when no one knew I was here.

I patted the pocket of my coat to make sure my cell phone was in there just in case I needed to call someone. When I made it to the greenhouse, I was glad there was a small roof overhang that'd kept the snow from forming underneath it. Just a small layer of fresh snow. A water drip came off the corner of the roof from where an icicle had formed and was starting to drip as the temperature began to warm a smidgen.

Carefully I turned the knob of the greenhouse door and opened it. The buzz of the heater and several plant lights filled the spooky air. I stepped inside and shut the door behind me. There were visible signs of the investigation as I walked down the one aisle of the greenhouse. Although I knew nothing about plants, I did know what a raid looked like, and I could tell from the aged, water-ringed spots that various plants had been moved around. The only types of plants being grown at the moment were various types of ferns. There didn't seem to be anything that resembled the hemlock photos I'd been looking at and reading up on in the books I'd gotten from Crooked Cat. And if they had been in there, I was sure Spencer had them moved to evidence.

With my curiosity satisfied, I headed back out of the greenhouse and stopped under the awning to zip up my coat so I could shield myself from the cold on my trek back to the truck. Then I noticed a shoeprint. One that had to been left since the snowfall and since the sheriff's department had been there.

I pulled my phone from my pocket and flipped the flashlight feature on to get a better look. It looked like a print from a tennis shoe and on the smaller side. Had the killer come back to get more hemlock? Did they find more hemlock here? Had Spencer not collected it all? Why would the killer have killed Abigail?

All these questions started to pop into my head. I only knew of one person who just might be willing to give me the answer.

Yvonne Moore.

Who was she covering up for?

CHAPTER NINETEEN

The truck's windshield was already covered with snow. It was coming down at a pretty good clip, and I knew if I didn't hurry up and talk to Yvonne, I'd not only have to wait until the roads were clear enough, but I wouldn't get the coffee shop open for any customer brave enough to get out in the snow.

"Can I help you?" Daryl asked from the speaker at the gate.

"Hi, Daryl. It's Roxy Bloom. I understand Yvonne is out…" I stopped talking as soon as I heard her buzz me in.

The lights on the trees lining the driveway were lit up, creating a magical scene with the snow on the ground. It was truly a spectacular winter wonderland, and if Yvonne did make it home to enjoy the scene one last time in the house, it would be bittersweet.

The snow globe blowup in the fountain was turned on and flooded me with memories of how my parents had kept the Christmas decorations on all day during Christmas Eve, all through the night, and all day on Christmas. That was when I knew Santa would come that night.

Daryl opened the door when I got out of the truck.

"Please take your shoes off." She pointed to the snow-covered boots. "Yvonne and Belinda are in the kitchen."

"Ho ho ho!" I did my best Santa impression and patted my belly when I followed Daryl into the kitchen. "I guess Santa came early for you," I told Yvonne.

The poor gal looked haggard. The big dark circles under her eyes told me she probably didn't sleep in jail, and her greasy hair told me she didn't shower.

"Roxy." There was a tone of relief in Yvonne's voice. She sat on one of three stools pushed up to the marble island. "I can't believe you stopped by in this crazy snowstorm. I had to beg one of the officers to take me home because I knew my mom couldn't drive."

"We really can't thank you enough." Belinda's face seemed less stressed. She grabbed the glass carafe from their coffee pot, grabbed a mug, and set it in front of me, at which point she filled it to the top with the brew. "You have to enjoy a cup of Christmas joy with us."

"I'd love to, but quickly." They had no idea how trained my esophagus was from all the years of brewing, testing, and remaking hot coffee I had under my belt. I was almost as much of a champion at coffee-brewing as Yvonne was at swimming.

I sat down on one of the stools and looked at the three-tiered display that was meant for food, but it appeared to be a catch-all for them, holding various envelopes, keys, and ink pens.

"You know you can get in trouble for interfering with a criminal investigation or even helping the killer if you are covering for someone," I blurted it out.

"I..." Yvonne looked taken aback by my sudden outburst.

"Listen, I have to know. Yvonne, you can't cover up a murder that's turned into a double homicide." It was not only illegal but immoral. "When you told Spencer you did it after we talked about the greenhouse, I knew you were lying. I recalled how you told me you hate being cold. I know you didn't walk to the greenhouse in your bare feet because you don't wear anything but heels. And you told me Ryan had hired Logsdon because you hated gardening. You lied. You lied to Sheriff Spencer about everything."

Belinda and Daryl looked back and forth between Yvonne and me.

"I thought maybe Abigail did it." She shook her head. "Not that I didn't want to bring Ryan's killer to justice, but I do love Abigail despite what happened between us. I'm probably more upset she's dead than Ryan only because I know that Ryan was the one who came on to her. I know she turned him down, but the second time, in the greenhouse, she was vulnerable and lost. If Ryan had not tried to kiss her in our kitchen a year ago, she'd never have tried to kiss him in the greenhouse."

How did she know about the greenhouse? My oh-crap-on-a-cracker meter started to tick. Had I been wrong all along? Did Yvonne really kill him?

I slid my eyes past the door frame and into the big family room. I could see the empty bookshelves where Yvonne's prized swimming trophies used to be proudly displayed.

"There is one thing that did disturb me about the night Patrick pulled you out of the water." I glanced back around to look at her feet. They were nicely manicured and small. Did the shoe print in the snow at the greenhouse just so happen to be hers? Did she really not own a pair of tennis shoes? "I had no idea you were a champion swimmer until I came here and your mom was putting your trophies in a box."

"Yvonne is home now." Belinda spoke up. "I don't like your line of questioning. You make it sound like you believe Yvonne did kill Ryan. How do you know Abigail didn't do it and then poison herself when she knew the police were getting closer to her as the murderer?"

"Good point." I could feel the air in the room get a little thicker and less… well… filled with Christmas cheer. "She has a young son. I spoke to her maybe within the hour of her death, and she sure didn't seem like she was in any mood to kill herself, though she said she felt ill."

"It's fine, Mom." Yvonne shifted in her chair to look at me. "What does me being a good swimmer have to do with anything?"

"I'm not sure why you didn't swim to the top. Maybe the amount of time it took Patrick to get you out and up on the banks would've been enough time to save Ryan. Unless you didn't want Ryan saved. Or even yourself." I stared at Yvonne. "Yvonne, did you slip Ryan the hemlock? Did you plan on not surviving a crash that night as well?"

"That is about enough." Belinda smacked her hand on the counter so hard that it got my attention. "I won't have this in my house. Get out!"

Yvonne sat completely still and kept my stare. She didn't flinch or budge. That was my cue that I better get out of there.

Slowly I got up, and when I turned around to go back to the front door, I noticed a pair of tennis shoes tossed on the drying mat next to the back door. One was placed on its side with the sole facing out.

"That shoe looks a lot like the shoeprint I took at the greenhouse this morning. And small like your feet, Yvonne." I pulled my phone out of my pocket and swiped to my photos, showing the photo face out.

"This is ridiculous." Belinda walked over to me faster than I'd ever seen her walk in the past few days. She pinched my arm in her grasp, pushing me toward the entrance of the house. "If you won't leave on your own, I'll be more than happy to help you."

"Ouch." I jerked my arm away from her and smacked over the three-tiered stand, sending it crashing to the floor and spilling out the contents.

"I'm sorry. I didn't mean to press any buttons." I bent down and gathered as many things as I could. "But I just can't wrap my head around why you'd confess. It's the lawyer in me."

I put the items on the marble island and noticed the nursing home pamphlet was one of them. It was creased opened to an image of a one-person room with a big red ink circle around it and Belinda's name accompanied by several explanation points.

"Belinda." I gasped and looked at her, then down at her feet. "Of course." I started that nervous laughing thing I did when I knew I was in a pickle. "Yvonne has your feet. You wear tennis shoes. You can walk pretty well. And Ryan wanted to put you in the nursing home. You poisoned him, but how did you do it?"

"I told Yvonne you were trouble," Belinda spat, her little-old-woman ways suddenly disappearing.

"Mom, please don't." Yvonne covered her ears. "I don't want to hear it."

"You're going to hear it, and we are going to get rid of her unless you do want to go to jail for knowing deep down that I did kill Ryan. And it was all for you." Did Belinda just really confess to killing Ryan?

"Belinda!" Daryl hurried to her side. "I don't think you know what you're talking about. We need to get you medication."

"Of course I know. You're the one who gave that young boy money and extra hemlock the night they went out to dinner. Don't be acting like this is all my fault, Daryl."

"What young boy?" Yvonne asked with a panic in her voice.

"The young man that works for the landscape company. He needed extra money. He said he was only hired for holiday work. The Logsdon Landscaping

Company was worried about being able to stay open because Ryan was going to run them out of business," Belinda snarled. "He was ruining everyone's life. He didn't care who he hurt. He cheated on you. He never was a father to Jo Beth, and he fired Gio for no reason whatsoever. He was going to take away all the livelihood the Logsdons had, and then you'd be here with nothing." She shook a finger at her daughter. "You were going to let him put me in that nursing home. I heard him telling you that the two of you were going to move and stick me in there alone. With no one."

"You mean to tell me you killed Ryan because he mentioned a nursing home and your name in the same sentence?" Yvonne walked over and stood nose to nose with the woman who had brought her into this world. "When Shepard said they'd found hemlock in the greenhouse and Ryan was poisoned with hemlock, I knew it had to be you that killed him. I was willing to take the fall for you, but when they let me go because Abigail had been killed the same way, I thought I got it wrong because you loved her. You have been begging me for the past twelve months to mend our friendship."

"I was until she came back here yesterday after I kicked her out. She figured it out. She came back here to tell me how she knew I was connected somehow while she sipped on some of my freshly brewed coffee." Belinda looked at me. "Was your coffee good?"

My heart sank. Did she really just let me know that she *poisoned* me? Instantly I felt sick.

"You hold on right there." Yvonne pointed at me to tell me to stay, and she grabbed her phone. "Yes. Please send an ambulance and the sheriff to the Ryan Moore home. This is Yvonne Moore, and my mother killed my husband and Abigail Porter."

CHAPTER TWENTY

"I was dreaming of a white Christmas, but I never figured it'd be this white." I had decided to pull my hair up in a bun and wear a black turtleneck and buffalo check A-frame skirt along with a pair of heels for the Christmas Day dinner. Most of my friends and family had only seen me wear the staple outfit, jeans or khakis with a Bean Hive logo shirt, which I covered up with an apron that had more spills on it than one could count.

"I'm just glad I'm spending another Christmas with you." Patrick was putting the final cloth napkins around the table in the coffee shop. "Glad you didn't test positive for hemlock poisoning."

"That was a scare." I sucked in a deep breath and continued to look out the window with a grateful outlook given how this time yesterday had turned out.

Yvonne had done the right thing and called 911. After they got there, the ambulance had whisked me off to the hospital, where they did all sorts of tests to make sure I wasn't poisoned. After Spencer heard I'd gotten the all clear, he was in my room lickety-split.

He told me they were on the cusp of pinning either Belinda or Daryl as the killer. Spencer had taken my leads about the busboy and gotten the video footage like he said he would do, and it revealed that the young man did work for the Logsdon Landscaping Company. Of course, Amy Logsdon had come out in the clear with my theory.

Then there was Abigail. He said he'd not put the puzzle pieces together until they'd used her cell phone. Shepard found phone pings from various cell towers where Abigail had been to see Belinda a second time that day after I'd seen her there. Phone records showed a call placed from the Moores' home to Abigail's phone, leading him to believe the killer was in the house and not Yvonne, because she was locked up.

"Hey buddy." Pepper sniffing my ankles brought me out of my thoughts. "You want to help me get the turkey out of the oven?"

I twirled around on the toes of my high-heeled shoes and headed to the kitchen. I took in all the beautiful details of what Patrick and I had created for our family and friends.

We had moved all the café tables to the side and formed a big U-shape constructed of three large tables we'd gotten from All About the Details. The Teagardens had brought down the table settings and placed them in front of each chair along with cloth napkins and poinsettias neatly used as centerpieces. The Christmas tree was lit next to the roaring fire.

But it was the turkey and all the baked goods that made it feel and smell like Christmas.

"That looks good," I told Pepper and Sassy when we pulled open the oven door and looked at the golden bird. "Stand back." I grabbed two potholders and pulled the big bird out, carrying it to the swinging door and backing out of it, where I found we'd gotten guests.

Yvonne Moore was there with Jo Beth and Gio. Boy, was I surprised.

"I'm so glad to see you." I didn't invite them, but we had plenty of food. "Please help yourself to something while we wait for everyone to come."

I pointed them to the snack table.

"We can't impose." Yvonne waved a hand. "We wanted to stop by and thank you. It seems you've done more for our little family than you could know."

"You aren't imposing." I insisted they stay. "We are all family and friends here."

"Are you sure?" Gio asked.

"Man, we are more than sure." Patrick had come over with the carving knife in his hand. "In fact, I'll let you do the honors since you're the real butcher around here."

"All right." Gio nodded, and off he and Patrick went.

"You don't need to thank me for anything." I put my hand on Yvonne. "I'm really sorry for your losses." My statement even included her own mother, who I knew was a big loss from her life, as were her best friend and husband.

One by one, all the people we loved came in from the snow and warmed by the fire. Once people stopped dribbling in, we decided it was time for prayer and food.

Patrick and I moved three of the chairs that I'd figured to be Bunny Bowoski's, Loretta Bebe's, and Floyd's if Bunny decided to bring him. They'd not showed.

We passed the food around. I was happy to see Aunt Maxi had recovered from her day-drinking experience and seemed to be much hungrier than normal. She even sat next to Mom. All the shop owners had come, and we were all talking when the bell over the coffee shop dinged. All the chatter stopped when we saw Bunny and Floyd standing there. My eyes shifted to Aunt Maxi.

I watched with bated breath, hoping she'd not say anything, but that was too much to ask for.

The sound of the chair legs scooting across the tile floor when Aunt Maxi scooted it away from the table cut the silence.

"We saved you two a seat. Roxy?" Aunt Maxi looked at me, giving me the eye to get the chairs back in place.

"Yes." I jumped up. "We didn't think you were coming, so we put them back."

I played along with Aunt Maxi's lie, one I could totally get my heart into.

"I've got it." Patrick grabbed my hand and stood up. "Sit. I've got it." He kissed me and pushed my chair back in for me when I sat down.

I took a deep sigh of relief. Patrick quickly got a couple of more chairs. Aunt Maxi grabbed a few more of the place settings I'd bought from Wild and Whimsy while everyone scooted around the big table to make room.

Once everyone was situated, the conversation began and filled the room with laughter, tales, and sheer love.

"Here, pass the green beans down to Floyd." I picked up the bowl and handed it to Patrick. Like an assembly line, we passed the food down to the happy couple.

Aunt Maxi winked.

There was definitely something about the spirit of Christmas that brought the unlikeliest of conflicts to an end... even if that meant a truce just for one day.

The End

RECIPES FROM THE BEAN HIVE

Burnt Sugar Cake
Gingerbread Softies
Twinkie Cake
Rich Potato Chowder

Burnt Sugar Cake

Submitted by Jeannie Daniel

This is an old-family, old-fashioned recipe.

Burn ½ cup sugar in a heavy skillet, carefully add ½ cup boiling water and boil until it is syrupy.

Sift together 1 ½ cups sugar, 1 teaspoon salt, 3 cups flour.

Dissolve 1 teaspoon of baking soda in a little warm water in a 1 cup measuring cup and then fill the rest of the way up with cold water.

Cream ¾ cup butter with 1 teaspoon vanilla.

Add 2 eggs and beat smooth.

Stir in the syrup mixture then beat in dry ingredients alternately with dissolved baking soda.

Bake in an 8 or 9 inch pan 30 to 35 minutes at 350 degrees

Gingerbread Softies

Submitted by Sharon Rust

Ingredients

- 1-18.25-oz box spice cake mix
- 1-8oz pack cream cheese
- softened ¼ cup (½ stick) butter melted
- 1 large egg
- ¼ cup packed Brown sugar
- 2 teaspoon ground ginger
- 1 teaspoon cinnamon
- 2 teaspoon vanilla

Directions

1. Take about ½ of cake mix and blend with the other ingredients until smooth then add remaining cake mix. (you might have to do the remaining cake mix with spoon unless your mixer is strong)
2. place by teaspoon full about 2 inches apart on prepared cookie sheet.
3. Bake 10-13 minutes in 350 degrees oven.

Twinkie Cake

Submitted by Robin Kyle

Ingredients

- 1 box yellow cake mix (I used Duncan Hines)
- 5.1 oz box instant vanilla pudding (the large box)
- 1 cup water
- 1 stick salted butter, melted and cooled slightly
- 4 large eggs, lightly beaten

Filling/Frosting Ingredients

- 1 stick salted butter,
- slightly softened
- 1/4 cup heavy cream
- 1 tsp vanilla
- 7 oz jar marshmallow creme
- 3 ½ cups powdered sugar
- Sprinkles

Directions

1. Preheat oven to 350.
2. Butter and flour 2 (8 inch) round cake pans and set aside.
3. In the bowl of your mixer, combine eggs and butter.
4. Add water, pudding mix, and cake mix and beat on medium for about a minute, until batter is smooth and thick.
5. Spread evenly in prepared pans and bake for about 20-25 mins or until tops spring back when lightly touched, or a toothpick inserted in center of cake comes out clean.
6. Cool cakes for a few minutes in the pans, then turn out on to wire racks to finish cooling.

For frosting/filling:

1. Beat butter and vanilla in your mixer until combined.
2. Add marshmallow cream and beat until smooth.
3. Slowly add powdered sugar until just combined.
4. Add heavy cream, increase speed to high, and beat for one minute, until light, smooth and fluffy.
5. Spread half of filling/frosting on bottom cake layer, then add the second cake layer on top of filling/frosting.
6. Spread the other half of filling/frosting on the top layer of the cake.
7. Add sprinkles on top.
8. Chill for at least 30 minutes and serve.

Rich Potato Chowder

Submitted by Chris Mayer

Ingredients

- 5 to 6 cups potatoes, peeled and cubed
- 1 lb. bacon, cut up before cooking
- 1 to 2 onions depending on size and your taste
- 2 ¼ cups water

Directions

In large stockpot fry bacon until crisp – DO NOT DRAIN
Sauté onion, THEN pour off drippings
Add to pot:
The potatoes and water
1 tsp. salt
½ tsp. paprika OR pepper, whichever you prefer
Bring to boil, cover and simmer 20 – 25 minutes, until potatoes are tender

Mix together:
2 cups sour cream
2 cans cream of chicken soup
3 ½ cups milk
Gradually stir into potatoes until blended
Bring to serving temperature over low heat, do not let it boil again

LEAVE A REVIEW

If you enjoyed reading this book as much as I enjoyed writing it then be sure to return to the Amazon page and leave a review.

Go to Tonyakappes.com for a full reading order of my novels and while there join my newsletter. You can also find links to Facebook, Instagram and Goodreads.

Join like-minded readers like YOU in the Cozy Krew Facebook Group for dream casting, fan theories, and live Q & A's. It's like a BIG GIANT BOOK CLUB! But if you want to have your own book club, be sure you let me know! I love to send goodies.

DEAD TO THE LAST DROP

A Killer Coffee Mystery

Book Eight

BY
TONYA KAPPES

ACKNOWLEDGMENTS

Gayle Shanahan! Thank you so much for submitting your Pecan Ball cookie recipe to the annual Kappes Christmas Cookie exchange. I'm so excited to have it featured here at The Bean Hive.

CHAPTER ONE

I liked nothing better than the smell of the freshly made coffees that brewed in the industrial coffee makers. The rich scent of my very own Peruvian roast curled around me like a warm blanket, and Pepper lay at my feet, warming them with his body heat.

Who knew how much a sweet Schnauzer could warm not only my feet but my heart? I reached down and patted him on his sleepy head, but he didn't move. The fireplace glowed with an orange flame and heated the Bean Hive to a perfect temperature for the customers who would arrive when we opened.

The coffee makers beeped to let me know the coffee had been fully brewed, sounding like a wonderful melody. The sound was music to my ears and a signal to get up off the couch and put the breakfast treats in the oven so they'd be hot, fresh, and ready for anyone who needed a little sweet with their morning coffee.

Pepper lifted his head to see what I was doing. "I better get those in the oven," I told him. "It's still coming down pretty good out there."

The entire front of the Bean Hive consisted of windows with a long counter-type bar in front of them. Behind the long bar stood stools for the customers who wanted to enjoy their coffee while taking in the magnificent view of Lake Honey Springs, the actual reason why Honey Springs, Kentucky, was a tourist town. Even in the winter.

"So pretty," I said with a sigh as I looked out at the freshly fallen snow down the pier and across the boardwalk. Then I turned to head back toward the kitchen of my coffee shop.

Bunny Bowowski, my only full-time employee, would be here soon. We took turns opening, and today was my day, which I didn't mind. I'd left my husband, Patrick, and our poodle, Sassy, at home and fast asleep, tucked into the warm bed.

After I went to Pet Palace, our local no-kill shelter version of the SPCA, Pepper had adopted me as his human, and Sassy and Patrick came along later. That reminded me to keep my ears peeled for Louise Carlton, owner of Pet Palace. She said she had a new cat for me to showcase at the Bean Hive this week.

I had gone through a lot of hoops to get the health department to even agree to let me showcase an animal from Pet Palace. Everyone deserved a loving home, and having an animal that needed a home here during the week was a perfect way for people to see how the animal acted and how they might fit together with that animal. I was proud to have been able to help all the animals I'd had in the coffee shop. They were all adopted out and living their best lives.

Louise had already told me a little about the sweet feline, so I was excited to get her into the shop to give her some good loving. It was still a little too early for Louise to show up, but you never knew whether someone was going to be early or not. I certainly didn't want her waiting outside in the snow with the cat.

I dragged the coat rack sitting next to the counter and used the rack to prop open the swinging door connected to the coffee shop and the kitchen just so I could hear if anyone was knocking.

The Bean Hive opened at six a.m. during the week and a little later on the weekends. There wasn't an exact time I opened, but six a.m. was when we got up and moved around. During the winter months I didn't open on Sundays, but I did come in to order and prepare the food for the upcoming week.

We were technically a coffee shop, but I liked to make everyone feel welcome and at home. Coffee was great for that, but a little something for the belly was also good. Each week on the menu I had a breakfast item outside of the usual donuts, scones, and muffins. I provided something like a quiche or breakfast-type casserole with a little more oomph for the hungrier customers. I offered a light lunch as well. These food items were the exact same for a week, so I made them in bulk on Sunday.

The kitchen had a big workstation in the middle where I could mix, stir, add, cut, or do whatever I needed to do to get all the recipes made. Someone might look at it and call it a big kitchen island, but it was where all the magic happened. There was a huge walk-in freezer as well as a big refrigerator. I had several shelving units that held all the dry ingredients and a big pantry that stored many of the bags of coffee beans I'd ordered from all over the world. I liked to roast my own beans and make my own combinations, but the coffee shop had pretty much reached its capacity of what I could roast, and the small roaster was in much need of a bigger upgrade. However, I rented the space from my aunt Maxine Bloom, and there was no room to expand on the boardwalk where we were located. On my right was the Queen for the Day spa, and to the left of me was Knick Knacks, a little boutique store with a variety of items. Aunt Maxi didn't own those, so expanding was pretty much out of the question because they weren't going anywhere anytime soon.

Quickly I put the muffin tins in the oven to get them heated up and ready to put in the glass display counter. Then I grabbed the dry ingredients I needed to make the coffee soufflé, which would sell out so fast. Every time I made it, it was a hit. Of course it was amazing. Who didn't like sugar, vanilla, and coffee?

"One envelope unflavored gelatin, sugar, salt and vanilla," I said to myself, plucking the items off the shelf as I found them. "Now for a little brewed coffee." I grabbed the carafe out of the small pot of coffee I kept in the kitchen for me and put it on the workstation with the dry ingredients. Then I went to the refrigerator to grab the milk and eggs.

Eggs didn't really need to be refrigerated, but for some reason I refrigerated them. Everything in the coffee shop was prepared with the freshest of ingredients. If I could get it locally, I did. My honey came from the honey farm across the lake from the boardwalk. The vegetables and eggs came from Hill's Orchard, and the coffee beans came from all over the world.

"Hi do!" From the coffee shop, I heard the familiar greeting from my Aunt Maxi. "It's me! Maxi!" she called out like I didn't recognize her voice.

But I knew she did it to let me know she wasn't some random burglar. Aunt Maxi owned the building where my coffee shop was located, and she had a key. She showed up whenever she wanted.

"Back here!" I hollered back just as I finished pouring the soufflé into a serving dish and putting it into the chiller to set. I had already made some earlier this morning, so I took those out of the chiller and was pleased with how they turned out.

"Oh, coffee soufflé today?" Aunt Maxi walked into the kitchen. She wore a bright-red wool coat with big purple buttons.

"Yes." I couldn't stop from smiling when I saw her.

She also wore a pair of snow boots with her polyester brown pants tucked in. She tugged off the purple knit cap that matched the color of her hair.

"What?" She used the tips of her fingers to lift her already-high hair in place.

"Your hair. I don't think I've ever seen it that purple." I walked over and kissed her.

"Honey, it's a new year. New me." She unbuttoned her coat and hung it up on the coat rack that continued to prop the kitchen door open. Her patchwork hobo bag hung across her body. She dug down deep in it to retrieve a big can of hair spray.

"Seriously?" I asked. "My food," I reminded her, but it didn't stop her from spraying.

"I've got an image to keep up now that I'm in the new play." And that was why she was here.

"Play?" I took the bait to hear all about her new adventure.

Aunt Maxi was always getting into something. I always enjoyed hearing about them even if not all of them had come to be. She was the reason I moved to Honey Springs after my divorce.

Aunt Maxi had always lived here, and when I was a little girl, my father would come to visit, bringing me with him. I loved being here so much I even started to spend my summers here. It wasn't until I'd gone off to college, earned my law degree, gotten married to another lawyer, and opened a law firm with my spouse that I realized our client policy was to help all our clients in more than just law.

Well... that was when I found my now-ex-husband, Kirk, doing counseling than was more than verbal, if you knew what I meant. It was then that I ran off into the arms of my aunt, who just so happened to have this space open while Honey Springs was in desperate need of a coffee shop.

I was still a lawyer and kept my license up. Good thing, too, because I give out so much advice around here that I find it soothes my lawyer side. But coffee was my passion. I loved all things surrounding coffee, and gathering with friends for a little gossip just might be my favorite thing of all. Gossip happened all day long at the Bean Hive. So technically, working here didn't feel like work to me.

"Mmmhhhh. Didn't you notice the new dowel rod flags on the lights around town?" she asked.

Aunt Maxi was referring to the dowel rods on the carriage lights that were all over Honey Springs and the boardwalk. Every season or occasion, the beautification committee had special flags to hang on the rods. It was a special touch to add to our small southern lake town.

"Well, I want you to know that Bunny Bowowski didn't vote for them, and neither did Mae Belle Donovan." She shrugged and curled her nose in disgust. "Low-retta Bebe is the producer of this year's local theater."

Aunt Maxi didn't have to say any more than that. I knew this conversation would need a cup of coffee.

"Grab those muffins and the stack of cookies," I told her. I grabbed the soufflés and the serving tray of mini breakfast quiches I'd made. The pastries were all ready to go in the display case "While we fill the display case, you can tell me all about it."

When both of us were through the door, I put down the items in my hand and moved the coat tree back. Turning back around to look at the inside of the coffee shop, I gasped at the beauty of the coffee shop.

"I'll tell you after I go to the bathroom." Aunt Maxi headed there.

Even though Aunt Maxi owned the building, she didn't give me a cut on the rent. I didn't expect her to since it was part of her income. Rent was a little steep, but I'd watched a few DIY videos on YouTube to figure out how to make the necessary repairs for inspection when I first decided to open the coffee shop. I couldn't've been more pleased with the shiplap wall, which I'd created myself out of plywood and painted white so it would look like real shiplap.

Instead of investing in a fancy menu or even menu boards that attached to the wall, I'd bought four large chalkboards that hung down from the ceiling over the L-shaped glass countertop.

The first chalkboard menu hung over the pie counter and listed the pies and cookies with their prices. The second menu hung over the tortes and quiches.

The third menu over the L-shaped curved counter listed the breakfast casseroles and drinks. Above the other counter, the chalkboard listed lunch options, including soups, as well as catering information.

On each side of the counter was a drink stand. One was a coffee bar with six industrial thermoses containing different blends of my specialty coffees as well as one filled with a decaffeinated blend, even though I never clearly understood the concept of that. But Aunt Maxi made sure I understood some people drank only the unleaded stuff. The coffee bar had everything you needed to take a coffee with you, even an honor system that let you pay and go.

The drink bar on the opposite end of the counter was a tea bar. Hot tea, cold tea. There was a nice selection of gourmet teas and loose-leaf teas along with cold teas. I'd even gotten a few antique tea pots from the Wild and Whimsy Antique Shop, which happened to be the first shop on the boardwalk. If a customer came in and wanted a pot of hot tea, I could fix it for them, or they could fix their own to their taste.

A few café tables dotted the inside, as did two long window tables that had stools butted up to them on each side of the front door. It was a perfect spot to sit, enjoy the beautiful Lake Honey Springs, and sip on your favorite beverage. It was actually my favorite spot, and today would be a gorgeous view of the frozen lake with all the fresh snow lying on top.

"Burrrrr. It's cold." Bunny Bowowski walked through the door, flipping the sign to Open. "Me and Floyd enjoyed your soufflé so much last night." She loved talking about her new relationship with Floyd.

Bunny's little brown coat had great big buttons up the front, and her pillbox hat matched it perfectly. The brown pocketbook hung from the crease of her arm and swung back and forth as she made her way back to the coffee bar. There, she'd grab a coffee before she hung up her coat and put on her apron.

"Did you notice the new lamppost flags?" she asked and waddled back over to the coat tree. Slowly she unbuttoned her coat and hung her purse and her coat on the coat tree. The sound of the water running in the bathroom caught her attention. "What was that?"

"Aunt Maxi is here, so maybe you shouldn't talk about the flags," I suggested, since they were probably talking about the same thing and clearly on opposite sides of whatever it was they spoke of. If it was no big deal to either of them, neither would've brought it up.

"Good thing she's here. I'm gonna give her a piece of my mind." Bunny brought the mug up to take a sip.

"Were you flapping your lips about me?" Aunt Maxi stood, glaring at Bunny with her fists on her hips. Her purple hair glistened in the light of the coffee shop.

"What are you doing here so early?" Bunny gave Aunt Maxi the once-over. "You trying to get to Roxy before me, huh?"

"Listen, we are open, and I don't have time for all of this." I looked between the two of them.

"Did you not see that snow out there?" Bunny asked. "It took Floyd almost an hour to get me here."

"It takes Floyd an hour to get anywhere without snow," Aunt Maxi muttered under her breath but knew Bunny could hear her.

"Ladies," I said in my warning tone, though I knew it wasn't going to work. "Everyone grab a cup of coffee, and let's talk about what is going on."

Bunny already had her cup and sat down at the café table nearest her. Aunt Maxi sat down at a different table near her. Instead of trying to get them to compromise at a neutral table, I simply let them stay, grabbed Aunt Maxi and myself a cup of coffee each, and stood so I could address them both.

"What are the flags about?" I asked Aunt Maxi, who was busy doctoring up her coffee with creamer and sugar. My eyebrow lifted as I wondered why she even bothered having coffee in the cup.

"They are about the play." She lifted her chin in the air and looked down her nose at Bunny. "Bunny and Mae Belle are mad because they didn't get an offer to be in the play, as I did."

"We don't care one iota about that, Maxine," Bunny chimed in. "We want to use the flags we had last year to promote all of Honey Springs for the winter instead of spending money on new flags when we could use that money somewhere else."

Bunny had a good point, but I didn't dare tell Aunt Maxi. She'd have a conniption right then and there. It wouldn't be a pretty sight.

"What good is doing a play for the tourists if they don't know about it?" Aunt Maxi snapped back. "We could put it in the paper, but tourists don't buy our local paper. We could put it on flyers in the shops, but look at that snow. Who is going to come out in the snow right now?"

Then I could see Aunt Maxi's point.

"Roxanne." When Aunt Maxi said my full name, I knew she truly believed what she was about to say. "I'm telling you, when Bunny thought she had a shot at the lead of Vi Beauregard, she was all over using whatever funds to promote it. Even had the boys at the Moose talking about what a good Vi she'd be."

"Why," Bunny said with a gasp, "I can't help it if the boys at the Moose like me over you, Maxine Bloom. I guess my niceness trumps your gaudiness." Bunny's eyes drew up and down Aunt Maxi until they fixed right up on Aunt Maxi's purple hair.

Aunt Maxi looked like one of those pressure cookers. I could feel her anger curling up from her toes and straight up to her hair. I swear, I thought I saw her hair stand up even more on its own.

"Why, Bunny Bowowski!" Aunt Maxi smacked the table so hard that when she got up, it almost tumbled over. "How dare you talk to me like that!"

Just as I was about to make sure Aunt Maxi wouldn't leap across her table to try to get to Bunny's throat, the bell over the door dinged.

"Welcome to the Bean Hive." Bunny's disposition turned on a dime. She planted a big smile on her face and stood up. Just as pleased as a peach, which I was sure was because she'd gotten the last word in.

She and Aunt Maxi knew I wouldn't stand for their bickering while there was a customer.

CHAPTER TWO

The morning rush came and went, and so did Aunt Maxi's rant. I assumed she got tired of waiting for Bunny to make a comeback at her, so she sat at one of the café tables sipping her coffee and talking to everyone coming in and out the coffee shop door. That didn't mean she was finished with Bunny. It meant she would be able to get her wits about her and come back for seconds.

Bunny knew it too.

Bunny was good at talking to the customers, though she was a tad bit slow on getting them their orders ready. They didn't seem to mind. In fact, I think customers liked Bunny waiting on them. She was sort of the grandmother type that gave advice when you didn't want it. Well meaning, she was, but still, she'd tell a customer they needed to get two muffins instead of one because they were too skinny… those types of comments.

I'd just gotten finished cleaning up the coffee station when Louise Carlton walked through the door with a cat carrier in hand and a folder underneath her arm. She looked so well put together with her silver bob hair nicely curled under. Her bangs were perfectly cut above her brows. She was such a beautiful middle-aged woman.

"I can't wait to meet our new friend." My eyes focused on the carrier that was a little too small to hold a dog, and Louise didn't seem to be having any trouble holding it until Pepper came running up to get a good whiff of the new furry friend she had brought.

"A beautiful cat." Louise lifted the carrier for me to peer inside. The bracelets on her wrists jingled. The big jeweled ring on her finger twinkled under the coffee shop lights.

"Hey there." The poor baby was as huddled in the back as far as it could be. The eyes' black pupils were the size of marbles. I slowly blinked a few times like Louise had taught me to do with the cats when I became a volunteer at the Pet Palace a long time ago.

Louise claimed it was a way for the cats to get a hug from you and to tell them you are nice or safe.

"What's the story?" I asked Louise. I motioned for her to follow me back to the counter where I'd display all of the cat's information and Louise's business card to attract potential fur-ever homes for the cat.

"A stray. A hunter found her and brought her into Pet Palace. She's been looked over by the vet and given the shots and has been cleared for adoption." Louise set the carrier on the floor of the coffee shop.

While she opened the folder, I made her a cup of coffee she could take with her and slipped a couple of coffee soufflés in a to-go bag. I knew she loved them, and I knew they'd be gone before we turned around. They were already selling like hotcakes.

"Mornin'," Perry Zella said, waving from the front of the coffee shop. A couple of his mystery club members had followed him inside. They had started meeting at the Bean Hive once a month for the past four months to discuss different unsolved mysteries and various mystery books they were reading.

I really enjoyed having them there because they loved to question me about the legality of everything, since I was a lawyer by trade and a coffee shop owner by heart.

"Good morning! I'll bring y'all a carafe in a second." I placed Louise's to-go items on the counter in exchange for the paperwork. "What is the cat's name?" I asked Louise.

"There is no name." She frowned. I could tell her heart was hurting as much as mine at the thought that this little baby had been outside in the woods, cold, hungry, and probably scared. "Why don't you name her?" Louise's eyes lit up at her idea.

"She is brown and tan." I couldn't help but notice she was probably a mix of different breeds because she didn't resemble any sort of breed I'd ever seen. "What about Mocha?"

"Perfect." Louise clapped her hands together and bent down. "Now, Mocha, you be a very good girl, and Pepper will love you so much," Louise told Mocha while I turned to the coffee pots behind me to start a carafe for Perry and his mystery friends.

"I'm sure we will be great." I wiped my hands down my apron and walked around the counter to get Mocha's cage so Louise could leave with peace of mind. "Why don't we put her on the cat tree and see how she does."

It wasn't really a question. Patrick had built a cat tree for the cats because when Sassy was around, she knew no boundaries with other animals and wanted to play with them all, so his solution was to make a nice tall cat tree that let them hide from Sassy. It worked pretty well too.

"Since Sassy isn't here yet"—I picked up Mocha's cage—"I'll let you know how she adjusts," I said to Louise and walked her toward the door on my way to the cat tree.

Louise had stopped to talk to Aunt Maxi on the way out. I heard Aunt Maxi telling Louise how Loretta Bebe had given her the lead part in the winter theater production put on by the community theater. Bunny let out a few huffs from across the room, showing her disapproval of how Aunt Maxi's already-inflated ego had gotten bigger. Or at least that was how I read Bunny's body language.

"Now." I lifted the cat carrier to the very top of the cat tree shelf and peered in at Mocha. "You are going to be so happy when you realize that you're going to have a magnificent family home here in Honey Springs."

I put the cage on the top and bent down to open the small door, a little box Patrick had built into the cat tree where I could store various cat toys and treats.

I grabbed a couple of the treats and opened the cage door, and I placed the treats right outside of it.

"You can come out whenever you want." I gave Mocha a couple of slower blinks and resisted putting my hand into the cage to try to pat her. She still had that scared look, and her pupils appeared to have gotten bigger. "Let's go, Pepper. You need to give her time."

Pepper was so good. He acted like he understood exactly what I was saying, and we headed back to the counter to get Perry's coffee for the group. Pepper followed me all over the coffee shop, but I noticed him stopping a few times to look at the cat tree in anticipation of running over and doing his usual greeting of smelling, sniffing, and licking. He might be surprised and get a claw.

"What are y'all discussing this week?" I asked Perry and set down the tray of mugs along with the sugars, creamers, and honey for the guests to use as they pleased.

"It's been quiet in the Kentucky mystery scene, and it's pretty slow right after the holiday, but we are sure it's going to pick up sometime soon. So we are having a little coffee and company this fine snowy morning." Perry smiled. The lines around his eyes deepened. His grey brows matched his short grey hair. "Maxine…" His smile grew bigger when he said her name. "I couldn't help but overhear you got the lead in the town theater production. Congratulations."

Aunt Maxi did something that I'd never heard her do before. A giggle. She giggled like a little girl.

"Oh, Perry." She blushed.

I looked at her with wide eyes and tried to wrap my head around the fact I was standing there, living and breathing, watching her flirt with Perry Zella.

"I honestly can't believe it. When Loretta called me to ask me to go through the formalities of auditioning but knew I was going to get the part, I was so honored." Aunt Maxi had put a hand on Perry's shoulder as she stood next to him.

"Well, I don't know anyone who could play a better dramatical part than you, Maxine Bloom." Perry Zella actually winked at Aunt Maxi while he patted her hand.

"Oh, Perry. You sure do know how to make a girl blush." She giggled again, patted him one more time, and then walked away with a big grin on her face.

"And what was that?" I asked her and looked under my brows toward Perry and his friends.

"She was making a fool of herself. That's what that was," Bunny said in a sarcastic tone and pointed at Aunt Maxi. "You ought to be ashamed of yourself, teasing Perry like that. He's a new widower and…"

"New widower, my foot. Carolyn has been dead for over two years now."

Aunt Maxi gave Bunny the side-eye. "He's just ripe for the pickin'." She sighed. "And I'm going to ask him to come to see me at the play."

"Of course you are," Bunny snarled before she put a big fake smile on her face. "How can I help you today?" she asked the two women who walked up to the counter.

"Yes. I'm looking for a Loretta Bebe. I'm to have met her here about ten minutes ago." The older woman of the two wore a long fur coat that looked real and long beige leather gloves that appeared to go all the way to her elbows. She picked at the tips of each finger and then pulled the gloves off her hands before smacking them into the hands of the younger-looking woman.

"This is Gretchen Cannon." The young girl acted as though we knew who Gretchen Cannon was. The girl wore a simple black puff jacket, her hair pulled back into a ponytail, and glasses that were too big for her face.

Gretchen Cannon had short flaming-red hair, an orange coat, and the brightest orange-red lipstick I'd ever seen. The wrinkles around her eyes and her lips were caked in makeup where she'd tried to cover them. The red-rimmed glasses were so large on her face that they were hard not to stare at. It appeared she was much more of a larger-than-life person than Aunt Maxi. And that was saying something.

"Hi. This is Roxanne Bloom, the owner of the coffee shop." Bunny didn't let the two women intimidate her. I chuckled on the inside. "We want to know what you'd like to drink."

"I don't think you understand," The young girl pulled her shoulders back.

"Thar you arrr," Loretta Bebe said, drawing her words out in her southern accent. "I'm Low-retta Bebe, and you must be the actress Gretchen Cannon sent." She looked between the two ladies.

"Gretchen. Gretchen Cannon." The young girl pointed at Gretchen, as though Gretchen couldn't speak for herself.

I lifted my coffee mug to take a sip.

"Oh dear," Gretchen gasped in some sort of accent that told me she wasn't even from the United States, but it was lovely. Maybe England? Ireland? I wasn't good at placing dialect or tones.

Gretchen looked Loretta up and down. "Honey, you've got to stop going to the tanning bed."

I tried, I really tried to stop myself from laughing at Gretchen's observation of Loretta, but I couldn't. I exploded. The coffee sprang out of my mouth and watered Gretchen's face like a sprinkler.

"My stars!" Loretta gasped. "Get me a towel!"

Bunny sprang into action and got them a towel, while I profusely apologized for my actions.

Gretchen tried to bat Bunny's hand away because Bunny was going to town so hard I was afraid she would wipe off Gretchen's skin.

"Oh my." Bunny gasped and looked down as a set of Gretchen's false lashes fell on the ground like a limp spider.

"Oh." Loretta whimpered and wrung her hands.

"Here." Aunt Maxi chimed in and ripped the towel from Bunny. "I'm sorry. They are babbling buffoons. I'm Maxine Bloom." Aunt Maxi gingerly patted Gretchen's face with the towel before she handed it to the young woman with Gretchen.

"I'm Gretchen Cannon, the star of the local play." The woman's voice dripped with pride.

Aunt Maxi's face went through a few different emotions as she bit her lip, then turned to stare at Loretta.

"I… um..." Loretta bit her own lip. "I'll get right back with you, Maxine."

Me, Bunny and Aunt Maxi watched Low-retta nervously shuffle the two women to one of the café tables near the fireplace.

I tried not to laugh, but it started all over again.

"Did you hear what she said about Loretta's tanning?" I asked Bunny.

"I did. Wait until she finds out Low-retta is one hundred percent Cherokee," Bunny said sarcastically in her best Loretta accent, sounding the way Loretta did when she claimed she didn't go tanning and it was natural.

Naturally fake down to her short hair, which was dyed midnight black, and her long acrylic fingernails. In fact, when Loretta was at Lisa Stalh's house, using the tanning bed Lisa kept in her garage, Lisa was in the house getting her manicure set together. She did Loretta's nails, though she'd take all this to the grave. But knowing this was part of owning the only coffee shop in town.

People gossiped. I loved to joke that the gossip at the coffee shop was as hot as the coffee. Truly, no one was above the gossip, and something about everyone in Honey Springs had been gossiped about around here.

"Seriously. What was that?" Bunny asked. "I thought you got the lead part."

"I'm not sure, but I'm about to find out." Aunt Maxi grabbed a couple of mugs and a pot of coffee like she owned or even worked at the joint, hippity-hopping her way over to the women.

Bunny and I watched as the four women conversed, and then it happened. Aunt Maxi's face turned all sorts of colors before it landed on red. I mean bright red. And all the way down to her neck, which I knew had fallen on her chest, and eventually making it to her hands, where it'd leave blotches.

"She's gonna blow," I warned Bunny right before Aunt Maxi started to let out a giant-size hissy fit.

"Now, Maxine. You wount the best for our town, don't youuu?" No amount of southern charm Low-retta tried to throw on Aunt Maxi would stick. No amount. "Now, be a doll and listen to me." She patted Aunt Maxi on the arm, trying to steer her away from the woman Gretchen and the young girl.

While Loretta walked Aunt Maxi towards me, I noticed none of this bothered Gretchen. The girl was a bit flustered and trying to talk to Gretchen, who was sitting calmly with her hands perfectly folded in her lap.

"You said this was your production. You said this was local, and now you've got some big producer coming here to do our town play. Where are you getting the funds?" Aunt Maxi drew her arms around the room. "Look around, Low-retta! It's winter, and we have very few tourists this time of the year."

"You aren't listening, Maxine Bloom," Loretta tried to whisper and eyeball me at the same time.

I shrugged and let her deal with the mess she'd created.

"You are still in the play, but don't you want to be a big star?" Loretta's dark brows rose dramatically, as did the southern tone in her voice, making it appear as if what she was saying was more important than the actual demotion. "I've called in a favor from Alan Bogart."

"Who the dag-burn is Alan Bogart?" Aunt Maxi questioned and crossed her arms.

This little exchange was particularly interesting to me. First off, Aunt Maxi didn't shut down or fall for Loretta's obvious attempt to get her not to throw the giant-size hissy fit and see things clearly. Secondly, someone owed Loretta a favor.

Now that alone was something extraordinary. Loretta never let a favor go owed for any long period of time since I'd known her. Trust me when I said that Loretta had a lot of pull in Honey Springs, though we didn't let her know that directly.

Oh, she knew it. She had the big head to prove it, but we'd never let her know that we knew. Regardless, I was all sorts of turned upside down to hear just exactly the favor this Alan Bogart owed her and who he was to our little local theater play.

"Why, Maxine Bloom," Loretta gushed. "A so-phist-i-cated woman like yourself doesn't know who Alan Bogart is?" The syllables in her words dragged out.

"Well, I know the name, but I'm so riled up I can't place it right now." Oh my, Aunt Maxi was so good at trying to lie her way through not accepting that she had no idea who this Alan Bogart was, and her idea was to blame it on being southern.

Something she was really good at.

"Of course," Loretta said with a pinched tone. A few beads of sweat formed on her upper lip. Loretta was a jumble of nerves inside but would never let it show on the outside. "I'm sorry seeing Gretchen Cannon, one of the best off-Broadway actresses, here to act alongside of you."

My eyes lowered as I looked at Loretta, knowing her game. Did she forget I had practiced law and could see right through her manipulation?

Ahem, Aunt Maxi cleared her throat when she heard the word "Broadway." I was certain she put the "off" part in the back of her memory.

"Max-een." Loretta's drawl was really strung out. "You are a star," she said with a widened mouth, ending in a smile. "You know Alan."

I could tell she was teasing Aunt Maxi because Aunt Maxi had no idea who Alan was, but Aunt Maxi would milk it for all she could.

"Yes. Alan is very... um... what is the word?" Aunt Maxi rolled her wrist as if she were trying to find the right words, but I knew better. It was her way of getting Loretta to finish the sentence without appearing she had no idea what Loretta was talking about.

"Motivated to make the best play possible, since he is a famous producer." Loretta's words caused Aunt Maxi to stiffen up.

Aunt Maxi drew her shoulders back and chin up, cocking her right brow.

"Yes, that's the word. Motivated." Aunt Maxi's gaze drifted ever so slightly to Gretchen Cannon. "I guess I could share the stage with Gretchen."

"You are so professional." Loretta let out a deep, gratified sigh.

The stress of Aunt Maxi had made Loretta sweat a little, which made her makeup slide off a smidgen and expose the white lines she desperately tried to cover that were created by the tanning goggles.

Loretta gave one last nervous smile before she turned and headed back to Gretchen and the young woman.

"She's on Broadway. Think of it." Aunt Maxi drew her hands in front of her like she saw her name on the marquee underneath the Broadway lights. "Maxine Bloom starring in the lead with Gretchen…" She snapped her fingers.

"Cannon." I helped her recall the actress's last name.

"Yes. With Gretchen Cannon as a supporting actress." Aunt Maxi's face softened as she looked out to the horizon. "I've got to make sure it says that at the theater," she commented as though visualizing exactly how the chalkboard outside of the local theater would look as well.

CHAPTER THREE

I'd like to say Aunt Maxi had continued with her dignified southern attitude, but the longer she sat at the counter and watched Loretta Bebe cater to Gretchen Cannon, the more her face twisted and turned like she'd been sucking on a dill pickle.

It wasn't until a peculiar-looking fellow walked into the shop that I saw Aunt Maxi's attitude shift from angry to curious.

"Who's that?" she muttered, watching his every move. "He looks like those artsy people. Another one of Low-retta's twists?"

I ignored her and greeted the gentleman when he walked up.

"Good morning." I smiled. "Can I help you?"

He had on one of those *go to hell* hats, or at least that was what we called them in the south. The kind that almost lay flat on the head with a little bill out in front. I think I'd seen actors from Ireland wear them. And he wore a nice brown canvas coat with shiny brown buttons and a corduroy collar.

"Yeah." He was too busy scanning the chalkboard menus above his head to notice me checking out his shoes.

Penny loafers. Shiny as the buttons on his coat.

"Get the chocolate souffle." Aunt Maxi took it as her in to get into a conversation with the man. "Roxy's special roast too. She has a small roaster in the back. She gets a big ol' bag of beans imported right from the grower. I don't mean any beans. High-dollar ones."

"Is that right?" The man smiled, his eyes dancing. The amusement of Aunt Maxi intrigued him. "You look like someone I ought to introduce myself to."

"I guess you ought," Aunt Maxi mocked, "if you want to know anything around Honey Springs because I know you ain't from here."

He laughed as Aunt Maxi kept on flapping her jaws.

"I'm Maxine Bloom. That there is my niece Roxanne Bloom." She pointed at me. "Now, she was a lawyer, but now she is making coffee like I told you, and she's married." Aunt Maxi rolled her eyes. "Get him a cup of coffee," she instructed me when I started to interrupt her about telling strangers my life.

His eyes shifted to me, and we both smiled.

"She should take her husband's last name, but she did that once, and well, she ain't married to him no more." I heard her telling my life story as I got him a cup of coffee.

"The condiments are over on the coffee bar if you need anything to doctor up the coffee." I gestured.

"Doctor up?" he questioned, giving me the same goofy grin he'd given Aunt Maxi.

"Creamer. Sugar. Things that don't make coffee coffee." I tried to cover my accent, but I wasn't an actress like Aunt Maxi was trying to be, and being myself was the only way I knew how to be.

"I gotcha." He gave a hard nod. "Just like it black."

That made me happy.

"Then you're going to love my special roast. How long are you visiting?" I asked and also took a vested interest in why he was here because he didn't look like our usual winter tourists who were here to do ice fishing and cold hiking through the woods.

"As long as the play has its run."

That made Aunt Maxi jump off the stool with joy.

"I'm the lead," she cried out. "Are you someone famous?"

"I'm a reviewer for the *Times*." The curious smile faded. His eyes held a question. "What do you mean you're the lead?"

"As in the *New York Times*?" The question gushed out of Aunt Maxi.

"Yes, ma'am." He picked up the coffee cup. "What do you mean lead? I thought Gretchen Cannon was the lead Alan Bogart had cast."

"Gretchen Cannon. Alan Bogart." Aunt Maxi snarled. "I've got to call Lowretta right now."

Aunt Maxi must've forgotten all about Mark and his *New York Times* gig, but I hadn't. Serving him up a piece of the chocolate soufflé would definitely get his palate moving and jaw flapping.

"Follow me." I moved around the counter and took him straight over to the table next to Perry Zella and his group of mystery club folks. "Perry, this is Mark Redding. He's here for the Times." I'd totally realized I never knew what he did, but I assumed he was here to do a piece on Honey Springs.

"I'm a theater reviewer and have covered many plays by Alan Bogart." Mark had a funny look on his face, one that told me he wasn't a big fan of Alan's. "I'm curious to see this small-town play when Alan is used to a little bigger."

"Oh. I know." I shrugged, giving a little bit of the gossip I'd heard earlier. "He owes Loretta Bebe a favor."

Perry laughed, as did the rest of his group.

"Oh boy, he must've really had Loretta do something to owe her a favor." Perry's brows lifted.

"Trust me when I say Alan Bogart doesn't do favors for just anyone, so I must meet Loretta Bebe." Mark sat down.

"Let me introduce you to my mystery club." Perry did exactly what I had planned when I'd picked the spot for Mark to sit. He'd taken Mark into the fold of the warm hospitality Honey Springs had to offer, now more important than ever.

Loretta wasn't the most welcoming citizen we had, but Perry and his friends would intrigue Mark.

"He does play reviews for the New York Times," I told Bunny Bowowski when she moseyed up to me to get the particulars on him.

"*New York Times?*" She drew her hand up to her chest. "That seems big time. Especially for our small theater."

"Mmmhmmm." I plated his soufflé and handed it to her. "You can find out all about it. I've got to get the lunch items started."

Leave it up to Bunny to sit down with Mark, where I knew she would pump him for all the information that would keep us in gossip until the end of the play's run, which I believed was two weeks. Or did I read that wrong in the Honey Springs newspaper? Either way, there was a story behind Loretta and this producer that I couldn't put in the back of my head.

Quickly I rushed through the coffee shop to clean up any dishes lying around, fluff the pillows on the couch, stoke the fire, and check on Mocha.

Her head was out of the cage, but her body was half in. Pepper was still in the bed up near the register where he took his morning nap. It was almost time for me to take him out to go potty and for our morning walk, so I made sure the tea and coffee stations were cleaned up and stocked before I took my apron off and slipped on my coat.

Pepper hopped to his feet when he heard me take the leash off the coat tree. He waited patiently while I put on his little coat and harness.

"We will be right back to start lunch," I told Bunny on my way past her.

Bunny was too busy talking, so she simply waved her hand in the air to let me know she heard me.

The boardwalk held fond memories for me, since I used to spend my summers here with my Aunt Maxi.

Pepper loved heading down the boardwalk and greeted people as he went. He knew he had to get to the grassy area in order to do his business.

All the shops were locally owned and pretty much boutique style. Wild and Whimsy was the first shop on the boardwalk. It was an eclectic shop of antiques and repurposed furniture. Beverly and Dan Teagarden were the owners. Their two grown children, Savannah and Melanie, helped them run it. Instead of installing a regular shingled roof, Dan had paid extra to put on a rusty tin roof to go with the store's theme. They'd kept the awning a red color but without the name. The Wild and Whimsy sign dangled down from the awning.

Honey Comb Salon & Spa was located next, and it was a fancy salon—for Honey Springs. Alice Dee Spicer was the owner, and from what I'd overheard through the gossip line, Alice had really gotten some new techniques from a fancy school.

Next to Honey Comb Salon & Spa was the Buzz In and Out Diner owned by James Farley. Bees Knees Bakery was next to the diner and owned by Emily Rich. All About the Details, an event center, was next to the bakery. A bridal shop, Queen for the Day, was right next to my shop, The Bean Hive.

The snow was still coming down, and it didn't appear to be stopping anytime soon. It was fine as long as the roads didn't get icy. The snow sure made for a pretty scene. The banners dangling from the lampposts had to have been the ones Bunny and Aunt Maxi couldn't agree on, but I'd bet it was safe to say it was the last thing on Aunt Maxi's mind.

Pepper did his usual sniffing around when we made it to the grassy area between the Cocoon Inn and the boat dock.

"Excuse me." I looked up when I heard someone walk up.

"Hi." I smiled when I noticed the young woman who'd been with Gretchen Cannon at the Bean Hive. "I'm sorry. I was just looking at all the boats in the slips with their covers on them. All tucked in for winter."

It fascinated me how Big Bib, the owner of the boat dock, was able to winterize so many boats. Though it didn't seem like a boat dock would be open during the winter months, Big Bib claimed this season was his busiest time of the year. He said repairing boats and slips was completed during the winter months because he didn't have anyone bothering him. I could see his point.

"Yeah, I don't know anything about those." She pushed her glasses up on her nose. "I'm Sydney O'Neil, Miss Cannon's personal assistant," she said in a stern voice.

Oh, so formal, I thought when she stuck her hand out for me to shake. An umbrella was attached at her wrist. A black bag hung from her shoulder.

"And Miss Cannon really enjoyed the coffee you gave her and would like to hire you to do the food service stand at the theater while she's in town."

Sydney put up the umbrella and handed it to me.

"Please hold this while I get out the schedule." She shoved it toward me, and out of reaction, I took it. She pulled the black bag around to her chest, stepped under the umbrella, and took out a piece of paper. "Miss Cannon doesn't like anything to be out of order, and if a single snowflake gets on this paper, she will not like it."

"That explains the umbrella," I said and wondered if Gretchen was hard to work for, since Sydney sure did make it seem that way.

"Among other things." Sydney relaxed a smidgen when she looked at me. "I guess I don't have to be buttoned up with you."

It was nice to see her jawline soften and a smile cross her lips.

"Why hello there," she said to Pepper when he ran up to us and sat next to her feet. "I saw you sleeping in the coffee shop."

"Sydney, this is Pepper." I always took pride in how good he was. He never jumped on people, though he did bark occasionally. He was a really good dog. "He is my constant companion."

"Gretchen is my constant companion," she said in a sarcastic tone. "Or maybe I'm hers."

"Sydney, I think you just made a joke." I laughed, and she smiled again.

"If you do decide to take the job to supply the coffee, I do have to warn you because you seem so nice." Her brows pinched. "She is very particular on how she likes things run, and coffee is one of those things." She handed me the piece of paper.

"I'm flattered she's asking for it." I wondered how hard it could be and then looked at the paper. "Oh dear. She wants me to be there early and a hot cup be brought to her dressing room." I bit my lip. "I don't think there are dressing rooms in the local theater."

I tried to think back to the last time I was in there and really couldn't recall.

"That's an issue." She took a pen from her bag and a notebook. "Call Loretta about the dressing room," she talked and wrote the reminder.

"Still, if there's no dressing room, I'm more than happy to supply the coffee but not sure if I can be there every day to hand her a hot cup." I didn't bother going into details on how I opened up, took the coffee to the Cocoon, then returned to the coffee shop to work the morning shift with Bunny. "I'm more than happy to give her a personal carafe for her room that'll keep warm all day even."

"I guess that'll be fine. She's just so used to getting what she wants." She pointed at another paragraph on this paper. "She'd like you to also bring over the maple pecan breakfast ring daily to have with the coffee."

"Maple pecan..." My mind drifted to what on earth we had in the glass counter that made her think it was a breakfast ring.

"She stopped at the Bees Knees Bakery on our way to check in at the Cocoon Hotel. That was where she had gotten it." She pointed at the paragraph underneath the demand for the breakfast ring. "It states here that you are to bring it with you daily."

"I'll have to check with Emily Rich on that." When I saw her frown, I knew she was confused. "Emily is the owner of the bakery, and she'd have to agree to make one of these daily for Gretchen."

"Miss Cannon," she corrected me. "She doesn't really like people she's not friends with calling her by her given name."

"I think I'll stick with calling her Gretchen if she wants my coffee." I wasn't going to bow down to some lady who appeared to be more washed up in her career than thriving.

"That's fine between me and you, but you've been forewarned if she bites you." Sydney seemed a tad bit frightened at the fact.

"I'm a big girl. I can take it, or I can take my coffee back." It wasn't a threat. It was a fact. I wasn't about to let Gretchen bully me. "In fact, I was a lawyer, and let me give you some free advice. If you don't like working for her, there are several more people out there who are nice and kind."

"I like working for her just fine." The buttoned-up Sydney O'Neil was back. "So if you agree to bringing the coffee and the carafe, please sign this paragraph so I have something to take back to her. Then please let me know what Emily Rich has to say about the maple pecan breakfast roll."

I signed the paper, and then she pulled a card from the pocket of her jacket and handed it to me.

"Can I ask you one thing?" I waited until I knew I had her attention. I handed her the umbrella back once the paper was safely back in her bag. Lord forbid the young girl get a tongue lashing from the old lady. "Exactly how did Gretchen Cannon get the role in the play?"

"Alan Bogart. She owed him a favor, and here we are."

"Gosh." I snorted. "Seems like everyone is collecting on favors."

"Huh?" she asked.

"Nothing." I tugged on Pepper's leash for him to stand. "Pepper and I have to get back to the coffee shop. Business never stops."

"Thank you, Roxanne." Sydney tried to seem personal, but it didn't appear to come naturally to her. Maybe it was too many years of putting up with someone as bossy as Gretchen Cannon.

"You're welcome." I almost told her to call me Roxy, but I only let my friends call me that, so I just let it be.

Besides, I couldn't wait to stop at the Bees Knees Bakery to taste this maple pecan breakfast ring. My mouth was already watering.

"Good morning," Emily Rich said in greeting when I walked into the bakery.

"Emily," I gushed and dropped Pepper's leash.

After she noticed he was with me, she grabbed one of the organic bakery treats she made for her fur customers and bent down to give it to Pepper.

"I've got to try this maple pecan breakfast ring."

"Roxy, you'll never believe it." She stood up and handed me a treat that I knew she meant for me to take to Sassy. "I made it by accident when I realized I'd forgotten to put the raisins in the raisin loaf. So I slapped on some maple glaze, and it's the best-selling thing I've ever made."

"I can't wait to try it." I looked over her shoulder to try to see the breakfast ring.

"I'm out." She shrugged. "When it slows down this afternoon, I'll make several more and maybe into the night."

"You're going to have to if you want to fulfill Gretchen Cannon's wishes." I snorted.

"The actress lady with all the orange on?" Emily asked. "Really, she shouldn't be wearing such a bright color. It ages her even more."

Emily cracked me up. At times she seemed so adult and others still the young, freshly turned twenty-year-old she was. Emily had worked for me in high school and used the kitchen to perfect her pastries. She tried to go to college to please her parents but didn't have the passion. It took a lot of coaxing on my end and talking to her parents to let them realize Emily had a dream that was very much in her grasp.

They ended up embracing their daughter's dream and let her fly off into the world, where she went overseas to pastry school and became a pastry chef. She ended up buying Odd Ink Tattoo Parlor on the boardwalk after it became available and opened Bees Knees, making it very successful.

I was glad too because it allowed me to cut back on making pastries to go with my coffee.

"She loves your maple pecan breakfast ring." I watched Emily rush around the bakery. "She'd like to have you bake her a fresh one daily while the play is in its run, and I'm more than happy to take it to the theater for you because I am going to take the contract to provide the coffee every morning." I laughed. "You wouldn't believe the demands she wanted, but I made sure we didn't have to deal with the drama."

"Yes. Orange is not good." She sighed and grabbed some papers off the counter. Then she shuffled them together in a pile.

"Right," I said in a bland tone when I realized she'd not heard a word I'd said.

She stopped and looked at me. She put the papers on the counter and held them down with her hand as if they were going to blow away.

"I'm sorry. I'm not with it today." Her face softened, and she smiled. "Can you repeat that?"

"I was just saying the actress would like to order one of your maple pecan breakfast rings while she's in town. And I'll take it every morning along with the coffee," I said.

Emily's response really caught me off guard. Usually, Emily would be really happy to have a client, and she loved making the daily goodies for the Cocoon Hotel's hospitality room where all the guest could hang out and grab snacks. The Bean Hive provided a lot of coffee contracts to area businesses, and I always tried to bring Emily's bakery in on the deals if I could.

The bell over the bakery door dinged. We turned around. Pepper was so good that he stayed next to me even when the man smiled at him. Pepper knew eye contact and a smile as a visual cue to show off and get some pats out of it.

"Dwayne. You're early." Emily looked from me to the man, who looked very professional in his winter overcoat, black hat, and briefcase.

"Business is never early." Hearing his words and seeing his eyes roaming around the shop made me pause. "It looks like the place has good bones."

"Roxy, I'd love to provide whatever the actress needs. You said something about you taking it?" Emily was trying to distract my attention away from this Dwayne feller by talking fast and walking Pepper and me to the door.

"Yes... I ..." I was going to finish my sentence, but she took a fur treat from her apron pocket and put it in Pepper's mouth.

"I'll have it ready for you in the morning." She practically shoved us out the door.

Pepper didn't seem to notice or mind how Emily had reacted. While he happily ate his treat, I lingered at the display window of the bakery and looked in at Emily and Dwayne, who was someone I'd never seen around these parts, which told me he wasn't a citizen of Honey Springs.

The two of them were looking at the papers Emily had gathered up and placed on the counter. Something very odd was definitely going on with Emily.

"She might think she can satisfy you with a treat," I told Pepper on our way back to the Bean Hive. "But it certainly doesn't satisfy my curiosity about whatever it is she's hiding."

CHAPTER FOUR

If I thought I would have any peace when I got back to the coffee shop, I must've had a screw loose. Aunt Maxi and Loretta were still bickering back and forth about the roles and who was playing what.

"I just don't understand why you think you can bring some big celebrity in here like that without *con-versing* with the theater committee. I'm a pretty smart woman." Aunt Maxi tapped her temple. "Why don't you explain it to me, Low-retta?"

"Maxine, I do not need to do any explaining to you." Loretta picked at the edge of her short black hair and turned her chin away from Aunt Maxi, avoiding Aunt Maxi's glare. "The committee voted me as the one in charge, and I can do what I please."

"Not when it's not your money." Aunt Maxi had a point. "It belongs to the Southern Women's Club."

Oh my. I knew those were fighting words between the women.

The Southern Women's Club was a whole southern social society that the name explained without explaining. The club determined who was who in Honey Springs. When I was invited to join—yes, you had to be invited—I was happy to use the coffee shop's busyness as a great excuse not to have the time to participate and therefore give my special invite to someone else in the community.

"Who said I used any of the club's money?" Loretta's head spun around. Her eyes narrowed on Aunt Maxi's, her fake lashes leaving a shadow on her cheek. "As if it were any of your business, Maxine Bloom, but I was owed a favor, and since I'm the one in charge, I called in my favor."

There Loretta went again with the favor.

"What kind of favor have you of all people been holding on to?" Aunt Maxi asked exactly what I had been thinking.

"A long-ago favor, Max-een." Loretta rolled her eyes.

"Low-retta Bebe, I've known you all my God-given life, and as sure as I'm livin' and breathin', you cash in them favors before you can do the favor you're cashing in for." Aunt Maxi's eyes drew wide open. She pinched her lips together, and her brows drew way up on her forehead.

"Max-een, you don't know me as good as you think." Loretta was about to say something else when the door to the coffee shop opened and a man larger than life stepped in.

"I'm here," he sang out, making everyone in the coffee house look at him. "And there you are." His words must have dripped with honey because Loretta seemed to be stuck to them.

"Alan," she said, her voice humming a southern melody. "My dear, dear Alan. I've been waiting for you."

It was like watching some old black-and-white movie with all the formal chitchat and kissing on the cheeks as the two of them walked to the middle of the coffee house, where they embraced.

I looked around and noticed all eyes were on them, especially the eye of Mark Redding's camera. The smile on his face and the look in his eye told me there was something between him and Alan, whoever Alan was.

"What the hell are you doing here?" Alan's glare and Mark's expression told me everything I needed to know.

These two men didn't like each other.

"Now, now." Loretta's lips twitched in a nervous smile. "I see there is something going on here." She politely turned to Mark, clasping her hands in front of her. Her face pinched the southern smile, the type of smile that actually squished the entire chin up to the forehead with squinty eyes like a newborn baby. And I'm not talking a newborn a few minutes old. I'm talking a right-on-out-of-the-womb look.

"Uh-oh." Bunny moseyed up to me with the coffee pot in her grip. "I better get everyone's mugs filled up because Low-retta is about to have a dying-duck fit."

"Mmmmhmm," I agreed and kept my eye on the situation transpiring in front of me.

As if it couldn't get any better, Gretchen sashayed into the joint with Sydney rushing behind her. Gretchen peeled off her glasses and took notice of the situation at hand.

"Well, well. I came in here to find our fearless leader." Gretchen's words dripped out of her mouth like the pearl necklaces around her neck. She pointed a direct finger at Loretta. "And here I find my answer." Her finger moved from Loretta and slowly between the two men.

She quickly snapped that finger with another one. Apparently, that was Sydney's cue to take over. Sydney gave Gretchen a hand fan. While Gretchen pretended to be having some sort of her own personal summer, Sydney's soft voice grew louder as she talked.

"Miss Cannon didn't know exactly when Mr. Bogart was going to show up, since she is here to make good on her favor to him." Sydney gestured to Gretchen. "Miss Cannon has a very tight schedule where she needs to get back to Broadway before the next run of her show starts."

"You mean off-Broadway to the show that hasn't sold one ticket since the opening?" Mark asked with a snicker under his breath.

"And secondly, we would like to call the police to have an escort for Miss Cannon because we read online how Mr. Redding was here to do a review, and Miss Cannon does fear for her life with him around, since he is trying to destroy her career." Sydney made an awfully bold statement.

"Now, just you wait a minute. Just because your play isn't a real play and I wrote an honest review doesn't mean I destroyed your career." Mark looked past Sydney.

"I agree. I don't want him anywhere near my play," Alan demanded and looked at Loretta. "And what do you intend to do about this?"

"Alan..." Loretta fluttered her eyes.

"If she flutters those eyes any faster, she's gonna start a windstorm." Aunt Maxi was having too much fun watching Loretta squirm.

"Hi," I interrupted, feeling like I needed to step in. I gave a slight wave to all parties involved. "I'm Roxanne Bloom. I own the coffee shop, and I'm so glad you're here. But I'm not sure if you want to air your business in front of all the customers."

"Of course they do." Mark folded his arms and sat back in his chair. Perry and his mystery club friends seemed to really enjoy the interaction playing out in front of us. "This is how they create drama and get people to show up at their pitiful shows. They've been practically shoved out of off-Broadway, and I couldn't resist the urge to show up here to see exactly how they ruin your small community theater."

"We will not stand for this!" Sydney spat before she hurried out of the coffee shop behind a cursing Gretchen Cannon.

"I'm not sure who will pay for this," Gretchen hollered as she went out the door. "But someone will!"

Loretta looked as if she'd swallowed a possum. Even the tan dripped right off her face as she stood there stunned.

"You fix this." Alan pointed at Loretta. "No favor is worth him. Do you understand?"

Alan also walked out, leaving Loretta stammering. She threw a look at me before she stomped over my way.

"Roxanne, don't just stand there." She jutted her finger toward Mark. The jewels glistened, causing little specks of light to dance along the ceiling. "Do something!" she demanded.

"Everyone," I proclaimed. Then I did something. "Free coffee on me!" I looked at Loretta.

A shadow passed over her face, darkening her features. Or maybe the color was coming back. Either way, she was on fire, and as she took off out of the coffee shop, I knew the wrath of Loretta Bebe had been bestowed upon me.

She slammed the front door of the coffee shop, rattling the glass windows. I turned on my heels to head back to the counter, where Aunt Maxi and Bunny were huddled together. The chatter of the coffee shop picked up and made me feel better.

"Oh my dear. This is going to be the talk of the town." Bunny and Aunt Maxi had sidled up to each other.

"I know. I can't wait to get to the theater tomorrow to get the lowdown." Aunt Maxi, again, was having too much fun.

"You two stop that gossiping. If what the reviewer said is true, I don't want them to ruin our local theater with a bad show." The concern was real. Loretta had flaws, but when she did something, she did it with the full intention of making it perfect.

"Honey, we ain't gossiping." Aunt Maxi winked at Bunny as she spoke to me.

"No, dear." Bunny shook her head. "We are discussing prayer concerns."

"Is that what we are calling it nowadays?" I questioned and grabbed a carafe for each hand. I walked off, letting the two of them beat the situation until it was dead, then pick it up to beat it even more to make sure it was dead.

CHAPTER FIVE

I'd never seen the likes. It always amazed me how gossip spread around Honey Springs like melted butter on a hot biscuit. Before I could even get people's free coffee for them, the phone was already ringing off the hook from people trying to figure out what on earth had happened.

"You can tell all your customers to get online this afternoon and begin reading my article on my stay here in Honey Springs." Mark Redding seemed awfully happy about what he had in mind for his piece today.

I carefully formulated the words in my head as I filled up all the mugs on the table.

"I'm not so sure if painting a picture of Honey Springs as volatile would show what our town is really about." I shrugged in hopes of getting him to change his mind.

"Oh, you and the town folk will be fine. It's Gretchen Cannon and Alan Bogart who will bring a halt to your town production. Have you read the play?" he asked me. There seemed to be a truly concerned look on his face. "I can tell you haven't."

He bent down and opened his briefcase up. He took out a stack of papers and handed them to me.

"You read this for yourself. You'll see just how they no longer have what it takes to bring a show, even a small-town show, to life. They don't like me because I give an honest review. Anytime a big name goes into a small town, we get so many readers. Usually, those big names do things to help around the community or give back in some way." He snickered. "When my boss told me they were coming here, together, I knew I had to cover it. The only thing they give back is a hard time. When they are together, there's nothing but trouble that comes out of it."

He took a newspaper out of his briefcase.

"Here. Check out this article I did before I got here. It's all the ways they singlehandedly ruined the careers of actors and actresses who thought they had an opportunity in these plays that were either produced by Alan Bogart or Gretchen Cannon starred in."

I took the paper from him.

"You know..." Perry's brows winged up. "There's not much happening in Honey Springs this time of the year. It might be fun to watch all this play out. Maybe our mystery group should focus on the play, since we don't have a reading pick this month."

I shook my head and headed back to the counter. The last thing Loretta needed was a handful of people hanging around the theater and putting in their two cents or just being nosey.

Pepper started to potty dance around my feet when I put the coffee carafe back in its place.

"Time to go potty?" I asked Pepper.

The tips of his ears perked up, and his little tail wiggled back and forth.

"Perfect timing." I patted him on his head. I untied the apron from around my waist and hung it on the coat tree next to the counter, and then I grabbed Pepper's leash. Taking him outside would also get me out of the coffee shop for some fresh air and regrouping.

"I'm leaving too." Aunt Maxi grabbed her coat off the coat rack. "You let me know if anything happens," she told Bunny as if they were instantly best friends. A deadly combination.

"Oh, I will." Bunny nodded and headed back to take care of the customers at the counter.

"Nothing like good gossip to bring a town together," I told Aunt Maxi on our way out the door and noticed Mocha was halfway out of her cage.

She was getting more and more used to being in the coffee shop. It was the normal progression with cats, and I wouldn't be surprised if after the morning coffee rush died down, she ventured out of the cage and sniffed around.

"It's not gossip." Aunt Maxi turned left once we walked out the door to head over to the parking lot on that side of the boardwalk. "It's about being informed. I'm going to the theater to learn my new lines now that I'm playing a different role."

"You seem to be okay with that." I was curious about how she went from being upset about losing the starring role to being happy with a role that was secondary if that.

"I'm going to see how all this plays out," she said as calmly as could be. "Don't count me out yet." She gave me a theatrical wink. With a giddy-up in her step, she bolted off in the opposite direction from Pepper and me.

With the snow starting to fall a little harder, I wanted to make sure I kept an eye on the weather report. If the roads started to get a little icy, there was no sense in keeping the coffee shop open. It wasn't worth the risk to put Bunny or my afternoon high school employees at risk.

All the shops were still open, from what I could tell when Pepper and I passed on our way to the grassy spot. He quickly did what he wanted to do and got ready to get back to the coffee shop, where it was nice and warm.

A loud knock on the Wild and Whimsy display window made my heart jump as we passed.

Loretta Bebe was standing inside of the antique shop, flailing her hand for me to come in. I could see Alan, Gretchen, and Sydney were in there, talking to Dan and Beverly Teagarden. For a second I thought of waving as if she were waving at me, but like Mocha, I was curious and half tempted to go inside to see what they were doing.

It took only one more of Loretta's hand gestures to coax me from out of the cold. Within seconds, Pepper and I were standing next to her.

"I was going to come back down there and let you know what is what." Loretta's face was crimson with fury. "I'm telling you, that reviewer needs to leave, and if you keep welcoming people like him with open arms, he will ruin the play for sure, just like he said these two amazing Broadway talents predicted."

"Loretta, I know you are passionate about his play, but do we really need two people such as them to even put on a small-town play?" I asked, trying to bring my lawyer reasoning skills to life. "I understand your precious name is on the chalkboard outside of the downtown theater and you take pride in what you do, but when you have big people such as those two, it also comes with big headaches."

"Of all people in Honey Springs," she scoffed, "I figured you, Roxanne Bloom, were the most sophisticated and would understand my position."

"I'm not saying I don't understand your position." I wasn't going to let Loretta's sucking up to me sway me from what I felt was something she'd taken too far. "But I'm asking you to think about it. Think about the good of the town. Mark Redding has as much right to be in Honey Springs as those three."

Loretta and I looked over at the group. It appeared as if Alan were picking out props for the play and Gretchen was agreeing to things. Sydney wrote profusely as they talked.

Loretta continued to fuss underneath her breath but abruptly stopped when Sydney began to walk our way.

"Put a smile on your face." Loretta had forgotten somehow that she was not Aunt Maxi because that was something Aunt Maxi would say and had said to me in the past. That directive was generally followed up by the statement that I could have put on a little lipstick.

I did. I put a big smile on my face.

"I'm so glad you are here. It saves me from coming to the coffee shop to find you." Sydney pushed her glasses up on her nose. "Miss Cannon would like you to go on down to the theater to get a feel for exactly where you'll be putting the coffee stand along with the pastries so we do not have to spend any time walking around trying to figure out where you put it. Also, we'd like confirmation that you know exactly where Miss Cannon's dressing room is located so you won't be delayed in placing the coffee carafe in there and be ready for her six a.m. arrival."

"Six a.m.?" Loretta drew back. "Why, honey, my eyes are barely open at six a.m."

"Then I guess it's a good thing you aren't on stage." Sydney's comeback threw Loretta off her rocker and me for a loop.

Not until Sydney was out of earshot did Loretta start in on the poor girl.

"That girl is wound tighter than a girdle at a Baptist potluck." Loretta was back to her snide remarks, and I couldn't help but smile.

In fact, the smile stayed on my face until I walked back into the coffee shop.

"Hey." Patrick's face lit up when he saw Pepper and me walk in. "You look happy even after what Bunny just told me about what happened here."

It was nice to see the shop had cleared, leaving a couple of guests sitting on the couches, enjoying the fire and a cup of coffee.

"This smile is about the exact same situation." I gave my husband a kiss and patted Sassy on the head. She and Pepper were busy greeting each other. "I'll have to tell you all about it later."

"I came here to grab Pepper from you. I'm going home. It's slow this afternoon with the weather, so the less you have to deal with, the better." He was always thinking about the good of our little family. "Do you think you'll stay open?"

"I'm not sure. I was thinking about the weather when I was stopped by Loretta and the crew about making sure my coffee station was exactly where it needed to be and how I can't hold up the famous Miss Cannon." I did a dramatic bow like she was the queen or something.

"Oh no." Patrick took Pepper's leash from me. "I can see this is going to be very interesting."

"Nah." I shook it off. "It'll all work out fine. In the meantime, I'm going to check the weather, let Bunny go home, and then stop by the theater on my way home."

"Perfect. Sounds like a plan." Patrick gave me one last kiss, and I gave the pups a last kiss before they headed out into the snowstorm.

Turmoil was brewing in the air. I could feel it. I wasn't sure whether it was about the situation with Loretta and Alan Bogart changing Loretta's lead actress or the situation between Alan and Mark Redding, but something was about to blow up along with the snowstorm about to hit.

"Patrick is right about me needing to watch the weather," I told Bunny while she was refilling the freshly baked cookies on the tray in the display case. I grabbed the remote control for the small TV we had above the fireplace and turned the television on. "The banner on the screen says it's still coming our way."

Bunny and I both stopped what we were doing and read the ticker at the bottom of the television screen.

"Right now is the best it's going to get." I was talking about the weather and noticed the snowflakes were getting bigger and covering more space. The bottom of the television screen said the temperature was in the mid-twenties, which was plenty cold for the snow to stick and make things a little messy.

"Why don't you go on home?" I suggested to Bunny. "I'll get things buttoned up here and text the afternoon staff to let them know we will be closing early and not to come in."

"I don't want to leave you in a lurch. Are you sure?" Bunny asked.

"Yes, ma'am, I'm positive. I've got to make some pecan cookies for Loretta, and I'll head over to get a look at the theater before heading home to spend a free evening with my husband and fur babies."

"If you're sure." Bunny had already gotten on her pillbox hat and her gloves, but she was just being polite, as we all did.

"I'll call you in the morning if things change for tomorrow." I waved her on out, and she didn't hesitate. "It's just me and you, Mocha," I told the sweet feline who was still huddled in her cage on the very top rung of the cat tree.

Something about her was so sweet and endearing. She was definitely shy, and I truly wondered how she got here. I knew that if I kept talking to her like I did the other animals, she'd venture out even more as the week dragged on.

"I guess it was a bad week to come here." I talked to her as I propped open the swinging door between the kitchen and coffee shop. While I walked and talked, I quickly pulled my phone from my back pocket and sent a text to the afternoon staff to let them know I'd rather they be safe and at home instead of coming in with the big snowstorm on the horizon.

"The snow and of course the crazy theater stuff, it sure can get loud in this small coffee shop." I continued to talk out loud to Mocha and slipped the phone back in my pocket.

On my way over to the dry ingredients shelf to fetch the pecans I needed to make the pecan ball cookies, I checked the oven to make sure it was not only on but also set to the three-hundred-and-twenty-five-degree temperature needed to bake the cookies to perfection.

I emptied out the full glass jar of pecans, which were probably too many, but what good was a pecan cookie if it wasn't full of the nut?

"I'm going to use the chopper now." I leaned a little to the right and peered out the swinging door where I could see the cat tree in full view. "Mocha?" I questioned when I noticed she wasn't sticking halfway out of the cage.

A squeak of a meow caught my ear. I looked down and saw the sweet feline had made her way into the kitchen and squatted underneath Bunny's stool, which was butted up against the preparation counter.

"Hey there." I greeted her with a smile and blinked my eyes slowly a couple of times to let her know I was friendly. "You aren't going to like this chopping noise."

Using my hand, I gathered pecans into a pile before placing the chopping machine over top of the mound.

"Normally, I'd chop these up with my knife, but I'm being lazy and in a bit of a hurry to beat the storm this afternoon, so cheating with a chopper is what we are doing." I reached underneath the counter and grabbed the chopper off one of the open shelves.

After pounding out a few chops, I looked to see whether Mocha had stayed or run off. To my delight, she was still crouched there, but her eyes were wide open.

"What if I gave you one of these?" For her courage in staying there and venturing out, I unscrewed the lid of the mason jar of homemade cat treats that I made for my cat-owning customers. Of course I had dog treats, too, but today, Mocha and I were going to worry about the cat treats.

I took one of the fish-shaped treats out and placed it on the floor. "You are going to love my special fur treats." I watched to make sure she ate it before I put a few more on the ground.

The little fish treat crunched in between her small teeth. I took a few more out and put them next to her before I went on with making the pecan balls.

"I knew you'd love those salmon treats. And they are good for you." I was pretty proud that the three ingredients I used were organic. The salmon was from the local butcher, the eggs were from Hill's Orchard, and the flour was organic and gluten free. They were all good for Mocha, and her loud purring told me she enjoyed them.

"I'm expecting you to come out tomorrow and engage with the people. You deserve a good home." I walked over to the refrigerator and pulled out the butter and vanilla, and on the way past the dry ingredients shelf, I grabbed the sugar and flour.

I glanced down at Mocha, but she was gone. I didn't bother looking for her because I knew she was simply doing the cat thing of exploring her environment while no one was around. Something I was sure she'd be doing all night after I locked up for the evening.

Quickly I combined all the ingredients but the powdered sugar and rolled several dozen balls from the dough before placing them into the oven.

The fresh Columbian beans needed to be roasted, so I grabbed the coffee bag that was imported from Honduras. It was one of the freshest bags of beans I'd ever gotten. They were hand-picked using the dry method, which was why the bag cost me so much.

I headed over to the small roaster I had in the corner of the kitchen, reached into the burlap bag, and scooped up about a pound of the light-brown coffee beans. I carefully dumped the beans into the loading hopper so I didn't drop any on the floor, with the roasting temperature set to three hundred and ninety-two degrees.

I flipped on the fan, which caused the fan in the cooling bin agitator to turn on as the arms of the fan circled. They waited for me to open the bean release lever, which would release the freshly roasted beans. I watched the coffee beans through the small window as they rolled around in the drum and couldn't help but think that each one of those coffee beans was handpicked using the dry method. I pondered all of what went into the process.

It was an age-old method of processing coffee and still used in many countries where water resources are limited. The beans were actually called cherries that were freshly picked and spread out on huge surfaces to dry in the sun.

Every day they racked the beans so the beans wouldn't spoil. Then the people covered them at night or in rainfall to keep them from getting wet.

This particular bean was produced in Honduras, so it would take the beans a few weeks for the moisture in them to drop to the 11 percent needed before the beans actually started to shrivel and look like the coffee beans I was watching in the roaster.

"Too bad my roaster isn't bigger." I talked to Mocha as if she could hear me all the way out into the coffee shop. "If I had a bigger roaster, I could do several pounds of fresh coffee."

Even though I knew the roaster hadn't reached the peak temperature, I pulled out the sample spoon on the roaster. It was a long steel piece with a canal down the middle in which I could pull out a collection of the coffee beans. The sample spoon allowed me to look at the coloring of the beans, since the roaster took the beans from a light brown to a nice rich dark brown but did not burn them. It was a very precise process and one I didn't like to mess up.

I pulled the sample spoon up to my nose and took in the aroma of the warm beans. It was a smell like no other. Not even a fresh pot of coffee smelled this good, though that smelled good too.

Quickly I replaced the spoon when I heard a noise from the coffee shop.

"What are you doing?" I wiped my hands down my apron and walked into the coffee shop to see what Mocha had gotten into. I was delightfully surprised to find it was actually Emily Rich standing in the middle of the shop with Mocha in her arms.

"Hi!" I was happy to have a human there and happier to see Mocha in her arms. "You found Mocha."

"Mocha, how adorable." Emily laughed and ran her hand down the cat's fur. Then she put Mocha back down on the ground.

"You must be the cat whisperer."

Mocha started to rub her side up against Emily's leg.

"Mocha has been hiding in her cage all day."

"She's really sweet. I love cats." Emily gazed down at Mocha and then looked back to me.

"What's wrong?" I hurried over to Emily, wiping the final pecan ball mixture off my hands so I could comfort her. "What's with the tears?"

"I'm not sure how to tell you this because you've been so instrumental in my career and life." Her voice cracked as the words tumbled out of her mouth, and the tears fell in big drops down her face.

"Are you sick?" I asked, hoping to help her tell me whatever it was she needed to get out.

She shook her head.

"Is someone in your family ill?" I asked since I knew her family well.

"Just let me get this out." She sucked in a deep breath and pinched her lips as if doing that turned the tear nozzle off. "When I walked in here while I was in high school, I just needed a summer job because my dad made me. Then I realized how much I loved the baking part. You talked my parents into giving up their dream of me going to college, then off to Paris I went." The smile radiated from her as she spoke fondly of the past. "Then I came back, and you helped me open Bees Knees Bakery. My dream was to open a bakery right here in Honey Springs."

I wasn't sure what was coming, though my gut told me Emily had some big news that would forever change not only me but her.

"Owning a business hasn't been easy. Especially in a small town like Honey Springs. Over the past year, I've come to realize how much more I love baking than being the owner of a shop. The business side I'm not good at." She shook her head and rolled her eyes. "My dad even took over about nine months ago since I wasn't even good at balancing the checkbook, but I still love to bake."

"Are you shutting down the bakery?" I blurted out with a cry of disbelief. "I can help you with the books."

"See, this is why you are so well loved. You offer to help anyone with anything, always putting you and the coffee shop second and third." She reached out and grabbed my hands. "But I'm an adult, and I need to do what an adult does and make some big-girl decisions. That's why I've decided to take a position as the head pastry chef at another bakery that's in southern Kentucky."

"You're moving?" My jaw dropped. I did not expect her to tell me she was shutting down the bakery, but for her to actually move a few hours away was downright shocking. I really did try to put on a happy face for Emily, but my head was having a hard time wrapping around what she was saying. "Leave Honey Springs? Close the bakery?"

"I was afraid of this." Emily's brows dipped. She gnawed on the edge of her lip.

"Afraid of what?" I asked her. Though I was only thirty, I had to remind myself that Emily was still very young and just entering her twenties. I didn't want to hurt her feelings, and by the look on her face, she was upset.

"How you'd take the news?" She swallowed hard. "I'm forever grateful for everything you've done for me, and it's not that I've taken it for granted."

"Okay, stop." I walked over to her and wrapped my arms around her for a comforting hug. "I'm not upset at all. I'm sad because I won't see you on a regular basis, but I also know that you need to spread your wings and grow. I'm so happy for you and super-supportive."

"Oh, Roxy," she gushed and hugged me tighter. We stayed like that for a couple of seconds longer. We let go. "I do think it's best. Like I said, I was losing the passion for baking because all the business things had me tied up, and then after I'd take care of those things, all my creative baking energy was zapped. I was struggling to do all the things."

"Trust me, I understand." Not that I wanted to make this conversation about me, but I felt like I needed to remind her of my past. "Remember, I spent all the money on law school and opened up my own firm with my now-ex-husband, only to come here to start my passion, where I'm so happy."

"And that's what I kept thinking about when I was feeling disheartened. I knew you had decided to leave your big lawyer job behind, not that people here don't always hit you up." She joked, but she was right.

Even though I wasn't practicing in a law office, somehow citizens knew I still had my certified law degree, which I did make sure I kept current, and would ask me to look in or help with various things. Just because of my nature to serve people—and, these days, coffee—of course I helped them if I could.

"What are you going to do with the building?" I asked.

"I don't know." She shrugged. "I know it's a bad time of the year to even think about putting it up for sale, but I've got to be there next week."

"Next week?" My jaw dropped, and my eyes popped open. "Wow, that's soon."

"Soon to you, but honestly..." She hesitated and looked down at Mocha rubbing up against her. "I've been working on this for months. The guy you saw in the bakery is buying all my equipment and inventory, which he's taking in a couple of days." She put her hands out in front of her. "Don't worry. I'll have all the pecan rings ready for you to take to the theater."

"I'm not even thinking about that." I shook my head and rolled my eyes. "Who knows if the show will go on?" I teased. "They are all about to implode with all the inner fighting. But I appreciate you getting those made."

I motioned for her to follow me back to the kitchen.

"I'm roasting some beans and don't want them to burn," I told her over my shoulder.

"I miss watching them spin," she whined on our way into the kitchen. "And I see you still haven't gotten a bigger one."

"Did I complain that much?" I asked her as we both noticed the temperature was about to reach the three-hundred-and-ninety-two-degree mark.

Just like old times, Emily, without me asking, turned the bean release lever just as the temperature was perfect.

"My favorite," she squealed as the dark-brown roasted beans fell out of the chute into the cooling tray, allowing the fan blades to circulate the beans while they cooled.

"I wish I had more space for a bigger one, but I don't," I told her as we both watched the beans being turned over and over and looked for any white beans.

"Found one!" Emily reached in and grabbed the white bean before the blades of the fan swept past and covered it up. "I'm putting it in my pocket."

"It still amazes me how some of the beans just don't get roasted." I laughed and remembered how Emily and I made a game out of who could find the most white beans after a roast. "Even though we haven't done this in a long time," I said, referring to us sitting there watching the roaster, "I'm sure going to miss seeing your face. But I'm incredibly proud of the woman you have become and are becoming. It took me well into my twenties to even consider going for what I wanted most in the world."

"You have no idea what that means to me." Her shoulders lifted to the bottoms of her ears, and a smile curled on her lips. "I have a great idea."

"Oh yeah?" I asked and started to scoop the full beans into Bean Hive coffee bags so customers could purchase them and take them home to grind. I also made sure to keep some back for me to grind so I could take them with me to the theater on my way home.

"Why don't you buy my building?" Her eyes lit up like the snow did in the sunlight.

"I don't want to be a baker." I laughed and headed over to the grinder.

"No, put a roastery in there. It would be great. You can give roastery tours. I've seen it in other cities." Emily nodded her head so fast that she looked like a bobblehead doll. "You can hold classes. It'll be great!"

"You know this all sounds good, but you are two shops down. It would be one thing if you were next door, but you're not." I hit the button for the grinder and talked over it. "Good idea, though."

"Think about it." She tapped the prep station with her fingertips. "I've got to go finish those pecan rings and make a few stops."

"How long do we have?" I asked.

"Less than a week." She frowned, but I could tell she was excited about her new adventure.

"Then all of us gals have to get together." I was referring to Crissy Lane,

Camey Montgomery, Fiona Rosone, Joanne Stone, Kayla Noro, and Leslie Roarke. All of us were about the same age and hung out sometimes, and I knew they'd all want to get together to say goodbye to Emily.

"That would be great!" Emily brought her hands up to cover her mouth. "You're the first person I told, so I'm going to be heading on over to Crooked Cat now to tell Leslie, then to the Watershed to tell Fione."

Those must've been the few stops she'd referred to earlier.

Leslie was the owner of the Crooked Cat Bookstore on the far end of the boardwalk, and Fione was a waitress at the Watershed floating restaurant on Lake Honey Springs. The restaurant was located in front of Crooked Cat.

"You let them know I'll be texting them to get together." I gave Emily one last hug and noticed the snow was really piling up. "Now get out of here before we both get snowed in."

"I'll see you in the morning to pick up the pecan rings," she trilled on her way out the door. "Bye, Mocha!"

CHAPTER SIX

The coffee turned out great. I went ahead and made two big carafes to take with me—one for the theater in case someone was there and one for home so Patrick and I could enjoy some coffee by the fire.

The roads were getting slick, and I made sure to drive pretty slow on the way into downtown Honey Springs, which was only a five-minute drive on a non-snowy day and a ten-minute drive today.

Downtown was a gorgeous small town. Central Park was smack dab in the middle of town. There was a sidewalk around it and different sidewalks leading to the middle of the park, where a big white gazebo stood. Most of Honey Springs's small-town festivals were held in the park. And I couldn't wait for spring to come back because I missed going to the farmers' market.

Dimly lit carriage lights dotting all the downtown sidewalks glowed and made a gorgeous picture with the falling snow. It was almost as pretty as the vivid memory of the colorful flowers and daffodils that I knew were hiding underneath the snow in the ground and would pop up soon to let us know spring was coming.

The courthouse was located in the middle of Main Street with a beautiful view of the park.

There was a medical building where the dentist, optometrist, podiatrist, and good old-fashioned medical doctors were located.

And the theater was near the library, which was across from the bank where Emily's dad was bank president.

Even the old theater looked great. It was a typical small-town theater with exposed light bulbs going all the way around the marquee, which was lit up on the top of the building. There were double doors and a small glass cashier window, where one of the members of the theater committee would sit and sell tickets for the show. The theater company did four shows a year, and those coincided with the seasons. Since we were still in the winter season, this was the winter show. With Loretta Bebe in charge of this one, I knew it was going to be over the top, just like her.

I made a U-turn in the middle of Main Street and parked in front of the theater. The street was empty, but the lights inside the theater were on, which told me someone was in there. I grabbed one of the coffee carafes and a plate of the warm pecan balls before I headed inside.

The Southern Women's Club took great pride in the theater. It was one of their works of philanthropy, and they made sure they did the necessary fundraising to keep the theater in the pristine shape it was in for its age.

They had replaced the long velvet red drapes along the wall with new velvet red drapes that were exact replicas of the originals. They also had the red carpet replaced to match the original carpet. The entrance was a long hallway that led right into the auditorium, where there were about fifty rows of seats with velvet covering the backs and bottoms. They were the originals and the most expensive to recover from what I remembered. But the Southern Women's Club did it.

The stage was the typical half-moon design, and there were two balcony box seats on both sides of the stage. Those were usually reserved for the mayor and other officials of Honey Springs.

I walked down the center aisle and headed to the left side of the stage, where the door led to the dressing rooms. I noticed Loretta had already put Gretchen's name on one of the doors, which made me happy because now I knew exactly where I needed to go in the morning with her sweet treat and special mug full of coffee.

Just in case she was in there, I gave a little knock before I opened the door.

"I'm sorry." I was shocked to find Alan Bogart, the director, in the room, standing over the makeup desk with the manuscript in his hands. "I... um..."

"What can I help you with?" He folded the manuscript and placed it under his arm.

"I was just making sure I knew where Gretchen's dressing room was before I showed up here in the morning with her requests from the coffee shop and bakery." I shrugged and noticed the briefcase lying on the makeup table was open and papers were spilling out of it.

"You found the right place. We are getting all the manuscripts to the actors before our morning rehearsal," he said with a stone face. "Did you happen to get rid of the reviewer?"

"You know, I live by the southern saying that I have no horse in that race, so that's something you're going to have to take up with him. But I am an expert on the weather around here, so you might want to get back to the Cocoon Hotel before it gets too slick to get back." I wanted to leave him with some friendly advice, but he didn't seem to be receptive to it.

"Are you also the weather girl?" he asked with a snide grin. "These little towns drive me nuts."

He pushed past me and out into the hall, leaving me at the door of the dressing room.

"I suggest you not be a half a second late in the morning, so you should watch the weather because Gretchen will eat you alive." He had turned around, walking backwards down the hall, giving me some advice with a huge smile on his face. "Better you than me." He let out a long, deep, evil laugh and turned around before he disappeared into the door that I knew led to the stage.

"Jerk," I muttered under my breath and took another quick look at the dressing room to see exactly where I would put the mug and pastry when I visited in the morning. Then I shut the door.

"That's ridiculous!" I heard the shrill voice of my aunt Maxi coming from inside the theater. "That is not what you told me!"

Oh man, someone was in trouble. I'd heard this tone from Aunt Maxi before, and I knew it was right before she threw a giant-sized hissy fit that no one wanted to see. Trust me.

Instead of just letting it go and her working it out so I could get in my car and get home to my little family, I sucked in a deep breath and prepared to head into battle—whatever battle she was griping about.

There she was standing on the stage in all her glory. Bleach-blond hair and all. If it weren't for her screaming and stomping, I would be shocked by the hair. I was used to all the different colors Aunt Maxi made her hair, but never had I seen her with short bleach-blond hair.

"Maxine..." Loretta Bebe danced around Aunt Maxi, using her pleading voice. "Alan is an award-winnin' producer. He knows what he's doing. I agree with you that it's a bit of a shock that we won't be doing the romance, but just think how much fun this little mystery will be."

"It's not the script, Low-retta," Aunt Maxi said with a growl. "It's the lead being taken away from me that I have an issue with. You asked me to be the lead. Not some dried-up actress."

"Well, Gretchen Cannon is dried up." Alan Bogart seemed to really be stoking the fire, the fire being Aunt Maxi.

"Who is calling who dried up?" Gretchen Cannon popped up from a chair in the front row.

"They can't possibly be talking about you, Miss Cannon." Sydney O'Neil jumped up to defend her employer.

"Nope." Aunt Maxi shook her finger directly at Gretchen. "I'm certainly talking about you. What was the last play you were in? Why are you here in Honey Springs? And you..." She turned her attention to Alan Bogart.

I squeezed my eyes closed in anticipation of what was going to come out of her mouth to help soften the blow to my ears.

"What kind of producer are you? One that doesn't take pride in his cleanliness, because I'm standing downwind of you and your stink is buckling my knees. And I'm sure Steven Spielberg doesn't stink." Aunt Maxi was on a roll. "Low-retta, you..."

"Now, Maxine..." Loretta had clasped her hands in front of her and was trying to calm down Aunt Maxi. "Why don't you sit a spell and simmer down."

"Simmer down?" Aunt Maxi raised a fist. "I'll show you how to simmer down."

"Hi!" I yelled from the back of the auditorium in hopes of stopping Aunt Maxi from taking up residence for the night in the Honey Springs sheriff's department. "What's going on?"

"There's my lawyer!" Aunt Maxi rushed over to the steps leading off the stage. She grabbed her coat and struggled with putting it on as she walked up the center aisle to meet me. "She'll get all this straightened out. Mark my words."

"Roxy, thank the Lord you are here." Loretta never praised me as such. "Can you talk some sense into your aunt?"

"Don't you listen to her," Aunt Maxi seethed through gritted teeth and slipped her hand into the crook of my elbow, guiding me toward the door. "She has lost all control of this production, and now those two have come in here and taken over." She turned around to face the group on stage. "I'm calling an emergency meeting of the Southern Women's Club. Do you hear me?"

Loretta let out an audible gasp. It was unheard of to call an emergency meeting with the Southern Women's Club and a tall threat when someone did.

"That'll give Low-retta something to chew on tonight." Aunt Maxi laughed. "Let's get out of here."

"Do you want to come to the cabin for some coffee and pecan balls?" I asked, knowing she needed someone to vent to and that I needed to talk her off the vindication I could see forming in her mind. "I know it's snowing and getting slick, but you got that truck."

"I'll meet you there." She gave a hard nod before she let go of my arm and started walking around the theater to the small neighborhood that was located behind the downtown business where she lived.

"Do you want me to drive you home to get your truck?" I asked.

"No. I need to walk off some of this steam and formulate exactly how I want you to help me." She waved a little wave in the air.

CHAPTER SEVEN

The roads had gotten a little more treacherous within the few minutes I was in the theater, but knowing the roads and all the curves down the winding road to my log cabin made it much easier to navigate, since the painted-on lines were completely covered.

Though it normally took me seven minutes to drive to work and just a few more minutes added on to reach downtown, it took me a good twenty minutes until I saw the cute little cabin come into view.

My heart filled with joy when I saw the little puffs of smoke coming from the chimney. Patrick and I loved a good fire in the small potbelly stove, and with the snowy night, it was a perfect setting to snuggle in with the dogs.

The front porch of the cabin happened to be my favorite place and was what really sold me—besides the low price. Aunt Maxi had several rental houses and over the years had accumulated furniture, so I was happy when she gave me the key to her storage unit and let me pick out anything I wanted.

The two rocking chairs my grandfather had made were a perfect addition to the cabin. I changed the pillows on the rockers to match the season, and the Christmas tree pillows I'd recently replaced with the cute snowflake pillows were a perfect match to the weather we were having. And they matched the deep-brown ladder-back-style rockers perfectly.

"Good evening." I walked into the one big room that combined a kitchen and dining room with my hands full of pecan balls and the coffee carafe.

I'd like to say Patrick was quicker than Sassy and Pepper to greet me, but he came in third.

"I'm going to have to jump the couch to beat them," he teased and took the items from my hands so they were free to give the pups some good loving scratches.

"Don't lock the door," I told Patrick after he put the treats on the small table and headed over to the door to lock it. "Aunt Maxi. . ."

"I can't hardly stand it, I'm so mad." Aunt Maxi pushed through the door.

"Is coming over," I muttered under my breath to finish my sentence. I gave Patrick a pinched smile, knowing he was looking forward to a night of the fireplace, the couch, snuggling with the dogs, and mindless television while the snow piled around us.

"Let me help you with your coat." Patrick was such a southern gentleman. He never complained about my mom or Aunt Maxi and their invasive ways when they just barged into our daily lives.

"Thank you. Thank God." Aunt Maxi threw her hands up in the air as if she were in her usual spot in the front row of the Honey Springs Baptist Church. "That Roxanne Bloom came to her senses and moved to Honey Springs and won you back over."

"Won him back over?" I laughed and walked into the kitchen to get the tray of pecan balls and three mugs along with the carafe of coffee.

"It took a lot," Patrick teased, knowing good and well how the story went. When Aunt Maxi turned away to walk into the family room ahead of Patrick, he pointed to her head and mouthed *her hair*.

I had to admit I was a little mean to Patrick when I first moved back. I wasn't in any shape to let a man into my life, but my heart softened as he not only fixed up the coffee shop to code but also changed out all the old knob and tube wiring in the cabin while I had renovated it.

With fond memories of how we reconnected the spark we'd started during my summer visits as a teenager and of my practically following him around everywhere, I looked around the cabin and could see how he had his hand in every room of our home.

The bathroom and laundry room were located on the far back right. A set of stairs led up to one big room that was considered the bedroom. The natural light from the skylights and the large window in the bedroom really made the room inviting, but today snow blanketed them, hiding any outside light, though it was really just a grey sky.

That might bother some folks, but I knew that just beyond the clouds was a beautiful sunny sky that would soon make its appearance.

"What's all this business of you being mad?" Patrick and Aunt Maxi headed over to the couches, but not without Pepper pushing himself on Aunt Maxi.

"Roxanne didn't tell you?" She looked between Patrick and me. She only used my full name when she was torn up about something. She was all torn up about this play.

"I just got home," I reminded her and sat down on the couch with my big mug of freshly roasted Columbian.

Pepper jumped up next to me and waited for me to curl up my legs and lay them to my side so he could nestle into their bend. Sassy hung next to Aunt Maxi, who had decided to stand up in front of the fire while she ate a few of the pecan balls.

"Loooow-retta Bebe has decided that our theatrical cast isn't good enough for her time as the head of the committee for the winter theater." Aunt Maxi put her fingertips down for Sassy to lick off the powdered sugar. I snapped my fingers at her, but she ignored me and kept talking. "She has taken my main part and given it to some dried-up actress who owes this director I've never heard of that owed Low-retta a favor." Her eyes narrowed. Her brown eyebrows were hooded like a hawk and did not match her hair at all. "Since when does Low-retta let a favor hang on and not cash it in right away?"

I knew Aunt Maxi was spitfire mad when she continued to pronounce "Loretta" the way Loretta enunciated her name with her southern accent. She was completely mocking her.

"Then..." Aunt Maxi smacked her hands together, making poor Sassy jump. "The producer tells us tonight that the play the committee had put together, the sweet little romance, has been changed to a murder mystery. One about a young girl who killed her aunt and kept her fur coat, something about a fur coat."

"Gretchen Cannon had on a fur coat. Maybe she is cashing in on her favor to have her play done?" I asked as only a suggestion, but it seemed to make

Aunt Maxi's face turn red, and it wasn't because of standing in front of the fire.

"I don't care if Woody Allen himself came to direct this play. It was written by the committee of the Southern Women's Club for the winter theater, and Low-retta or anyone else on the committee *cannot* change it without a vote, and Low-retta didn't do that." Aunt Maxi stomped and made sure she exaggerated her words to get her point across. "And now!" she screamed and jerked some folded-up papers from her pocket before shaking them up in the air. "I only have two pages of script, since I'm nothing more than the maid!"

She took a couple of steps closer to me before she shoved the papers in my face, and she needed to sit down to catch a breath.

"What is this?" I asked and noticed it was really only her part of the play. "Where's the rest of it?"

"That's the crazy part. He said that we don't need the full play and that we will only get the pages when we are on the stage." She shoved a few more pecan balls in her mouth then poured herself a cup of coffee.

She took the time to sip and eat while I read through her lines. It did appear Gretchen had all the lines and Crissy Lane had the lines of the young woman.

"I had no idea Crissy Lane was in it." Reading her name reminded me that I needed to text the group of gals about Emily. "Which reminds me..." I knew I was going to go off subject, and probably the best thing was to get Aunt Maxi stewing on something else. "Emily Rich is closing Bees Knees Bakery and moving out of Honey Springs."

"Moving? Out of Honey Springs?" Aunt Maxi seemed more shocked at this news than what she was mad about. "How could she do that? What about her parents? I just saw Evan down at the bank today, and he didn't mention a word of it."

"I don't know anything about that, but it's a done deal. She's sold all the bakery equipment and even has a moving date for next week." A deep, sorrowful sigh escaped me before I took another drink of coffee.

"This is great coffee, by the way." Patrick's arm was lying across the back of the couch and was long enough for his fingertips to scratch at my back. "New roast?"

"Mmm-hmmm, the Honduras bag." I couldn't help but well up with pride because he was right. It was a nice, full-bodied, rich coffee that I knew was going to sell well when I debuted it for the spring collection. "Which I was roasting when Emily came in to see me before I left for home. She actually said something that made me think."

"Uh-oh." Patrick smiled. "When you start thinking about something, I know something is going to happen."

"She mentioned something about me taking over the bakery space for a roastery." Saying it out loud actually gave me a little tickle in my belly which told me there was a little something to it. "She even suggested having roastery tours and maybe some roasting classes."

"I can see by the fire in your eyes that you're thinking on it." Aunt Maxi smiled. "So maybe her leaving isn't a bad idea. I could use the distraction."

"What?" Patrick and I both said in unison for her to clarify.

"You're going to need someone to run it. I am the perfect person." She shrugged and popped another pecan ball in her mouth.

"First off, you're going to get sick." I uncurled my feet, causing Pepper to jump up, and leaned over to grab the tray before I got up and took the sweet treats into the kitchen. "Secondly, you don't even know how to use the roaster I have now."

"I might be old, but this old dog does learn new tricks." She straightened her shoulders back and lifted her chin in the air. "I don't need you to pay me."

"It's not that, Maxine." Patrick also took the liberty to chime in. "But you're retired. Enjoying your life. Why would you want to spend your days roasting coffee?"

Though I knew Patrick was trying to sway her as I wanted him to, what he said really got my attention.

"So...." I hesitated and stopped in front of the couch where he was sitting. "You think it's a good idea and I should buy the building even though it's not next to the Bean Hive?"

"I think that Queen for the Day is looking to expand. Even though the Bees Knees isn't as wide on the inside as Queen for the Day, it's got more square footage in length and exactly what Tamara McFee is looking for." Patrick would know, since he was the contractor most businesses used. "She was seriously considering moving off the boardwalk to find a bigger space, but this might work out perfectly."

"Then I could take her shop, which is right next door." The idea was coming together.

"If the city council agrees." Aunt Maxi just had to throw a wrench in it. "But I know people." She gave me a wink.

"If I give you a job?" I asked, knowing her wink came with a catch.

"Mmmhhhh," she ho-hummed with a big smile across her face and then took another drink of her coffee.

CHAPTER EIGHT

The alarm went off so fast that I didn't even feel like I'd gone to sleep. Last night, after Aunt Maxi seemed to calm down about her small part in the play, we talked about the possibilities of what a roaster could do for Honey Springs.

While the men went on their fishing trips, we could offer a roasting class for the women along with some cool facials and spa treatments using coffee if I could get the Honey Comb Salon to agree. They were a few doors down, and we could make it a package. I'd even go as far as putting something together for All About the Details and the bridal events they hosted. Bridal parties were always coming into the Bean Hive to grab coffee while they were waiting for the appointment with Babette Cliff, the owner.

Honey Springs was a destination for all things romantic. Most of the tourists rented cabins for honeymoons, girls' weekends, family trips, and other gatherings. Maybe a roastery would just add to the experiences our small southern town offered.

Still, it was definitely something for me to consider, and I would ask Crissy Lane when I texted her about Emily. Aunt Maxi always told me God made everything happen for a reason, and though I hated to see Emily move away from Honey Springs, I couldn't help but think Aunt Maxi's way of looking at things just might be right in this case.

Like always, Pepper and I got up out of the comfy white iron bed suite that I'd also gotten from Aunt Maxi's storage unit when I moved in. I tiptoed down to the bathroom to get ready.

This was the reason I kept my work clothes in the laundry room. I didn't want to have to wake Patrick since my wake-up time was around four-thirty a.m. and his was around six.

Sassy wasn't about to budge and Pepper curled up in his little bed in front of the potbelly stove that still glowed red through the small window on the door.

After I took a few minutes to get ready and throw another log on the fire so Patrick and Sassy would have a warm house to wake up to, Pepper and I were out the door.

"It looks like the road crew really worked hard last night." I talked to Pepper, who was busy standing up on the arm of the door and looking out the window as if he could really see something through the darkness.

The sun wouldn't pop up until around seven a.m., and the sunrise would only start to get earlier, since we were headed into spring. The long, dark, and really cold mornings were almost behind us, and a new life would soon bring Honey Springs alive with fresh Kentucky bluegrass, daffodils, lilacs, and spring mix that painted the season of spring.

It only took us seven minutes to pull into the boardwalk parking lot. There weren't any lights on in any of the stores on the boardwalk when we passed, which was normal for our usual start time. But I knew to expect a lot of the owners to start trickling into their shops in about an hour, stopping at the Bean Hive to get their morning caffeine fix.

"What do you think about a roastery?" I asked Pepper and stopped in front of the Queen for the Day clothing boutique. "I can totally picture a small roaster in the display window to pull in customers."

Pepper danced around my feet, and I took it as a sign that he totally agreed with me.

"Pepper..." I looked down at my sweet Schnauzer and into his big round black eyes. "I think we are in trouble. I've already got the roastery details in my head, and when I get something in my head...."

He darted off to the front door of the Bean Hive, and I followed him. Then I unlocked the door.

"Good morning, Mocha," I called out and ran my hand up the wall to flip on the interior lights of the coffee shop.

Pepper had already darted inside. Light or not, he never waited.

I was happy to see Mocha was curled up in the dog bed in front of the fireplace. She didn't run off when Pepper hurried over to greet her. She simply stretched out her arms and gave a great big yawn.

"We need to get this fire going." I noticed it was a tad bit chilly. I peeled off my coat and laid it across the arm of the couch. I started to stack up kindling and some newspapers before I threw the match in the wood fireplace to get a nice bed of coals going there.

After Pepper greeted Mocha, he left her alone and sat in front of his bowl.

"I know, you're hungry." I grabbed my coat, and when I passed Pepper and his empty bowl, I reached down and scratched the top of his head before I hung my coat up on the coat rack. I retrieved a scoop of his food. "Here you go."

He chowed down, and I walked along the industrial coffee pots behind the counter, flipping them to brew. Then I headed back into the kitchen, where I turned on the three ovens for preheating and flipped on my little coffee pot filled with the new Columbian coffee I'd just roasted yesterday.

The sausage casserole was pretty much a staple around here for customers during the winter months. It was a comfort to the soul, and all the cheese made it perfect. We southerners loved a good comfort food.

I retrieved a couple of the glass casserole dishes from the walk-in freezer and took them over to the oven, where I set them on top of the stove while I waited for the ovens to preheat.

"Hey, you two," I said, greeting Pepper and Mocha when they came into the kitchen together. "I see you've made friends."

Though it made me happy to see Mocha making friends with Pepper, I really needed her to make friends with customers so we could get her into her forever home.

"I need to text Crissy and the girls." It might seem odd to some people that I talked to the animals like they were human, but they made me feel happy and kept me company. There was nothing like a great conversation with an animal because no matter how wrong or misguided, as we like to say in the south, about how we might feel about something, the animals always appeared to agree with me.

Hey girls! I'm sure y'all are as sad as I am about Emily moving, but we all want what is best for her. I would like to invite everyone to the coffee shop so we can discuss how we can send off our dear friend with a see-you-soon party because we know this isn't goodbye. Please let me know if late afternoon today works to meet. We don't have a lot of time to plan. Xoxoxo Roxy.

"There. That should do it." I put my phone down just as someone was knocking on the door. "It's a bit early for Bunny, and I don't have to pick up the pecan ring from Emily for a couple of hours," I told Pepper and Mocha on my way to see who was at the door.

The pitter-patter of their feet made me smile, telling me they were following me to the door. If it weren't for the sweeping lashes and great big smile, I'd have mistaken the blond-haired woman for Aunt Maxi, but Crissy Lane was standing at the door in all her glory, waving, when she noticed me walking to let her in.

"Hi do, Roxy." Crissy walked through the door, wearing a bright-blue fluffy coat. She gave me a hug, and though the coat looked like something my grandmother would have covering the lid of her toilet, it was soft to the touch. "I just got your text on the way to the salon, so I figured I'd just stop right on in and grab my coffee early so we can discuss."

"Good morning." I laughed at Crissy's typical behavior.

We southerners liked to just drop in. We didn't bother calling or texting when we were about to stop over. If the desire to pop in washed over us, we just did it, and we weren't expected to call either.

"I'm glad you're here." I locked the door back after she came on in. "That's Mocha, the Pet Palace animal of the week. Isn't she a doll?"

Crissy was like me. She loved all animals.

"How about a cup of coffee while we talk?" I loved seeing her bright smiling face in the morning.

"Yes. It's so cold out there. I can't believe the snow was so heavy it snapped the internet lines." The red freckles on her face widened as she frowned, which was how you knew she was a natural redhead. Her false eyelashes swooped down her cheeks, drawing a shadow along her cheeks.

"The internet is down?" I questioned and headed right on over to the register, where we used the Square application on the iPad.

"Yeah. Of course, I tried to get on social media first thing, and when I couldn't connect, I nearly had a heart attack. I flipped on the radio and heard the weather report about how the snow was so heavy on the lines that some power is out and the internet is out." While she told me her whole morning routine and how this was going to affect her day, I tapped and poked the iPad alive, only to find out she was right.

I would still be able to take orders and process credit cards through the Square. The payments were just going to have to be offline. They would quickly recover automatically once the internet came back.

"I hope it comes back on before we open." I glanced up at the clock and realized that was in only an hour.

"The radio report said it could be days in some areas." Crissy made herself at home, which was expected. She waved her phone in the air. Her dime-store square solitaire diamond flashed as she wiggled it around.

Like Patrick and I, Crissy and I had formed a relationship when I was visiting Aunt Maxi on all those summer vacations. Crissy was loud, boisterous, and fun, making it easy for her to make friends and enjoyable to be around.

When I moved to Honey Springs, she'd gotten me into a community of girlfriends that made my transition to living here very easy.

"I'm going to have to show Bunny how to process a sale without the internet." Not that it was too difficult, but Bunny was up there in years, and I tried to make working, or, as she put it, *getting out of the house*, easy for her.

"I can be here later today. I've got to run through rehearsal then color Mae Belle Donovan's hair." She made herself a big cup of coffee in a mug, which told me she would hang out for a minute.

"I heard you were in the big production that seems to be causing a lot of controversy." It was my chance to poke around, and Crissy was the perfect person to do it with because she loved to talk, so she had the perfect job.

"Let me tell you how it happened."

She moved around to the stool on the side of the counter while I headed over to stoke the fire. Then I started to refill the coffee-and-tea station, since I didn't do it last night before I left.

"I was already in the play Loretta had written." She rolled her eyes and took a sip of coffee.

"Keep talking," I called to her over my shoulder on the way back to the kitchen. "I've got to get the casseroles in the oven."

"Loretta was in my chair, getting her hair dyed, which we all know is from the bottle, though she'd as soon die as admit to it." Crissy always told it like it was, and I admired that about her.

She talked about Loretta for a few more minutes, giving me the opportunity to get the casseroles in the oven and a few of the other frozen pastries out of the freezer. I dumped some of the pecan balls I'd made last night on a serving platter. Then I reached under the preparation island to grab one of the mini chalkboards to place beside the platter in the glass display case.

"She told me she needed a scene in her play where the heroine is getting her hair done for the ending of the wedding. She wanted it to be real with real language and all, so of course she came to me." She shrugged, bringing her shoulders up to her ears. "I'm always about helping people out."

I grabbed the piece of chalk next to the register and quickly wrote the name of the pastry on the small chalkboard then put it in the glass case.

She gave me a theatrical wink. You know, the long and slow type with her lip hiked up really high to one side?

"Yeah. You're for sure that." I patted her shoulder on my way across the coffee shop to the coffee bar. I opened the bar stand cabinet and took out the contents that needed refilling—the small packs of differently flavored coffee creamers, the various sugar packets and non-sugar packets, coffee stirrers, and a few lids, just to name a few. "Who do you think you're talking to? You can't pull the wool over my eyes," I teased and went behind the counter to retrieve the free-standing coffee carafes just in time for the kitchen timer to ding.

"Just as luck would have it," she continued when I went into the kitchen to retrieve the casserole and put more casseroles in the oven to heat through since I'd already pre-cooked them. "Alan loved my small performance, and when he changed the play, he said I was perfect as the murderer."

"Murderer?" My head shot up when I put the casserole dish on the counter and took off the oven gloves. I left the casserole dish there to cool so I could cut really nice thick slices.

"Yeah." Crissy and I both looked back at the door when it dinged at Bunny's arrival. "It's an awesome story."

"Good morning," I said to Bunny and helped her with her coat. "You're a little early."

"I wanted to make sure I gave myself plenty of time if the roads were bad, but they weren't." She took the bobby pins that had spilled out of her pillbox hat from her hair and started her routine of putting her coat, hat, and pocketbook away while she grabbed an apron. "What's going on with you today, Crissy?"

"Oh the usual, being a star and stuff." Crissy loved to pique everyone's interest about what she had going on. "I was just telling Roxy how Alan Bogart loved my acting skills and moved me to the second lead in the new murder mystery play."

"Is that right?" Bunny asked and kept hitting the keys on the iPad so she could sign into her time card.

"Internet is down," I whispered on my way back into the kitchen so as not to disrupt Crissy's story because she kept on talking. Didn't miss a beat.

"It's really good. There is an old lady, played by Gretchen, of course, who is a grandmother to this killer, *moi*." She had her hand on her chest when I walked back into the coffee shop with the other casserole.

Bunny had already taken the liberty of cutting the cooling casserole and putting the slices in the brown wrapping made specifically to keep the items warm. Then she set them on a tiered tray in the glass counter where I'd placed the mini chalkboard.

"The granddaughter kills the grandmother. It's fabulous. Like no other murder mystery you've ever seen." Crissy stood up and walked over to the coffee bar, where she retrieved a to-go cup.

"How do you know all the plot?" I questioned. "Aunt Maxi only got two sheets of her role. She said Alan didn't want people to worry about the other roles or something like that."

"Yes," she said with a gasp. "I'm the only one with the full manuscript," she squealed. "But I must go. The stage calls."

"Which reminds me that I need to get my coffee over there before the big seven a.m. curtain call." I shook my head and waved to Crissy.

"I'll see you there, and I'll be back this afternoon for the see-you-later party planning." She waved goodbye to Bunny and me before she disappeared into the dark morning.

"See-you-later planning?" Bunny asked and walked over to the fireplace with a salmon treat each for Mocha and Pepper.

Pepper didn't care whether it was a cat treat or dog treat. He just liked treats.

"I have unfortunate news about Emily Rich." I headed over to the shop door and flipped the Closed sign on the door to the Open side. "She's closing Bees Knees and moving out of town. So the gals and I are going to throw her a see-you-later get-together instead of a goodbye party."

"I never thought of anyone leaving Honey Springs." Bunny loved our little small town so much. She was a staple of our community and a very good person... when Aunt Maxi wasn't around.

"I know I'm not going anywhere." I untied my apron from around my waist and took my coat off the coat rack. "Do you mind putting a couple more carafes on? I've got to get these down to the theater and come back to take those to the Cocoon."

I did a few clicks of my tongue to get Pepper's attention so he knew we were heading out the door. Plus it was a great time for him to go potty.

"No problem. Be careful out there," Bunny called on my way out the door. "And I don't mean the weather. I mean all the big heads at the theater."

I giggled, knowing exactly how right Bunny was about the divas all in one room. Unfortunately, a tickle in my gut told me to hold on because we were in for a big production, and I was not sure it would be worthy of a five-star review.

CHAPTER NINE

"You be on your best behavior," I told Pepper after we walked into the theater. "Not that I don't expect you to behave, but there's a lot of people in there."

My hands were filled by the pecan ring Emily had given me on my way here and the carafe of coffee. While I tried to focus on getting Gretchen's request into her room, my mind continued to wander because of the question Emily posed when I picked up the pastry. She'd asked me if I'd thought about the idea of turning the bakery into a roastery.

I did tell her that the idea interested me, but there was a big issue that stood in the way... the other two buildings.

There was really no time to worry about that right now. What was important in this moment was getting the pastries in Gretchen's dressing room before she noticed they weren't there.

All the lights were on inside the theater, and people were milling around. Most of them I knew I liked and some of them I didn't.

"Good morning, Bev," I said to Bev Teagarden when she passed me with a big flower arrangement I'd seen on display in the Wild and Whimsy.

"Hiya, Roxy." She shuffled past, making sure she didn't whack me with the arrangement. "This whole change of plans has really thrown a wrench in our day. I'm not sure if this producer knows exactly what he's doing."

I smiled, trying not to gossip about my thoughts on Alan and how he had handled the switch over of props and actors for the new play he'd implemented. Then I headed straight to the craft table, where I set up the table of goodies for the crew of the production. Next, I headed off to Gretchen Cannon's dressing room with her own personal treats, which Sydney had requested.

"Knock, knock," I said to announce my entrance when I pushed open the door to Gretchen's dressing room with my toe, happy to see the door was cracked. "Good. Not here yet."

The lights in the dressing room were off, but the lights from the hallway added a nice glow to the room. That way, I could see the exact spot I'd scoped out the night before to put her pecan ring and coffee.

I'd put a few napkins with the Bean Hive logo in my bag to go along with the display in Gretchen's room to make it a little more presentable. Emily had put the pecan ring on a plastic decorative tray Gretchen could throw away when she was finished.

"Not here yet?" Mark Redding stood at the dressing room door, catching me off guard. "Sorry if I scared you."

"I'm good. I wasn't expecting anyone. I was focused on getting this set up just right before Gretchen gets here." I smiled and added the finishing touches to improve the presentation.

"Southern women sure do like everyone to feel at home." Mark Redding walked in and fiddled with the briefcase.

It was the same briefcase I had seen Alan digging through, and I wondered why he left it in there. The thought quickly slipped my mind when I heard voices.

"I'm getting out of here before I have to interact with anyone." I grabbed my bag from the floor and met Mark out in the hallway, where he was busy patting Pepper. "So, let me guess, Camey Montgomery is going out of her way to make everyone welcome."

The voices were coming from the front of the theater down the left, so I took a right with Mark following next to me.

"She's amazing. I've never stayed at a hotel so welcoming." He twisted to the side when we passed someone so he didn't bump into them. The glare the man gave Mark didn't go unnoticed. "This is turning out to be a big deal. I see Alan's production crew is here."

"So that's where all these people came from," I said since I'd noticed a lot of faces that I didn't recognize hurrying around. "Let me guess, they all can't stand you."

"Only because of him." Mark's head tilted to the stage when we walked into the side door of the theater.

For a couple of seconds, we watched Alan Bogart as he directed people to go here and there. What I figured was the manuscript was folded in half under his arm.

"Go down! Down! I said go down!" Alan screamed at the top of his lungs with a vicious tone and pointed at the lights.

As he yelled some more, the lighting guy was tilting, twisting, and rotating until Alan had agreed it wasn't perfect but would do.

"See, he just can't give compliments or be nice. I swear after he had that heart attack and needed a blood transfusion, they gave him blood from the devil himself." Mark's words made me giggle. "It's true. The reviewers thought his life-changing surgery would make him a little more compassionate, but it made him worse."

"That's a shame." My eyes swept up to the entrance, where the center aisle started, and I noticed Gretchen and Sydney were standing there. "They're here."

"And everyone else better get here or Gretchen and Alan will have what you guys around here call a hissy fit." He pointed at the front row, and I followed him there. "Might as well have a front-row seat to the show."

We slipped into the seats with no one even noticing. The crew was busy making the adjustments to some of the props Bev Teagarden had brought, and another crew member helped take out some of the props that were supposed to go with the original script by Loretta Bebe.

"Okay, everyone!" Alan clapped his hands. "It's time for the morning meeting per your schedule. Time is money, and money is time."

"Schedule?" I whispered to Mark.

"Oh yeah, he keeps a pretty tight schedule to keep everyone moving. That's one of the reasons so many actors won't work for him. If they are even one second late, he fires them." Mark's brows rose. "Back in the day, his heyday, it worked. Not too many agents or lawyers involved. But up there."

I followed Mark's eyes as they shifted up to the balcony.

"Those are lawyers and agents." He'd pointed out the group of about ten people gathered in the balcony with their heads buried in their phones. "The actors claim all sorts of things if things don't go their way."

"I have to say that I'm glad I'm no longer a practicing lawyer." I smiled.

"Get out. You?" Mark drew back. His brows furrowed. "Sweet and southern you were a lawyer?"

"I'm still a lawyer, just not practicing full time."

The lights went down, and we shifted forward to watch the stage.

"This is not going to do!" Gretchen hurried onto the stage. Sydney had stopped shy of the steps going up to the stage. "I have three pages of lines, and I want the entire manuscript."

"Here we go." Mark leaned over and continued, "Gretchen has been a pain all morning. Starting with the hotel. I could hear her clear up to my room, fussing with someone in the lobby. I couldn't make it out, but I think it was Alan. It was a man's voice."

"Really?" I asked and made a mental note to ask Camey all about it... over a cup of coffee, of course.

"Thanks for the coffee." Loretta Bebe had snuck in behind us and leaned on the back of my chair. "This has been a nightmare. I'm a little upset I called in my favor now."

I reached around with my hand and patted her arm. Loretta had to be upset if she was thanking me for the coffee. Normally, she'd just go on about her business.

"We had a sweet love story, and now he's doing murder. I'm beside myself over it, and I've got to get all the committee to up my budget so I can change the marketing materials. I had hearts on everything. Now I guess I've got to put knives or some sort of dripping blood." She shivered. "The thought makes me so upset. What will the church group think?"

"You're the one who didn't question him." Alan shrugged.

Uh-oh, I thought when Loretta jerked back, glaring at Alan. She stood up, tugged on the edges of her pink suit coat, and straightened herself to look presentable before she marched off.

"What was that?" he asked while we both watched her march up the steps and engage in the meeting Alan was having with the actors, including Crissy and Aunt Maxi.

"You've just gotten on Low-retta Bebe's bad side." I laughed.

"I seem to do that to a lot of people." He nodded toward the stage then took out his camera. "Here we go. The real show is about to start."

"I told you that I'm not going to play some old lady!" Gretchen's hands fisted. "You told me I'd be playing a young, vivacious actor."

"That was before I got my hands on the new script." Alan jerked the papers from his armpit and shook them in the air. "That was before the mystery."

"That wasn't the favor I called in on, Alan Bogart, and you know it." Gretchen's lips were moving a mile a minute, and the spit flowed out from her mouth like a sprinkler.

Sydney practically tiptoed onto the stage and around the group, making her way over to Gretchen.

"Stop this nonsense right now!" Alan pointed directly at Gretchen. "If it weren't for me, you'd not be here." Then he looked directly at Loretta and pointed. "If it weren't for me, this little romance production you had going would have brought this theater under!" Alan held his hand up over his eyes and looked out into the crowd. When he caught sight of Mark Redding, he pointed at him. "I told you never to show up to anything I'm doing! Get out of here, or I'll make sure you don't have a job at the *Times* when you get back to New York!"

Alan sucked in a big deep breath before turning around to face all the actors.

"I want five minutes to myself. In that five minutes…" He held up his hand. He had stubby fingers. "If you do not want to be a member of this cast and crew, I suggest you clear your things and leave. There are plenty of people around here that I can make a star! And younger."

The last jab had to be for Gretchen because he looked directly at her.

"You'll regret this." She stomped off the stage with Sydney in tow.

"I'm guessing this is my time to leave or at least hide." Mark excused himself.

The only people left on stage were Aunt Maxi and Crissy. Both had shocked looks on their faces.

"You stay," I told Pepper, who was lying underneath the theater chair. "If you were to go up there and scratch the floor, Alan would have you banned."

Pepper's ears perked up.

"You're a good boy." I made my way to the steps and over to Aunt Maxi and Crissy. "That was harsh."

"I agree about him changing the script." Aunt Maxi harrumphed, crossing her arms.

"I'm the opposite. I've been practicing my lines all night." Crissy held up the thick manuscript.

Aunt Maxi's jaw dropped.

"Is that the full play?" she asked Crissy.

"Mmm-hhhhm. I've got the biggest part, and I'm the killer." Crissy took real pride in claiming that.

"There's one thing for sure. Low-retta is not happy." I couldn't help but look over where she'd disappeared, but everyone was gone. Everyone but Alan Bogart, who was looking at his watch.

"Here he comes." Crissy stiffened and shifted toward the little circle the three of us had formed.

"I see we have two actors who'd like to get instructions from me." Alan's chin lifted. "There's something to say about you two ladies and the pride you take in your craft."

"I'm beyond thrilled to be playing a killer," Crissy started to say, but the ropes dangling behind us flew up in the air, smacking the velvet curtain behind them.

"Watch out!" I yelled and pushed Aunt Maxi out of the way when I noticed the ropes were attached to the sandbags overhead that kept the equipment in place.

Aunt Maxi and I fell to the ground just in time. She looked at me with wide eyes.

"Are you okay?" I asked her and used my hands to push myself up on my knees to help her up. I glanced above my head when I heard some footsteps.

Was someone up there?

My eyes narrowed to see through the dark for any shadows. A sliver of light peeked through what appeared to be a door opening then closing quickly.

"Yeah. I'm fine. I think." Aunt Maxi brought my attention back to her. She patted around her body and then took my outstretched hand to help her up.

"I'm not!" Crissy yelled.

I looked up and across Alan's body to find one of the sandbags had landed on Crissy's leg.

"I think my leg is broken." She winced in pain as Aunt Maxi walked closer to her.

"I think he's dead." Aunt Maxi stood over Alan Bogart's body.

CHAPTER TEN

It didn't take long for Spencer Shepard of the Honey Springs sheriff's department to show up and not too long after that for Crissy Lane to pour on the tears so Spencer could console her.

Granted, Spencer was single and very handsome in his sheriff's uniform, and his sandy hair and piercing green eyes weren't bad either.

"I don't know what happened," Crissy whined to Spencer's question he'd had for her about the time of the incident. She was still sitting on the floor with her hand on her leg while the EMT put a brace on it. She whimpered as they hoisted her onto a stretcher that was waiting for her off stage where the audience would sit. "One minute we were discussing my leading role, and the next minute I heard the cord of the sandbag zipping up the curtain, and before I knew it, I was knocked on the ground. When I looked up, Roxy and Maxine were over there, and Alan was between us." Crissy batted her eyes at Spencer.

I wasn't sure whether or not he noticed her flirting between the whines and whimpers, but he sure didn't lead on. He kept his eyes on the notebook in which he wrote down what she'd been saying.

"Spencer, can I talk to you privately?" I asked when I noticed Gretchen Cannon, Sydney O'Neil, Loretta Bebe, and Mark Redding were standing stage right in a huddle with their heads together.

Every once in a while, Loretta popped her head out and chin up over the heads of the others to see if she could hear what was going on. In true Loretta fashion, she reported back what she could hear. Trust me. I knew her gig because I'd been in various situations in Loretta's little huddle.

"Sure." Spencer nodded. "Can you please get Crissy on over to the hospital to get her leg checked out?" he told more than asked the EMT. "Does anyone else need to see the EMT before they head on out?" Spencer asked the crowd but looked at Aunt Maxi since I had pushed her out of the way, making her fall.

When no one, not even Aunt Maxi, stepped up, he gave the go-ahead for them to take Crissy.

"I'll call you when I leave here," I assured her and walked her out of the theater so she wasn't alone. Pepper trotted next to me.

"I might need you to bring me some magazines if the internet doesn't come back up soon." She waved her phone in the air.

Her leg must not have been hurting her too badly if she was worried about her social media.

When the EMTs got her into the ambulance, she gave the most pitiful wave before they shut the door. Pepper and I stood there watching the ambulance drive off.

"You can sit in the car for a few minutes," I told Pepper and put him in the car, where he immediately snuggled up on his blanket in the passenger seat. "And you have water too."

I took out the dog bag I kept in the door's storage holder. I put his water bowl on the floorboard and filled it halfway with the bottled water and set a few treats next to it.

When I walked back into the theater, I noticed Spencer had walked over to Kevin Roberts, the coroner. They whispered a few words before Kevin pointed to Spencer's neck. He handed Spencer a clipboard. Spencer signed something, which I assumed was the paperwork needed for Kevin to remove Alan's body because Kevin had already gotten Alan on the gurney. He tugged it up and rolled him down the ramp with the clipboard on top of Alan's body.

"What was it that you needed?" Spencer walked over to Aunt Maxi and me. "Hello." He waved his hands in front of me.

"Sorry. I was just looking at Kevin." I gnawed my lip. "You know, I don't know him that well. The only time I see him is when there's been a murder, and I'm not so sure this was an accident."

The only reasons I used the word "accident" were that I'd overheard the others answering Spencer's questions by saying what a terrible accident this was and that Spencer had even referred to it as an accident.

"Roxy," he said in an exhausted tone. "You and I both know this old theater is so rickety and outdated. It's used four times a year, and ropes start to deteriorate."

"I agree, but when I was helping Aunt Maxi up after I'd pushed her out of the way, I heard footsteps up there." I glanced up. "Shortly after I heard them, I saw a sliver of light shine through an open door before it closed."

Spencer moved his face towards Aunt Maxi but kept his eyes on me for a few seconds before he finally asked Aunt Maxi, "Did you see or hear anything?"

"Not a darn thing. All I know was one minute I was about to complain about my two little pages of script, and the next I was thanking the good Lord above for sparing me the knock on the head. Now that I see it took out Alan, I'm very grateful for the shove." She nodded at me with big eyes.

"Are you absolutely sure you heard footsteps?" He shifted back to me. "I mean, you were under a lot of stress in that moment."

"Yes, Spencer. I heard footsteps and saw a door open. I know what I saw." There was no mistaking what I'd seen, and I had a hard time believing the cords had simply deteriorated and no one had noticed.

"You didn't see who it was?" he asked, and I slowly shook my head. "Man? Woman?"

"Nope. Just footsteps. But give me a few hours, and I'll see if I can remember anything else." It was a technique I used to use with my clients when I was a lawyer.

If they called me after a traumatic experience and they had to be questioned by the police, I suggested the police wait to interview them because the client was so shocked or ridden with anxiety they weren't thinking as clearly as they could. Generally, it would be days or even weeks after their mind relaxed that they would recall small details that helped paint the bigger picture. I was no different.

Though I didn't believe I was in shock, I could've been, and I could've blocked any sort of details to tell whether this was an accident or homicide.

"Plus there aren't a lack of suspects that would love to see Alan Bogart in the state he's in now." The words accidentally left my mouth, and I threw my hand over it.

"All right." Spencer's eyes narrowed suspiciously. "What is going on in that head of yours?"

"Nothing," I lied. "What did Kevin say?"

"At initial glance, it appears as if the sandbag hit him perfectly on top of his head, breaking his neck and causing instant death. Probably didn't see it coming." Spencer frowned.

"Spencer." Loretta stalked over, and her little gossip group had all turned to watch her. "Just when do you think this little fiasco will be cleaned up? We have a play to rehearse." She clasped her hands together in front of her. "The play must go on."

"Alan would've wanted that," Gretchen said and dabbed the edges of her eyes, adding a little sniffle.

Mark Redding wasn't about to let this moment pass without taking photos and getting comments from the various actors and crew members.

"I think you're done for today. We need a little time to process the scene," he told Loretta with a follow-up glance to the group.

"Process the scene?" Loretta asked nervously. "That's normally not done unless you think there was foul play."

The group of actors and crew members walked over in full earshot of what Spencer had to say.

"Let's just say I'm not ruling this out as a homicide. We'd like to make sure there isn't any evidence of that, and it'll give us time to process your statements and where each one of you were during the time of the incident."

Spencer might've had their attention when he addressed them, but the one word that had caught my attention was that he'd changed from his previous statement of "accident" to "incident." Two very different scenes in the investigation world.

"Who on earth would want to harm Alan?" Gretchen asked and looked around.

"Oh, come off it." Aunt Maxi pointed a finger at Gretchen. "By the way I hear tell, you had the biggest beef with him about your role in this play, and he owed you a favor. Some favor payback for him to switch your role at the last minute, and if you're all worried about your career, becoming the B-class actress he insinuated you're becoming is humiliating."

"I mean, Maxine might have a point." Loretta chimed in like she was trying to take the heat off her. "You did just ask me to put you back in the lead role."

"I cannot believe my ears." Gretchen's mouth dropped. She looked to Sydney to save her.

"Those are ridiculous accusations. Miss Cannon has nothing but love and respect for a producer as amazing as Alan Bogart." Sydney took Gretchen by the shoulders. "I honestly can't believe you."

"Me?" Loretta pointed at herself.

"Yes, you." Sydney was direct. "You just asked Gretchen for more help on the production, and now you go pointing fingers at her as if she killed someone when she isn't obligated to stay here, since she no longer has to fulfill the favor to Alan now that he's dead."

"Another motive to have killed the man," Aunt Maxi muttered, elbowing me in the ribs.

"I just can't help direct." Gretchen brought the hanky back up to her eyes and dabbed them again. "I just can't do it all."

I watched Spencer's amused reaction while the group of actors turned on one another.

"But you said you'd help me." Loretta had already moved on from pointing out Gretchen's flaws with her fingers and practically began to beg for her help.

"I can't take this stress. You claim I killed my friend when you have the best motive to have killed him." Gretchen's tears dried up awfully fast. "He owed you a favor, and when he switched the play from the two-bit romance you wrote to this genius murder mystery, your head spun around five times on your shoulders. You have a reputation to uphold in this community, and if you think for one second that I believe that you don't lie in a tanning bed, you're crazy!"

Loretta went from a southern lady to a hot mess within half a second.

"Now, now, ladies." Sydney stepped between the two feuding women. "Tearing each other down isn't going to get us any closer to production. Let's let Mr. Shephard do his job and we collect our thoughts. If we need a production manager, I'm more than happy to step up to the plate."

"She does have her degree in film." Gretchen nodded.

"Agree to regroup tomorrow?" Sydney looked at everyone for confirmation. Everyone nodded. "Great. I have the text thread from Alan, so we will continue to communicate through that."

After it was all said and done, Spencer was busy looking around, and everyone else had gone their separate ways. Everyone but Aunt Maxi, Loretta, and me.

"That woman," Loretta spat, referring to Gretchen Cannon. "She's so sorry I wouldn't wave at her if my arm was on fire."

"Don't you pay her any mind, Low-retta." Aunt Maxi took her by the arm and guided her out of the theater. "Our town will love our play no matter who is in it or who produces it."

"Not if we have a murder on our hands." Loretta looked at me with the most pitiful downturned eyes. "Do you think they think I'm a suspect?"

"Don't you worry yourself about that until Spencer comes back with Kevin's report." I tried to make Loretta feel better, but I'd been around this block a time or two.

I knew what I heard and what I saw, and I was pretty positive Spencer's report would come back as an official homicide.

CHAPTER ELEVEN

"What on earth is going on over at the theater?" Bunny Bowowski couldn't hightail it over fast enough to me when she saw Pepper and me come through the coffee shop door.

That there were so many customers shouldn't've surprised me because whenever there was a situation in Honey Springs, including simple gossip, they loved to come to the coffee shop to have a cup of coffee and hear the rumor mill.

I'd like to say it was awful that they did this, but it was good for business.

"You aren't going to believe it," I muttered under my breath and took a look into Mocha's cage on my way back to the counter. Bunny followed on my heels.

"Roxy!"

I was slipping off my coat and on my way back to the counter to hang it up when I heard someone calling my name.

"Roxy!"

"It's that reporter." Bunny snarled and put her hands on me to guide me back to the counter as though she were protecting me. "He's trying to get the scoop."

"The scoop? He was there." I hung my coat up and waved him over to me. "He might have some good information for us."

"For us?" Bunny jerked back. "Oh no. Don't you dare tell me you're going to stick your nose into this." She waited for me to respond. When I didn't, she threw her arms up in the air. "Of course you are going to. Why wouldn't you? You think that producer was murdered, don't you?"

"Bunny, Mark and I are going to go into the kitchen." I scanned the glass display case to see what I needed to thaw and replace while I was back there. "I'll grab some more donuts, blueberry scones, and some maple glazed long johns."

"And that blend you had."

"Blend?" Frantically, I turned around and looked at the small container I'd roasted from the very expensive Honduras burlap bag.

"Yeah. That stuff sold out fast." She shrugged and waddled back over to the register when someone came up to pay. "I want to know every single detail of what happened after I get some of these people out of here."

Mark followed me through the push-through door into the kitchen.

"You can sit there." I pointed to the stool butted up to the workstation.

While he got situated, I headed straight to the freezer and grabbed the few items to thaw and restock.

"That should keep us until lunch." I was mainly talking to myself like I always did, but Mark nodded in agreement. "And while those thaw..." I continued and tugged the big dry-erase whiteboard from underneath the workstation, laid it on top, and grabbed the dry-erase marker from the drawer. "We can talk about who had the most motive."

"Whoa!" Mark eased up onto his feet. His jaw dropped when he noticed I'd written Alan Bogart's name at the top and the word Victim under it. "What are you doing?"

"Obviously one of the crew or the actors killed Alan." I quickly wrote down Gretchen's name. "But who?" I wiggled the marker toward him. "I saw you talking to the crew, and I don't know them, but I'd love to read your notes."

"Wait." Mark's mouth opened, closed, and opened before his head tilted to the left, and he pursed his lips. "Are you saying Alan was murdered?"

"Well, yeah." I noticed his state of befuddlement. "Don't you?"

"I never thought..." He hesitated. "But the officer guy said the theater was old and the rope was probably deteriorated."

"Deteriorated my patootie!" Low-retta swept through the door with Aunt Maxi on her heels. "The theater has an inspection once a year in January. And it passed with flying colors. Nothing about the ropes and nothing about the sandbags."

"I did hear something from the catwalk right before the bags came down, and I saw the door up there open and close right after the bags fell," I told them. "I told Spencer too."

My words met with a collective gasp.

"Think about it. Gretchen Cannon was here for a favor. It was no secret she wasn't happy he changed the script. What was the favor?" I tapped the marker on the whiteboard as I tried to collect my thoughts. "Then you and Alan sure did have a volatile relationship." I pointed at Mark and then wondered if he should be here.

"Me? I was sitting with you the entire time. I don't know my way around the theater." He scowled at me. "Besides, we don't even know if he was murdered."

"You know what?" I grabbed the hand towel sitting on the workstation. "You're absolutely right." I wiped off the board.

"What are you doing?" Loretta cried out. "I need your help. I might be a suspect."

"Fiddlesticks." I shook my head at Loretta then gave Aunt Maxi a subtle wink when she started to open her mouth. "I'm sure the inspector didn't check out those old ropes and Spencer is right. We are just being busybodies like we always are."

That seemed to settle Mark down a little. He put his bag on the stool seat and took out his notebook.

"I'm going to finish up my article for today, and I wanted to get a statement on what you saw today. That's why I'm here." Mark opened the notebook and clicked the top of his pen, ready for the statement.

"You can actually grab that from the police report." I smiled, grabbing the thawed maple glazed long johns. "I've got customers. I'm sure you understand."

I hurried out the kitchen door with the platter. While I was putting them into the display case, I was happy to see out of the corner of my eye that the three of them had filed out of the kitchen. I'd also gotten a text from Crissy.

According to the message, the bag had come down on her shin bone, bruising it badly but not breaking her leg. She said she'd be here this afternoon for the girls' meeting about Emily's see-you-later party and told us not to start without her. She texted that she had some really great ideas for the girls, and that made me a little nervous.

Crissy's great ideas were far from my great ideas. Maybe we could meet in the middle somewhere. I didn't have time to worry about that now that I knew she was okay, so I turned my attention back to the group standing in the middle of my kitchen.

Mark, of course, didn't think anything of my sudden change of heart. He had stopped when he saw Perry Zella and his mystery group at the middle table of the coffee shop.

"What was that about?" Aunt Maxi had dragged Loretta over to the counter. "You know as well as I do that Alan was murdered. It's just gonna take time for Spencer to figure it out. And we could be suspects." She gestured between her and Loretta.

"And so could he." I slid my gaze to Mark Redding. "Think about it. He and Alan had the most public fights, and it was no secret Alan despised him. Not to mention how each said to the other that they could end each other's career."

"Oh." Loretta's eyes grew as big and round as her lips. "You are so good."

"Top in my class for body language." It was true.

It was taught in law school how very important it was to be able to read body language, and I ended up being very talented in that department.

"Mark Redding's body language told me he knew more about what happened than he's letting on. Maybe he's not the killer, but he knows something." My brow rose, and I shut the display case.

The bell over the door dinged. A smile as big as the day was long grew across my face, and my heart went pitter-patter when I saw it was Patrick.

I watched him weave in and out of the tables, shaking the hands of the folks he knew before he made it to me.

"Can I talk to you? Privately?" he asked after he gave Aunt Maxi a hug and patted Loretta on the arm.

"Listen here." Loretta leaned into him. "If I'm a suspect, I expect your wife to help me."

"Suspect?" He laughed. "Suspect in what?"

"Gossip," Aunt Maxi said and jerked Loretta's sleeve. "Let's go grab a coffee."

Aunt Maxi knew Patrick so well that she knew if he even heard I was sticking my nose into another murder investigation, he just might lose it or I just might lose him.

"Listen, I've been thinking about the idea of the roastery, and I think we can do it. I called Tamara. She said that it just might work out, and I'm going to meet her this afternoon. I called Emily, and she can too." He stopped talking and gave me a shifty look. "What's wrong?"

It didn't take Patrick long to look around the coffee shop and then at Aunt Maxi before he knew something was up.

"There are a lot of people here that aren't normally here at this time." He pointed at Loretta and Aunt Maxi. "I thought they had rehearsal."

The door of the coffee shop swung open like the curtain was rising on opening night before Gretchen Cannon walked in, the fur coat draped over her forearm. She handed it off to Sydney.

"You simply have to get this cleaned." She stomped back with me in her sight and used a very loud outside voice, putting all eyes on her. "Now that Sydney has looked at the script, she's going to. . ." Gretchen hesitated and made the sign of the cross, the first inclination the woman even believed in the big guy in the sky. She dabbed her eyes with the handkerchief and stumbled over her words. "I just can't. I can't. Simply can't." She motioned at Sydney.

"She simply can't believe Alan is gone." Sydney held the fur out over the counter for me to take.

"Gone? Y'all ran him off already?" Patrick laughed and looked around to see our reactions. "What? Y'all act like someone died."

"And I thought southern men were supposed to be gentleman," Gretchen scoffed and marched toward the door.

"Here." Sydney thrust the big fur coat at me and then took off after Gretchen.

"What was that?" Patrick stood there with a dumbfounded look on his face.

"Alan is dead," I whispered over the counter with the darn coat in one hand. I picked up one of the maple glazed long johns and practically stuffed the entire thing in my mouth.

"You literally ate that in one bite, which tells me you are stressed. Kitchen. Now." He pointed to the kitchen and took off in that direction.

"What am I going to do with this fur coat?" I asked Bunny.

"Perry Zella is right over there. Maybe his laundromat can clean it." She made a very good suggestion.

Perry and the mystery group were discussing Alan with Mark when I walked up.

"I'm sorry to interrupt, Perry, but do you think you could clean this fur for me? Coffee was spilled on it, and I believe they need it for the play." I tried to look around the darn thing for the coffee stain but couldn't find it.

"No problem. I can have it ready tomorrow afternoon."

"Great. That's great news." I pointed to the coat rack next to the front door. "I'll put it over there so you can grab it on your way out."

"Sounds good. I'll see you tomorrow afternoon," he told me and went back to his group while I headed back to the kitchen.

"Let me guess." Patrick didn't leave me any space to explain about Alan before he started in on me. He began the usual lecture I got when he didn't approve of me doing a little snooping around. "You think he was murdered. The whiteboard gave it away."

"In Roxy's defense..." Loretta Bebe had pushed her way into the kitchen and the conversation. "If Alan's death is ruled a homicide, I will be a suspect, Patrick. I don't do well in jail." She gnawed her lip. "Not that I've ever been in prison, but I don't do well under high stress. I start breaking out in hives." She started to scratch.

"Who does she think she's fooling?" Aunt Maxi had also joined us. "Unfortunately, there's no tanning bed in prison, so she's worried we'll all find out she's been lying all these years," Aunt Maxi said in a hushed tone while Loretta did her best to convince Patrick she needed my expertise in the law field.

"Thank you, ladies, but I think I'll talk to Patrick alone." I gestured for them to leave us alone and turned around to face him when they were safely out of earshot. "We aren't sure if he was murdered or not."

"How did he die?" Patrick asked.

While I told him the entire story, I grabbed some Kentucky burgoo from the freezer and part of today's lunch special since it was pretty near time for the lunch crowd.

"And you have already declared it a murder even though Spencer hasn't claimed it to be a murder?" Patrick shook his head.

"I'm claiming it now." Spencer walked into the kitchen. "Roxy, I'm going to need your full statement because after we inspected all the ropes and the rope in particular that snapped and gave Alan his fatal blow, it was cut, and the knife was found on the catwalk."

Spencer pulled out his phone and showed me a few photos.

"Geez." Patrick ran his hands through his hair. "You're not going to try to solve this. Tell her, Spencer. Tell her to stay out of this one."

"I'd like to do that, Patrick, but one problem." Spencer slid his gaze to me. "You're our only witness to someone being up there, and I'm afraid if they saw you looking up at them, you could be in danger."

That startled me into a wide-eyed expression.

CHAPTER TWELVE

I'd like to say Patrick's attitude turned around after Spencer gave me a time to be at the department to give my statement, but it didn't. One, he was mad because it was the same time he wanted me to meet with Emily and Tamara. Two, he didn't want me to be the next victim. He remembered other circumstances when my big nose got me into a situation in which someone had literally set my cabin on fire to keep me from snooping.

Of course I'd spent twenty minutes trying to convince Patrick I was safe and it was all good. Then he got a text from Walker Peavler, Camey's husband. They wanted to know if we wanted to come to the Cocoon Hotel for dinner. A little couple's night.

It was a no-brainer for me that I wanted to go since I knew I wanted to get the scoop on what Alan and Gretchen had been arguing about so loudly, according to Mark.

Patrick was going to meet with Tamara without me and afterwards take Pepper home for me.

Still, I couldn't wait to get to the sheriff's department to talk to Gloria Dei, one of the employees of the department. She wasn't a deputy, just a secretary who knew it all.

Though it was Bunny's afternoon to stay before the afternoon gals relieved her, I told her to go on home because there was really no sense in me leaving.

When the afternoon staff arrived, it would be time for me to head on over to the department, then come back to meet with the girls about Emily's see-you-later party.

The first building on Main Street was the Honey Springs Church. I couldn't stop the memories of when Patrick and I were teenagers. Both our families made us go to church, but little did they know that we'd slip out the back door before Sunday school started. We weren't doing anything bad, just acting like two teenagers who liked to spend time down on the shore of Lake Honey Springs. Aunt Maxi said that if I didn't watch it, I was going to lose my religion on that lake. I didn't know what she meant at the time.

Next to the church were the firehouse and the sheriff's department, where I needed to be. Across the street from that was the Moose Lodge. I pulled in the only free spot that looked to have been cleared from the snow and headed to the front door of the department, but not before grabbing the box of sweet treats and a thermos of coffee.

I rarely went anywhere without taking some coffee and sweet treats. Especially the department, where the treats not only helped me get information out of Gloria but also out of the deputies. Not like they'd come out and tell me something on purpose, but coffee and treats did make people chat and get them to say things they normally wouldn't just blurt out.

"Roxy!" Gloria rushed over to me when I walked in. "I was supposed to get off at three, but I saw on the ledger of the Bogart file you were coming in." Her eyes drew to my hands. "Are those...?"

"Treats." I smiled and handed them to her.

"Not that I was waiting around for those, but I will have one." She gestured by nodding for me to follow her over to the small table, where the coffee pot carafe was completely stained around the glass pot where the hours-old coffee had sat without being dumped. "The deputies are great at their jobs, not great at coffee."

"That's why you have me." I patted her on the back. "So you've seen the Alan Bogart file?"

"Mm-hmm." Gloria was busy looking into the bag of goodies I'd brought before deciding on one of the cranberry scones with the sparkling hard sugar crystals on top. "Let me tell you, no one was more surprised than Spencer when the forensic team came back with the rope in the evidence bag."

"I'd like to get a look at that rope." I wasn't so subtle.

"I knew you were going to say that, and I can't get over how you are the only witness." She took a bite and glanced around the department. "Spencer had to go back to the theater for a second because I'd heard there was another piece of evidence they wanted him to see on the catwalk, so I'm going to go tell the deputies there's a few goodies out here, which might take me a few minutes."

I followed her eyes as they shifted from me to the yellow file on her desk.

"Gotcha." I winked and smiled, since this was how she and I danced around her not showing me the file but telling me it was on the desk.

Granted, I could get a hard talking-to if I got caught looking through the file, but if I got caught taking photos of anything in there, then that'd be a whole other story.

Which I did. I had taken out my cell phone and took a photo of the file's photo of the severed rope. Even though it might have appeared to be just a cut rope, the way the fibers were cut would be able to tell a real forensic team exactly what type of tool was used to cut it. The murder weapon was definitely the sandbag, but the tool used to cut the cord would probably lead us to Alan's killer.

There wasn't a whole lot in there that blew my mind or that I didn't expect to see in an initial autopsy report Kevin had performed. Alan Bogart's death had been caused by a broken neck. Kevin had ruled it instantaneous, which gave me a little bit of relief since Alan didn't even see it coming. For that, I was grateful.

In the file there appeared to be next of kin, and it was marked that they'd been contacted. I couldn't get to the dictation of the conversation, since the sounds of chatter and feet were coming back down the hall.

"Roxy, glad to see you got here on time." Spencer was with the group. "I was a little surprised when Gloria told me you were here and alone with the file." He grabbed the file from Gloria's desk. "Not that I'm accusing you of looking at it, but I'm not putting it past you either."

"Spencer," I said with a gasp. "Me? Unethical? I'm just sitting here twiddling my thumbs."

"Roxanne Bloom, twiddling her thumbs when there's been a murder." He scoffed. "Y'all hear that?" His questions were met by a few nods along with some laughs from the deputies, who'd already started to munch on some goodies and make themselves a cup of coffee.

"Ha, ha." The sarcasm was in my tone.

"I actually asked you down here to talk about exactly that. Follow me." He waved the file at me to come with him.

There was a nice long silent pause between us. Another technique I learned in law school. So many times people talked through awkward silences or pauses, but if you could just beat the silence and not give in, the other person would start talking. I didn't want to add anything to my conversation with Spencer at all. He was the law, and anything I said could be held up in court. I was on an answer-only basis with him at this point in the investigation.

He took me into an interrogation room I'd been in before. I sat down in the chair before he even asked me to and watched him get all the equipment together.

"I'm glad Crissy is going to be okay." He set up the microphone and recorder before he planted himself in the chair.

"Me too," I said and watched him open the file, take out his little notebook, and click his pen.

"State your name, occupation, date of birth, and why you were at the theater." He knew he didn't need to tell me why we were here. It was the official statement he needed for the investigation now that Alan's death was ruled a homicide.

I told him the story of how someone's movement caught my eye when I was helping Aunt Maxi up to her feet where I'd knocked her out of the way, followed up by my noticing someone going through the door. Then Spencer turned off the tape recorder.

Interesting.

"You're our only witness." He said it again, but his tone was different from when he'd first mentioned this at the coffee shop. "I didn't want to talk about it in front of Patrick because I know how touchy he is when you get a little too involved. But it's been brought to my attention that none of these people get along."

He pulled a piece of paper out of the file I'd not been able to flip to.

"I also know they've all been to the coffee shop." He pointed at the photos of all the suspects I had in my mind. "I talked with Alan's production crew. All of them have worked with Alan for a long time, and they all know how he works. According to them, they know exactly how he likes everything set up, and when they were putting up the overhead lights for the production, there weren't any sandbags up on the catwalk or overhead. I've been trying to get in touch with Butch Turner to get a copy of the last inspection, since Loretta Bebe kept saying it had passed."

"You're beating around the bush." I could tell he was circling around to get to why I was really here. "Just cut to the chase."

"Fine." He sucked in a deep breath and looked cautiously at me, as if he were trying to assess whether to ask me something or tell me what he wanted to tell me. "I wanted to see if you could get any information out of these people at the coffee shop or just keep your ear to the ground. I was going to put someone on you since I'm worried that the killer saw you, but if we don't come out and publicly say we have a witness, then I think you'll be safe. Besides, I don't think you'd let me put someone on you, and I know if I told you Loretta Bebe was in fact a suspect, you'd end up helping her in some shape or form." His shoulders relaxed as he got the words out. "So I might's well use you to my advantage and get a report on what you hear so we can get this thing solved."

"Spencer Shepard." A big grin crossed my lips. "You do think I'm pretty good at solving crimes."

"Now, now. Don't be thinking you're getting a gun or badge," he joked. "Honestly, it's not looking great for Loretta. Especially since we have two witnesses who she told if she'd known he was going to change the script, she'd rather he'd crawled in a hole and died. They also mentioned some sort of verbal fight between the two." Spencer took out his phone and laid it on the table. "And without internet, we've got to go back to good ol' foot-and-mouth investigation."

"The internet is still out?" That was more shocking than Loretta being a suspect.

"Yep." He shook his head. "We rely on emails, cross-references, and even looking up phone numbers to call over agencies when we get a homicide. Those things are only found on the internet in this day and age. Really making it much harder and take longer to get to even the slightest bit of information needed for a murder investigation."

Spencer was right. We'd gotten so used to having technology at our fingertips and instant gratification that it took something like a big snowstorm that knocked out the internet to really get us back on our toes.

"Luckily for you"—I pointed at him—"I've never had the amazing technology you've had to figure out a couple of your investigations and had to rely on the sleuthing I know." I tapped my nose. "Being nosy, asking questions, and kinda doing things not on the up and up."

"Those are things I don't want to know, but I do want to know if you hear anything." He closed the file. "And are you sure you don't want someone in plain clothes to be hanging around in case the killer tries to come after you?"

I tilted my head to the side, with my jaw relaxed and an eyebrow tugged up.

"Just had to make sure." He and I both stood up at the same time. "Who do you think did it?"

This was such a turning point in our relationship, and I was very excited about it. Given that he knew I was a lawyer, he knew I would be smart.

"I'm a little on the cautious side with Mark Redding."

Spencer flipped the file back open.

"He's the reviewer with the *Times*."

"Yeah, yeah." Spencer nodded. "I've got a call into the *Times* so I can get information on him from his boss. I can't even get things like background checks with the internet down. Warrants. Nothing."

"He's a talker. He's really gotten invested in Perry Zella's mystery club. I'll see what I can get out of Perry when I drop by there tomorrow to get *Gretchen Cannon's fur coat,*" I said in a fancy tone of voice. I ran my hand down my front like I had on a fur coat.

"Don't be getting yourself into any situation that can harm you," Spencer warned.

"Don't worry. I love my life and am not ready for it to end." I pulled my phone out of my pocket and waved it over my shoulder on my way back down the hall. "I'll call you."

CHAPTER THIRTEEN

Now that I had clearance from Spencer to stick my nose in places where it didn't need to be stuck, I was actually excited about getting the meeting with the girls over with and going to the Cocoon Hotel, where I would meet up with Patrick, Camey, and Walker for supper.

All my suspects were staying at the Cocoon, and someone had to have overheard something. The only problem I was going to have was Patrick. I'd rather face any killer than face Patrick. He'd have a conniption for sure if he knew Spencer had even asked me to snoop.

I had to put all my sleuthing ideas and questions away when I got back to the Bean Hive and found all the girls who would be going to Emily's see-you-later party were already there and having coffee and a dessert.

Crissy Lane, Camey Montgomery, Fiona Rosone, Joanne Stone, Kayla Noro, and Leslie Roarke had pushed together some tables and were too busy chatting to even notice I'd come in.

"How's business been?" I asked the young girl who worked for me in the afternoon.

"No one has come in until your friends. Then Camey brought the morning coffee carafes, and I washed those." She shrugged and then pointed at a schoolbook on the counter. "I've been studying for a test I have tomorrow."

"No internet still?" I asked, hoping it'd been restored in the few minutes' drive it took me from downtown back to the boardwalk.

"Nope, and it's making me anxious," she said.

"Don't be anxious. If you can't get on your social media, then none of your other friends can." I could see the anxiety starting to rise. "You can pack up and go on home. I'm going to close early, since no one will be out in this weather."

"You know it's not that I want to see what they are doing, but this week is the week we are all supposed to hear what college we got accepted into, and we're all pretty much competing for spots that are hard to get." She flipped her book closed. "I'm dying to know if I get in. The schools send out emails now instead of big packets in the mail. It's killing me not to have access to email."

"I'm sure you're going to get into all the schools you've applied to." I tried to assure her and put her at ease.

Even though she smiled, I could tell her mind was jumbled with her thoughts.

"There you are!" Camey hollered across the coffee shop. "Come join us. I think we've already got it planned."

"That's good." I did a quick sweep of the coffee shop to see what I needed to do before the girls left and I had to close up. "Hey, Mocha." I reached up on the top of the cat tree and gave her a few chin rubs and pulled away before she'd had enough.

"We've decided to get the room at the Moose Lodge and get a little bluegrass band." Crissy was no worse for the wear. She looked as good as ever. "I'm not going to be able to do much line dancing since I've got this nasty bruise."

"Yes." Fiona's eyes grew big. "I can't believe you were at this murder too."

Fiona had been a great witness for me in the last case I'd stuck my nose in, which just so happened to be a murder. One I'd like to forget about.

"I was telling Fiona that you needed to not think about a roastery and open up a private investigation office." Leslie Roarke caught me off guard.

"Who said anything about a roastery?" I questioned.

"Emily. When I asked her if anyone was interested in the space, she mentioned it." Leslie pulled a book out of her purse. "I brought this book from the bookstore about different roasteries in Kentucky."

"And I had a few reference books I'd pulled from the library but forgot them." Joanne Stone, the librarian, frowned as she twirled the braid she'd styled her long red hair into.

"Thank you," I told them both. "It's super-early stages of talking. It wouldn't make any sense if the roastery was a few doors down."

They all agreed but thought it was a great idea.

"What is this about the Moose?" I asked.

"We figured you could provide coffee. Fiona is going to see if the Watershed would give us a great deal on some simple finger foods. Camey said she and Walker could decorate and use some of the stuff they have in storage for the Cocoon Hotel." Crissy got confirmation from each of them. "We will all pitch in to pay and make sure we clean the Moose up afterwards."

"I'm going to get the band the Bee Farm uses during the summer tours." Kaya Noro was the owner of the Bee Farm, which was located on the island across from the boardwalk across Lake Honey Springs.

She had to use a boat to get across the lake to the mainland when she needed to come over.

"And we have internet." She was smiling so big. "I have no idea how we have it, but we do, and I'm dying to catch up on my Instagram, so I've got to get going."

"You are a very bad friend," I told her and held up a finger for her to wait before she left. "Camey, can you help me box up a few things for the girls to take home?"

"Sure." She readily agreed and got up to meet me behind the counter.

"Listen." I grabbed her arm. "I need to get some information about some of your guests, mainly Gretchen Cannon, Alan Bogart, Mark Redding." I snapped a finger. "And Sydney O'Neil."

"Are they suspects?" Her eyes glowed with excitement.

"To me they are. Spencer has pegged poor Loretta, who'll just die if she hears." I left out that Loretta had already mentioned to me she was worried they might make her a suspect.

"She'd just lie down and die herself rather than go to jail." Camey shook her head slowly and took the to-go box I'd given her.

"I'd heard there was some arguing going on this morning." I wanted to give her a little intro to what I wanted her to expand on.

"Some?" She drew back and sighed loudly. "I've not been the hostess I like to be as the hotel owner. I've traded my sweet and southern hospitality for a referee shirt." She scanned the display case and picked out a few more treats for each one of our friends to take home. "They are all at each other's throats, and I can't make heads or tails of it."

"The main body of one of the tails is dead." I filled another box and started to pick out more of the treats for another box. "Be sure to get some of the quiche in them too. I can't reheat those tomorrow, and these have been thawed from frozen."

Usually before Bunny left her shift, she was good at picking out the items that might go stale and taking them down to the church for the few homeless folks we did have in Honey Springs. Today she was just happy to get out, and I loved giving my treats to my friends when I could.

"I heard Gretchen was giving someone a fit." I didn't tell her how Mark had mentioned it, and she didn't ask.

"That woman treats everyone badly, and I don't see how they stand it. Coffee?" She pointed.

"Yeah. You can put as much of it in the to-go boxes as you'd like." I loved the boxes, which had nozzles and were big enough to serve eight people. "The afternoon girls are so good about making coffee for the after-supper coffee drinkers, but I don't think anyone is coming out tonight."

"You mentioned Gretchen. She had an argument with Alan, Sydney, and Mark this morning. If I was that assistant of hers, I'd quit."

"Sydney has a degree in film or something like that." I remembered hearing something about it in passing. "Gretchen even mentioned Sydney taking over production."

"What would be Gretchen's motive to have killed Alan?" Camey asked, just in earshot of Crissy.

"Oh! Are we trying to find Alan's killer?" Crissy bounced on her toes. "I loved when we did all that sleuthing last time."

We laughed at the memory of the three of us cramming into Crissy's VW Beetle. The laughter and merriment spread to the rest of the group, ending my conversation with Camey.

They were all happy to get the treats and take the coffee home. Camey said she'd see me in a couple of hours for our couples dinner date, which would give me time to get the coffee shop ready for tomorrow morning, but instead I had a different idea.

"Kayla..." I stopped Kayla on her way out. "Do you mind if I hitch a ride over the lake and use your internet?"

"You're sleuthing again, aren't you?" Her brows arched.

"You know it." I laughed, remembering how I did help her and Andrew out once when they were in a bit of a pickle. "I just can't let Spencer think Loretta killed that producer. Who knew the internet could really hinder a case?"

"You know I don't mind. In fact, it's exciting, and I'm so happy to help. I can even say I had a small part in your becoming a famous detective," she joked. "You ready?"

"Absolutely." I hurried over to Mocha and made sure she was okay. I also wanted to make sure she had plenty of food and water. "I will check the heat because we want her to be toasty."

"You don't have someone to adopt her yet? She's a doll." Kayla walked over to Mocha, and Mocha let Kayla pick her up.

Mocha batted at Kayla's shiny brown hair, which had Medusa-like waves. She had on her typical Bee Farm tee, tucked into her khaki pants, showing off exactly how tiny she was.

Mocha was becoming very comfortable with people touching her, and I loved it.

"She just got here, and then we had this crazy snowstorm, so not a lot of people have gotten to meet her." I turned up the heat a smidgen, checked the fireplace to make sure it had died down, turned on the radio for Mocha, and resigned myself to the fact that closing everything for the shop was going to have to wait until the morning.

It was my turn to open, and I wasn't sure where we stood on providing coffee and the pecan ring to Gretchen, so I made the administrative decision to simply shut the lights off, lock the door, and head on over to the Bee Farm island to use Kayla's internet.

Both of us bundled up. It was cold on the boardwalk, but when we got out on Lake Honey Springs, it was going to be downright frigid.

All the shops on the boardwalk looked as though they were closed. It was the off season, and it was normal for most of us to close early, but this early was rare.

"I can't wait for all this snow to melt." Kayla led the way down the boardwalk to the ramp of the boat dock.

"I love Honey Springs in all the seasons but not this cold." I shivered just watching the wind whip up on the lake. Parts of the lake were frozen on top, and some parts weren't. "You can get your boat through that?"

"Oh no. Big Bib is really helpful when the lake is like this." She opened the door to the marina's shop. Big Bib was in there watching television and eating some chips from a bag.

"Hey, Roxy." A smile crossed his lips, though you couldn't see it under that big thick beard of his. "What are you doing here?"

He got up and grabbed the soft flotation key ring with a small boat key on it. When he stood, it showed off just how big and burly he was, true to his name. Granted, his legal name was Big, but it was also Bib. Around here, it wasn't unusual to go by two names or even a nickname. Nickname in Big Bib's case.

"I'm going to head over to Kayla's for about an hour and a half." I pointed at Kayla's box. "I've got some goodies for you if you'd come back and get me then."

"You are awful." Kayla simply laughed and opened the box. "But I understand these tasty treats can persuade anyone to do anything. That's Roxy's secret weapon."

"And a mighty good one too." He looked in the box, rubbed his hands together, and reached in for a maple glazed long john.

"Here." Kayla put the box of long johns and the box of coffee on the counter. "I don't need all those calories. You can have the whole box."

"What about Andrew? He might want some." Big Bib was trying to be nice, but it was written all over his face how much he wanted all the goodies.

"No way. He needs to watch his sugar intake." Kayla shook her head. "He's already eating too much honey."

"We better get going." Big Bib grabbed a handful of pecan balls and then gestured for us to follow him to the boat ramp, where one of his boats was tied up snug to the dock. "Be sure to grab a life jacket." He popped a couple of the balls in his mouth.

Kayla and I helped each other adjust the straps, tugged the life vests over our coats, and snapped them into place. Meanwhile, Big Bib revved up the engine and untied us from the slip.

The lake was a little rocky and choppy. I held on tight as he maneuvered the boat around some of the ice patches, and I kept my head down so I'd not get the brutal part of the wind in my face.

The engine slowed after ten minutes. I looked up, and Bib was steering us right on into Kayla's dock at a perfect angle. He was so good at getting the boats in slips the first time. It would take me several attempts of backing up and pulling forward before I'd ever get it just right. Not Big Bib. He was perfect each time.

During the summer months when the Bee Farm was open for tours and tasting, Big Bib made great money as the only type of transportation for tourists who didn't have a boat docked at his marina.

Even in the dead of winter, visiting the Bee Farm was amazing. It took up the entire island. There were many trails and different stops along the way, and Andrew had posted signs there about which bees lived where. They had devoted the entire island to the species and taking care of the ever-dying bee population.

During the warmer months, Andrew and Kayla had a nice building on the island with a unique roof shaped like a honeycomb, which was a perfect place for tourists to take selfies. On most summer nights they had a live band playing while the tourists enjoyed the various honey-tasting stations. There was a small store where Kayla and Andrew sold fresh honey.

It was the only honey I used for the Bean Hive. I was happy to promote other local businesses.

"Thanks." Kayla handed Big Bib some money. "Don't forget tomorrow."

"I won't." He stuck the money in the pocket of his heavy Carhartt jacket. "I'll be back to get you in about an hour and a half."

"Sounds good." I took his hand and let him help me off the boat while Kayla grasped the edge of the boat, keeping us butted up to the dock.

She and I waved goodbye to him while he pushed the boat's gear into reverse and manipulated it around some more ice.

"He's so good at that." I couldn't help but bring it to her attention. "Just like we are all good at our jobs. This entire island is amazing. Even in the snow."

"Andrew does most of it by himself. Crazy." Kayla headed off down one of the many trails the island had and that they'd made as part of the tourists' tours. "Our house is this way."

The trail was amazing. It wasn't one I'd ventured down before, since it truly wasn't marked as one for tourists because it led up to their private property. The snow along the trail must have been patted down with some sort of machine—I noticed there were tracks. It was too cold to ask or talk, so I observed as we walked along.

Tall evergreen trees lined each side of the path, and before too long, we came to a bridge that crossed over a small creek.

"This is my favorite spot." Kayla had stopped midway across the bridge. "Andrew built this bridge all by hand. He used dead trees and salvaged what pieces of wood he could. He made all these boards and crafted it." A big smile curled up on her face. "It's where he proposed."

"I love it. So romantic," I said with a sigh and took in a nice deep breath of the chilly air. "How did you get the island?"

"Andrew and I grew up here. He inherited it from his grandfather because his parents live really close to your Aunt Maxine, but they didn't want to live on the island." She started to walk again. "Sometimes during these months, we can't get off the island, and we still have to tend to the bees. Andrew was the only one who truly cared so much about them that he went into the family business, and all his family is thrilled."

"You? You don't mind being alone all out here when you know you can't get across the lake?" I asked because I knew it would drive me crazy.

Even if I didn't really need to leave the house, knowing I couldn't would make me want to.

"We have so much to do around here I don't even notice. And we have plenty to keep us occupied." She winked, given the romantic scene.

"Yeah. Still..." I hesitated. "I'd go nuts."

"Nah. You'd just make more coffee."

The trail opened into about an acre of flat land. Their cottage house was located in the middle.

"Isn't that amazing?"

"Wow," I literally gasped at the picturesque sight of their little yellow cottage house with its sloping snow-covered roof and the woods surrounding their property. All the trees had a nice layer of snow on the branches.

"See, I don't mind being iced in." She gestured for me to follow her. "Let's go inside and get some coffee and on the computer."

The inside of the cottage was much larger than it appeared from the outside.

"The cottage was Andrew's grandparents'." Kayla and I sat down on the small bench just inside of what was pretty much a log cabin. "They wanted the look of a cottage on the outside but used much of the wood and resources from the woods on the inside."

Kayla took off her shoes and walked over to the kitchen. I took off my shoes and let her make the coffee while I toured around the open space.

"Crazy how I have never been back here." I looked out the back window and noticed another small house that was in the woods. The insides glowed a warm yellow from the lights. "What's back there?"

"That's another house we have for the bees." Kayla made all sorts of noise in the kitchen, but I was too busy looking out at the landscape and watching for Andrew's shadow to pass across the window of the other little cottage to pay her any attention. "Instead of furniture, it's all the bee houses."

"It's amazing out here." I turned around when I heard her walking towards me. "I could probably be okay out here in an ice- and snowstorm now that I've seen it."

"Too bad you gave away our sweet treats or we could have had one with the coffee." She handed me the laptop from her hands. "I'm joking."

"I know you are. But when he brings you back tomorrow, you stop in the coffee shop, and I'll have a new box ready for you to bring home."

"You can just open it up. We don't have the internet password protected because no one is out here to worry about."

I took the laptop over to the couch, opened the computer like she said, and clicked on the browser icon.

"I just can't get over you having the internet." I was tempted to check my email and a couple of my social media accounts but held off because I only had a limited time until I had to catch my ride back across the lake.

"It's crazy how well Andrew's grandfather could see far into the future and the property, how he really did build an amazing electric and data system. So we've never had an issue." She worked around the room while I started to type, starting my investigation of who the killer could possibly be.

"Gretchen Cannon." I typed her name, and the search engine brought up her IMB account with all her details and biography on it.

Nothing in there made me pause, so I hit the back arrow to scan down the results from the search.

My eyes scanned down the page. There weren't any glaring words that stood out until… I arrowed over to the next Google search page and saw Alan Bogart's name in the text. I clicked on the highlighted link.

There were several articles about a romance between Alan and Gretchen along with some paparazzi photos.

"Oh my," I said with a gasp.

"Find something?" Kayla hurried over to the couch with two cups of coffee in her hands. She set them down on coasters and sat next to me. Then she looked at the screen where I had pointed out the article.

"Gretchen Cannon and Alan Bogart had a romance." My jaw dropped. I looked at Kayla with wide eyes.

"Scorned love is a great motive for a murder," she said in a singsong voice. "Click on the images."

When I did that, all sorts of photos popped up, citing various articles.

"I was thinking the same thing about scorned love. Let me see what it says about the breakup." I Googled their names and added "breakup" to the search.

"There's one." Kayla was so excited. "Click it." She picked up a coffee and handed it to me while we both sipped on them and read the article.

"According to this, they had a public fight and broke up. It doesn't say who did the breaking up, but it definitely is weird they'd be doing a play together here." I took another drink. "In fact, she owed him a favor. Trust me, if I was in an argument with someone as public as this… I don't think I'd be fulfilling any sort of favor."

"Is there any article saying they made up—or any articles about them since this one was published because this was five years ago?" Kayla had a good point. "A lot can happen in five years."

"I'll switch the filter on the search engine to the newest information." I changed the filter and hit Enter, but nothing came up as current or even from the last three years. "This was three years ago at some award ceremony."

We sat next to each other on her couch with our coffee mugs in our hands, reading the article.

"It says they went to great lengths to ignore each other," Kayla pointed out in the article. "What was the favor?"

"I don't know, but I'm going to try to find out." I exhaled a deep breath.

"What about Mark Redding?"

"The paper guy?" Kayla asked.

"Yes. Alan despised him. They had a few public fights here and there." The one in the coffee shop as well as the one in the theater right before Alan was murdered stood out. "I'm going to see if there's anything on these two."

I set the mug back down on the coaster and typed in both of their names. Instantly, a legal document I was very familiar with popped up as the first thing, which told me it was the most searched document pertaining to the two.

"What is that?" Kayla pushed back her long hair over her shoulder as she leaned into the screen.

"It's a restraining order." I knew the form pretty well from when I was a lawyer on divorce cases. My client was either serving one or being served. "Good grief." I shook my head as I read through it. "Alan had a restraining order against Mark."

I scrolled down to check out the details of the length and the terms.

"The end date was a year ago, and it looks like Alan didn't go back in time to renew it." Most restraining orders contained a grace period of time in which they could go back to court and get the documentation and reason for the restraint without going through the whole ordeal. The judge would either grant the extension of the order or void the order altogether.

When I typed in more necessary information in the search engine, it appeared the order had run out and Alan was no longer restricted to the terms.

"Does it say why Alan had one on Mark?" Kayla asked.

"Let me see." I toggled back to the restraining order and scrolled down. "As if it couldn't get worse." I shook my head and read. "Apparently they were at one of Alan's rehearsals, and it was a medieval play."

I read ahead so I could summarize what I was reading to her.

"They had a fight, and Mark picked up one of the axes and swung it at Alan. Alan was in fear of his life and didn't want Mark anywhere near his productions." I blinked a few times and reread the conditions of the restraining order.

Quickly I typed in their names with keywords such as "feud," "reporter," and "legal documents."

"Look here." I used the cursor to point to the one article that said Mark was let go from his job as theatrical reviewer because of producer Alan Bogart's restraining order held against him. "And that is a motive."

"You think?" Kayla asked in a sarcastic tone. "I think I'll just stay on my own little island with Andrew and the bees. I'm happiest here."

"Do you have any vacancies?" I joked. "All kidding aside, I wonder why Alan didn't petition to extend the order. If someone came at me with an axe, I sure would make sure they didn't come near me again for the rest of my life."

"You've talked to Mark, right?" Kayla asked.

"I've talked to him here and there. A few conversations, but he made it seem like he was the victim of Alan's rants and that it was really Gretchen and Alan who had the biggest beef." I snapped my fingers when I remembered him coming to the coffee shop today. "He came in the Bean Hive, and I started to make a suspect list. He was very interested. Then I pretended to get busy so I could have him leave." I shook my finger in the air. "I had a feeling he didn't need to be there, but I'm still not sure I get 'killer' from him. Gretchen, she's a whole other story. Evil seeps out of her."

"How so?" Kayla asked and leaned back into the couch.

I set the computer on the coffee table and joined her with my coffee in hand.

"She has no regard for others' feelings. She's not nice to her assistant. She is demanding, and if she doesn't get her way, she lets you know it. And she stormed in here like this was her production and a play written just for her."

All the not-so-pretty sides of Gretchen twirled around in my head, making me wonder if she was the one who killed Alan.

"Think about it." My eyes slid over the rim of my mug as I took another drink. "She and Alan had a very public breakup. They were seen at an event three years ago where their people had made special arrangements for them not to interact, and then she shows up here because she's cashing in a favor?"

"Or was it her opportunity to murder him in this small-town play?" Kayla's eyes narrowed. "It's almost time for Big Bib to get you."

"Do you have a printer?" I asked.

"Shoot. That's the one thing I was going to pick up. Printer paper. We are out, but I'll get some tomorrow." She and I stood up. "What do you need?"

"I wanted to print off a few of these articles to give to Spencer. It can wait. Maybe the internet will be up tomorrow." I crossed my fingers in the air and got my coat and boots back on before I backtracked to the boat dock, where Big Bib was already waiting for me.

CHAPTER FOURTEEN

There wasn't much chitchat between Big Bib and me because it was too dang cold and my breath would've frozen in mid-air.

Cocoon Hotel was a sight to behold from the water.

The historic white mansion that was built in 1841 had been in Camey's family for years. Camey had hired Cane Construction to help rebuild the old structure into an amazing hotel that was situated right on Lake Honey Springs and was able to keep the cozy character. The two-story white brick with the double porches across both stories was something to behold. It was difficult not to gasp out loud when it came into view. It was that spectacular.

It would be a perfect cover for any issue of one of those southern magazines you'd see while standing in the checkout line at the local grocery store.

"Here's your stop," Big Bib joked after he'd safely pulled into a slip, tied off, and shut down the engine.

"Thank you, sir." I couldn't help but smile at him. He looked so scary under his big burly size and that beard of his, but he was a teddy bear underneath. And someone who'd do anything for you. "Do you have a time you're going to get Kayla tomorrow?"

"Nah. She usually texts me." He put his hand out for me to take as he helped me off the boat. "You need something?"

"I might have to go back over and didn't want to create too much of a fuss." I walked alongside of him on the wooden dock towards the front of the marina. "I'll ask her in the morning."

"Where you off to?" Big Bib asked when I took a left to take the path to Cocoon.

"I'm going to have supper with Camey and Walker. Enjoy your treats." I snuggled my hands in the pockets of my jacket and hurried down the path toward the hotel.

It would be nice to have dinner with friends. Patrick and I rarely did it, since he was busy running Cane Construction and I was busy at the Bean Hive. Tonight was going to be nice—getting out of the rut of going back to the cabin and trying to figure out what was for dinner, since I cooked and baked and served coffee all day. Though I loved doing all those things for Patrick, sometimes it was just something I didn't want to do at night.

I'd hit the jackpot with Patrick. He could always tell when I was exhausted, and he'd come up with some sort of alternative. Like tonight.

Camey had also hit the jackpot with Walker. He'd come to town on business, and when he and Camey locked eyes... it was all she wrote. They were smitten with each other. She had bent over backwards to make his stay at the Cocoon Hotel a very nice and memorable one. So much so that he upped and moved to Honey Springs and brought Amelia, his granddaughter, who he had custody of, with him.

All in one big swoop, Camey had the instant family she'd always wanted.

It truly was a perfect union. He and Camey were both in their fifties, and Honey Springs was a fantastic place to raise a child. Camey, Walker and Amelia were one big happy family. Tourists always referred to Camey and Walker as Amelia's parents.

Amelia would smile and not dare correct them. She treated Camey and Walker as if they were her biological parents. And Camey treated the little girl as if Camey were Amelia's mom and loved her as such.

Camey had decided to keep her last name when they got married because of her business but recently had said how much easier it would be for Amelia and school documentation if they all did have the same last name. She'd never mentioned what solution they'd come to, so I should probably ask and check on my friend.

"My goodness," I blurted out when I saw Newton Oakley out with a dry paintbrush, brushing the snow off some purple type of plant. "What on earth grows in this type of weather?"

The wheelbarrow was full of shovels, spades, and all sorts of gardening tools I didn't even know the name for but recognized. Gardening was not my thing. My thumb was not green, nor did I have the desire to make it such.

"Cold-hardy camellias." He had pride written all over his face. "Maybe not the ice but in snow. I make sure I come out here every day during the snow and uncover them to make sure the investment Camey put into them is a good investment."

"You have so much joy in your work, Newton. I need to remember that when I make terrible coffee." I jogged up the steps with the warmth of the inside in my head.

"Now, now, Roxy. Your job brings a lot of joy to people around here—and warmth. Literally." He laughed and went back to using the dry paintbrush to carefully sweep the snow off.

The inside of the Cocoon was just as gorgeous as the outside. To the left of the big entry was the guest counter for check-ins and anything else guests needed. To the right was a huge room that Camey had turned into the hospitality lounge. It was also where I supplied her daily complimentary coffee and a few sweet treats for her guests.

The crackling fire could be heard over some laughter. When I peeked my head inside the room, I was pleasantly happy to see the laughing was coming from my group.

"Roxy!" Patrick smiled and put his cocktail glass on the table. He hurried over to kiss me and help me out of my coat. "Get over there in front of the fire to warm up. You look like you're freezing."

"I am." I took Patrick's advice. I hugged Camey and Walker when I passed them on the way to warm my hands in front of the fireplace. "I'm so glad we could do this."

"We are too." Walker reached over and rubbed Camey's back. "Amelia had dance lessons, and it's not our night to carpool, so we thought we could get in some good dinner."

"Speaking of all that, we better get to the restaurant." Camey gestured for the men to lead, but she wasn't kidding me none. She wanted to scoop on what I found out.

"You won't believe it." I used my hand to cover a little of my mouth so Patrick couldn't hear because if he did, it'd ruin supper.

"Restraining order?" Camey gasped. "And they were both staying here." She did a quick jerk of the neck when we walked past the stairs that led up to the guest suites. "Spencer is up there now going through Alan's room. He even has a warrant to go through Gretchen's and Sydney's rooms."

"Really?" I was happy to hear Spencer was looking into other people besides poor Loretta. "I wish I could go tell him what I found on the internet, but it wouldn't go well with dinner."

"Internet? What did you find on the internet?" Walker asked. "You know you can't believe everything you read on the internet."

"But if it's on the internet, it has to be true." Patrick made Walker laugh with his comment.

"You two think you're so funny." Camey shrugged and led us through the restaurant bar to get us to her special table in a secluded room.

"If you'll excuse me for a second, I need to go to the bathroom." I smiled and tried not to look Patrick in the eyes because he'd know right away I was not telling the full truth, but I wasn't lying either.

I did have to go to the bathroom right after I talked to Sydney, who I just so happened to see sitting at the bar when we walked past her.

"What do you want?" Sydney's usual happy-go-lucky demeanor was a bit on the sour side. She picked up the glass and swigged down whatever was in it, and then she picked up her phone and tapped it a few times before she angrily smacked it on the bar top.

"The internet isn't working. Snowstorm." I shrugged and tried to break the ice between us.

"Of course. That's what we get when we come to these small towns." She rolled her eyes in disgust.

"Are you okay?" I asked and noticed the empty stool next to her.

"I'm fine. It's a Coke." She shook her head. "I don't drink. And if I did, I couldn't because you never know when Gretchen is going to need me."

"You must have a hard job." I sat down next to her and ordered a water when the bartender pointed at me. "I couldn't imagine the schedule you keep."

"She is demanding, but she's a great boss. I'm just tired of all the cops and people asking if she killed Alan. No way." Sydney was sure of it. "Alan and Gretchen had a long-running relationship."

"Yeah. I read somewhere they'd been romantically involved." I casually mentioned it, making Sydney laugh so hard she held on to the bar as if she were going to fall off the stool.

"That was a marketing ploy." Sydney smiled. "And you fell for it. See, it all works."

"Marketing ploy? You mean they did it for publicity?" I asked.

"Yeah. Alan's career was tanking, and Gretchen had just gotten that Tony Award. His people called her people. They all got together. Next thing I knew Gretchen's calendar was filled with dinner dates, a yacht date, and an airplane trip to nowhere just so the media would take photos of them to help jumpstart Alan's career."

"So that's the favor he owed her." I ran my finger along the rim of the glass of water and pondered what Sydney had said.

"Don't you dare tell her I told you. I just feel like I need someone to talk to now that we are going to stay here. If we wanted to leave, that cop guy said we can't." Her shoulders slumped. "I'm afraid they are going to arrest Gretchen because she honestly doesn't know how to stop arguing with people."

"You seemed to have mastered it." I wanted to give her some confidence. She looked defeated. "Not only do you cater to her, but now you're going to be doing the producing."

"As much of it as she'll let me. She's been rewriting the manuscript Alan had changed all day long. Of course making her part bigger, which she should. I'm not saying she shouldn't. She is the star, after all." Sydney thanked the bartender when the bartender slid a fresh Coke in front of her.

"What exactly was the favor Gretchen called in from Alan?" I decided to just go for it. I couldn't pretend I was in the bathroom all this time. I had to hurry and get to the point.

"Do you even know Gretchen's career?" Sydney asked.

"Honestly, I do not." I felt bad, but watching plays or even movies had never been my thing. "I was a lawyer, so my nose was always in a book."

"Wow." She jerked back. "That's cool. How did you go from that to making coffee?"

"See. Right there is why I need to open my roastery." I knew she didn't know what I was talking about. "I don't just make coffee. I actually roast it from the raw bean. It's an art. Like the theater."

"That's amazing. Can I stop by, since I'm stuck here, and see you do it?" She was all sorts of impressed, making me think the roastery was a great idea.

"I'd love for you to." I was always happy to talk about coffee. "So what were you saying about Gretchen's career?"

"She's always been the second leading lady. She's never gotten the big roles. She's good enough, but there's a chain of command, and she's not kissing no one's you-know-what to get her to the top." Sydney was alluding to all those rumors about directors and producers I'd recently seen on the news. "She'd rather get there by clawing her way to the top, so when she stopped getting a lot of calls for even the secondary roles, she knew it was time to cash in on the favor Alan owed her where she helped get his career back on track."

"I thought they hated each other." None of what Sydney was saying made sense. "They were always at each other's throats."

"In public, but are you kidding me? Just last night we were all in Gretchen's suite, watching a movie and eating popcorn. It was all an act, so Gretchen is upset about his death. That's why she'd vowed to make this the best play ever. She also made a deal with Mark to get it in all the papers for big reviews," Sydney muttered under her breath. "It's him that I'd be looking at if I were the cops."

"Sheriff." I finally corrected her.

"Huh?" she asked with a confused look.

"We don't have cops in Honey Springs. We have a sheriff's department." I waved my hand in the air to wave off her trying to understand it. "It's a county, city Kentucky thing."

"Oh." She looked off into the distance like she was trying to process my words.

"There you are." I felt someone's hand on my shoulder. "It's time to order."

"Oh, Patrick." Inwardly I cringed that I'd been there so long that he had to come looking for me. "This is Sydney O'Neal, Gretchen Cannon's assistant."

The two of them exchanged pleasantries.

"Are you coming?" he asked with a not-so-pleasant tone.

"Yeah." I slid off the stool. "Sydney, stop by the coffee shop anytime, and I'll roast some special beans just for us to enjoy."

"I'll do that." Sydney waved goodbye.

Patrick put his hand on the back of my arm.

"Where are your manners?" he scolded me like I was a child. "Our friends are hosting us for supper, and I'd like to think you were just exchanging hellos with that woman, but I know you all too well."

"Patrick, she's a guest of Camey's hotel and a customer of the Bean Hive. I wasn't going to be rude." I tried to answer as any good southern woman would. Turn the attention at hand to a mannered thing, and then any sort of underhanded reason I'd be talking with her would be forgotten, since it appeared as though I were being a good southern host.

"Roxanne Bloom Cane. I know you better than that, and I know for a fact you just can't stop sniffing around when there's a fresh murder down at Kevin's morgue."

"Keep your voice down." I shushed him, which he didn't like once we got to the table. "We will talk about this later."

"Talk about what later?" Camey asked and handed me the menu. "Try the glazed salmon. Tonight's special."

"I'll have that," I told the waitress, who was apparently waiting for me to return to the table to get our order. "We were discussing the murder of the producer because on my way to the bathroom, I noticed Sydney, Gretchen Cannon's assistant, sitting at the bar. I was simply checking in on her."

"Can you believe he was murdered?" Walker asked.

Poor, poor Walker. He had no idea what he'd just stepped into. Camey and Patrick both eased back in their chairs—Camey for reasons much different than Patrick. She knew he didn't want to discuss it, and he didn't want to discuss it.

"That reporter told me all about the restraining order that guy had against him." Walker started to tell the story of how he and Mark were having early-morning coffee when Mark just told him all about the fight they'd had.

Only Mark turned it around and made himself the victim, not Alan.

"How is Amelia doing in school?" Patrick abruptly changed the subject in a very nonchalant I-do-not-want-to-talk-about-the-murder way.

Camey kicked my shin under the table. I bit my lip not to cry out. It was her way of trying to be secretive about Patrick's behavior.

"She's doing..." Walker was a little apprehensive, as though he were trying to figure out Patrick's sudden attitude change.

"Great!" Camey's voice rose an octave. "She's gotten so involved with everything and keeping us busy."

"I can't thank Camey enough for taking such good care of her." Walker reached over and put his hand on top of Camey's. He looked at her with the most loving eyes. "I go out of town for work, and I am so thankful for her. I'm able to go on my trips knowing that Amelia is safe and happy, all because of this woman."

Patrick and I glanced at each other when Walker awkwardly leaned over and kissed Camey.

"Here we are." The waitress had brought the big tray of food out.

Each one of us pushed back from the table so she could put our plates in front of us. Most of the dinner was just chitchat about town but no mention of the murder or play. I knew if Camey had hit me under the table, she was probably doing the same thing to Walker.

It wasn't until Walker invited Patrick to look at the HVAC that Camey finally mentioned his odd behavior.

"And what was all that about?" She rubbed her cloth napkin over her mouth and laid it on top of her plate along with her knife and fork.

"When he came looking for me, I was sitting at the bar, talking to Sydney. He knows how interested I am in figuring out who killed Alan, but he's taken the stance that he doesn't want to know anything about it." I took a drink of the water and flipped the coffee cup over on the saucer for the waitress to give me a shot.

"He told you he didn't want to know?" Camey asked and flipped her cup over too.

"No. His actions told me. I mean, look at how he rudely didn't want to talk about it when Walker brought it up tonight." I gave a slight shake of my head when I saw the men coming back into the room with Amelia.

"Are you ready?" Patrick asked.

Amelia climbed up in Camey's lap. The love among the three of them warmed my heart so much. I was so happy to see that they'd come together.

"Camey." Newton walked in with a concerned look on his face. "I'm sorry to interrupt, but I was cleaning up to go home, and I noticed the ax is missing from my wheelbarrow. Did you borrow it?"

"No." Camey looked at Walker.

"I didn't take it." Walker looked back at Newton.

"I can't find it anywhere." Newton scratched his head. "The last time I used it was yesterday, when I cut down a few of the dead roots of a couple of bushes because they were too thick to use shears."

"Don't worry about it." Camey was so good at not stressing about too many things, a trait I wished I had. "I'm sure it'll turn up."

"If not, we can get a new one. Probably about time we replace a lot of your tools anyways." Walker brushed off the missing tool.

We all said our goodbyes.

"Do you want to ride with me and I can just bring you back in the morning?" Patrick asked.

"I'm going to open, since it's still so cold out." I forgot to text Bunny that I'd just open again. "I need to tell Bunny."

While Patrick and I walked in the cold to our cars, there was a frigid air between us, and I wasn't talking about the outside temperature.

To avoid it, I sent a text message to Bunny. After I sent it, I checked to see if there was internet.

"Oh. I think we've got internet." I quickly typed in Gretchen and Alan's names in the search engine, but the wheel of death continued to spin, which told me we didn't have the internet.

"I'm sorry." Patrick put his arm around me on our way to the parking lot.

"It's okay. We rely too much on the internet anyways." I slipped the phone back into my jacket pocket.

"No. I mean I'm sorry how I acted tonight." Patrick stopped in front of my car. "I know we can talk about this at home, but I worry about you. I know you're a lawyer. I know you have formulated all sorts of suspects in that little mind of yours. I love your mind. I love you, but it still doesn't keep you safe."

"I'm fine. You do worry too much." I wrapped my arms around him and looked up into his big brown eyes.

"Even Spencer said you were the only witness. That's what has been on my mind all day." He brought me closer to him and hugged me. "I don't know what I'd do if something happened to you."

"You don't need to worry about that. Let's get home and see the kids."

CHAPTER FIFTEEN

The wind whipped up during the night, waking me from a sound sleep. My mind started to wander, and Alan's murder played in my head, keeping me from falling asleep again. There was only another hour until my alarm went off, so I peeled back the covers and met Pepper in the family room.

He lifted his head from his dog bed in front of the fire, his ears bent back as if he were ready for me to say something to him.

"Hey, buddy." I squatted on the floor next to him and felt the warmth of the fire on my back.

It was a little too much excitement. He wanted more than a few rubs. He jumped into my lap with his front paws on my chest, doing his best to get in some good-morning kisses on my chin.

"You're such a good boy." My voice was a cross between a sigh and small giggle. "But it's time to get to work. I know it's early, but we have some sleuthing to do."

I would love to say he was eagerly excited about the sleuthing we were going to do by the way his tail was wagging, but he wasn't. He ran to his dog bowl and looked at it with the most pitiful eyes when he noticed there wasn't any kibble in it.

"Fine. I'll let you have some, and I'll make a coffee." I dumped enough kibble to hold him over until we got to the Bean Hive and brewed just enough coffee to hold me over until I got there.

In lickety-split time, I was showered and out the door before Patrick or Sassy even had time to roll over.

Pepper and I did our usual routine in opening the Bean Hive. Mocha had started to follow us around, which was a good sign she was getting comfortable. The knock at the door was a much-welcomed Emily Rich, who saw my light on early. She was going to the bakery to clean out the office.

"I heard the meeting went well between Patrick and Tamara." Emily reminded me that the meeting had totally slipped my mind.

"Oh brother. I was so wrapped up in Alan Bogart's murder investigation, I forgot to ask Patrick." A long sigh escaped me. "How could I be so selfish?"

"You? Selfish?" Emily shook her head and helped me get the coffee shop ready to open.

It was nice to have her there with me. She did work for me while she was in high school, so she could probably do it better than me.

"I don't know. You knew me as single Roxy. He's my husband, and I really should make it a point to ask him how his day is." I took out Mocha's food.

"Here. I'll feed her." Emily took the cat food and walked over to Mocha. Mocha meowed and rubbed up along Emily's leg.

"You know, she's putting her scent on you." I watched as Mocha continued to rub against Emily and dot her tail in the air, which was a sign of love. "She would make a great companion to someone who is moving to a new town."

"Oh no you don't." Emily wagged a finger at me. "I know what you're doing."

"I'm just making an observation. Trust me. I know." I reminded her that I was in her boat a few years ago, which was how Pepper came home with me.

"Let's talk about the murder. If Patrick won't listen, I sure will." Emily and I made our way back into the kitchen.

All the items were in the oven. The coffee was brewed, and soon it would be time to get the carafes ready for the Cocoon Hotel hospitality room.

"Well." I was all too happy to engage in what I'd discovered and eagerly grabbed the dry-erase board, propping it up on the prep table. "As I see it, we have three suspects. Only two, I think, had real motive."

I listed Loretta, Gretchen, and Mark.

"Loretta's only motive was that he changed the play on her. It did make her mad, and it bruised her ego a little, which made her talk bad about him, but you and I both know Loretta Bebe couldn't hurt a fly, much less a grown human man."

I moved on to Gretchen.

"Gretchen and Alan had pretended to be in a relationship when Alan's career was on the downward slide. They made sure they had public photos together and all sorts of appearances." I told her how Sydney had told me about it, and she'd know, since she'd been Gretchen's assistant. "She also told me how Gretchen agreed to it, and when she needed a favor, he'd have to give her one."

"I can see where this is going." Emily glanced over when my personal coffee pot beeped, having brewed a full pot. She walked over and made two cups of coffee while I continued the investigation into why I believed Gretchen could've been the killer.

"Gretchen's career is now on the way out. A has-been, like he said. So she called in her favor, which was..."

"To put her in the show." Emily finished my sentence with disbelief in her tone.

"When he changed the play, he also changed her role to a minor role as an old woman who gets killed." Emily and I both knew no woman liked to be called old. "Can you imagine what it's like to be an actress and have the industry not give you roles because they have dubbed you old?"

"Society already puts so many stipulations and opinions on us regular folk. I couldn't imagine if I were famous." Emily held the mug between her hands.

"Right? And Alan was public in calling Gretchen old." I didn't go into details or tell Emily the exact words, but she understood what I was saying. "Think about it. He moved her larger role to a smaller role, not only still keeping her career tanking but also hurting her overgrown ego."

Emily simply shook her head and drank her coffee while I wrote down all of Gretchen's motives underneath her name on the whiteboard.

"Then we have Mark Redding." I tapped his name with the marker tip. "Why? Why would a big-time reporter come here to our little town when there are so many big shows opening up on Broadway?"

"Umm… why?" Emily asked as though it were a trick question.

"Exactly." I smacked the counter. "Why? Well, he's getting back at Alan for putting the restraining order against him after Mark threw an ax..." My jaw dropped. "An ax. Oh no."

"What?" Emily watched me frantically feel around my body for my phone.

"Mark Redding is the killer," I called over my shoulder on my way out to the coat rack to get my phone out of the pocket of my coat. "Alan had a restraining order against Mark, but he let it go and didn't renew it. Mark had thrown an ax at Alan. Granted, it was a prop at a medieval play Alan was directing, but Mark did it."

I clicked on my photos and used my fingers to blow up the photo I'd taken of the evidence of the severed cord.

"Mark saw the ax in Newton's wheelbarrow, and he took it to the theater." I racked my brain while I paced back and forth in the kitchen. "Where was he when I went on stage right before Alan was killed? I don't recall seeing him, so he could've gone up on the catwalk with the ax, and that's when he cut the rope at just the right time—when Alan was standing under it."

"Ax? Newton's wheelbarrow?" Emily was so confused. "I have no idea what you are saying, but I'll take your word for it."

"Good. I've got to call Spencer." I took the casseroles out of the oven and replaced them with more goodies that just needed to be heated, then refreshed my coffee so I could sit down with my phone, call Spencer, and give him my full attention.

Emily got the carafe for the Cocoon Hotel together for me and decided she'd just go on and deliver it, telling me she'd talk to me later.

On the phone with Spencer, I went through the whole story from the internet search to the conversation I had with Sydney in the bar to the missing-ax story that ended my day of sleuthing. "I'm telling you, if you find the ax, you will find the fingerprints of Mark Redding," I told him.

"Kayla and Andrew have internet?" Spencer asked on the other end of the line.

"That's all you have to say after I just handed you the killer on a silver platter?" I asked.

"Thank you. I'll get it all checked out, but for now, I'm going to head over to the Bee Farm and get on their internet." Why didn't I think of that? "Keep your ears to the ground. Stay out of harm's way and let me know if you come up with anything else."

"Do you know when the internet is going to come back?" I figured he'd at least get some sort of sense.

"No. But I am planning on bringing this up at the next town council meeting. Honey Springs needs to invest in the fi-optics or some sort of internet that won't be taken out by a snowstorm. Ridiculous in this day and age." He seemed more upset about the internet than Alan's murder.

"Fine." I felt a little defeated. Spencer wasn't exactly as happy as I'd hoped he'd be, but maybe it was his way of trying to keep a level head.

Either way, I just knew Mark Redding had gotten his final revenge...and finished the job with a very fitting object... an ax.

CHAPTER SIXTEEN

"An ax?" Aunt Maxi laughed from her dressing room when I told her about my theory. "Roxanne Bloom, you've lost your mind. The sandbag is what killed him."

"I know that, but someone had to have cut the cord." I showed her the photo on my phone.

I made sure I'd brought the coffee items and pecan roll over to the theater a little early so I could stop in and talk to Aunt Maxi. Bunny had gotten to work, and everything was done thanks to Emily, so it was easy leaving Bunny by herself for a little while.

"If what you said about Mark having a restraining order put on him by Alan because of an ax is true, I'd say you have something there." Loretta nodded.

"Did I hear someone say my name?" Mark Redding curled around the doorframe of the dressing room door. He had his big camera strapped around his neck.

"Where's the ax you cut the cord of the sandbag with?" Loretta was about as subtle as a screen door on a submarine.

"You think I killed Alan?" His brows furrowed. He looked up and down the hall before he stepped into the dressing room and shut the door behind him.

"What are you doin'?" Loretta took a couple of steps backwards. "You open up the door right this instant."

He lifted his finger to his mouth and said, "Shhhhhhh."

"I'm gonna scream," Loretta warned him. "You come a step closer."

"Seriously?" Mark didn't appear threatening, but I was cautious like Loretta.

"Why did you shut the door?" I asked.

"Because I don't want the real killer to hear us." He shrugged, putting his hands up.

"How do we know you're not the real killer?" Aunt Maxi asked. She'd picked up the pair of scissors in a stabbing hold, pointed it at Mark, and stepped in front of Loretta and me with her other arm out, motioning for us to get back.

"I told the *Times* people who are from here are crazy." He turned and put his hand on the doorknob like he was leaving.

"Crazy?" Oh... that set off Aunt Maxi, and that was a side you never wanted to be on. "Do you want me to show you crazy?"

"Listen." Mark jerked around. "Alan Bogart and I had our differences. We both love the theater and in the end knew that about each other. We still didn't like each other, but he knew I respected his work. That's why I'm here." He threw his hands in the air. "We had a fight. I threw a plastic ax at him. Plastic prop. The media made it out to be some sort of crazy moment, but it wasn't like that. Alan had to put a restraining order against me so he'd get good publicity. It's how it works when you're big time. Then I started to do reviews under a pen name, and it was all fine."

He pulled a card out from the camera case strapped on him and held it out.

"That's my pen name. Check it out." He laughed. "Not that I need to tell you three anything because the sheriff just left, and my alibi checks out. It must've been one of you that told him I was the killer."

All three of us looked at one another with downward-turned mouths and shook our heads. Each denied it, even though we knew it was me.

"And just so you know it, I had gotten a call from your good friend Perry Zella about coming to speak at his mystery group this afternoon. So my call log and Perry's call log proved it. I'd stepped out of the theater to take the call. When I came back in, Alan had already been killed."

His alibi seemed simple enough to check out, and I was sure he was right about Spencer looking into it.

"Are we done here?" Alan asked.

All three of us nodded.

"Maxine and Loretta, when the two of you are finished gossiping, I need to get some headshots for the review." He turned the knob and walked out the door.

"I guess he didn't do it. It just added up so good." Aunt Maxi patted me.

"That's the problem," Loretta griped. "All them crime shows make it out to be the obvious one as the main suspect, then boom!"

Aunt Maxi and I both jumped when Loretta yelled boom.

"The killer is no one you'd expect at all." She shrugged.

"This ain't no crime show. This here is real life, and if Mark didn't do it, it leaves Gretchen Cannon. And I'm going to get that fur coat from Perry Zella because it'll give me a chance to question Gretchen when I give it to her." I tapped my temple. "And I'll question Perry about Mark's alibi."

"Why would you do that if Spencer already checked it out?" Aunt Maxi asked and finished putting on the final touches of her makeup before the rehearsal's curtain call time.

"You never know." I didn't have an answer for her.

Maybe I needed to hear Mark's alibi from someone I trusted, like Perry. Or maybe it was curiosity to see if it did align with Perry's recollection of time.

Still... as a lawyer and now as a part-time sleuth, I left no stone unturned.

Going to the dry cleaners would be simple, since it was located right downtown. I even walked over there.

Perry's business was a simple little block building. The words Dry Cleaners were stenciled on the front window, and it was as simple as that. When you walked inside, the smell of the dry cleaning products hit you like a brick. There was a small counter in front of the guts of the cleaners.

Perry did his own laundering. He didn't send it out like most services.

"Hello, Roxy. I've got something so interesting to tell you." He pushed a button from underneath the counter, and the mechanical carousel with all the dry-cleaned clothes moved in a circular motion until Perry took his finger off the button.

"Yeah? I've got something to ask you." I watched him take the fur coat off the carousel.

"You first." He hung the heavy thing up on the metal hanger.

"Did you call Mark Redding yesterday morning?" I asked, not very sure of the time.

"Yeah. Actually, Spencer just left here after asking me the same thing. I even showed him my phone." He had the cleaning ticket in one hand and punched the register with the other hand. "I guess they are trying to cross suspects off their list of the murder of the producer."

"I'm guessing it all checked out?" I looked down at the screen and saw the total of the dry cleaning, which nearly knocked me off my feet.

"Sure did." He looked up and nodded towards the direction of the theater. "While we were talking, I heard all the sirens and then saw the ambulance. That's when he said he had to go because something was happening in the theater. Later he called me back to confirm him coming to the mystery meeting, and that's how I found out about the death."

"Crazy, right?" I tried to play off why I was asking and making it seem as if I was just curious, but it seemed Spencer was one leg ahead of me in this investigation.

"Here's something that's so crazy awesome I can't wait until our meeting tonight to tell the guys." He opened the fur coat and revealed a tag. "This is a true mystery right here. This was a real fur coat of Amanda B. Suculant."

"Is that someone from Honey Springs?" I asked with no idea who this person was.

"Are you kidding?" His eyes grew big and bright, his voice escalated. "Amanda B. Suculant was a true crime mystery. My club even read the unofficial autobiography. I really think this was her coat. She was murdered by her granddaughter. The granddaughter took off and went on the lam."

"I wonder how Gretchen got it." I looked a little closer at the tag.

"Amanda had all her coats made for her, and they all have these tags in them. Do you know how much one of her coats sold for at auction years ago?"

"No." I had no idea, but it was still an ugly coat.

"Over a million dollars. I can't believe it. I took so many photos of this so I could show my group." He was like a kid in a candy shop over this mystery. "They still never found the killer."

"I thought you said 'granddaughter'?" I asked and took the coat from him.

"They think it was the granddaughter, but they never found her." He held on to the coat, making me tug a little harder to get it from him. "I just wish I could take this to the meeting."

"Well, you can't. It's Gretchen's. Maybe she's the one who bought it for a million big ones." It made sense because she probably could afford it.

Plus, she would be the type to drop that kind of money down on something like this. Just in case it was this million-dollar coat, I told myself that I would lay it in the back seat of my car carefully when I got back to the theater, since I'd walked over to the dry cleaners.

When I shut the door, I noticed Butch Turner, the inspector who passed the theater, was walking into the Moose Lodge. There was no better time than the present to go over and check out the space for Emily's see-you-later party.

After all, it was my job to make sure the coffee was placed perfectly.

The Moose Lodge was a staple in practically every town in Kentucky. At any given time of the year, you'd find a wide array of activities to participate in both as an individual and as a family.

The events ranged from holiday parties, dances, sports, themed dinners, and live entertainment. There was a membership fee that let you use the lodge for those activities, but the bar was open to everyone in the community.

The bar was exactly where I found Butch, along with a pack of his cigarettes next to him.

"Howdy." I slid up next to Butch. "It's a little early for a drink."

"I know, I know why you're here." He reached over for the glass of water sitting in front of him. "And I'm not drinking. I'm meeting your husband here for an early lunch."

"Oh. Are you inspecting the building next to the Bean Hive, Mr. Inspector?" I teased and realized I couldn't've picked a worse time to have decided to come here.

Patrick.

"Code Enforcement Officer," Butch corrected me with his official title. "Yep. That's why we are meeting."

"I bet you don't know why I'm here." I leaned back on the bar, facing out into the space. "You obviously know, since you're meeting with Patrick, that Emily is closing the bakery and moving."

He gave a slight chin raise.

"Well, me and a few of our friends are giving her a see-you-later party here at the Moose, and I'd love for you to come." I pushed off the bar and nudged him. "I know you two have a fondness for each other, since you did give her a hard time about those pesky smoke detectors when she was building the bakery."

"We fought." He remembered. Dang.

"I wouldn't say you fought. I'd say you had very different views of the law." When I noticed he wasn't impressed with my interpretation of the event, I decided to just stroke his ego. "And you were right, just like you were with the Bean Hive."

"I better not come in there and see any sort of animal in that kitchen." He was oh-so charming.

"I think I'll put the coffee stand over there for the party." I pointed at the side wall and changed the subject. "I guess I better get going. I'm going to be heading on over to the theater because I have to drop off some coffee they've hired me to deliver."

It was my subtle segue to the real reason I was here.

"Speaking of the theater"—he met my words with a deep sigh—"I guess you heard about that sandbag falling on the producer."

"Mm-hhmm," he ho-hummed. "What are you beating around about?"

"Me? I was just making chitchat." I shrugged and kept my peripheral vision on the entrance in case Patrick came in.

"You know me enough. I'm not a chitchatter. You and I worked side by side a couple months before you opened, and we really worked in silence." He let out an even bigger sigh than before.

"I'm trying to figure out when you did the inspection last on the theater because the sheriff's department is pointing out something about the cord." I pretended that I didn't know the cord was cut.

Even though I didn't think Loretta was the killer, if she did come up and need my services, I was getting a jump on it. Though, technically, I'd get copies of the report if it came to that.

"I already turned everything in to Spencer." His words made my jaw drop. "You should know all about the last inspection because your husband had replaced the doors on the dressing rooms because the old ones weren't in good shape."

He jarred my memory of the Southern Women's Club fundraiser in which they needed to make repairs to the theater to keep it going, but I didn't recall

Patrick saying his donation was because Butch had ordered the doors to be replaced.

"Dang. Spencer is ahead of me again," I muttered and decided it was high time to try to get into Spencer's brain to see exactly his next move.

"And he also knows that Loretta Bebe insisted on using the lowest grade cord possible to pass inspection. So I'm not saying the cord didn't deteriorate with age, and I'm not saying someone didn't cut it." Butch was no help at all. "All I know is that it passed inspection, and I stand by my work."

"Well then." I clasped my hands in front of me and rocked back on my heels. "I hope we see you at the party tomorrow night."

"Tomorrow night." He gave a hard nod. "I just might show up for that coffee you're going to put right over there."

Did I mention how I was first in my class in the department of body language? Of course I did. I could tell by his body language that he'd already known I was there to pick his brain, not to look for a place for the coffee station.

"Yes. I think that's perfect." I squeezed my nose up and waved goodbye on my way out the door, thankful I didn't run into Patrick.

When I hurried across the street so Patrick didn't see me, I got into my car to text the group of girls before I gathered my thoughts about how I would ask Gretchen about the fur coat when I took it inside the theater.

My text to the group was about the space in the Moose and how it looked great as well as the perfect spot for the coffee. My text started the follow-up text, with everyone giving updates on their progress on their tasks for pulling off Emily's party. All of it was coming together, and everyone pulled their load, which was a blessing. I was fortunate to have such a great group of friends who were trustworthy, kind and all-around good people.

Checking to see if the internet was back was also a high priority. I wanted to Google Amanda B. Suculant and see if Gretchen did waste that much money on a fur coat.

I clicked on the internet icon and typed in Amanda B. Suculant only to be met with the rotating wheel of death. Meaning...the internet was still down.

The knock on the passenger-side window made me jump. Aunt Maxi was standing outside, laughing her head off.

"I just scared you to death," she mouthed and then pointed and continued to laugh. She opened the door and got in, putting her big hobo bag on the floor.

"What in earth is in there?" I asked.

"Things I need because I've gotten a bigger role." Aunt Maxi beamed with excitement. "At first I was worried about Loretta agreeing with Gretchen to let Sydney take control, but now that I've got a bigger role, I'm all good."

"What things do you need?" I glanced down at the bag, which overflowed with papers and tissues.

"I've got my makeup bag in there. Water. Spritzer for my skin." She patted her cheeks. "Plus notes on my performance." She shimmied her shoulders. "I had to do old-school acting in front of the mirror because I was going to watch some YouTube videos but that darn internet."

"It's ridiculous that we can't bring our town up to the technology to match the world." Suddenly I pictured Aunt Maxi in front of her mirror, making stabbing motions or whatever the mystery script had in it. I pinched my lips together so I didn't laugh at the image in my head. "Spencer said he was going to take up the internet issue with the town council because it's really hindered the investigation."

My phone chirped a text from Kayla.

Come anytime. I've already been to the mainland and back so I'm home all day.

"Who's that?" Aunt Maxi leaned over to see who was texting me. Her bag fell over, and she bent down and tried to shove everything back in her bag.

"Kayla. We are talking about the party for Emily. I hope you're coming."

"Crissy told me about it, and I plan on being there as long as we are out of rehearsal." Aunt Maxi hoisted the heavy hobo bag into her lap. "Speaking of rehearsal, I better get in there before we start."

"I have to take Gretchen her fancy coat." I pointed at the coat.

"How much do I owe you?" Aunt Maxi asked.

"Nothing." I didn't tell her the cost because it was ridiculous.

She opened the door.

"I'll be right in."

I waited until she was inside the building before I got out of my car and opened the back door to get the fur. But first I wanted to snap a photo of the label to be sure that when I did Google it, I had the correct spelling of the name.

I didn't want to go accusing anyone of anything if I didn't have all my T's crossed and I's dotted.

With the coat slung over my forearm, I headed into the theater and straight down the hallway to Gretchen's dressing room.

"Hi, Sydney."

Sydney was sitting in one of the chairs in Gretchen's dressing room, looking over what appeared to be the play's script.

"You got the coat back. That was quick." She smiled, stood up, and walked over to get it. "Gretchen will be thrilled." She leaned in and whispered, "Though she'd never tell you that."

"How's it going?" I asked with genuine concern.

"You know, since I saw you last night it's actually a little better. I went back up to the room, and Gretchen had made some great changes to the manuscript and really turned it into a nice play that I think will not only be well received by your community but even Broadway." She did seem much more relaxed. "In fact, she's doing an interview right now with Mark Redding. I haven't seen her do any press junkets for years. She offered Mark a job as her press secretary to get some gigs with different media outlets, since he knows so many people."

"Really?" I questioned.

"Yeah. Strange how she and Alan have spent so many years trying to boost each other's careers by all these favors when it was his death that really got the needle moving in her favor."

My heart skipped a beat. Did Sydney just give me another motive for Gretchen Cannon to be Alan Bogart's killer?

Sydney telling me how Gretchen's career had started to soar with the news of Alan's death only fueled my curiosity to see if she had any connection to the fur coat or the story of Amanda B. Suculant.

The only way to find out any answers in today's age was surfing the web, and last I checked, the internet was still down. But I was happy to see some work crews and big trucks working on some lines. I had no idea if those lines were for the internet, but I was putting all faith and hope that it was.

When I parked my car at the marina to have Big Bib boat me over to the Bee Farm, I noticed some papers on the floorboard of the passenger side where Aunt Maxi's hobo bag had dumped out. When I reached over to pick them up, I noticed it was her play's manuscript.

"Great," I said with a groan and looked up out of the windshield where Big Bib was looking back at me, waiting. I put the papers in my bag and decided they would have to wait until I got done with my business at the Bee Farm and then took the manuscript back to the theater.

Within minutes, with Big Bib's help and Bunny's willingness to stay at the Bean Hive for the whole day, I found myself back on Kayla's couch, enjoying another cup of her coffee while reading the fascinating story of Amanda B. Suculant and her life.

"She was a wealthy widow, and her husband was an oil man." I didn't read in too much detail about that. "It says here she was a big supporter of the arts."

I grabbed my bag and took out Aunt Maxi's play manuscript to grab the notebook I'd put in there. I wanted to take notes on the article, since Kayla had forgotten to get copy paper when she did boat over to Honey Springs.

"Gretchen," Kayla said, gasping.

"And look." I pointed at a photo I'd found of Gretchen and Amanda together at a big charity event. "If they weren't friends, they knew each other."

"According to the article, Amanda was found dead in the freezer in the garage." I didn't want to picture it.

"Chopped up?" Kayla made a crunched-up face and dragged Aunt Maxi's manuscript off the coffee table. She sat back and started to thumb through it.

"No. All in one piece like her killer cared about her and really tried to preserve the body or something. I'd read a case once where someone had been murdered by a family member and put them in a stand-up freezer at their family restaurant in a brown sack that others thought was frozen meat." I vaguely remembered the case, but it was the conclusion that stuck in my head. "The family member who killed subconsciously wanted to be found out and did want the body to be preserved so they could eventually have a funeral. I bet it was the same with Amanda. That's why they think it's the granddaughter that killed her."

"It makes sense. But what does this have to do with Gretchen?" she asked.

"That's a good question." I picked up my phone and showed her the photo of the label I'd taken of the fur coat. "According to everything I've found so far on here, Amanda's coats were auctioned off, and there are photos of them. Nowhere did I find this coat. I'm not saying it couldn't have been sold outside of auction. So I'm not sure. It just seems odd this dead woman's coat is on Gretchen and now the producer is dead."

"Roxy!" Kayla gasped and jumped up, waving Aunt Maxi's manuscript in the air. "I think we have our answer." She shoved the pack of papers in my face. "Have you read this?"

"No. Aunt Maxi said it's great and is excited about it. Why?" I put the laptop on the coffee table and stood up next to Kayla to look at what she was overly excited about.

"This play reads a lot like Amanda B. Suculant's life, only the names have been changed." She handed me the manuscript.

"What?" I looked down at the papers in my hand while Kayla pointed out the various similar accounts that we were reading on the internet.

"I'll get us another cup of coffee while you read that."

My head was in a tailspin as I scanned more of the manuscript. The similarities were uncanny.

"I'll get that coffee later." I quickly texted Big Bib and asked if he could come get me. I knew it wouldn't take him long since the temperature was up, the snowstorm had long passed, and the ice on the lake was melting. "I need to get Aunt Maxi out of that theater."

"It does all add up. Gretchen came here cashing in on her favor. She and Alan had all those fights." Kayla blinked several times, recounting all the things I'd told her. "But don't you think it's dangerous for you to go in there? Don't you think you should call Spencer?"

"I want to get Aunt Maxi out of there, then I'll call Spencer." I gathered all my things, shoved them into my bag, and walked out the door. Down the path I went.

CHAPTER SEVENTEEN

Not that I wasn't grateful the crew was working on the lines, but it was just annoying how they'd stopped traffic while I finished up one of the wires. Traffic wasn't bad—it was only one other car and me—but there I sat. In my car. Stopped. Annoyed.

"Hi." I had rolled down my window and called out to the lady with the stop sign.

She walked over.

"Is this going to take long?" I asked.

"No. We just need to get the bucket down so we can move over to the last box and get the internet up and running." She was pleasant, even though she shivered from the cold.

"Great. How long do you think it'll be?" I asked.

"Before you can go or the internet comes up?" She wanted clarification.

"Both?" I asked with a smile in hopes I wasn't annoying her.

"Looks like you're about to go now and in about an hour for the internet." She flipped the stop sign to the other side and motioned for me to go.

When I got to the theater, Aunt Maxi was on stage with Gretchen, who was directing her. She was totally into her part. Aunt Maxi was playing who I considered to be the character equivalent to Amanda B. Suculant, and Crissy appeared to be playing the relative. I stood there with my eye on Gretchen.

Aunt Maxi didn't appear to be in immediate danger, so the more nonchalant I was, the better.

The play seemed to take a turn in the middle. When I read it, it appeared that the ghost of Amanda B. Suculant haunted the family member who killed her, so it wasn't exactly how the true crime went but close enough to get my attention. None other than Gretchen played the ghost.

While they played out the scene, I continued to type in the Google search on my phone to see if the internet was back up. I knew the lady had told me about an hour, but I could pray it would be earlier.

"Granddaughter of Amanda B. Suculant," I said out loud and typed into the search engine.

"Cut!" Sydney's voice boomed over the actors. "I don't think the lighting is right. George, do you think you could lay off the purple tone and do a simple sunrise blue?"

George, who I assumed was one of the crew's lighting guys, waved a hand and started to push all sorts of buttons on the control panel from his area in the back of the theater where all that stuff was kept.

"Take five!" Sydney held her hand up in the air. "Good work, people."

From the way the actors were smiling, I could tell Sydney's directing was a far cry from how Alan had handled them.

I couldn't help but watch Gretchen leave the stage. I got up to follow her out into the hall, where I bet she was going to her dressing room. When I peeked inside, she wasn't there, but the briefcase was on the table.

Alan's briefcase. The one I'd seen him with when I walked in on him when he was in here reading his manuscript.

"Hey there." Sydney walked up behind me. "What's going on?"

"I was looking for my aunt Maxi. She left her script in my car." I pulled it out of my bag and followed Sydney into the dressing room.

"She must've memorized it because she's doing great. She's a natural." Sydney sat down with her papers in her hand and pulled the pencil from behind her ear. "Dang. Tip is broken off." She looked in the briefcase, shuffling through before she found another pencil.

"Is that yours?" I asked about the briefcase.

"Yeah. I got it back in film school." She sat down and started to mark on the paper.

The sound of dings came from my phone and her phone, then vague, distant sounds of dings went off down the hall. A few woohoos could be heard in the distance.

"I think we just got internet. That would be great!" Sydney was so excited.

I pulled my phone out, wondering if I was standing there with the real killer. While I pretended to be paying attention to my phone, various things started to pop into my head that would actually make sense if Sydney did kill Alan Bogart.

When I looked at the internet on my phone, my search engine popped up the last thing I'd Googled, Amanda B. Suculant's granddaughter. A photo of a young woman with brown hair popped up. I looked up at Sydney and tried to picture her with brown hair that was not the deep brown.

She looked at me and smiled.

"The internet is a good thing." She went back to her phone.

I looked back and forth a few times between the photo on my phone and her. The granddaughter's name was Carrow Suculant. The girl in the photo didn't seem as meek and quiet as the woman sitting in front of me.

"Are you okay, Roxy?" she asked when she looked up and I was just staring at her with a blank face.

"Why?" I knew it was her when I noticed the eyes were the same. "Why did you kill your grandmother?"

"What?" She laughed.

"This." I wagged Aunt Maxi's copy of the manuscript. "You killed your grandmother. You knew Gretchen from the arts where your grandmother took you. I'm not sure how you got to working for Gretchen, but somehow you went to college for film then wrote this transcript where you detailed the crime you committed but tweaked it enough with the ghost to throw people off."

She started to laugh. Her attitude only fueled me more.

"The other morning when I was delivering the coffee and the romance play was still the production, I was dropping off Gretchen's personal requests, and I found Alan in here. I thought he was looking at his briefcase, but he found your life story in there. This." I wagged the papers even harder when I recognized her facial features had turned a little sterner. I knew I was on the right track. "When you found out Alan had stolen your manuscript, you killed him. I honestly thought it was Gretchen after I picked up the fur from the cleaners and Perry told me about the tag and the history of your grandmother. I couldn't understand why Gretchen had the fur, but now I know it's a prop. A prop in your sick manuscript."

"Aren't you just the nosiest citizen in this little town?" Sydney's head tilted. "You know nothing about my life."

"Oh. I think I'm right. Look at you. You're shaking, you're so nervous." I pointed out how the papers in her hand were shaking.

"I'm fine." She put the papers in the open briefcase but still held the pencil in her grip. Her hands fisted. "You just don't understand. This business is cutthroat. Alan stole from me."

"You thought writing the manuscript was going to clear your conscience of killing your grandmother?" I started to pepper her with questions to try to confuse her more and buy me time to come up with a way to get the heck out of there.

"She cut me out of her will," Sydney seethed and lunged towards me with the pencil above her head.

I smacked her arm out of the way and fell to the side.

"There's no way you're going to get out of here alive." Her eyes were on fire. She shut the door of the dressing room and locked it.

"Help!" I screamed.

"These doors are soundproof, like most doors in theater dressing rooms, so actors can rehearse lines." She thought she was so clever, but she didn't know Honey Springs dressing rooms. They were not anything special. Like Butch had said earlier, Patrick had donated the doors from a pile he had left over from another job at Cane Construction, and they weren't fancy, noise-proof doors.

"Help!" I continued to scream as she got closer.

I swung my bag at her as she shifted from side to side. Each time she got a little closer, she swung her arm down, trying to stab me with the pencil. I knew I couldn't die from a pencil, but it might stop me from getting away from her.

I kept one eye on her and one eye on the path to the door, only she continued to hop around like a little jumping bean.

"You think you can turn me in? Now that I have reached a level of fame in my career and no longer need to be under the control of Gretchen Cannon?" She came at me a couple of additional times.

"Help!" I continued to scream, hoping anyone would be walking past the door and hear me.

A thud and splintering wood shard flying in the air made Sydney and me turn to the door.

"Hold it right there." Spencer Shepard was staring down the barrel of his gun, which was pointed directly at Sydney O'Neal.

CHAPTER EIGHTEEN

"Tell us one more time how you figured it out?"

I stood in the middle of the coffee shop, telling Perry Zella and his mystery group all the details of how I'd figured out that Alan's killer was Sydney, also known as Carrow Suculant, the granddaughter of Amanda B. Suculant.

On the night of Sydney and Gretchen's arrest, Perry still held the mystery club meeting at the coffee shop, and I was all too happy to tell them about it.

"After Kayla had read the manuscript while I was looking up Amanda, she said it was eerily like Amanda's life. I remembered seeing Alan in Gretchen's dressing room with the briefcase. He'd found the manuscript and took it for the play." Of course I had hand gestures and facial features to go along with my story to make it a lot more interesting.

I continued.

"When the internet pinged on my phone, it was then that it brought up my last search, which was the photo of Carrow. I recognized by the eyes it was Sydney and that it was her briefcase Alan had taken the new play from. It was hers. She had written it as a way of letting out her feelings about killing her grandmother."

"It was her sick way of making herself feel less guilty," Perry said and looked around at his club. "This has happened in crimes before. The killer needs closure for themselves."

"Right." Mark Redding chimed in and continued to write in his little notebook.

"I wasn't sure how Gretchen fit in, but according to Spencer, she somehow figured out Sydney was the killer, and she blackmailed her into working for her. Even taking one of Amanda's fur coats in exchange for helping Carrow change her identity." It was crazy how it all turned out, and I was still trying to wrap my head around it and the danger everyone was in. "Gretchen and Sydney knew Alan had stolen the manuscript from the briefcase, so they hatched a plan for them to create a big argument. While Gretchen made a scene, Sydney slipped off stage. She knew all about the ins and outs of the theater, since it was her degree, and she knew if she cut the rope, the sandbag would kill Alan."

"So she did take the ax from Newton's wheelbarrow?" Perry asked.

"She did. When they saw Newton's tools, they'd devised a plan the night before in their hotel room to carry out the plan." It was crazy how many details Gretchen had put into it. "Gretchen was the mastermind that fed Sydney's guilt. Gretchen also thought that she could get out of being under arrest for murder since she didn't actually cut the rope, but that's not how it's going to go down."

"This is crazy." Perry shook his head. "And to think a big murder like Amanda B. Suculant from years ago would be solved in small town Honey Springs."

The days following the big arrests were kind of crazy. Gretchen and Sydney had been transported to a federal prison while they went through the legal process. I'd given my statement. Loretta had changed the play back to the sweet romance, and everyone was happy with their parts and the simplicity of just entertaining the citizens of Honey Springs.

It did take a few trips and the community coming together to switch out the props, but in the end, it all worked out.

Even Emily's see-you-later party was fabulous. It was a big time, and she was thrilled to see all the people coming together.

Though I was happy for her moving and getting on with her life, I was even more excited about what was happening today.

"I can't believe this is happening." I reached over to Patrick, who was sitting in the chair beside me in front of Evan Rich's desk at the Honey Springs National Bank. I squeezed Patrick's hand.

Evan was busy eating a couple of the pecan balls and sipping the coffee I'd brought him. He watched the printer spit out the papers needed for me to sign to make the Queen for the Day building, which was next to the Bean Hive, all mine.

Tamara had already purchased Bees Knees Bakery right after Emily moved away from Honey Springs.

"I'm excited about the roastery. I think it'll be a cool addition to our town." Evan slid the papers across his desk in front of me and put a pen on top. "As soon as you sign the loan papers, I'll get the necessary paperwork over to Penney, and she'll finish the closing."

"Sounds good." I couldn't stop smiling.

"Speaking of Penney, how is she?" Evan asked about my mom, who was the local real estate agent.

"She's doing great. In fact, she has been on a vacation, and Patrick and I are meeting her at her office after we leave here so we can discuss all the crazy things that took place while she was gone." I signed on the line and pushed the papers back to him. "How is Emily doing?"

"She's settling in. And Mocha." He shook his bald head and smiled. "Emily loves that cat."

"Great. I'm so glad it worked out for both of them." When Emily had come into the Bean Hive to give me her final goodbye, she couldn't leave without adopting Mocha. The match was purr-fect for them both.

"Well, congratulations." Evan, Patrick, and I stood up. Evan shook our hands. "It looks like you're going to be busy with construction the next few months."

"Good." Patrick spoke up. "Anything to keep her mind occupied with something other than murder investigations."

Evan was right. I was going to be busy the next couple of months getting the building ready for the new roastery and maintaining my tour schedule, but if another murder investigation came up, I was not so sure the roastery would occupy me that much.

What was Patrick thinking? I thought with a simple smile on my face.

RECIPES FROM THE BEAN HIVE

Pecan Balls
Salmon Cat Treats
Coffee Soufflé
Maple Pecan Breakfast Ring

Pecan Balls

Submitted by Gayle Shanahan

Ingredients

- 1 stick butter, softened
- 2 T sugar
- 1 C flour
- 1 t vanilla
- 1 C ground pecans
- Powdered sugar

Directions

1. Mix all ingredients, except powdered sugar, well.
2. Form into small balls.
3. Bake 15 minutes at 325°.
4. While still warm, roll cookies into powdered sugar.

Enjoy!

Salmon Cat Treats

Ingredients

- Can Salmon
- One Egg
- ½ cup flour

Directions

1. Pulse the canned salmon in a food processor and chop finely.
2. Combine salmon, egg, and flour in stand-up mixer until it forms a dough.
3. Roll out dough to 1/4 inch thickness on a floured surface.
4. Use a cookie cutter (I recommend a 3/4 inch cutter) to cut into pieces.
5. Put the treats on a baking sheet and bake at 350°F for 20 minutes.

Coffee Soufflé

Submitted by Andrea Stoeckel

Ingredients

- 1 envelope (1 tablespoon) unflavored gelatin
- 1 1/2 cups brewed coffee, cooled
- 1/2 cup milk
- 1/2 cup white sugar, divided
- 1/4 teaspoon salt, divided
- 3 eggs, separated
- 1/2 teaspoon vanilla extract

Directions

1. Combine gelatin and cold coffee in a small bowl; set aside for 5 minutes to soften.
2. In a heat-proof bowl or the top of a double boiler, combine coffee mixture, milk, 1/4 cup sugar, 1/8 teaspoon salt, and the egg yolks.
3. Set the bowl over a pan of simmering water.
4. Stir until sugar is dissolved and gelatin has melted.
5. Whisk in remaining 1/4 cup sugar, 1/8 teaspoon salt, and the egg yolks.
6. Cook and stir until mixture is thick and creamy and coats the back of a metal spoon.
7. Remove from heat.
8. Whip the egg whites (with a pinch of salt, if desired) until stiff peaks form.
9. Fold egg whites and vanilla into slightly cooled custard.
10. Pour into a serving dish or lightly greased mold.
11. Chill until set, at least 4 hours.

Maple Pecan Breakfast Ring

Ingredients

- 1 cup milk
- 1/2 stick butter (1/4 cup)
- 1/4 cup sugar
- 1/4 cup softened butter
- 1/2 cup finely chopped pecans
- 1/4 cup sugar
- 1/4 cup brown sugar
- 3 tbsp pure maple syrup
- 1/2 tsp maple flavoring
- 2 tbsp softened butter
- 1 1/2 cups powdered sugar
- 1/4 tsp vanilla
- 1/4 tsp maple flavoring
- 1 tsp salt
- 1 package yeast
- 1/4 cup warm water
- 1 egg, slightly beaten
- 4-5 cups flour

Directions

1. In a large microwave-safe bowl, heat the milk, butter, sugar and salt until the butter is just about all melted.
2. Stir to melt the rest of the butter.
3. Cool slightly. In a mixing bowl, combine the warm water and yeast until bubbly.
4. Add the egg to the milk mixture and then add to the yeast.
5. Either with a dough hook attachment on a heavy-duty mixer or with brute strength of your arm and spoon, add the flour and knead 5-10 minutes.

6. Cover in a bowl and let rise one hour until doubled.

Directions For Maple Pecan Breakfast Ring:

Punch down and roll out to a large rectangle (20 inches long).

Spread softened butter all over to edges.

Combine remaining filling ingredients and sprinkle evenly all over.

Roll up, jelly roll style.

Cut roll in half lengthwise and turn the cut sides up, next to each other.

Prepare large round pan and grease the outside of a ramekin, too.

Place the ramekin in the center of the round pan.

Twist the two halves of the cut dough and gently pick it up and place it in the prepared pan to form a ring. Pinch the ends together.

Cover and let rise 30 minutes.

Bake in a 375° preheated oven for 35-40 minutes or until golden brown.

Remove from oven and let cool in pan.

Make glaze by stirring softened butter into powdered sugar.

Combine the flavorings and a little water and add to the sugar/butter mixture.

Stir until smooth.

Add more water if necessary until you get the consistency you like.

Pour glaze over the top.

Serve warm or at room temperature.

LEAVE A REVIEW

If you enjoyed reading this book as much as I enjoyed writing it then be sure to return to the Amazon page and leave a review.

Go to Tonyakappes.com for a full reading order of my novels and while there join my newsletter. You can also find links to Facebook, Instagram and Goodreads.

Join like-minded readers like YOU in the Cozy Krew Facebook Group for dream casting, fan theories, and live Q & A's. It's like a BIG GIANT BOOK CLUB! But if you want to have your own book club, be sure you let me know! I love to send goodies.

FROTHY FOUL PLAY

A Killer Coffee Mystery

Book Nine

BY
TONYA KAPPES

ACKNOWLEDGMENT

I'd love to thank my review team, Kappes Review Krew, for being so amazing. A big thank you to Meryl Lustig Markowitz for her amazing review that also helped me write the blurb for Frothy Foul Play.

Xoxo

Tonya

I couldn't stop myself from smiling when I noticed Tom had gotten off the boat and walked up the boardwalk toward the Bean Hive.

"Maybe I should call Birdie and tell her to be nice to him," I told myself and was a smidge relieved when I watched him take a hard right down the pier, across from the Bean Hive. "Tom Foster, you don't seem like the fishing kind." I made the observation as I watched him walk into The Bait Shop, which was located in the middle of the pier. You had to walk through the little store to get to the other side of the pier.

Shortly after I said that, he walked out the other side, which gave him zero time to even look around or purchase anything. I watched as he approached another person wearing a long brown trench coat with a hood, hands shoved into the pockets.

"What is that about?" I asked myself when I noticed the two appeared to be arguing and watched closely.

As if I were watching a movie, the drama played out before me, and not too long into the drama, I saw the trench-coat wearer pull what looked like a gun out from the pocket.

For a second I stood there, stunned. Was this really happening? I questioned what I was seeing. Tom Foster stumbled forward a little before falling to the ground, and I realized there had been no shot.

"Help!" I screamed. "Call 911!" Frantically, I bolted past the lady who had come back out to see what on earth was I yelling about. "Silencer! Someone used a silencer!"

I fumbled with my cell phone as I tried to call Spencer Shepard, the Honey Springs sheriff, to tell him I'd just witnessed a shooting and get an ambulance to the pier. When he didn't answer, I called Gloria Dei.

"Gloria, I'm so glad you answered," I gasped and ran down the path toward the boat dock. "I was just at the Bee Happy Resort."

"I'm dying to get off work so I can get over there. I told Big Bib that—"

"Gloria, stop talking!" I screamed into the phone. "Listen to me." I slowed down to tell her exactly what I'd seen while in front of me, Big Bib drove the pontoon up to the Bee Happy Resort dock with even more guests.

"I'm sorry. You have to wait," I told a couple of the guests waiting to get a ride back over to Honey Springs. "Listen, I need you to put this thing in high speed and get me across the lake. Someone was shot."

"Shot?" Big Bib looked at me with a confused look.

"Yes. Tom Foster, the man you just dropped off, was shot on the pier. I saw it with my own two eyes." My chest heaved up and down at the thought of wasting any more time to save Tom. "Go!"

I slid my gaze over to the pier by the boat dock in anticipation of what I was going to find once we got across lake. A chill scurried up my legs, leaving a trail of goosebumps and bringing me back to this morning's thought when my feet had hit my cold floor. I had known it was going to be a chilly day—I just didn't know how chilly until now.

CHAPTER ONE

Morning was always my favorite part of the day. Maybe it was the feeling of a fresh start. Maybe it was the amazing sunrise that lit up the sky with glorious oranges and reds that skidded across the calm water off Lake Honey Springs. Or just maybe it was the smell of the freshly brewed coffee that filtered throughout the Bean Hive, my coffee shop.

I sighed as I shifted my gaze away from the boardwalk and peered over my shoulder at the clock on the wall behind the counter.

Soon, my only employee would be walking through the door, and shortly after that, she'd be followed by our first customer of the day.

I was very appreciative of my customers, but the sound of Pepper, my schnauzer, snoring lightly, all snuggled up in his bed next to the fireplace, sparked a joy deep in my heart.

With a mug of hot coffee nestled between my hands, I turned my eyes back on the sunrise, inhaling a deep breath to get the most aromatic whiff possible of my cup of wake-me-up, and then closed my eyes. I felt the first warm rays of sun reach down the pier and across the boardwalk and kiss my face.

"Welcome, sun," I whispered and opened my eyes, pushing my black curly hair behind my shoulders.

I set my cup down, firmly planted my elbows on the long bar that ran across the front of the entire coffee shop, and rested my chin in my hands as I reflected on what the day ahead was going to look like.

With all this Zen talk from Crissy Lane about her new Bee Happy Resort adventure, I thought she might be converting me over to the quiet life.

Drip, drip, drip.

The sound of the industrial coffee makers working was music to my ears. The smell of the freshly roasted beans I'd created in my own roastery blanketed the coffee shop, lending warm and cozy comfort to what was a cool morning.

With what few moments I had left to myself before the hustle and bustle, I closed my eyes again. I couldn't stop myself from smiling when I thought about Crissy Lane. She told me that if I outwardly smiled, then I'd smile inwardly too. She was right. Or it was the coffee. Either way, I was willing to give her the credit.

Knock, knock, knock.

I opened one eye to see who on earth was tapping on the picture window in front of me.

There was no denying that the big-haired shadow standing right in the way of the morning sunrise was in fact my aunt, Maxine Bloom.

"Whatcha doing in there?" she mouthed through the glass before pointing with her free hand to the door, motioning for me to open up while using her other hand to steady her bike, which she refused to put in the bike rack on the edge of the boardwalk.

Instead, she propped it up against the front of the coffee shop and jerked her hobo bag out of the wire basket strapped to the front.

Pepper heard her and came running to the door, wagging his little tail in anticipation of the treat he knew Aunt Maxi had for him.

Aunt Maxi bolted into the door once I unlocked it. "I said, 'What are you doing with your eyes closed?' Are you tired? Are you and Patrick having problems?" She gasped, dropping her bag to the ground and throwing her hands over her mouth. "Oh my gawd! You're pregnant!"

"No. No. And no!" That last "no" definitely ended in an exclamation point. Not that I didn't want children, but Patrick Cane and I hadn't been married too terribly long, and we still just wanted to enjoy our time together. "The only kids I've got are Pepper and Sassy."

I picked up her bag, shooing Pepper from it, and handed it to her.

Aunt Maxi cocked her head to the side and shook the bag before resigning to the little silver-and-white dog begging at her feet.

"I reckon you do have these little babies." She wagged her finger, gesturing for me to open her bag. Once I did, she reached in and pulled out a plastic baggie with the Walk in the Bark logo printed on the front and tasty homemade dog treats inside. "Where's Sassy?" she asked, looking around for the black standard poodle that I'd gotten with the marriage.

"Patrick took her to work with him today. He's got a few things to finish at the Bee Happy Resort before Crissy's big weekend. Sassy loves running around the island while he works there." The sun's rays had finally made their way across the entire shop, giving it an inviting glow.

"New hair color?" I asked when I noticed the bright-yellow color and purple streaks in her hair.

"I like it." She raked her hand upward through her hair. "It's bright and cheery."

"It is that." I gave her a hug. I loved how she was her own person and never cared what others thought about her ever-changing hair colors. "I'm guessing Crissy's new replacement did that?" I asked after I gave her another quick hug.

Aunt Maxi only pulled out a can of hair spray from her bag.

"Oh no. Don't you be spraying that in here," I told her and reached around to flip the Closed sign on the door to Open, even though it technically wasn't opening time.

Did she ever listen to me? Nope.

She pressed her finger on the aerosol cans nozzle and sprayed it at full strength all over her head, missing most of her hair.

"Pft, pft." I spat and waved my hand in front of my face as I passed her on my way to the back of the coffeehouse.

There was no time to dillydally. I had to get the rest of the coffee shop ready to open, and that meant the opening ritual.

"Stop spraying that stuff in here. It might get on the food," I said as I went over my mental checklist of tasks like refilling the coffee-bar condiments and the tea bar.

"It's no different than dog hair or cat hair or whatever else Louise Carlton will be bringing in today." She shrugged and put the can back in her bag as she weaved in and out of the tables on her way back to the counter.

"I don't know what animal Louise is bringing in this morning, but I'm excited to give the baby a fur-ever home." I delighted in the fact that I had a small hand in giving the homeless animals in Honey Springs a warm and loving home.

There was no doubt that I'd jumped through a lot of hoops to get the health department to even approve the collaboration I had with Pet Palace. It was what some towns called the SPCA, but since Honey Springs was a small Kentucky town, there weren't any sort of funds for a local SPCA. That's when Louise Carlton had opened the nonprofit no-kill shelter, where I volunteered once a week like most of us around here.

In fact, I'd had a terrible case of loneliness when I moved to Honey Springs permanently and opened the coffeehouse upon being nudged by Aunt Maxi. I'd met Louise when she came in to get a cup of coffee, and she'd told me she had the cure for my lonely nights. That cure was Pepper.

I knew I had to help other little furry animals find homes, so each week, I began featuring one of the Pet Palace animals at the coffeehouse, and we'd had a one hundred percent adoption streak.

"Did you know all the rooms at the Cocoon Hotel are booked?" Aunt Maxi made small talk while I checked on the status of the coffeepots, which were in full percolating mode.

I nodded and got out the container of creamer to fill up the little ceramic cows on all of the café tables that dotted the inside of the coffeehouse. "That's a good thing for Crissy. I'm excited for her."

"I'm gonna help you so that I can sit with my niece for a good cup of coffee this morning." Aunt Maxi looked back at the door. "Where is your employee, anyways?"

She hung her purse on the coatrack next to the counter in exchange for one of the Bean Hive aprons I required the employees to wear while they were working.

Aunt Maxi looked around and immediately started to work on the checklist for opening the coffee shop.

I loved that about her. Even though she didn't work here, she always wanted what was best for me and helped me whenever she could. Plus, she had never been one of those people who was good at idly sitting around while things needed to be accomplished. She was one of those people who could just pick up a task before being told to do it. She had an eye for seeing what needed to be done and doing it.

"Thank you for helping me." I loved her so much. She was the reason I'd come to stay here every summer and the reason I lived here now. "I'm sure Bunny will be here any minute."

"Why aren't these youngins doing all of this at closing?" Aunt Maxi huffed even though she loved when I praised her. She made her way over to the far end of the L-shaped counter, where the tea bar was located.

"Hmm. Let me see." Aunt Maxi reviewed the station to see what needed to be done. She moved various packets of tea and opened the base cabinets to get more single-serves and refill the loose tea containers of stir sticks, sweeteners, and condiments like honey.

"It's hard to find good help nowadays," I said and made sure the centerpieces on each café table were properly placed.

When I'd opened the Bean Hive, I knew it had an atmosphere that was warm and inviting. The coffee was just a bonus, along with the cozy community.

"Hi, do," Bunny Bowowski trilled when she shuffled through the door, letting the cold air rush in behind her.

"Speak of the devil," Aunt Maxi said under her breath and brushed the edge of the apron along the top of the tea bar before she headed to the opposite side of the counter to tidy up the coffee self-serve bar.

"What on earth does that mean, Maxine Bloom?" Bunny gave Aunt Maxi a hard stare as she pulled from her hair the pins that were holding her pillbox hat in place. It was no secret they weren't the best of friends, and Aunt Maxi was good at poking the bear.

"Roxy was saying how it was hard to get good help, and well"—Aunt Maxi shrugged—"you walked in."

"Oh, stop it. I wasn't talking about you." I rushed over to help Bunny with her things. She was elderly and slow, but she was good at making customers feel welcome. Plus, she needed something to do during the days, so when she'd asked for a job, I was delighted to have her.

"We were talking about the afternoon kids completing the checklist, like restocking the coffee and tea bar." I put the creamer container on the table and gave Aunt Maxi a little bow. "Which I'm grateful Aunt Maxi is doing for us."

"Doing for Roxanne." Aunt Maxi made it clear she wasn't doing Bunny any favors.

"I don't know what I'd do if you two ever got along," I teased as I placed Bunny's handbag underneath the counter and headed back through the swinging door to the kitchen, where I needed to get another container of creamer to have on hand at the counter and check on the sweet treats in the oven.

I wasn't back there for too long by myself because Bunny, Aunt Maxi, and Pepper had followed me. Aunt Maxi planted herself on the stool that butted up to the metal workstation where I did all the preparing for the cooking and baking.

Aunt Maxi licked her lips when she noticed the donuts I'd taken out of the fryer earlier this morning and placed on the cooling rack so I could get them iced and displayed before the first customer of the day. "I love a good donut."

"Your favorite too." I opened the oven door to check on the muffins then set the timers for a smidgen longer since I noticed they weren't quite done.

The other oven had the breakfast quiches, and they were still a little jiggly in the middle, so I upped the time on those too.

"We need to keep an eye on the quiches," I told Bunny on my way over to the walk-in refrigerator to get the container of creamer.

"Strawberry and cream?" Aunt Maxi's eyes grew, and she licked her lips like she could taste them.

"Those aren't for you," Bunny told Aunt Maxi in a sharp voice. "Let me get you a coffee." Bunny made her way over to my small coffeepot that I kept in the kitchen for us and made herself, as well as Aunt Maxi, a cup of coffee.

"Mm-hmm," I said and bent down to grab the creamer from the refrigerator. "And the donuts are for book club tonight, so none this morning." I put the creamer next to her on the workstation so she could doctor up her coffee.

"All of those can't be for book club." Aunt Maxi leaned a little to the left to look around me at the cooling rack of all the donuts. "One little, tiny one?" She used her thumb and pointer finger to show me just how tiny she meant, with her eye looking through the space between them.

"Nope." I stopped and took a treat from Pepper's treat jar since he was so cute sitting next to Aunt Maxi, hoping she would get a donut and accidentally drop a morsel for him. "You haven't told me why you're out so early this morning."

The bell above the door in the coffeehouse dinged, and we all looked at one another. I nodded over to the muffins, cookies, and bagels I'd already gotten on the display trays.

"Everyone grab a tray. We've got an early one." I walked through the swinging kitchen door with the creamer in one hand and a glass pie plate holding a blueberry tart in the other. Aunt Maxi and Bunny both followed me with their hands full.

"Good morning," I called out to our first customer of the day, who was next to the self-serve, pay-by-good-faith coffee bar. "I've got the coffee coming right up. Just got finished brewing."

I put the creamer on the counter along with the tart, and then Bunny's eyes met mine, and she knew what I was thinking. She began to put all the treats in the display cases, write their names on the small chalkboards on the front, and write all the specials on one of the big chalkboards on the wall while I continued to put the coffee carafes on the coffee bar.

The Bean Hive was located in the middle of the boardwalk, right across from the pier and was a perfect stop for anyone who worked in downtown Honey Springs or even just the tourists who came to visit our little town.

I was very proud of how I'd transformed the old building and kept the exposed brick walls and wooden ceiling beams in their original form.

With some elbow grease—and binge-watching DIY videos on YouTube to figure out how to make the necessary repairs to pass inspection—the Bean Hive had become a great success over the years, and the friendships I'd built had become priceless.

"To answer your question from a few minutes ago—I dropped by to ask if you were going to book club and wanted to pick me up tonight," Aunt Maxi said.

"Yes, I'm going, and yes, I'll pick you up." Not that I was planning on leaving the coffeehouse today, since the book club was at the Crooked Cat, the bookstore at the end of the boardwalk.

I was involved in a lot of committees in Honey Springs, and some days, it was just easier to stay at the coffeehouse all day instead of driving to my house, which was really only a seven-minute drive. Plus, there was always something to do here.

"Is there anything else we can get you?" I asked the customer and received a shake of his head before he dropped his dollars in the good-faith jar. "We have some delicious cream cheese–topped carrot-and-raisin muffins that pair well with our in-house New Year Blend I noticed you got."

"No. I'm sure I'll be coming back for some more later this week." He sounded pretty confident, and that made me curious as to why he was in Honey Springs, since I didn't recognize him—which told me he was a tourist.

"Are you here for pleasure or business?"

He turned around when I asked him the question and unzipped his coat as he surveyed the coffee shop.

"I guess you could say both." He offered a smile.

I looked into his black eyes to see what kind of man my customer was and whether or not I could read his personality from his body language.

"My wife begged me to come and do an article on the new health and wellness spa. Honey Happy or..." He trailed off as he tried to recall the right name. "We just pulled into town and are about to get our room."

"Bee Happy Resort?" Excitement filled every part of me, knowing how much work Crissy had put into her new retreat resort over the past nine or ten months.

"Yes, for the retreat, but we aren't staying at the resort itself," he said with a stiff voice. He rolled his hand in the air, with a stir stick between his fingers. "Anyways, my wife likes all the holistic stuff, and I write for *Healthy Women's Magazine*." He looked around. "In fact, I just might like to do an article on this little gem." He smiled again, and this time, his dimples deepened above the beard.

"Really?" This seemed like a nice opportunity for me and one I didn't want to pass up. "I'd love for you to." I hurried over to the counter and plucked a tissue from the box. "Let me get you some strawberry-and-cream donuts to take back to your wife as well as one of the carrot muffins."

"I wouldn't want to..." He was going to try to stop me, but I wasn't going to let that happen.

"I insist." I actually put two muffins in the box. "I think you're going to fall in love with our welcoming community while your wife is enjoying her time at the Bee Happy Resort."

The door of the coffeehouse opened.

Crissy Lane walked in, and with the sun up over the trees, the rays sprinkled in and cast yellow highlights on Crissy's sun-washed blond hair, which wasn't at all as natural as she proclaimed.

"Speaking of Bee Happy Resort." I turned his attention to Crissy as I waved her over. "This is the owner, Crissy Lane."

"Crissy, this is—" I turned to my customer. "I'm sorry. I didn't get your name."

"Tom Foster." He took the box of treats from me.

"Crissy, Tom and his wife are here for the opening of Bee Happy Resort." This was great because that meant there were two people going to her grand opening weekend.

The reservations for the weekend retreat had been slow when she'd opened them up a couple of months ago and had started her marketing campaign to push for clients. She'd been driving all of her friends crazy about coming because she needed warm bodies to fill the camera space since she'd sent out all the media releases with free treatments for the first five reporters and social media influencers to sign up.

"It's so nice to meet you early." Crissy smiled, batting her long, fake eyelashes at him.

Pretty much everything on her was fake, down to her ta-tas. She had a heart of gold and truly did love all things spa. Since she was already a nail technician as well as a hairdresser, opening a resort was in her wheelhouse, and she was good at it.

However, I did love her natural red hair over her box-dye job. She had the cutest red freckles along her cheeks that made an adorable bridge across her nose and were the same shade as her real hair color, but she tried to cover those, too, with all sorts of makeup.

"He's with *Healthy Women's Magazine*." I bounced on my toes at the thought of him actually doing an article on the Bean Hive.

"Then we have to sit down, and you can let me show you the ins and outs of the spa. I think your readers are going to love it." She curled her hand into the crook of his elbow, her long nails capturing the fabric of his shirt like a cat clawing its prey. "I insist on giving your wife a free facial that she'll never forget." Crissy's twangy voice dripped with Southern charm as she steered him away from the coffee bar. "Where are y'all staying?"

"The Cocoon," I overheard him tell Crissy. I smiled since it was so good Crissy's new endeavor was bringing in business for Camey Montgomery, the owner of the Cocoon Hotel. And Tom was probably on the boardwalk this morning taking a stroll when he just so happened upon the Bean Hive for a great cup of coffee, if I did say so myself.

"What's all the nonsense about?" Aunt Maxi asked, both of us watching as Crissy took him over to the couch next to the fireplace and helped prop his back up with a few of the pillows.

"Crissy being Crissy." I laughed and turned back to Aunt Maxi. "I'll pick you up around five for book club."

"Mm-hmm. Did you tell her?" Aunt Maxi threw a glance over at Crissy.

"No." I shook my head and knew that after her little meeting with Tom, I had to tell her I didn't have anyone to work at the Bean Hive for the weekend, so I wasn't going to be able to go to her grand opening. "But I will."

"I don't envy you." Aunt Maxi patted me on the arm. "Anyways, I've got to get going." She grabbed her hobo bag from the coat-tree and pulled it across her body. She put her hand in the bag and pulled out a small thermos. "I've got to meet an Airbnb client in about ten minutes, so I wanted to grab a couple of donuts and a cup of coffee to take." She unscrewed the lid and put the thermos under the coffee carafe, filling it up.

"You are brilliant." I couldn't help but smile at her coming here to get my coffee to entice her new tenants. "Make sure you leave a Bean Hive business card next to the goodies. I'll be sure to bring you a couple strawberry-and-cream ones at the book club." I buttoned the top button of her coat for her. "Make sure you bundle up. I have no idea why you rode your bike, anyways. It's still not spring, and it's cold."

"I'll be fine. I'll see you at 5:00 p.m. sharp." She gave me a long, level look that reminded me of how she liked to be on time.

Honey Springs was such a small community that every business was pretty much independently owned, and we relied on each other to promote and support our businesses. That's why I used the Bee Farm's honey in all of my recipes that called for honey, kept the information for the Cocoon Hotel at the counter, and promoted adoptions for Pet Palace, among many other things.

"I'll be there," I assured her but didn't commit to an exact time in fear I wouldn't be able to close on time since I didn't have any help this afternoon.

I walked her to the door and watched her secure the thermos and to-go box of donuts in her wire basket before she tried to pedal off, nearly running over Louise Carlton in the process.

"Bunny," I called over my shoulder when I saw Louise Carlton say something to Aunt Maxi before Aunt Maxi left in the direction of the Cocoon Hotel. "Do you mind changing the menus? Louise is here, and it looks like she's got a cat in the carrier."

"I reckon I can." Bunny tried not to show how much she really did like to draw on the chalkboard menus that I'd opted for instead of paper menus.

When I originally opened the Bean Hive, I had attached the chalkboard menus to the wall, which forced me to either take them down or stand on a stool to write on them. Patrick decided he'd had enough of worrying about me falling off the stool, so he created a pully system that allowed us to move the boards up and down with a chain, making it easier for Bunny to take over that job.

"The specials are written on the piece of paper next to the register," I told her and headed over to the door to let Louise in since her hands were full. "Don't forget to add the cream cheese-topped carrot-and-raisin muffins."

It was a new recipe that I had given great consideration when I'd made the New Year Blend at my roastery. I wanted to create a menu that married the food with the coffee choices. Since we weren't open on Sundays, I spent most of those afternoons testing and trying out various combinations to come up with just the right pairing. I was very proud of this new muffin-and-coffee combination.

"Good morning!" Louise's smile was as bright at the morning sun. Her eyes lit up underneath her bangs as the sun bounced off the silver bob that made her look so sophisticated. "You aren't going to believe this little beauty."

She held up the cage of the cutest smoosh-faced black kitten.

"Achoo!" The loudest sneeze came from Tom Foster, making me jump all the way to heaven.

"Good night!" Bunny hollered, throwing her hands up to her chest. "You almost made me pee myself."

"Is-is-is…" He stood up from the couch where Crissy had had him pinned, his nose curled and his eyes squinted. "Is that a—achoo!" He snorted. "A cat?"

CHAPTER TWO

"How was I to know he was allergic to cats?" I felt bad. I really did.

Apparently, Tom Foster was deathly allergic to cats, and even just the smell of one would give him hives. I'd come to find out he wasn't allergic to dogs, and it was a good thing Pepper was a schnauzer, which just so happened to be a hypoallergenic breed.

The poor man ran out of the Bean Hive so fast but not quickly enough to outrun the large red bumps and swelling cropping up around his eyes. He looked like he'd been stung by hundreds of bees from over at the Bee Farm.

"What can I do to make it up to you?" I asked Crissy to try to get anything out of her besides sobs. "Anything."

"Anything?" Her head hung almost to her cup of coffee.

"Anything." I was sitting next to her on the couch and pushed back a dangling strand of hair so I could see her face.

"You can just be there all weekend." She tilted her head and smiled at me. "I know you didn't know. I didn't know. Glad I didn't get a resort pet. I can give his wife some great treatments to help ease the pain. But just having you there is apology enough."

I gulped and tried not to look at Bunny, who was snickering behind us and trying to write the specials on the menus.

She and Floyd, her boyfriend, who was also in his golden years, were leaving for a trip this afternoon to visit some of his cousins out of town. It was something she'd been looking forward to for a long time. That was why I didn't have staff for the afternoon and wasn't sure I could be at Aunt Maxi's at five on the dot.

"You know I wouldn't miss it for the world." I patted her. "I'll even bring some coffee for the guests."

"Oh, no." She shook her head. "You don't need to do that. I'm only offering kombucha and other homeopathic treats."

"Sounds great." I blinked a few times, thinking I'd never even heard Crissy mention anything about this being a holistic place. "I thought you were doing a spa."

"I am. I also have chanting classes, meditations, yoga—a full retreat." She sighed. "What did you want to talk to me about? I thought I'd just buzz over before I went to the retreat this morning."

"Nothing." I stood up. "I've got to finish the menus before the breakfast crowd starts to get here."

"Yeah. Sure." She got up and glanced at the counter. "Those donuts really have a lot of sugar, don't they?"

"Nah." I gestured over to them. "You haven't opened that fancy holistic place yet. One more sugary donut ain't gonna hurt you." I winked.

"You're the best. Only one." She held up a finger and trotted over to the counter to pick out the one she wanted while I moseyed over to the shorter side of the L-shaped counter to check on Bunny.

"If you think I'm going to cancel my trip with Floyd, you've got another thing coming to you, Roxanne Bloom." Bunny wrote down the selection of breakfast casseroles and drinks we were offering this week on the third chalkboard menu, which hung over the counter with those items on display.

"I'd never ask you to do that." I knew I was in a bit of a pickle but had no idea who I could plead with just so I could make good on my promise to Crissy. "Don't forget that we have kombucha drinks."

"I don't know how to spell that, and it doesn't even sound good." Her face pinched like she'd been sucking on a dill pickle.

"I'm teasing," I told her, even though she knew. "Now that we have all that out of the way"—I had made my way over to Louise, where she was sitting at one of the café tables with adoption paperwork spread out—"who do we have here?"

I bent down and looked into the plastic crate, where a tiny kitten was hunkered down in the back right corner, its yellow eyes so big that I could see the fright all the way down to its little heart.

"Oh, it's a baby." My jaw dropped in pleasant surprise. "We rarely get babies."

Carefully, I pinched the door hinge to open the cage and reached in to take out the sweet and very scared kitten.

"It's okay." I snuggled the little one up against me and was greeted with several meows that got Pepper's attention. "Excuse me?" I asked him and laughed, as did Louise when Pepper stood up on his back paws and planted his front ones on my leg, with his nose stuck straight up in the air to get a whiff of the kitten.

"You better get used to him." Louise reached up from her chair and scratched the kitten on the head.

"Yes. Pepper will be your best friend." I bent down a little so Pepper could get a sniff of the baby. "Whoa." I moved slightly back when the kitten got scared and started to claw its way up my chest, where it landed on my shoulder. "Maybe we will let him sniff you while you are in the cage just so you can get used to him."

Pepper danced around me as I put the kitten back in the cage, where it scurried right back into the corner. I kept the door open so the poor little thing could freely come and go when it was comfortable. Pepper was so good. He knew not to stick his head into the kennel, so he patiently walked around it to smell the kitten before he walked back over to his bed next to the fireplace, where he would stay for his morning nap.

My theory behind this whole animals-in-the-coffeehouse thing was to not only find them fur-ever homes but to also let them roam freely so the potential adoptive parents would be able to see how they'd react in a home-type environment.

"I don't think we will have any problems getting this one a home." Everyone loved babies, and generally, Louise sent me adult or older animals to rehome. "Do we have a name?"

"We don't. I found her in a box on the steps of Pet Palace when I went to work a couple of weeks ago. She was so tiny that we've been bottle-feeding her."

I frowned.

"What's wrong?" Louise asked.

"I wish I had someone here so I could resume my volunteer duties at Pet Palace, that's all. I'd have loved to have been able to bottle-feed her." Even though my main job at Pet Palace had been to clean all the cages, which involved the yucky task of cleaning out their potty boxes, I did enjoy getting to know them. It was very good therapy and good for my soul. "Let me know if you hear of anyone needing a part-time afternoon job."

"What happened to the school kids?" she asked, referring to the high school students who'd always worked after school.

"They had to quit because it's the last semester before they go to college. They are studying for all those college entrance exams and taking classes on how to pass them." I really did miss the help I'd had over the years. One of my employees had even gone off to start her own bakery in another town.

"I'm sure someone will come along." She pushed the file across the table with all the particulars for the kitten inside. "As you can see, the veterinarian places the kitten at about seven to eight weeks. She's had all her shots, and there are some photos of before and after."

I opened the file to find all the contents as well as the adoption papers and Louise's contact information at Pet Palace.

"Perfect." I picked it up and got up to put the file next to the register where we kept them so when people asked about the animals, we would be able to have the information on hand. "Pepper, give the baby some time," I said to him when I noticed he was lying in front of the kitten's cage with his head nearly stuck inside.

Pepper didn't listen.

"Are you going to be at book club tonight?" I asked Louise and got her one of her favorite sweet treats from the coffeehouse—a blueberry scone—and put it into a to-go bag alongside a cup of her favorite Christmas coffee blend with a splash of almond milk.

"I will be there. I'm picking the next book, so I'm hoping the library is open because I've asked Joanne to pick me out a very good one." Louise fanned her hands out in front of her. "Lots of romance."

"Romance? Who's having some romance?" Loretta Bebe pushed on through the front door of the coffeehouse in all of her Southern glory. "Did you say you are having lots of romance? I'm gonna need a strong cup of coffee to wash down this bit of information."

"Coming right up." I winked at Loretta and left her and Louise to talk.

"There you go again, spreading gossip, Low-retta." Bunny Bowowski felt like she was old enough to have earned the right to call people out as she saw fit.

I, as the peacemaker of our group, had to nip any sort of arguments in the bud before they got started. After all, it wasn't even 8:00 a.m. yet. Gossip flowed as freely as the coffee did around here, and sometimes, it was hard to distinguish between a tease and the truth. That's when and how most of the gossip around Honey Springs got started.

"We were talking about our new book for book club." Louise had gotten up from the table and walked over to the counter to get her to-go items. "I hope I see y'all there tonight."

She bent down to look at the kitten on her way to the door and gave her a few smoochy kissing sounds.

"Thanks, Louise. I'll keep you posted about the kitten. And I'm excited to read a romance." I went back to the supply closet that was next to the bathroom and dragged out the small cat tree, which Patrick had made for one of the past Pet Palace cats, and pushed it up into the corner of the coffee shop near the front window so that people on the boardwalk could see the kitten—if and only if the kitten decided to come out of the kennel.

"Why do you have to be so nasty?" Loretta shook her jeweled finger at Bunny after Louise had left.

"You point that finger at me one more time, and you'll be drawing back a nub." Bunny's face stilled.

Slowly, Loretta pulled back her hand.

"Why, Roxy, it sure is hard to find good help nowadays." Her gaze shifted back to Bunny. Bunny jerked forward, making Loretta jump. "You're cray-zeee." Loretta drew the word out in her Southern accent. "I don't understand why Roxanne keeps you here."

"Bunny, can you go check the ovens? I think I heard those timers going off," I said, even though it was a lie. I needed to shoo her away before there was a

Southern smackdown right here in the middle of the coffeehouse and certainly before any more customers showed up. "What can I get you?"

I moved the kitten's kennel next to the cat tree, took some of the catnip from the bag Louise had set on top, and sprinkled it on the top shelf of the cat tree to try to entice the little guy to come out.

"I came in here to see if you still had a job opening." Loretta nearly stopped me in my tracks on my way back to the counter.

"You're looking for a job?" I asked, a little confused, and leaned my hip against the back of the glass display case, eyeballing her.

Loretta Bebe, work? As in an actual job? She was a pro at volunteering for anything and everything. She was the president of the Beautification Committee and the Southern Women's Club. Those came with honors and accolades, which Loretta Bebe loved to bask in, as any true Southern woman would. But to have a physical job where she had to take instruction from a boss was far from who Loretta Bebe was at her core.

"No. My granddaughter is coming to live with us for a while, and she needs a job." She looked away, as I am sure she didn't want to see the shock on my face.

"Granddaughter?" I questioned since I'd never even heard her mention a daughter, much less a granddaughter.

"Mm-hmm." She sighed and patted around her short, coal-black hair before she pulled out a compact from her purse and blotted some very dark powder onto her already very tan face—coloring which she claimed was from her Native American heritage.

But we all knew it was from the tanning bed over in Lisa Stalh's garage.

"I'm assuming you can keep a secret." She let out a long sigh and glanced over at the coffee bar, where there was already a line of people ready to grab a cup and go. It was one of the most popular features I had at the coffeehouse.

"Cross my heart." I was more excited than I thought I would be at Loretta finally telling me something, as I was always left out of her little circle.

"She needs a little raising. She needs a heavy hand to make her do well in school, work, and go to church." She gave me the good old Baptist nod I was used to getting around here. "If you know what I mean without me saying it out loud." Her penciled-in eyebrows drew up, and her lips flattened. "Her mama and I don't agree on things too often, but she's had a time with her. She even stole some things at a store, and now she's in trouble. And…" Loretta took a second to suck in a deep breath and lift her chin into the air as if she needed to gear up some confidence. "She's been on drugs. Now, she's been clean for about a year, but she is still fragile. I've got to rule with a heavy yet loving hand as the grandmother."

"Well…" I hesitated because I wasn't sure if I needed help that badly and I was a wee bit unsure about all the baggage the poor girl would be bringing along.

"The one thing I thought about here is that she did work at one of those fancy coffeehouses before. She was good at it." That made me feel a little better. Loretta continued, "She knows how to run a register—granted, she did steal from the place—but with her here in Honey Springs, I think it'll do her good to get away. A fresh start. She's smart. I mean, really smart in chemistry, so when you need someone to mix all them beans back there in the roaster, she's your girl."

"I don't know." I wasn't sure how to tell her no.

"I think you better not throw stones in glass houses." She stared. "In fact, from what I know about you, you quit your job as the fancy lawyer, got a divorce, and moved to Honey Springs for your start, and look at you now. You just needed a community like me and"—she shifted her gaze over my shoulder to look at Bunny, who was happily waiting on a customer at the counter—"her too. Look at you. You have a thriving business, sometimes you offer legal advice to people, you're newly married, and you opened the roastery."

"She's good at chemistry?" I asked and tried to buy myself some more thinking time because Loretta wanted an answer right then and there, on the spot.

"Who told you?" Loretta drew back, her eyes narrowed to crinkled slits.

"Told me what?" I asked.

"About her chemistry teacher." Loretta had me all sorts of confused. "Oh." Her eyes opened again. "I guess you don't know, but my granddaughter did get accused of trying to poison her chemistry teacher, but all of that was figured out."

"Poisoned?" I gulped back a shudder. "I don't know, Loretta."

"I'm thinking you can give her a chance." Loretta gestured around the room, her pocketbook swaying back and forth on her forearm. "You don't have much of a choice. It's either you work yourself to death with no help"—she slid her glance to Bunny—"and I do mean no help. And your marriage suffers because you're here all the time, or you can use a little help with my granddaughter."

"When you put it that way..." I gnawed on my bottom lip. I'd always tried to make my marriage come first in my life, but it was hard when you were the owner of a business and you wanted it to succeed. "Don't make me regret it."

"You're a doll. She'll stop by later this afternoon to talk to you." She put her hands together, causing the stacked bracelets on both wrists to jingle against each other. "She can even start right away. I'll be sure to tell her."

"Wait." I stopped her. "What other sorts of things did she get in trouble for in school?"

If the poor girl was sent to live with Loretta, that seemed like punishment enough, but I wanted the entire picture. Not just the things Loretta was willing to share with me—not that stealing or trying to poison her teacher wasn't enough.

"Birdie is too smart for her own good. I honestly think she was bored in school, so she used her skills." Loretta drew in a long breath before she just let it all go. "I have no idea why that girl doesn't use her God-given brain and her amazing abilities in chemistry and biology to do good in the world by going to college and getting a degree. I told her mama and her daddy that she needed to be a pharmacist or something. She's a whiz in the chemistry lab at school. Though she did blow it up on purpose after her teacher gave her detention after she tried to poison her."

"Was she trying to kill her teacher?" I gasped. "I mean, what if I make her mad? I would be her boss, you know."

"No." Loretta waved her hand in front of her. "Nothing like that. Just trying to get back at her. She gave her teacher something to make her sick to her stomach and miss work. She needed a break from the teacher, that's all. All of us need a little break sometimes. Even the best of us."

"Oh." My brows knitted. There was a worry in my gut. "I don't know, Loretta. Maybe I spoke too soon."

"Uh-uh." Loretta shook her head. "You said you'd hire her." Loretta's eyes lowered. "Fine. What do you need from me to give her a chance?"

Was this the moment I'd been waiting for? My big break into Honey Springs society?

"Hmm." I brought my finger up to my temple, trying to tap something in there that I could pull out to use for this exact moment. I had to use the opportunity of her offering to do something for me and get something out of it instead of just being kindhearted by giving the troubled girl a job. "I'd like to be added as a member of the Southern Women's Club."

"Don't press your luck." She drew her eyes down me. "But I guess I could ask the gals if we have room for one more."

"I think you do. In fact, I know you have room for one more." I had the opportunity here at hand and took my gamble. I'd been trying to become a member for a while now because these were the cream-of-the-crop women in Southern society.

It was rare to see one of them come to the boardwalk and shop. They liked high-dollar stores, and if I could get in with one of them for catering one of their dinner parties, then I just might have another revenue stream. I already did cater some events, but the women of the club had big parties that would bring me even more business.

"Honestly," she huffed. "You Blooms like to take advantage of every situation." She turned on the balls of her shoes and called over her shoulder, "I'll be in touch."

"I'm looking forward to meeting your granddaughter," I called over the sounds of some chattering customers coming through the door. "What's her name again?"

"Birdie!" She hollered and traipsed out onto the boardwalk.

CHAPTER THREE

The kitten had finally come out of the kennel and made a trail up the cat tree after I'd gotten the homemade cat treats out. Pepper was good at hanging back but did gobble up the treats the cat left behind.

Pepper sure did like the treats—she liked any treats, really. Since they were made with the finest ingredients and no by-products, he was welcome to eat them, as was any human. I'd just figured the salmon in them would entice the little kitten, and I was right.

"What's her name?" Debbie Cane, my sister-in-law, was bent down next to my nephew, Tim, who we used to call Timmy until he asked us to do otherwise and who had no fear of being scratched.

As soon as they'd walked into the coffee shop, Tim had grabbed the snoozing kitten from the top of the cat tree and snuggled her.

"Oh, Mom, can we keep her?" Tim asked.

"I don't think so. We already have our hands full." Debbie was a single mom who'd already gotten a pet from me and juggled a career with being a mom.

"I think this kitten likes one-on-one and not more pets." I made the comment to help Debbie out, knowing all the begging my nephew would be doing. "Let me grab you a coffee."

Debbie pushed back her long amber-colored curls and looked at me. "Thank you," she whispered.

"But you can play with her while you're here," I told Tim and walked away to finish sweeping up from the lunch crowd and grabbing Debbie's coffee. "People sure do miss their mouths." I made the observation with a snicker and used the broom to sweep up all the crumbs.

"I don't know how you do it with a smile on your face all day. Have you found anyone to take the afternoon shifts?" Debbie asked and headed over to the tea station, where she liked to get a nice hot steeped tea, her usual.

"I did, and think she'll be here any minute." I could hear Bunny getting her stuff together from behind me since it was past her time to get off work. She'd been really good about helping me out in the afternoons.

"The Bean Hive." Bunny jerked the phone receiver off its hook on the wall as it rang as she headed past it.

It took me by surprise because the landline phone rarely rang.

"Wow." Debbie's mouth formed an *O*. "I've not heard an actual telephone ring in a long time."

"What was that?" Tim asked with a snarled nose.

"That's what you call a telephone, from when I was a little girl." Debbie reached over and ruffled his hair. He jerked away and swatted at her, jumping to his feet and handing her the kitten.

"Can I go outside on the boardwalk?" Tim asked.

He used to love coming in here and hanging out with me for the day, but as he'd gotten older, he didn't care as much for hanging out in the coffeehouse listening to all the gossip.

Debbie gave him parameters. "You stay right in front of the coffeehouse, mister. Don't make me worry about where you might wander off. You hear me, Timothy?"

"Yes. I hear you," he mocked and hurried out the door, slamming it behind him.

"I tell you—he's going to be the death of me." Debbie shook her head. "That's why I have to come in here and get some sort of afternoon pick-me-up on my day off. He is constantly go, go, go now that he's old enough to be involved in sports. And don't get me started on those video games."

"It wouldn't happen if you didn't buy them for him," Bunny butted in and pushed the bobby pins up in her hair to catch the edge of her pillbox hat. She looked at me. "Camey Montgomery is on the phone for you."

"What does she want?" I wondered. "Why didn't she call my cell?"

I patted the pockets of my apron and realized it wasn't in there.

"Mm-hmm, she did." Bunny's eyes drew down to the empty pockets. "That's why she called this phone."

The bell chimed over the door and in walked a young woman with blond hair in a pixie cut, who was as thin as a rail and wearing a top that looked like it'd been hacked off midway with a saw.

"I'm out of here." Bunny waved her fingers in the air. "I'll see you next week."

"Have a great time," I called out to her as I noticed the young girl was looking around for someone. "Don't do anything I wouldn't do."

"Oh, we will!" Bunny chuckled.

"Can I help you find someone?" I asked the young woman.

"I'm looking for Roxanne Bloom." She stopped walking, shifted her hip to the side, and folded her arms across her bare midriff.

"I'm Roxanne. Can I help you?" I asked and wondered if she felt the slightest chill since it wasn't warm enough to go without a light coat, much less with half of a shirt.

"I'm Birdie Bebe. My grandmother sent me down here to talk to you." She gave me an I-don't-care-about-nothing attitude.

"Chirp, chirp," Bunny called before she opened the door. "Don't forgot about the phone call, and Timmy is climbing on the rail."

"My goodness. That kid!" Debbie shoved the kitten into Birdie's hands before she darted out the door with Bunny right behind her, leaving me with Birdie.

"Well. Let's talk." I heaved a big ole sigh that would blow out a candle and wondered how on earth I was going to tell Loretta that Birdie wasn't going to work out. "You have a seat with my kitten friend, and I'll be right back after I take this phone call."

She took to the kitten, which made me feel somewhat better about the poor girl. Not that she looked like she had anything wrong with her, but for one thing, if she was here for the job, she should've dressed better or at least in a whole shirt. Secondly, she had an attitude that wasn't fit for the kitten, much less for customers.

"Hey, Camey, what's up?" I asked and laid the phone between my shoulder and my ear. The long cord stretched to the back, behind the counter, where I took the opportunity to clean up where Bunny had left off. I started two fresh new pots of coffee and noticed the jar of special-blend beans was already empty.

I made myself a quick mental note to go and grab some after I got off the phone with Camey and shooed Birdie back to Loretta's nest. I didn't want to be in the Southern Women's Club that badly.

"We've got a few guests staying here for the opening of Crissy's new resort, and I'm already out of coffee and those thumbprint cookies you made. Can you possibly run some down? I'd send Walker, but he's gone to take Amelia to the doctor. She's been running a fever for a couple of days, and well, I'm just shorthanded this afternoon." Camey sounded like she was in worse shape than me.

"I'm so sorry she's sick. Do you know what it is?" I asked and watched Pepper wake up from his nap. He looked around, and when he noticed Birdie sitting in the chair, he got up, stretched, and trotted over.

"She's got the sniffles. I think it's a winter cold, but you know Walker. Anytime our granddaughter has the slightest ache, he takes her to the doctor." Camey laughed.

"Better safe than sorry. Does that mean you aren't coming to book club?" I asked.

"I was, but now that I have to work since Walker will be with Amelia, I guess I've got to skip. That's another thing. Can you let the gals know I won't be there?" The favors kept coming, and I didn't mind, but I, too, was having my own issues.

A couple of customers came in the door and walked up to the glass counter. Birdie seemed to notice them. She had the kitten in her lap and was scratching Pepper's head with her other hand.

"Of course. I'll tell Leslie you won't be there, but there's no way I'm going to be able to bring you any coffee or thumbprint cookies. Bunny has already left for her weekend trip to visit Floyd's family, and I don't have any more afternoon staff since it's the ending semester for my seniors and they are taking those ACT classes." I looked up when I heard Birdie scoot her chair away from the table. I continued to talk and watch her. "I'm going to have to close early for book club."

"Ahem." One of the customers cleared her throat in a way that told me she was ready and waiting.

"Camey, hold on a sec," I told her, ready to move the phone from my shoulder when Birdie came around the back of the counter, took Bunny's apron off the coat-tree, and put it on, tying it snug around her midriff and covering up the bare skin.

"I've got it," she said with an air of confidence. "And you can take whatever it is they needed on the phone. I could handle this place with my eyes closed."

Maybe a little too much confidence.

"Camey, it looks like I can run the coffee and thumbprints down there now." I watched Birdie go from ugly duckling—by attitude, not looks—to a lovely swan as she rolled her shoulders back, put on a smile, and actually looked like she wanted to be here. That was definitely not the same young girl who'd walked in the door.

"I'll be with you right after I wash my hands." Birdie used the hand sink behind the counter and quickly dried them. "Did you see today's specials? The New Year Blend is amazing. As you can see, the canister is already empty, which means we are on our last little bit of the day, and there's still a few hours before we close. So you better get it if you're thinking about it."

The customers looked at each other and nodded.

"Great. Extra-large?" Birdie was up selling them, something Bunny would never do. "What about a few orange-and-raspberry scones to go with it? From what I understand, the palate delights in the tartness of this particular scone coupled with the bold taste of the New Year Blend."

"I was going to go with the chocolate chip muffin, but I think I'll take your suggestion." The customer smiled. "Thank you. You're so knowledgeable."

"I try. I love anything coffee and sweets. That's why I work here. And because I make a couple of dollars over minimum wage." Birdie looked at me. "Right, Roxanne?"

"Roxy," I told her. "My friends call me Roxy."

CHAPTER FOUR

"Wait." Aunt Maxi was all situated in the car with Pepper right on top of her lap as we headed the few minutes back to the boardwalk where the book club was meeting at Crooked Cat. "She just took right over?"

I'd told her about my afternoon with Birdie Bebe and how she was a natural at not only running the coffeehouse but with people.

"I don't get it. Granted, at first she wasn't very pleasant, and I can't say I like her choice of clothing, but we do have the apron and a shirt, so that will resolve that issue. When she got there, I took a call from Camey, who said she needed refills for the hospitality suite due to all the guests checking in for Crissy's spa. Birdie saw I needed some help, and literally, she jumped right up. You should've seen her up-selling all the customers." I shook my head, leaving out the part about how Birdie had swindled me for more than minimum wage.

We drove past Central Park, which was located in the middle of downtown Honey Springs. It was the epicenter of town and where most of the festivals took place during the year. From the looks of it, the Beautification Committee was already getting ready to start the initial process of setting up the annual Honey Festival that took place during the spring.

It was a great venue for a lot of events with the gorgeous gazebo in the middle, and by the time the Honey Festival rolled around, all the carriage lights that dotted the downtown sidewalks around Central Park would be accompanied by the specially made banners for the festival.

Those, along with the vibrant daffodils that would be popping out of the soil around the park, made the downtown area come alive and welcomed so many tourists, which was what little shops like the Bean Hive thrived on.

"Honestly..." I drummed my fingers on the steering wheel, excited about what I was going to say. "If Birdie keeps up-selling like she did today, I won't have to rely on the money the festivals bring in to keep us afloat."

"Is the coffeehouse in trouble?" Aunt Maxi looked at me with big eyes.

"No. I was just thinking how Patrick pours over the Bean Hive numbers, and since we are a tourist town, we do rely on the good festivals to keep open all year around. Not like a big city coffeehouse where there's never a down season."

"She's nothing like Low-retta?" Aunt Maxi said Loretta's name in the slow Southern drawl.

"I've not really gotten to know her well, but I do plan on getting the down-low on what is really going on with her." I couldn't help but wonder if Birdie just needed a little guidance, and maybe I was someone who could help her.

"Don't let her steal you blind like she did from the past employer." Aunt Maxi groaned.

"From what I understand from Loretta, Birdie's lived in a bigger city, but I've yet to really get any sort of details from Birdie herself." I was actually looking forward to getting to know the young woman.

From the little time that I'd gotten to talk with her and practically throw the extra set of keys for the Bean Hive at her so she could close up, I could tell she was like that chocolate topping that hardened over ice cream once it was poured on—hard on the outside but soft on the inside.

I bet Birdie was like that, but for now, her secret would be safe with me. After all, I did understand teenage girls somewhat since I'd been around them at the coffeehouse for the last couple of years. The Bean Hive had become a big hangout before school for them to grab their shots of caffeine, and after school, they lingered by the fire to catch up on what their friends had been doing all day at school or the latest gossip.

"I'm just sayin', that's all." Aunt Maxi shrugged. "Say, that guy that came into the coffeehouse, the one allergic to cats—"

"Don't remind me." I didn't want to think about what type of things he was going to write in his article. I was just going to assume he didn't even mention me at all.

"He and his wife rented my little cottage next to my house." My brows winged up as my mind processed what she'd just said.

"They did?" I questioned and kept my eyes on the road for the short drive back to the boardwalk. "Really? I thought he mentioned something about having a room at the Cocoon Hotel. Maybe I didn't hear correctly when he mentioned it to Crissy."

"I got his deposit, and he even gave me extra money to have it stocked with some vegetables and in-season fruits. I reckon I'll be going to see Jean Hill." Aunt Maxi unbuckled her seat belt as we pulled in to the parking lot.

I put the car in park and reached around to the back seat to get my book and purse.

"I guess we're going to find out what happened from Crissy." Aunt Maxi opened the door, and before I could even get out of the car, she was already walking up the ramp to the boardwalk.

My cell rang just as I slammed the car door and went to hit the lock button on my key fob.

"Hey there." I was happy to find out it was Patrick. "Did you get Pepper?"

"Of course I did. Who's the new girl?" he asked.

"I'm curious to see what you think about her." Patrick literally had become the love my life when I was a teenager and visited Aunt Maxi. We ended up kind of being boyfriend and girlfriend, only it was difficult when I was with my parents during the school year, and when I thought I would stay in Honey Springs forever after high school, we'd had a huge disagreement. It was then that I'd decided to go off to college, go to law school, get married, and open a law practice with Kirk, my first husband.

Luckily, Kirk and I didn't have children, and I'm not sure Kirk even realized he'd had a wife, but that was a different story for another time. Needless to say, when I came back to Honey Springs, a little older and much wiser, I recognized Patrick was still the man for me. Thank the Lord I did.

"She's nice. Different, but nice. Sassy really liked her," he said. Patrick and I both knew that our dogs were great judges of character. "She didn't have much to say, but I did watch her get into a little argument with some guy."

"Some guy?" I asked. "Anyone we know? And he asked for the special blend?" I wondered if it was Tom Foster but knew he didn't have a girlfriend.

"He said he was there earlier, but this time, he took some Benadryl or something weird like that."

"Oh. I bet it was Tom Foster and his wife. They are here for the opening of the resort, and he works for the *Healthy Women's Magazine*. He said he might do an article on the coffee shop, but he is highly allergic to cats, which was probably why he mentioned the Benadryl. I'm actually surprised he came back." There was no way I'd come back somewhere if I'd gotten big red welts like that.

"Well, your new girl told him she just didn't want to make any of the new blend because it would require her to clean up since it was closing time and yada yada."

"Oh no." I groaned and stopped shy of the ramp to walk onto the boardwalk near the Watershed Restaurant.

"What?" There was some reservation in his tone.

"The new girl, she's Loretta Bebe's granddaughter." I let out a big sigh and then sucked in a deep breath, which gave me a brilliant idea. "But he's staying at Aunt Maxi's cottage, so I can literally have coffee delivered to him every morning he's here to make up for it."

"Nope. He's staying at the Cocoon Hotel, because his wife said she'd tried your thumbprint cookies at the hotel. I told him who I was and that we'd have him an entire pot of the New Year Blend delivered to Camey in the morning." Patrick knew exactly how to make customers happy.

"He told you he was staying at the Cocoon Hotel?" I questioned and really hoped Camey was able to come to book club tonight because I felt like I was going crazy.

"Yep, but he still wasn't happy. And Loretta is a grandmother?" Patrick sounded exactly as surprised as I was when she'd first mentioned it. "When did that happen?"

"I guess about seventeen years ago." I'd yet to tell Patrick about Birdie's history and her being a recovering addict, and I had no idea what she'd been addicted to, but I knew he wouldn't be very happy. I didn't even want to imagine what he was going to say when I told him she'd tried to poison her teacher.

Not that he didn't believe in second—or apparently in Birdie's case, several

—chances in life, but leaving her alone there the first night without any training and only Loretta's word wouldn't sit well with him.

Patrick owned and ran Cane Construction, a family business that was run very smoothly. He was always telling me how they did things in the business department, and it sounded great. No matter how many times I tried to tell him construction and the food industry were complete opposites, he still believed businesses were businesses and should be run as such.

Not me.

I was delivering more than food and business. My coffee delivered an experience from the time a customer walked through the doors of the Bean Hive until they threw away their cup. I'd made sure to build a warm and cozy environment with the interior layout—the comfy couches near the fireplace, the strategically placed stools up along the front window's bar that looked out at Lake Honey Springs, the self-serve tea and coffee bar for convenience, as well as the décor that'd come from several shops around Honey Springs and the finishing touches on the homemade pastries made from ingredients from the local small businesses.

The Bean Hive was an emotional experience you just couldn't get when you only took in the bottom dollar like Cane Construction's business plan did.

"I remember when her son left Honey Springs, but I completely forgot all about him until now." Patrick blinked several times. "Huh. When did you interview her?" he asked.

"Um..." I hesitated and closed one eye before I said, "About five hours ago."

"Roxanne, you know that you can't let someone new take over the coffee shop alone." He was talking, but I heard someone call my name.

"Roxy, come on. We are starting." Leslie Roarke, the owner of the Crooked Cat, had peeked her head out of the bookstore door and gestured me in.

"Honey, I have to go to book club now. We can talk when I get home. Love you." I hit the red dot on my phone screen to end the call before he could protest. "I'm coming," I told Leslie and put the phone back into my purse.

I had very fond memories of the Crooked Cat bookstore. When I was a child and came to Honey Springs for the summer, Aunt Maxi would bring me here. Sometimes, I'd get so wrapped up in the books, Aunt Maxi would spend almost an hour looking around the store for me. She would always find me in the display window, curled up in the sunlight with a book.

Several times, Alexis Roarke, Leslie's mother and the original owner who had since passed away, would talk Aunt Maxi into letting me hang out with her, which took me off Aunt Maxi's hands for a much-needed break for the both of us.

It was a very fond memory. I was delighted Leslie had taken over the bookstore and not sold it or let the building on the boardwalk go vacant. Every town needed a bookstore, and it was located in the perfect spot too.

A lot of the time, tourists would buy a book and wander down to the Bean Hive to enjoy a cup of coffee while reading. It was a wonderful sight to see, and naturally, we had our book club after-hours since Leslie was now in the club.

"Sorry about that." I greeted the women who had formed a circle of chairs in the middle of the banned books section, which happened to be my favorite section in the entire shop.

Other than Leslie Roarke, I was happy to see Ida Combs, the clerk from the courthouse; Kayla Noro from the Bee Farm; Camey Montgomery; Morgan Keys; Fiona Rosone; and my mom, Penny Bloom, who were among those who had all joined us for our book discussion. Only I knew it wasn't the book we were going to talk about. They didn't have any interest in that. They only wanted to gossip about Crissy Lane's new adventure.

"I still can't get over how quickly it went up without me even noticing all of it." Literally, the view of the island was right across from the coffeehouse.

"You did take some time off." My mom jogged my memory. "Plus you and Patrick had gone on the week-long vacation. Not to mention your hours are much shorter during the winter months."

"And you kept your nose in the addition where the new roaster is located and that doesn't have a lot of windows." Aunt Maxi was right. Since we'd bought the building next door and the installation of the new roastery I'd been busy creating and testing and redoing all the newest blends coming to the coffeehouse.

"I guess you're right." It was true, I didn't pay too much attention to what was going on around me when I was mixing and creating all the beans.

"Maxine was just telling us how you hired Low-retta Bebe's granddaughter with the sordid past." Kayla Noro looked around the group, but I gave Aunt Maxi a good, hard stare.

I knew better than to tell her anything.

"What? Was it a secret?" Aunt Maxi stared right back at me. "You think these ladies won't be in the Bean Hive over the course of the next week and see your new help? They might's well know who she is going in instead of gossiping about it while they are there."

As much as I wanted to have a good comeback for Aunt Maxi, she was right. I could only imagine what they'd all say if they did come in and get hit right in the face with the young lady, since we knew pretty much every child in Honey Springs.

"Honey." My mom came up and put her arm around me. "She's just worried about you, and you are, too, or you wouldn't've told her. Now, why don't you sit down before we get started and tell us all about this granddaughter."

"You know." Morgan Keys, the owner of Walk in the Bark, pushed her side bangs even further off to the side. "I forgot all about Loretta's son. He left here so long ago, and he never comes back."

"Come to think of it…" Fiona Rosone had to take her stab at the situation. She uncorked a few of the bottles of wine she'd brought from the Watershed, the restaurant where she was a waitress and sometimes bartended. She began to fill the flutes on the card table, which was set up with all sorts of chocolate candies and a tray of strawberries.

I guess it was her idea of the perfect snack, because she was in charge of the book we'd read, and that meant she was in charge of the food. We'd read a romance, which was synonymous with wine, chocolate, and strawberries.

"I did overhear Loretta mention something about her son coming home or sending someone home." Fiona continued her train of thought and put the wine bottle down after she had poured some in all the glasses. "We can let that breathe while we discuss the book. *A Scoundrel for a Lover*." She giggled, wiggling her shoulders back to her chair before eased down ever so seductively.

We all laughed.

"Did she say why Elliot sent Birdie here? He couldn't even stand Loretta and her nosiness from what I recall. Even sent the sheriff after Loretta once when Loretta whopped him with a fly swatter," Gloria Dei said and nodded and pointed her book in the air. She knew all about who and what was going on down at Sheriff Spencer Shepard's office since she'd worked there forever.

I was shocked she'd even mentioned the calls to the sheriff's department, because she and Loretta were part of the Women's Club and on the church's Baptist Committee. I guess I shouldn't've been so surprised. Their telephone prayer chain was really just a cover-up for gossip. They weren't fooling anyone.

This group of women made me smile. We were all of various generations with different backgrounds yet had a lot in common—books and coffee, a perfect combination if you asked me. I fit right in, and I wondered to myself why on earth I had taken Loretta Bebe's deal.

A little regret settled into my bones. Maybe Birdie would still be at the coffeehouse, and I could just let her know I was sorry but it wasn't working out.

"I don't know." Joanne Stone, Honey Springs's librarian, opened her book and rested it in her lap. "Elliot is always calling and putting books on hold for Loretta. Things about parenting an adolescent teen, teen drug problems, and other issues like that. Loretta never picks them up. I think Elliot has been trying to prepare Loretta for months. Now she's pawning her off on you."

"I don't think it's pawning her off." It sounded horrible, and now my feelings were leaning toward keeping Birdie. She obviously needed someone in her corner to champion her.

"She seemed like a sweet young woman." Kayla spoke up. "She came over this morning to pick up some honey for Loretta. I didn't get to really talk to her much. I met her at the boat dock, and she didn't even get out of the boat. Big Bib pulled up, and I handed her the honey, and she said thank you, and off they went."

Poor thing. I was willing to give her a chance until she proved me wrong. Not much differently than her, I also had run to Honey Springs to get a better life. I was also thirty years old when I came here. Maybe, just maybe, she'd get a leg up on her future by moving here now.

"I guess we'll just have to wait and see. If it weren't for Birdie, I'd not be able to go to the grand opening of Bee Happy Resort." I put a positive spin on it.

"Speaking of Bee Happy, did you know Crissy has all sorts of hocus pocus stuff going on over there?" Gloria Dei asked. Instead of discussing the hot and heavy action in the romance book, she wanted to discuss all the strange things Crissy was having at the grand opening of her spa.

"Who on earth ever heard of meditation in a circle under a hot tent?" Joanne asked, nudging Gloria from her chair.

"It's really a good thing to cleanse the soul and your pours." Fiona spoke up, and she was young, so she understood, like I did, the reason Crissy wanted to bring a new place like Bee Happy to Honey Springs.

"There's honestly nothing wrong with yoga, meditation, and any sort of soul-searching activities if you're into that sort of thing." It actually sounded really nice to me. Anything to help alleviate stress always seemed like a good idea.

"I agree, but when you pair it with some of that out-of-this-world stuff she's promising, then I'm not sure it will go over very well with, well, you know—" Morgan Keys's head bobbled on her shoulders before she whispered— "the church."

"The church is against yoga?" I laughed.

"I said it's not yoga. It's all that 'awakening to your highest potential' talk and metaphysical classes." Morgan sat back in her chair and folded her arms. Her brows ticked up then slowly fell back down.

"Don't forget hydrocolonic cleanses." Joanne snickered.

"Hydro-what cleanses?" Aunt Maxi asked and sat up a little taller like she was thinking on the "colon" part. "Is it what it sounds like?"

"Yep." My mom's head drew up, and then she gave a pointed nod before she pinched her lips together.

"You mean to tell me that people want to have it cleansed?" Aunt Maxi's contorted face made me laugh. "I was throwing my hands in the air in a big old hallelujah when Dr. Kels told me I didn't need to have another one of those in my life. Why would someone want to do that?"

"Voluntarily too." Joanne laughed.

"That just don't seem right." Aunt Maxi couldn't wrap her head around this cleansing concept that'd been around a while, just not in Honey Springs.

"What is 'transformation breath work'?" Kayla Noro had a brochure I'd yet to see.

"Can I see that?" I asked, and Kayla passed the brochure around the chair circle to me. "She's even got massages and farm-to-table organic food. No wonder she didn't want my coffee and sweet treats."

"Kombucha. Whatever that is." Aunt Maxi's voice held sarcasm.

"Honestly, this stuff has been around a long time. Crissy is just ahead of the times here, and good for her. I bet she's really got a neat setup out there." We all looked over at Kayla.

"Don't even ask me to tell you. She's been so secretive on that side of the island that she didn't let Andrew trim any of the vegetation for the winter. He's beside himself about what it might do for the bee population." Kayla and Andrew had seen somewhat of a decline in their business about two years ago.

The community had come together to help them get out of the red, but Andrew said he never wanted to be that way again. He'd ended up taking a few acres off the backside of the Bee Farm, which was located on its own little island in the middle of Lake Honey Springs.

"It's the craziest thing you ever saw." Kayla hugged the romance novel to her chest as though she were protecting a secret.

I looked around to see if anyone else caught her body language. I didn't notice anyone, but I was actually great at reading body language since I was a former court lawyer. Even though I didn't have an actual law firm today, I still kept my license in case friends and family needed my services.

Who knew I'd pay all that money to go to law school just so I could open up a coffeehouse and do wills or financial trusts on the side?

Regardless, the formal training and being thrown into a courtroom really did give me a good sense of people and how they reacted to certain situations or questions, and Kayla Noro had my body language–reading skills on high alert.

"Where on earth did Crissy get the money to buy the land from y'all?" I asked.

"You know, I asked her the same thing after she came in and got the paper I drew up." My mama crossed her leg and shook her foot.

"Kayla?" I shifted my focus back to her.

She wiggled around in her seat and curled her leg up under her, sitting on her foot.

"That's all Andrew's dealings." She pulled the book from her chest and held it up. "I think we need to get to this amazing book Fiona picked before we all have to get home. After all, it's a work day for most of us tomorrow."

Kayla was awfully quiet for the discussion of the book, which made me even more suspicious that something odd was going on, especially since she'd wanted to start the discussion first.

There was no doubt she didn't want to discuss anything to do with Bee Happy or Crissy's business adventure, making me even more interested in snooping around. Not that I felt anything illegal was going on. It was that little hint of lawyer in me that always kept my curiosity up, and I had to research it. It was something I just couldn't turn off, even if I didn't practice on a regular basis. It was an ingrained, almost innate quality that I'd grown to love and embrace.

It was actually what had made me a great lawyer.

"I'm so glad you made it," I said to Camey Montgomery. "I need to ask you about one of your guests."

"Who?" Camey asked before she put the flute up to her lips and took a sip of the wine. Her lashes were so long that every time she blinked, they'd brush against the tips of her thick bangs hanging perfectly across her brows.

"Tom Foster. He's a reporter for the *Healthy Women's Magazine*. His wife is in town for Crissy's resort, and I was hoping Crissy was here so I could ask her about him. I saw her car outside." I picked up a glass of wine.

"I don't have a Tom Foster staying at the hotel, but if you do talk to him, tell him I would desperately love to be in his magazine." She pushed back her scarlet hair.

"Strange. He told Crissy and Patrick he was staying there, but he also rented a cottage from Aunt Maxi." I took a drink. "I know it's none of my business, but I'm still curious."

"Are you sure it's the same person?" she asked.

"Pretty sure, but not entirely sure." I laughed. "Does that make sense?"

"No. Not at all." She smiled. "I'll double-check and let you know in the morning, but I've got to hurry back to the hotel. I told Walker I was just going to pop in for one drink since it's cocktail book club."

"How is Amelia?" I asked.

"She's got bronchitis. Poor little girl. And we are making sure we extra-spoil her." Camey made a wonderful grandparent to Amelia and an excellent wife to Walker. I was so glad she was happy.

"Tell her I'll send her a special treat down tomorrow." I knew exactly what she'd want and was excited to get to the coffeehouse bright and early to make it.

"You do spoil her, Roxy." Camey put her hand on my arm. "I'll send up

Walker to grab the coffee carafes for the morning since you're short-staffed. What time do you think I should send him up?"

"I'll be there around five or five thirty at the latest. I told Birdie to get the pots ready, and she said she would, so I just have to flip on the switches." Though Birdie had a lot of baggage from her seventeen years on this earth, she did take my instructions to heart. Maybe I needed to talk to her about customers being right, even if Tom was a little bit of a jerk.

"I was surprised to see you were open so late," Camey said.

"Late? We closed at the normal time." It was the winter-hours schedule we were on, and the last call for special drinks was at four thirty with the doors locked by five.

This weird seasonal time between winter and spring was always slow for the coffeehouse, and not many customers came in when it was dark before five thirty. My closing hours changed with the seasons, so soon, I'd be open until eight p.m.

"Oh." Camey blinked a few times. "I thought I saw some lights on when I passed to come down. When you said you'd left to run a few errands and pick up Maxi, I figured you'd already started your extended hours even though it's a tad bit early."

"No. Birdie should've closed up, and Patrick said he saw her, so maybe she left a light on." I thought I'd better run down there after book club and make sure the lights were off and the doors were locked before I took Aunt Maxi and myself home.

"Who knows what I saw?" Camey smiled. "I'll see you at the grand opening tomorrow?"

"Yes. I'd not let Crissy down for the world." Even though I did have my reservations about Birdie, I was grateful she was there. Maybe she just needed a little polishing, and I was in no position to try to spit clean the poor girl like a good piece of fine silver. "Don't you think it's odd how Kayla acted when I asked her about who helped Crissy buy the land?"

"I noticed that too." Camey gasped and grabbed my forearm, squeezing as her eyes got bigger. "I was going to say something to you about it in the morning when you bring down the items for the hospitality room, but now that you brought it up..."

Our conversation was interrupted as a few of the book club members were going home, which made it a perfect timing for us to escape to make sure the lights of the coffeehouse were turned off and make sure Birdie had done the checklist.

"I'm going to hitch a ride with Penny," Aunt Maxi told me, making a few of us stop in our tracks since Mom and Aunt Maxi weren't exactly always on the same page.

It involved a long history with my dad, who was the blood relative to Aunt Maxi, bringing me here during the summers. My mama wasn't a big fan of Honey Springs or Aunt Maxi. She never came with us, and when I begged to stay the first summer I was here, my mama about killed my dad when he didn't bring me home. My mama held that against my father even after his death.

The repair of Mom and Aunt Maxi's relationship was seen here and there, one of those moments being now.

"Sure. I'm going to go check out the coffeehouse, then." I gave her and Mom a hug.

"Then I'll stay." Aunt Maxi looked at Mom. "I don't want you going down there alone. You never know what kind of trouble is lurking in the darkness, especially now that we've got a criminal for an employee."

"We?" I rolled my eyes, glad Camey decided to speak up before I got into an argument with Aunt Maxi.

"I'll walk with her." Camey smiled and tugged her purse strap up on her shoulder.

"That settles it. Let's go," Mama said to Aunt Maxi. Mama gave me a sympathetic look that told me she understood where I was coming from when it concerned Birdie and to let Aunt Maxi be. Both of us knew Aunt Maxi was set in her ways, and there was no way she was going to change.

Both of them told me they'd see me in the morning.

"Do you need any help cleaning up?" I asked Leslie and took a quick stroll over to the newly released books section. I was always drawn to the cozy mysteries and noticed a new series about a campground in Kentucky.

"Nope. I've got some inventory to put on the shelves, so you two can go on." She glanced around. "Besides, there's not much to clean up but empty bottles of wine."

"Yeah, I guess we were a little thirsty," Camey joked. "You ready? I've been gone long enough. I bet Walker needs a break. Amelia is sick."

"Oh no." Leslie held up the palm of her hand. "Wait right here. I got this amazing new coloring-book-and-colored-pencil set in today. I was holding one back for her because I'd love it if she could color a few and let me hang them in the shop for display."

"She'd love that." Camey held her hands to her heart. "Thank you, Leslie."

"Be sure to lock the door," I reminded her even though it wasn't too terribly late. It was late enough that none of the shops were open, and it was already dark, though the daylight savings time change was on the horizon.

"I will. Hold on—let me get Amelia's present." Leslie hurried back to the storage room that also doubled as the Crooked Cat office, emerging with the gift for Amelia in a Crooked Cat bag.

"Tell her I hope she feels better." Leslie gave the gift to Camey and followed us to the door. She waved us off into the dark, and the sound of her locking the dead bolt echoed into the night, waking up my senses.

The sound of the breeze flitting across Lake Honey Springs sent an eerie noise into the dark night that echoed off all the trees along the banks. You could hear the lapping of the waves around the posts of the boardwalk. The lamppost along the boardwalk was a nice touch that added to the cozy feel of our community and the spectacular ambiance of the moonlight hanging over head.

The stars were showing off, and it was a much-welcomed sight after the long and gloomy winter we'd had. Some of the trees would be in full springtime bloom with their radiant lime-green leaves. The bluegrass was already showing a hint of the blue undertone fed by all the limestone cliffs around the lake.

"Back to Crissy," Camey started off, bringing me out of my senses. "She didn't make that much money doing nails and hair at Honey Comb Salon and Spa. Let's face it, Alice Dee Spicer isn't that kind with her money." She was referring to the owner of the only salon in Honey Springs, where Crissy worked.

"I know Crissy pays her a rental fee for the space, and I guess she could've been saving her tips and money for the new spa." I wanted to give Crissy the benefit of the doubt even though I knew there was no way she made enough money to open such a fancy spa.

Slowly, we walked down the middle of the boardwalk where the Bean Hive was located. It was a perfect spot for tourists. Many times, they'd stop after they shopped at the boutiques before my coffeehouse and enjoy a snack before they strolled to the rest of the shops. Plus, the pier was directly in front of my shop, and many people loved to fish from it. I'd been known to make delicious treats that fisherman loved to bait the fish with. Even our scaly friends loved what I had to offer.

"I guess we won't know until we show up tomorrow," Camey said and stopped in front of the Bean Hive. "It looks like it's all closed up now."

"Yeah. Sure does." I put my hand above my brows and looked through the dark window. "Even the new kitten is snuggled up on the top platform of the cat tree, so I'll just head on home."

"Okay. I'll see you in the morning. Do you want to take the ferry over at the same time?" Camey was making plans for us to get over to the island by way of the marina's only ferry ride.

"Yep, if Birdie comes back in the morning like she's supposed to." I hugged Camey goodbye.

"Loretta will have her hide if she doesn't."

"Very true. See you tomorrow." I turned back toward the bookshop to walk to the parking lot but stopped briefly when I heard a noise coming from the pier.

I gulped, and my heart began to race. I wasn't sure why. I'd stood here many times before, even later in the evening, but tonight, there was something not sitting well with my soul.

CHAPTER FIVE

The drive to my little cabin was a short one from the boardwalk. I longed for the warmer days where I could hop on my bicycle with Pepper nestled into the basket and pedal to work. "Soon," I sighed as my car hugged the curves of the country road that ran alongside of Lake Honey Springs. A good old-fashioned two-wheeler was a means of life around Honey Springs. Everything was knitted together so tightly that driving a car when the temperature was over fifty was almost a sin.

I'd brought the old cabin back to life when I moved here and really loved the smallness and simplicity it offered me. Patrick lived in Aunt Maxi's old house that was huge, modern, and overlooked the lake, while my little cabin was across from the lake. When we'd gotten married, Patrick expected me to move in with him since he knew I loved Aunt Maxi's old house, which he was right about—I loved it for her, not for me or the stage of life I was in.

I'd gotten really good at recognizing I didn't need stuff after my divorce. Even at my young age, I'd learned that lesson. Patrick did put up a little bit of a fight, but if he wanted to marry me, he and Sassy were going to have to move in with me and Pepper. We never regretted our little cabin-in-the-woods home.

The road between the boardwalk and my house was winding but truly just a short car ride. I could see the television's glow coming from our window when

I pulled into our driveway and parked. I peeked into the window and could see my sweet little family sleeping on the couch.

Not for long. As soon as Pepper heard my key slip into the lock, he jumped down and ran to the door, barking and scratching, waiting for me to walk through.

"Hey, babe," Patrick greeted me in a sleepy voice and rubbed his eyes as he looked over his shoulder from where he was sitting on the couch in the family room, which was connected with the combination kitchen-slash-dining-room. "How was book club?"

"Good." I patted Pepper and Sassy. "Who wants a treat?"

"I do!" Patrick laughed.

"I bet you do," I teased and stepped into the kitchen, which was directly to my right.

The cabin was literally one big square room on the bottom. The kitchen was small, with a long countertop along the left side with the stove and sink but no dishwasher and a small, two-person table on the right below a small window with a view of the wooded scenery and the lake across the street.

The family room was open to it, and I had a longer couch facing opposite the kitchen in front of our wood burning stove, a small television stand in the corner, and a small love seat for more seating. Behind the family room and kitchen, I had a larger table with more seating. A door stood off to its left and two off to the right as well as a back door that led to the back porch.

The rooms off the makeshift dining room were a second bedroom, a bathroom, and a laundry room. The steps were also tucked back there and led up to our loft bedroom-and-bathroom combination. It sounded weird to have a bathroom in the bedroom when it wasn't really a *room*, but I had a nice big claw-foot tub behind a folding-type panel I put up, so it seemed like it was off to itself.

The cabin was a great investment for when the tourists who came to Honey Springs for vacation gobbled up the rentals. It truly didn't matter what time of the year it was. People loved to come and rent cabins, though summer was the busiest.

"Do you want something?" I asked Patrick before I grabbed a water from the refrigerator.

"Nah. I'm good." He yawned, reaching his arms way above his head. He patted the couch. "Come sit with me."

I unscrewed the lid and took a drink with the Crissy situation still on my mind. I plopped down next to him and offered him the bottle, but he shook his head.

"Uh-oh." He sat up a little and looked at me with his big brown eyes. He gave a soft, tender smile that set in his chiseled jawline before he asked, "What's going on in that little head of yours?"

It was one of those questions that I wasn't sure how to answer when he asked. There were two ways he could respond. One would be that it was none of my business, or two would be that I shouldn't snoop around, which was essentially the same thing.

When I told him how I was curious to know just how Crissy Lane paid for or was financing the spa, I got both answers. "It's truly none of your business, and why should you care?" He took the water bottle from me and sat it on the coffee table before he pulled me into his arms to snuggle me. "You don't pay her bills, so you just need to be happy for her."

"I am happy for her." I took a deep inhale and got a faint whiff of his cologne, which brought a smile to my face. "I'm just curious."

"Your curiosity leads to more than just scratching a little question." He was right. Every time I stuck my big nose into something, it always uncovered something else.

"You're right." I sighed and patted Pepper, who'd jumped up on the couch to find a nice cozy space behind the crook of my bent knees. "I'm just not sure I can let it go. I mean, come on. She's got farm-to-table food—where is that coming from? She wouldn't take my offer to give her coffee."

"So that's what's got your feathers ruffled." His words made me push away from him and sit up, causing Pepper to jump down and head over to his bed next to Sassy's by the fireplace. "You're upset because someone in Honey Springs doesn't want to provide your coffee to their customers."

"No." I blinked a few times to think about what he just said. "I don't think so. It's just that it's not cheap." I pushed up off the couch and walked over to get the brochure I'd put in my purse, which was on the small table located just next to the door. "Look at this brochure. You can't tell me Crissy has been hoarding her tips and the little take-home pay she gets from the Honey Comb."

"You don't know what she makes." Patrick Cane had me fuming inside. Why couldn't he just listen and not talk?

"You're right. I don't. But I am a business owner like you, and we know what it costs to start up a business. At least I do." My eyes lowered.

"Wow. Is that a jab at me taking over my family's company?" His eyes lowered. He cocked his head to the side.

"I'm just saying that I didn't get a business handed to me. And I know Crissy didn't either. So maybe you don't know what it's like to start a business from scratch."

"I'm going to bed." Patrick got up from the couch. "You need to go to bed too. You are cranky."

"Patrick?" My jaw dropped when he walked off and up the steps to the bedroom. "Pepper? Sassy?" I questioned my had-been-loyal fur babies when they followed him up to go to sleep. "I can't believe you're acting this way."

If he thought I was going to let him go to bed without talking to me about it, he had another thing coming to him.

"I think it's great Crissy started a new business and she's able to bring more economic development to Honey Springs. I'm sad she didn't ask me to build the development, because from what I hear, it's pretty cool. She's your friend, and you should just be happy for her."

"I am happy for her. I can't have a conversation with my husband about it?" I grabbed my toothbrush.

"And the rest of the gossiping women at book club too."

Dang it. He knew me too well. So we ended it, agreeing that it was truly none of my business, but I couldn't help to think about it all night.

I had resigned myself to the idea that I'd just have to see for myself tomorrow with the hope Birdie would show up and actually work out. Who would've ever thought that Loretta Bebe had a granddaughter, much less that she'd be the one to help me out in a pinch?

CHAPTER SIX

"We better get going," I whispered to Pepper after the alarm went off at four thirty. He was snuggled in a ball between me and the edge of the bed.

I glanced over at Patrick. The alarm didn't faze him like it used to when we first got married. He didn't have to be at work until nine, lucky dog.

So I didn't disturb him. I carefully pulled back the covers, which was Pepper's signal to jump off the bed. My feet hit the floor, and a rush of cold shivered up my spine. It was going to be a chilly day—I could already feel it in my bones.

I slipped my feet into my slippers, and my mind instantly went to the to-do list I had on tap for the day.

The first thought that hit me as I headed to the potbelly stove to stoke the leftover coals from last night so it would warm up the nippy morning air, before I made it to the kitchen to pour my first cup of coffee for the day, was what sort of condition Birdie had left the coffee shop in when she closed last night.

I slightly regretted that I'd not taken the time to stop in and see when Camey and I had left book club last night, but if I was going to really give Birdie a chance, unlike some of the people I knew, then I had to have trust from the beginning. I knew that and there wasn't anything I could do now, so I simply put it out of my head and moved on to the next thing on my list.

"I guess you want to go potty?" I asked Pepper and then looked over at Sassy, who was sleeping away on the couch. She started out in our bed, but with the four of us, she'd get hot and make her way to the couch, where she could spread out.

She'd stay there until Patrick got ready for work. She was going to go to work with him, which was what she normally did. Good thing too. She wasn't very fond of kittens. She liked cats, but kittens were too playful for her and tested her limits.

With my coffee in my hand, I opened the front door and let Pepper out. He darted off the porch and into the darkness. Even though I knew he wouldn't run off, I still didn't like to leave him outside at this dark hour of the morning. Coyotes loved to hang around dusk and dawn, and Pepper would make a tasty treat for them, so I grabbed one of the blankets I kept rolled up in a basket on the front porch and curled it around me before I sat down in the rocking chair and sipped on my coffee.

This was a morning ritual I truly loved before heading off to work, where I did another morning ritual of having another cup of coffee there while looking out over the lake.

I'd heard so many times in my life that if you loved the work you did, then it wouldn't feel like work. It was definitely true for both careers I'd had.

Being a lawyer was something I thought I'd enjoy when I was younger, but it turned out that it wasn't rewarding at all. The only time it had been fulfilling was when someone here in Honey Springs needed some advice or help. That was rewarding, but the coffee shop was the best of all. I enjoyed getting up this early and going into the coffee shop to make delightful treats and drinks for everyone to enjoy. The smile and the relief a good cup of coffee put on people's faces just made my day.

"What do you think Crissy meant by not accepting my coffee?" I asked Pepper as my thoughts turned to how I could get Crissy to rethink not wanting my coffee at her fancy-shmancy resort retreat.

"We could make some of her favorite chocolate chip muffins," I told Pepper on our way back into the house, knowing that I had to get the cream cheese-topped carrot-and-raisin muffins into the oven when I got to the Bean Hive this morning.

I put the thought in the back of my mind and headed to the bathroom to get ready for the day, and before I knew it, Pepper and I were in the car heading toward the boardwalk.

"You're so cute." I reached over and patted Pepper on the head. He sat in the passenger seat like a little human with his little coat on. His leash was attached to the seat belt. I'd had a wreck before, and it taught me a good lesson—to make sure that Pepper was buckled in too.

He didn't like it at first because he loved the freedom of sticking his head out the window or at least making nose prints on the window, but like all things, he got used to it. He was so smart, though, so he would start to get antsy when he knew where we were going.

"I'll let you out in a second." I pulled into the parking lot of the boardwalk and looked down the lit path toward the Cocoon Hotel and wondered about Tom Foster. Was he or wasn't he staying at the Cocoon? It was yet another question to occupy my already curious thoughts.

After a quick release of my seat belt and Pepper's, Pepper darted out the door when I opened it. He knew exactly where to go, running toward the Bean Hive door, where I soon found him sitting when I caught up to him.

"I'm hurrying." I dug down into my purse to get the coffee shop keys so I could let us in. "Here, kitty," I called as I ran my hand up the inside wall to flip on the lights. "There you are."

The sweet little ball of black fur was snuggled on the shelf of the cat tree in a little blanket that I didn't recognize. For a second, I wondered how it'd gotten there, but Pepper got my attention, dancing back and forth between me and the counter where I knew he wanted his breakfast.

"All right," I told him but gave the kitten a quick little scratch on the head, pleased to see the little one didn't run from me. "You are needy this morning," I teased my salt-and-pepper companion when I nearly tripped over him to get behind the counter, where I opened the cabinet to retrieve a scoop of kibble for his bowl. That would keep him occupied while I traded my light jacket for an apron hanging on the coatrack and headed to the kitchen.

Both ovens were going to be required this morning, so I turned them on to preheat while I headed to the freezer to get some of the donuts, muffins, and scones I'd already made for this week's menu. I placed them on the workstation to thaw to room temperature before I popped them into the oven for a light warming. In the refrigerator were mini quiches that were ready to be baked, and once I got those in the oven, I grabbed a quick cup of coffee that'd brewed thanks to the timer for the employees in the kitchen and headed back into the coffee shop.

I sipped on my coffee and read down my checklist, which I knew by heart but still used because I loved the feeling of checking things off as I completed them. "I've already turned on the industrial coffeepots. I got the cookies out of the freezer for the Cocoon, which reminds me to ask Camey if she snooped around for me." My head jerked up when I heard a light tapping at the door.

I looked at the door when I heard someone peeking in, knowing it was way too early for a customer. Pepper started to bark and ran over to the door.

I smiled when I caught Birdie's eye then Loretta's.

"Good Lord, what does she want at this hour?" I asked Pepper under my breath with a smile on my face.

"Good morning, Roxy." Loretta's slow southern drawl told me she was gearing up to tell me something more. "I'm thrilled you hired Birdie on the spot, but being out at all hours of the night is something I will not tolerate at her age. After all, she will be starting school on Monday, and she'll need to get her beauty sleep."

While Loretta was talking, Aunt Maxi had walked in and caught the tail end of what she was saying. "Mm-hmm," Aunt Maxi quietly hummed as she sauntered past me, pulling off the scarf around her neck. "Only one thing stays open after midnight, and that's legs."

"What did you say?" Loretta glared at Aunt Maxi.

"Grandma," Birdie tried to interrupt. "Please stop," she pleaded.

"Grandmamaw, dear." Loretta even corrected her own granddaughter.

"She wants me to call her grandmamaw." Birdie rolled her eyes and peeled her sweatshirt off over her head before she went to the coatrack and hung it up in exchange for an apron.

"What's wrong with that? I don't call you 'chirp, chirp' even though that's what a bird does." Loretta sighed, rolled her shoulders back, and sucked in a deep breath. "You can imagine my shock and how hard it was for me to keep my mouth shut when my daughter-in-law told me what they'd named my granddaughter," Loretta whispered.

"I can hear you, you know." Birdie rolled her eyes again at Loretta.

"Honey, I'm sorry you got Low-retta for a granny." Amusement rested on Aunt Maxi's face. "Which means you best get a straw because that just plain sucks."

"No wonder my dad never wants to come visit." Birdie crossed her arms and huffed. "I want to go home."

"See that? Kids do not respect their elders these days, and that's why I'm here. There will be no working on Sundays. Birdie will be going to church with me and sitting in the front pew."

"Here we go again." Birdie threw her hands up in the air.

"Don't you—" Loretta jutted her finger in Birdie's direction, only Birdie had pushed through the swinging kitchen door.

Aunt Maxi dropped her hobo bag and slouched off her coat, sticking it on top of one of the tables as she followed Birdie.

"Don't you dare let Maxine Bloom talk to my granddaughter." Loretta's eyes snapped in the direction of the kitchen. "That woman never had any kids of her own, and she'll ruin what little innocence my dear sweet Birdie has left."

I smirked to myself since there was no way I was going to think out loud on any sort of matter about children. "Aunt Maxi is harmless, and honestly, she's just trying to get under your skin. But I'll talk to Birdie even though I don't have any experience with teenagers other than them working here. She really is a good young woman, and I just might have a few chemistry tricks up my own sleeve." I had a few ideas that might keep Birdie occupied with her smarts and keep her from being so mischievous.

"And what might be up your sleeves?" Loretta cocked a brow and looked at my sleeves like there was literally something about to pop out.

"Birdie obviously likes to be around coffee and here." I smiled and put my thoughts into words, which sounded pretty good. I could attribute that to being a lawyer. "Not to say that I was any shape or form of a chemistry whiz, nor did I want to be, but I did know a thing or two about cooking, baking, and roasting beans, which some would argue is a bit about the chemistry between ingredients."

As my words fell onto Loretta's ears, her shoulders dropped, her eyes softened, and her head tilted before I saw a small grin forming on the edges of her lips.

"Though the Bean Hive is a specialty coffeehouse, customers on the boardwalk love to come in and grab something to eat." I reminded Loretta how I'd come up with the cooking one item for lunch that was the offered for a week. Because we were closed on Sundays, it was easy to come into the coffee shop, flip on my music, and bulk-bake or -cook something that would last all week. "I'd love for her to join me after church on Sunday and see what her creative skills are in the kitchen and even the roastery."

Loretta didn't say anything, so I kept going.

I gestured for Loretta to look around. "The place was spotless this morning. She even did the whole closing checklist. So she is already a great employee. I say you give me a chance to talk to her, not about her actions outside of the coffee shop, but in here, and I bet you'll see a change out there." I gestured to the outside world and kept the story Patrick had told me about Tom Foster coming in last night and having a little tiff with Birdie to myself.

The young lady already had Loretta to deal with, and that was handful enough for one person. It would be my place to mention it to Birdie since I was technically now her employer.

"If you think you can get through that thick head of Birdie's, I'd be much grateful. No wonder they sent her to me. You know I didn't let Wyatt get away with all the sassy back talk." And she wondered why the boy never came home to visit his mom. "Just so we are clear, she gets no favors." She wagged her finger between me and her.

"Very." I gave her a hard nod to emphasize I understood since she had a way of carrying on about things. "I've got to get the coffee carafes down to the Cocoon now that Birdie is here."

"I guess I'll be seeing you at the grand opening of the Bee Happy Resort this afternoon?" she asked.

"Yes, if Birdie is okay to close up again by herself." I knew she'd be fine, but I could see Loretta did have a sense of pride about Birdie being pretty independent. "You do know that Birdie is very smart. She catches on quick, and she's great with customers." Maybe not so great with all the customers, like Tom Foster, but at least she was great when I saw her in action.

"I don't expect any less of her." Loretta's chin lifted as the pride settled on her face. "She takes after me. I'm a quick learner."

"Is that right?" I smiled and glanced over her shoulder when the bell dinged from a customer entering.

"Good morning," I greeted the young man coming through the door while waving goodbye to Loretta. "Welcome to the Bean Hive."

"Thank you." The young man pulled off his knit cap and rubbed his hands together. "It's a bit chilly this morning."

"It sure is. You just reminded me to start a fire." I made my way around the counter and headed straight to the fireplace. "You can go ahead and look around if you'd like something from behind the counter, or you can help yourself to our self-serve honor-system tea or coffee bar."

"Thanks." He smiled and walked along the front of the glass display case while I put one of those easy-fire starter logs in the fire place.

Birdie and Aunt Maxi were laughing when they emerged from the kitchen. Both of their arms were filled with plates of the mini quiches I'd gotten from the freezer this morning and popped into the ovens. It was nice to see her and Aunt Maxi smiling and joking.

Aunt Maxi wasn't fooling me any. She didn't have children, but she knew exactly what to do with them, and that's why I'd decided to come back to Honey Springs. Aunt Maxi was just able to communicate a point without explicitly stating the lesson to be learned.

My dreams of living in a large and bustling city were something I talked about every summer I came to the small cozy town. Aunt Maxi had a great way of reminding me what small towns had to offer, which was what I'd craved after my divorce. Looking back now and at how she was interacting with Birdie, I could see very clearly the same relationship Aunt Maxi had established with me, and there was a settling in my soul. The initial road with Birdie just might make my springtime a little bumpier than I'd anticipated, but by summer, I was sure it'd be all smooth sailing.

"Who gave the kitten the blanket?" I asked as I waited for the young man to select what to purchase.

Birdie moved around me and out from behind the counter. "I did. The kitten had moved from the cage to the small house built into the cat tree while I was doing the closing checklist and straightening a few items on the tables. She let me pet her, so I just took the blanket and put it up there so she could curl up." Birdie took something out of her apron and laid it next to the kitten. "We were super slow last night, and I noticed your recipes in the kitchen, so I made a variation of one of your dog-treat recipes for the cat."

"That's wonderful, Birdie." I was delighted to see that she'd taken the initiative to bake. "I hear you're really good in chemistry, and you know, mixing the right amount of ingredients to get a desired taste in any sort of baking and cooking is kind like chemistry?"

I felt a little elbow nudge from Aunt Maxi when she passed by me to look at the status of the industrial coffeepots. "I can see what you're doing, and I think you're doing a good job. She's a smart girl." Aunt Maxi winked and nodded, saying it low enough so that Birdie didn't hear from across the coffee shop.

"I wrote it down in my notebook if you want to see it," Birdie said with a flicker of apprehension in her voice.

"I'd love that. In fact, I'd love for you to make some for the customers, and you can have all the money from the sales."

"Are you serious?" Birdie looked at me in surprise.

"Honey, if Roxanne is one thing, she's not a big jokester, and whatever she says, she means." Aunt Maxi had taken off the industrial pots to get them ready for the Cocoon Hotel and replaced them so we could start the next round of coffee because she and I both knew the morning crowd would be bursting through the door any minute.

"Thank you." Birdie picked up the kitten, kissed her, and put her back before she headed into the kitchen. "I'll get started on them right away. Let me know if you need me out here."

"I will." I glanced at Aunt Maxi, and both of us laughed.

The bell over the door dinged again.

"Good morning," I said to the customer when she stepped inside. "Welcome to the Bean Hive. We have a self-serve coffee and tea station with the honor system for paying, or you can get anything you see on the menus."

"How adorable," the woman gushed as she looked around the coffee shop. She was probably a few years younger than me and had black hair that went down her back in one long braid. She had deep-brown eyes that were nicely framed with thick brows. Her face and spirit lit up with her smile. "Camey Montgomery told me that you'd be down there any moment with the coffee for the hospitality room, but I have to be over at Bee Happy Resort this morning so I can get ready for my demonstration."

"Demonstration? That's exciting. What are you doing for Crissy?" I asked and snapped my fingers a few times after Pepper decided to get up from his bed next to the fireplace and check out the customers.

"He's fine." The lady smiled. "I love dogs. Hey, Casper," she said to the other customer who was still walking between the display counters to see what he wanted to eat.

"Angela. How are you?" The two seemed to know one another, since they locked hands and greeted each other the French way by kissing each other's cheeks.

With a little more caffeine in me and more light filtering through the windows, I could see Casper a little better. He had short black hair, a pointy nose, and a strong jawline with a little bit of stubble that seemed to be for looks. When he turned a little to the right, he looked like a model. He was very well groomed, and by the way his sweatpants fit, he appeared to be as toned as Angela.

"I'm good. I had no idea you were coming," Angela said and put her hands together in a prayer-type pose, putting them up to her third eye and giving me a little bow. I'd seen this many times in yoga classes, though I was never big on the exercise. My mind raced too much for me to ever stay still for too long. It was possibly from too much coffee, but I didn't care. I loved it.

"I just couldn't miss all the new honey-type products they will be using and the new organic body-wrap treatment." He bowed slightly to her. "I'm guessing you're here for the enhanced listening chant?" That was something I'd never even heard of.

"Yes. I couldn't pass it up. The last time I did it was in India, and I immediately got trained. It was a very enlightened experience." The two of them talking really piqued my interest and curiosity about this new adventure for Crissy. "I'm so excited to share it with the world."

Organic body wrap? Listening chant? Who on earth had Crissy Lane become since she went to that fancy retreat in California? Plus, none of this stuff was free.

"I'm guessing you're here for some last-minute caffeine?" Casper laughed and held up one of the cups from the self-serve area.

"Yes. Kombucha only gets me so far. I've tried and tried to get completely off caffeine, but as you can see"—she lifted her hands and her brows—"I've not been able to master that technique."

Casper turned back to the counter and pointed one of the strawberry-cream donuts out to me then held up two fingers as he continued to talk to Angela.

"I am teaching drum yoga for Crissy. Only at sunrise tomorrow, though. Where are you staying?" Casper asked her.

When the bell over the door rang, all of us looked up.

Tom Foster was back. Only this time, he had red bumps all over his face.

"You probably shouldn't be in here," I said even though I hated to make anyone leave. "The kitten is still here."

"Oh, don't you worry." He waved a hand. "I took my allergy pills this morning, and no amount of hives or kittens will keep me from getting a cup of coffee."

"Are you sure?" I asked with a smile on my face in hope he was going to write a little something good about the coffee shop in the magazine.

Out of the corner of my eye, I noticed Angela and Casper had turned their heads and moved away from the counter as if they didn't want Tom to see them. It kind of reminded me of when I would see someone down the aisle at the grocery store that I didn't really want to talk to. I'd literally turn my head so they couldn't see my face and push my cart the other way so I didn't have to run into them. Angela and Casper were displaying that sort of behavior.

"I think your coffee gave me diarrhea. I had the worst cramps, but my wife, she loved it. I told her I'd get her a coffee and a treat before I head over to the Bee Happy Resort with her." His monotone voice didn't necessarily exude excitement.

"Help yourself." I suggested he go to the coffee bar and noticed he looked behind me when Birdie came out of the kitchen with a piece of paper in her hand.

"I wanted to ask about..." She looked up as Tom cleared his throat. She set the paper on the counter and walked over to him.

I gulped and kept an eye on them so they wouldn't start another argument. I was going to let Birdie try to handle this herself.

Tom didn't seem to notice Angela and Casper. Birdie and Tom spoke in a low murmur, nothing too loud, so I assumed Birdie was making peace before he quickly headed back out of the coffeehouse. I had given him complimentary strawberry-and-cream donuts in hopes they'd make up for the coffee he didn't like and he'd possibly talk about my delicious food instead of the coffee if he did end up doing an article on Honey Springs. Was it too much to hope he didn't even mention the Bean Hive at all?

"I'm staying at the Cocoon," I overheard Casper tell Angela when I went back to manning the counter while other customers filed in and ordered food.

It was hard to listen to everything they were saying but not for Aunt Maxi. She'd grabbed a cup of coffee and sat down on the couch in front of the fire with Pepper in her lap. She was taking in every word, and I would hear exactly what was going on after they left, so I tended to the customers and let Birdie do her baking in the kitchen.

"The sweets are out of the oven." Birdie popped her head out of the kitchen door to let me know the treats for the Cocoon were ready to be taken down with the coffee.

Angela and Casper carried their conversation over to the coffee bar, where they ended up doing the self-serve after all. Honestly, I'd positioned myself so I could interrupt since Crissy had been all hush-hush about the resort and what she was doing over there. She'd only said it was a big surprise and was going to let everyone see it for the first time. These two acted as if they knew her.

"How do you know Crissy?" I asked and busied myself with rearranging the various sugars and sugar substitutes on the coffee bar.

"Oh." Angela put her hands on her heart. "She's an angel. We were so lucky to meet her when she came out to my retreat a few months ago."

"And I was there doing a talk on the future of the holistic community. She was very interested in the business side," Casper said.

"And if anyone knows how to do business in a space that's a new concept to the world, Casper is the guru." Angela placed her hand on Casper's arm. "Not only is his drum yoga electrifying to the soul, but he has a knack for business plans."

"So you are Crissy's business partner?" It totally made sense for him to be the mystery person.

"Oh no." He wagged a finger. "I am a consultant and gave Crissy and her partner some advice for some big bucks. When I met Crissy in LA, I knew I had to introduce her to Angela to help fulfill her dream of opening a holistic retreat in Kentucky. The connection had to be made. After all, Angela had over four hundred attendees at the event." He was very fond of Angela and Crissy. "Angela has magical hands."

"It was meant to be." Angela sucked in a deep breath, bringing her shoulders up to her ears before they slowly fell back down as she let out a long steady breath. "Crissy is a deep soul who has some amazing ideas that we'd love to see brought to life."

"She's a wonderful person." I agreed with them but was a bit taken aback by how they were describing Crissy. I'd never known her to be so earthy. "As a business owner, I know the cost of things, and there's no way opening up a big retreat like you're talking about comes cheap."

"Not an expense was spared. That's why she's here." He gave a slight nod to Angela. "She doesn't come cheap."

"I've not heard who her business partner is." I tried not to sound too nosey, but I wanted to know. "I bet I know her."

"I have no idea. Never met them." Casper looked at Angela.

"I will say there was barely room for negotiation, and I had to send Crissy's partner a free admission to my session." Angela took a few sips of her coffee and put it back under the nozzle to fill it up again. "I guess I better get back to the hotel. I've got to get some of my things together." She placed a hand on Casper's arm. "I do hope I see you over there." Then she turned to me. "You should come to my sesh. It's the first one after the opening ceremonies. Around lunch-ish."

"Yeah. I'll try to do that." I wasn't going to make any sort of commitments to any sort of chanting anything. But I still put on that good old Southern smile and waved them out the door.

Even though Casper claimed he didn't know who Crissy's partner was, I caught the fact that whoever she was had asked for a free pass to Angela's class.

I looked up at the clock and realized I had to get the hospitality room coffee down to the Cocoon Hotel or Camey would be calling soon.

"I think I will go over to the Bee Happy Resort at lunch. Do you think you'll be okay here?" I asked Birdie as I untied my apron and hung it on the coatrack. "I need to take down the donuts and coffee to the Cocoon for the hospitality room."

"I'm leaving too." Aunt Maxi also got her things. "Will you be okay here alone?" she asked Birdie.

"I've got the kitten and Pepper. We will be just fine." Birdie was confident in her abilities, and I liked that about the young woman. When I got back, I'd be sure to ask her about where she was last night.

"See you in a minute." I grabbed the items and walked Aunt Maxi out the door, telling her goodbye as we went in opposite directions down the boardwalk.

The marina was already a hopping place. Big Bib, the owner, had a pontoon that was the only transportation over to the island, and people were already waiting on the boat to go over. I looked at each of them with their life jackets around their necks and snuggled tightly around their waists. Big Bib always played by the rules of the lake, and I was sure the police were somewhere around there in their police boat. They had a habit of stopping Big Bib once a day to make sure he was in compliance.

I tried to make out which customers were heading over to the Bee Farm and which ones were the resort-going type. A few of them had on large-brimmed beekeeper hats, and if I were a betting woman, I'd say they were going over for the freshest honey Kayla and Andrew had to offer this morning.

There were a few women who had on coats and leggings, who I would say looked to be stereotypical yoga students and figured they were probably going to the spa. Everyone on the boat appeared to be excited and sat up a little straighter when Bib took his place as the captain of the boat, revving up the engine.

With a slight acknowledgement to Bib via a quick nod of my chin, I hurried down the sidewalk that took me straight to the Cocoon.

The Cocoon Hotel was gorgeous. Camey Montgomery had turned the old mansion that had the most perfect views of the lake into a hotel and since added on to it for more guest rooms. Luckily, they didn't hurt the integrity of the two-story double porches that lay across the hotel so guests could sit and rock all day long as they enjoyed the lake.

Since it'd been an original home, Camey had kept the Kentucky bluegrass yard that flowed down into a sandy beach area that met the lake, which was perfect for swimming.

Just a year ago, I'd gotten married to Patrick on Halloween in this very hotel and had an impromptu wedding reception on that very lawn during the Halloween festival. It had literally been a surprise to everyone.

I couldn't help but pause and recall the memory. It was a magical day, even though we had to trick everyone into thinking our bride and groom outfits were costumes and not really wedding attire, no thanks to Mama and Aunt Maxi.

My mama had moved to Honey Springs, and she and Aunt Maxi had been working on their relationship. That went out the window after Patrick proposed. Each one of them had their own ideas for my wedding, neither taking into consideration what Patrick and I wanted. That was when we got the idea that Patrick would dress up as a groom and I would dress up as a bride, but in reality, we'd had it set up where we were going to get married in the hospitality room in the hotel. It went off without a hitch and was perfect. Our wedding day ended up being exactly what we wanted.

A long sigh escaped me as a chill swept across my neck and brought me back to the here and now, which meant I needed to get these industrial coffee thermoses and treats into the hotel.

"Good morning," I said to Camey when I walked into the front doors of the hotel. "How is Amelia?"

"She's so much better," Camey gushed, coming from behind the registration desk to help me. Her almond-shaped brown eyes held relief. She had her scarlet hair pulled back at the nape of her neck, and her thick bangs hung perfectly across her forehead. "Her fever broke in the middle of the night. I told Walker to just let her sleep and that she'd get up on her own, because he worries her to death." She took one of the carafes from me and walked into the room to the right, which she'd turned into the hospitality room where she served treats to her guests all day. "Every time he opens her bedroom door, she wakes up. He's not the quietest, you know."

"What man is?" I teased and shook my head.

She cleared out some space on the large credenza for me to set the industrial coffee carafes next to each other.

"Did you happen to check on that guest I asked about?" I asked her in a low tone just in case guests came in because I didn't want them to hear me.

"No. There's no one with the name you gave me." She opened the cabinet of the credenza and took out the fancy paper plates, napkins, and cups, placing them next to the treats.

"I think Patrick is confused, or maybe Tom was wrong, because a guest of yours came into the coffeehouse this morning to get what I guess would be her last cup of caffeine for the day. Angela…" I snapped my fingers. "You know, I didn't get her last name, but she has a long braid down her back."

"Yep. I do know her." Camey moved and scooted and arranged the food to make it perfect like she did everything in the hotel. "Angela Paul and her boyfriend are staying here."

"Boyfriend? Did he have brown hair, a strong jaw, and is really good looking?" I asked.

"No." She laughed as if I'd made a joke and stopped when a few guests did come in and made their way over to us.

We took a step back so they could get their coffee.

"I brought you some of these too." I took the box of donuts out of the bag and left the room to wait for her, which only took a few seconds before she met me in the lobby.

"Now, what were you saying about Angela?" she asked.

"She came into the shop, and she knew the customer already in there, but I thought they seemed to not realize each other was here, which was odd because they knew each other so well. If they were close, wouldn't they know they'd be seeing each other in Kentucky of all places?" I pondered my own question.

"Roxy, you are putting too much thought into Crissy's spa. Honestly, just come with me today and enjoy what she's offering. She's helping the economy just like me and you. No different." Camey waved to a couple of her guests as they walked out the front door.

"You're right. Though it just seems so out of Crissy's character to open such a place." I sighed.

"I recall it wasn't too long ago that you too did something that was out of your character too." Camey gave me that all-knowing grin that always reminded me that she was older than me and had lived life a lot longer, which meant she'd experienced a lot more than me.

"You're right." Life had happened to me. After law school and getting married to Kirk, my life was about work, making more money, and accumulating stuff. Now, I was simpler and only used the things I needed, so I could relate to people changing. "I still want to know who her partner is, though."

"Maybe you should just ask her about it." Camey's suggestion was silly, so I changed the subject.

"Since you suggested I go with you, I'm guessing Walker is going to take care of Amelia while you go?"

"I'm also letting him sleep in so he is well rested to take over the front desk. Everyone and their brother is going to the opening, even my staff. Amelia will be happy watching some of her television shows or playing her video games while he can sit here and read all day."

"Let me know when you're going, and maybe we can catch a ride over together," I told Camey before I headed out the door. "I've got to get back. Bunny is off, and Birdie is there alone." I waved behind me.

On the way back to the coffee shop, the sun popped out, and the rays felt so good on my face. For a moment, I closed my eyes to let the relaxation blanket me.

"Oops!" I nearly tumbled over my own feet and knocked someone else over in the process. "I'm so sorry. I had my eyes closed because of the sun." I threw my hand up over my mouth when I noticed it was Angela and she wasn't alone.

"It's fine." She laughed with her Bean Hive coffee cup still in her hands.

"I still can't get over how the hives are gone from your face." I gushed over how the spots on Tom's face had gone away.

"So, your kitten was the one who gave him the reaction?" Angela burst out laughing. Tom didn't seem to be amused by the glare he'd given her. She rested her hand on his chest. "I'm sorry. It's funny how these things happen to you when you're out of town."

His body stiffened to her touch. Slowly, she moved her hand away and cleared her throat.

He put a smile on his face and said, "I was just telling Angela about your New Year Blend."

"Were you?" I asked and didn't let him know my little secret about how good I was at reading body language. By the way the two of them were acting, I could tell that I'd interrupted something before I nearly bowled Angela over.

"He was," she said in a low tone. "But I told him I went for the house blend." She held up her coffee.

"I understand you and my employee had a little disagreement yesterday, and since my aunt owns your rental, I know exactly where to bring your morning coffee," I told him.

"There's no need to do that. All under the bridge." He was kind enough to not hold it against me. "I don't want anything to interfere with my article."

"Article?" I asked. "You've actually decided to do an article?"

"Yeah. Last night I decided to do that feature about Honey Springs, and don't think your little coffeehouse won't be mentioned." He gave me a hard look. "It was good seeing you again, Angela," he said to her before he excused himself and walked down the wood walkway that led to the marina.

His words made me gulp.

"Have you ever read his work?" Angela asked.

"No. I've heard of the magazine, though." Of course I'd seen it several times while I waited in line at the grocery store.

"He's going to crucify this place." She shrugged and turned to go down the same path to the marina.

"What?" I blinked and tried to wrap my head around such a terrible word.

"Oh yeah. All we have in this life is our reputation. Especially in this business, at least, which is my life." Angela scoffed. "Once Tom Foster ruins someone's reputation, you better go find a different career."

I stood there watching her and Tom as Big Bib greeted both of them. Tom had put his hand on the small of Angela's back as it appeared he was introducing her to Big Bib. If Tom Foster thought I was going to find a different career, he had another thing coming to him.

CHAPTER SEVEN

"'Crucify'? She said 'crucify'?" were Camey's exact words when I told her about my literal run-in with Angela and Tom Foster after I'd left the hotel this morning to go back to the coffee shop.

The wind off Lake Honey Springs had really whipped up, literally forcing the two of us to huddle up to ward off the chill, even though we were somewhat shielded in the back of the pontoon, with Big Bib standing at the wheel in front of us.

"Maybe it was you those two were talking about," Big Bib said and turned around to look at me.

"I had no idea you eavesdrop." I was a little tickled by the fact that this big burly man with his full scraggly beard and baggy overalls had a knack for listening in on people's conversations. "And I love it."

Camey snorted, shaking her head. "You're in for it now," she warned Big Bib.

"What were they saying?" I asked.

He shot me a look.

"Oh, come on. You wouldn't've said anything if you didn't want me to know."

"I will tell you that neither of them are looking forward to this fancy drink Crissy seems to be serving up." He gave me the side-eye.

"Kombucha." Camey nudged me in the ribs with her elbow.

"Yeah." Immediately, I tried to rub the pain out. "I know."

"It don't even sound good." Bib picked up his thermal mug and held it in the air. "Good old black coffee is all anyone needs." His dark eyes looked at me. "Right, Roxy?"

"Dang straight." I gave him a hard nod. "So, they were talking about my coffee?"

"Sure were. Even said something about how you seemed to over-roast your beans." His words brought me from being on cloud nine to being down in the dumps.

"Over-roast?" I gulped as the images of what Tom Foster's article might say popped into my head. *Burnt. Amateur. Leave the big beans to a big city. Small-town roastery should be left in the backwoods.* All sorts of headlines began to come to mind, leaving me with one mission when I got over to the Bee Happy Resort.

Find Tom Foster.

"Aw, don't worry about him. Burnt or not, you still make the best coffee around here." Big Bib had pulled up to the dock and patted me on the back before he leaned over me and Camey to throw the loop of the rope connected to the boat around one of the piers.

"You're right." I folded my arms over my chest and gave a hard nod. "I just might not serve him anymore of my delicious coffee."

"That's right." Bib smiled and moved to the middle of the pontoon to throw the rope there and then up front before he started to let the other passengers off.

"I wish you'd listen to Big Bib, but I know you." Camey stood up since we were the last on the boat to get off. She pushed her hair back behind her shoulders and tried to rake down her bangs the best she could since the wind from the boat ride had made a mess of them. "You will worry about this until you make Tom Foster the best cup of coffee you've ever made."

"I just want to know why he thinks that." I pushed myself up to stand and looked at the island, wondering in which direction I might find him. "I'm not opposed to learning from him if he knows some tricks and secrets."

"Learning from him?" Camey laughed and tugged on my sleeve to get off the boat. "I'd like to see that."

"Or I could just poison him before he gets a chance to write the article," I teased, shrugging and walking past her with a sly grin on my face.

"I don't think you should do that." Big Bib took my hand to help me off the edge of the front of the pontoon. "We need the Bean Hive to stay open, not close down because you'd be in jail."

"I'm a lawyer. I can find various ways to get myself off the hook." I winked and stepped off the boat, on the opposite side of where Big Bib normally dropped off guests for the Bee Farm.

"Can I interest you in a shot of kombucha?" asked a young woman with a long flowing dress and sandals on her feet.

"Aren't you freezing?" I asked her.

"Oh, no. The kombucha warms the soul." She spouted off some sort of guru language that I was certainly not getting and did not care to understand.

I was only here for the grand opening, and that was it. Nothing more, and I probably wouldn't be back. Anything I needed done to me, I could find at Touched By An Angel Spa, where you could get a simple massage and facial. *Simple.*

"No, thank you." I recalled the word "simple," which was exactly how I liked my drinks. Just black coffee. "You have mine," I told Camey when she went to try it.

I walked past Camey and the young woman, smiling to myself when I noticed the young girl had goose bumps clear up her arms and on her neck. I followed the stone path from the beach as it wound its way into the woods.

Wooden signs dotted the pathway, displaying various words like Serene, Quiet Your Mind, Bliss, Pure Indulgence, Calm, Cozy, and Relaxation. I figured this was where Crissy wanted everyone to start to get into the Zen mood.

The three-tiered mosaic building appeared in an opening that just a few months ago was completely wooded and thick with brush, trees, and critters. The clay roofs popped above the trees and over the open living areas of the spa.

"This is definitely a step up from Touched By An Angel," Camey gasped from behind me.

"Yeah." My mouth opened and closed a few times when I couldn't verbalize the jumbled-up thoughts in my head.

"Let me by. I'm going to get my free massage." Camey nearly knocked me over when she shoved past me.

There was just something so strange about this whole thing. Now that I'd seen it with my own eyes, I had more questions than ever on how on earth Crissy Lane, of all people, pulled this off.

I could only imagine what the path and the foliage would look like in the spring and summer, with all the barren trees in full bloom and the Kentucky bluegrass vibrant from all the limestone found on the island.

"I would never let you do that." The familiar voice coming from the depths of the woods had a quiet and ominous tone.

I took a step off the path, and the rustling of leaves from my first step abruptly stopped me from moving forward. Luckily, whoever was in the woods didn't hear me.

"I'll expose you for what you really are." The voice clicked when I recognized it.

Tom Foster.

"I can completely wreck your reputation, and unfortunately, in our world, that's all you have." The voice dropped in volume. "Do you comprehend what I'm saying?"

I listened closely to see if whoever he was talking to had comprehended the warning, because in my opinion, when Tom Foster made a threat, it was to be taken seriously, which was why I had to talk to him.

Not that he'd threatened me directly, but since he did say he was doing an article on the Bean Hive, or at least mentioning the coffeehouse in the write-up, and after hearing he thought my beans were over-roasted, I had to make good.

"I thought so" were the last words I heard from the woods before Crissy snuck up behind me.

"So, whatcha thinking?" Crissy asked with her hands clasped behind her back as she sashayed up to me. She blinked her fake lashes underneath that bleach-blond hair that was even brighter against her black turtleneck. "What are you doing?" She glanced at me and then into the woods.

"Nothing." I planted a smile on my face and took a step back on the path. "I'm looking at the woods, and I'm just shocked at how all of this turned out."

"Shocked because it's so amazing?" She smiled and giggled.

"Shocked because I never knew you wanted to do something like this. I mean, not that you aren't holistic—maybe you are—but the Crissy I know is all about the big hair, colorful nails, and loud..." My eyes ran up and down her body. "Loud, um, everything."

"Why, Roxanne Bloom, if I didn't know better, I'd think you were giving me a compliment," Crissy gushed, fluttering those lashes.

"How on earth did you get all of this built without anyone seeing large quantities of building supplies going across the lake?" I asked.

"Honey." She shifted her hip to the right and planted her fist on it. "There's more ways to get on this island than Big Bib. And there's this side where you can't see Honey Springs."

"Oh." My brows knitted when I figured she was right. There were several sides to the island, and we only used the cleared side of the Bee Farm, and Crissy did clear the opposite side. "Who on earth helped you?"

"Now, that is my silent partner, who does wish to remain silent." She grinned and leaned in to my ear. "I will tell you a little secret. You do know my silent partner. Very well too."

She straightened up, pursed her lips, and cocked one brow. She brought her finger up to her lips. "Sh. I can't tell." She laughed and looked beyond my shoulder when the sound of leaves crackling caught our attention.

Tom Foster emerged from the woods with his phone in his hand.

"Tom," Crissy scolded, "you know you should've left your phone at the Airbnb."

"Are you kidding, dear?" He greeted her with a kiss on each one of her cheeks. "I had to get some of these amazing photos into the magazine so they could make it to deadline." He winked.

His smile faded when he noticed it was me standing with her.

"Ms. Bloom." A big sigh escaped him. "You seem to be everywhere in this little town."

"I am here to support one of my dearest friends since childhood." I wanted him to know that I was watching him, and if he was doing something sneaky, then he needed to stop.

"I'm glad you both are here. And as for all this Zen stuff"—Crissy reached out with both hands, grabbing my hand and his, squeezing them—"I love that we can all coexist in harmony together."

"On that note, I'm going to go grab something from the pool bar before I go to the meditation chant." Tom headed up the hill, on a real path this time.

"Angela Paul is teaching that, right?" I asked to confirm since I was fully aware that there was some sort of funny business going on between her and Tom. Plus, I didn't forget how Angela had mentioned the silent partner had asked for a free voucher for the class, which meant I was definitely going to cash in the free voucher Crissy had given me so I could get the answers to my questions.

"Yeah," Crissy gushed with a wide-open look. "She's amazing. I saw it with my own eyes when I was in California. That's how I knew this whole wellness resort thing was going to be huge, and I thought, 'Crissy, you need to get in on the action.'" She talked about herself in third person. "I went to the library, where Joanne gave me a bunch of awesome books on how to start a business and how to put together a business proposal. I just so happened to run into..." She curled her lips in as her brows knitted together. "Let's just say that my business partner literally bumped into me, and it was fate. That's when I told my partner, well before they signed the deal, about my great idea. And all the money was put up for it that day."

"Your silent partner put up all the money?" I asked.

"Let's just leave it at that. My silent partner said you'd be asking all sorts of questions and that I shouldn't let that lawyering side of you get me to answer them." She wagged her long finger at me. "Smart one you are."

"How do you know if you got a good partner if you didn't have a great lawyer?" I asked.

"Who said I didn't have a great lawyer?" She gave me that smirky smile before she turned her head when someone called her name. "I've got to go. Don't forget to go take a tour of the resort rooms where guests can stay overnight. You won't believe the woods and lush garden views. Breathtaking. And there are a few with panoramic views of the pier. You can see the Bean Hive perfectly."

This was getting stranger and stranger by the moment. All the secrecy drove me crazy. I didn't like it one bit. If someone went to great lengths to tell Crissy not to tell me, then I felt like something was off. Just like Aunt Maxi would tell me as a kid, "If someone tells you to keep a secret from your parents or me, then you know they are doing something wrong." I lived with that statement all through my life, and that meant law school, when it came in very handy during a few trials.

"I wouldn't miss your opening for the world." I smiled and nodded toward the person calling out to her. "I think someone wants you."

"Just follow the signs," she hollered over her shoulder as she scurried off, leaving me standing there with even more questions than before. "You won't be disappointed!"

I waved her off and looked at the signs she was talking about. There were various signs nailed to a six-foot-tall wooden post, pointing in various directions.

"Pool bar. Hmm. Isn't that where my friend Tom Foster was going?" I questioned aloud and headed up the same path.

When I got to the top, I stood there trying to take in what Crissy had created. It was nothing short of amazing, and it felt like I was on a tropical island far away from Honey Springs.

The infinity pool overlooked Lake Honey Springs and had a large concrete patio along three sides with several round, black outdoor tables with tan umbrellas and cushioned chairs. There were several rattan lounge areas along with some firepits. Even though this place looked like it would be much better to visit during the warmer months, Crissy had gone to great lengths to get portable heaters and firepits to accommodate anyone who needed to be outside.

The bar was located along the back side, and by "bar," I wasn't referring to liquor. It was some sort of juicing bar along with really odd-looking foods.

Tom Foster sat in the very last stool at the bar. I could hear the bartender telling Tom about the drink he'd just served him. Tom looked down into the purple concoction before he took a sip.

"Hello, mademoiselle." I was greeted by a man with a French accent. He was wearing a chef's uniform with "Pierre" embroidered in the spot where a name tag might go. "Can I interest you in a vegan juice to go along with your detox today?"

"Detox?" I asked.

"Ah, you must be a native to the land of Kentucky." His smile reached his eyes. "I can tell by the accent of the South you have."

"Southern. Yes. I'm from Honey Springs. I own a coffeehouse on the pier." I saw a visible switch in his attitude.

"Ah, yes. I've heard of your coffee." He moved his eyes down to Tom. "In fact, one of our very special guests says he must go to have a coffee across the way because the juicing isn't his thing."

Tom held up his glass and gave me an air cheers.

Pierre scoffed. "Aw, you two know each other?"

"Yes. He's been into my coffee shop." I gave Tom a little wave, still curious about what his story was, and wondered if he knew who the backer was for Crissy's spa.

"Really, none of this is his thing. But I can see you are curious and possibly interested in trying what we have to offer, which is a vegan-style menu that will go along with what you'd like to accomplish while you are here today."

"Accomplish?" I questioned.

"Are you here for a detox? Massage? Clearing of the mind? Cupping? Rebirthing?" All the words were as foreign to me as his accent.

"Rebirthing?" Now this was all a little too woo-woo for me. "I think I'll just have a water."

"Suit yourself, but I think you'd be very interested in the cupping along with a detox from all the coffee," he suggested as he handed me a fancy wine glass of water with a lime slice in it.

"Thank you. I'll keep your recommendation in mind." I excused myself and turned back to Tom.

"What are you doing over here if you aren't here for detox? Juicing?" Tom chuckled and picked up his glass.

"I'm here to support my friend Crissy and um..." I pretended to forget the silent partner's name in hopes Tom would just finish my sentence, so when the uncomfortable silence hung between us a second too long, I opened my big mouth again. "What's the name of her partner?"

"You don't know it either, huh?" He cocked a brow. "I've been trying to get to the bottom of it myself. I've put out a few feelers and possibly one might know and let me know later today."

He picked up his cell phone and looked at the locked screen.

"Is that your wife?" I asked when I noticed it was a photo of him and a brown-haired lady. He gave me a strange look.

"My Aunt Maxi recognized you and said that you and your wife rented her little cottage in downtown Honey Springs. Remember I suggested bringing you coffee?"

"Yes. This is my wife." He held his phone up for me to see the photo, but the problem was that the time was plastered over her face, so I couldn't really get a good look at her.

Between the numbers of 2:45 I was able to get an eyeball and some parts of her cheeks.

"And I'm guessing you and Angela are just friends?" I made the statement more of a question.

"Why would you say it like that?" He drew back and slid his phone into his pocket.

"I couldn't help but notice when you came into the coffee shop this morning that she and her friend Casper sorta slinked out of your sight." I just couldn't stop my nosey lawyer side.

"Goodness, maybe you should be writing an article instead of me." He stood up, downing the rest of his drink. "Because you're better at research than me. So let me know if you find out who the silent partner is, and I just might put your name on the article as a contributor with this amazing little coffee shop."

"In the lawyer world, we call that a bribe." I smiled and took a drink of my water.

"You own a coffee shop, and you're a lawyer. That's good for the article too." He wiggled his brows, gave Pierre a nod, and walked away.

Pierre and I had a quick moment where he gave me a shady grin like he'd heard my conversation with Tom. He was toweling off a glass. I gave him a slight shrug before I turned around and propped my elbows on the bar behind me as I leaned back and let my eyes glaze the edge of the infinity pool. Crissy was right. The view from up here was amazing.

"There you are." Camey had found me. "Where did you get that water? I need to get that nasty kombucha-whatever-is-in-it taste out of my mouth. Yuck." She did a little shimmy with her shoulders.

"Chef Pierre prepared it." I gave a quick head tilt over to Pierre, who was already waiting on another resort customer.

"I'll be right back. Do you need anything?" she asked and left when I told her no.

I turned my attention back to the view. Big Bib was guiding his pontoon back across the lake, full of a lot more guests arriving at the spa. I followed his boat and watched him pull up to the pier, doing his usual routine of how he liked to hook his boat up to the dock.

He helped everyone out of the boat, and I noticed a passenger get on.

"What are you staring at?" Camey walked up with her lime-water wine glass. I gestured ahead. "Wow, look at this view." Her attention span was about as long as her granddaughter Amelia's. "Let's cash in our free vouchers." She pulled them from the back pocket of her pants. "I think I might try the shamanic sound healing."

"Is that the chanting thing?" I asked, knowing it was Angela's session and that I certainly needed to go to it.

"Yes. It's supposed to give you deep peace and inner harmony using sounds, vibration, and some chanting." She was all excited about it. "Why not? It's free."

There was no amount of humming, chanting, or gonging that was going to offer me any inner peace until I found out exactly who was financially behind this operation. There was something that bothered me about the entire situation.

Whoever it was didn't want me to know, which made it all the more curious to me.

"I was going to go check out the guest rooms, but I'm going to go with you to that chanting class instead." I drank the last bit of my water and put the glass on the bar, making it ting and catch Pierre's attention. "Thank you," I called out to him before we left.

"I'm actually really excited to be going to the chanting class, and I'm quite surprised that you're excited," Camey said as we headed back down the path toward the front of the retreat.

I was sure there was a quicker path to the building where the chanting class was taking place, but I didn't really know my way around here yet, though I hoped to by the end of the afternoon.

"You can't help but feel a little calmer here." I loved how the trees were starting to bud and slightly hung over the path. I was sure the paths were strategically placed, which gave them a cozy and intimate feel. The faint sounds of wind chimes and low gongs could be heard through the trees. When I looked around, I didn't see where the sounds came from. I bet Crissy had placed them in hidden areas.

"It almost feels like we are in a tropical paradise and not Kentucky," Camey observed.

"I don't know." I shrugged. "I think Kentucky is a paradise."

"Of course you would." She snuggled her hand in the crook of my arm as we headed down the path. "I'm glad we are here together."

"Me too. Two heads are better than one," I told her. "Who could possibly be helping Chrissy fund this resort?"

"Who cares?" She squeezed my arm. "Just let go of any thoughts and let the Zen take over."

Both of us laughed and moved past the subject. Well, Camey had changed the subject, but I'd not in my mind. I had an itch that needed to be scratched.

When I looked around, everything I saw seemed like it would cost a lot of money. So whoever was her big secret partner was for sure wealthy. The buildings were stucco with terra-cotta roofs, the trails were well laid, and the flowers were perfectly planted. Even in the cold temperature, everything looked as though it was alive and thriving. Even Angela said at the coffee shop this morning how she came with a price, as did Casper.

Speaking of which, I'd not seen him here.

I kept my eyes open for him as we took the next trail to the building where the chanting was going to be taking place.

The room was exactly how you'd picture it. The wide-open space with a vaulted ceiling and hardwood floors was perfect for the echoing of any sort of chants and, apparently, instruments that would be played during the hour-long class. There wasn't any furniture. The lingering scent of polyurethane curled around me as the young lady at the entrance politely handed me a purple yoga mat.

"Thank you," the young girl said and gave a slight bow of her head.

"Oh, no, thank you for the mat." I felt like it was her I needed to thank.

"You're very kind," she said in a soft, gentle voice with a pleasant smile on her face.

"If that's what this chanting will do for a body, I'm all in," Camey, who had grabbed her mat, whispered to me after we stepped out of earshot of the young woman.

I glanced back, and it seemed like the young girl did the same thank-you ritual with everyone who walked in. I would put money on it that her fancy yoga outfit that showed off her toned arms, midriff, and legs was Lululemon.

"No joke," I scoffed and turned to look for a spot for us to lay out our mats.

"Wow," Camey said with a shocked look. "There's a lot of people in here. This chanting business must really work. Crissy did say that it would melt the stress away."

There wasn't a single clear space for us to put our mats. Both of us looked around, and finally, after I had to stand on my toes, I spotted an empty area in the front right corner.

"Over there." I pointed, and Camey nodded, following as I led the way.

We weaved in and out through the mats, where people were already seated with their legs crossed. Each person had a variation of where they put their hands. Some had their hands resting on their knees, while others had their hands in prayer position up to their hearts, and still others took the pointer-finger-and-thumb-pinched-together approach.

"I'm so glad to see you here, Roxy." Angela had spotted us right off since we were next to the stage where she was set up. "Welcome." She gave Camey a slow nod. "I hope that you find chanting will deliver exactly what you seek."

"Did you see her husband?" I asked Camey as both of us bent down to roll out our mats.

"She doesn't have a husband." She glared at me. "Take this seriously, Roxy. Maybe you can find a little calm in that head of yours. It's always going, and right now, it's going a hundred miles an hour."

"There you are." I heard Aunt Maxi's familiar voice behind us. It bounced off the walls. I grinned before I turned around to see her. "'Scuse me, 'scuse me."

She nearly took off people's heads with the end of her yoga mat as she plowed through the room on her way over to me and Camey.

"There's no room up here," Camey told Aunt Maxi.

"Why, there sure is." Aunt Maxi stuck the yoga mat up under her armpit and wagged her finger. "Scooch over a little that way," she told me. "And you, scooch over a little that way," she instructed Camey.

"Then our mats will be touching," Camey snarled and looked up from her mat.

"And?" Aunt Maxi's brows rose. "Go on. Scooch."

Instead of getting up, which would've been much easier, I did what she said and wiggled over a little while pulling my mat with me so she had enough room to lay her mat between mine and Camey's.

Once she was settled, she let out a long sigh and looked at me with a smile. I craned my neck to look around to see if I recognized anyone in the darkly lit room. Everyone pretty much looked the same in the eyes-closed, seated position.

"Welcome, everyone," Angela's soft and soothing voice came over the loud speaker.

I turned around and focused back on the stage, where I noticed there were four people joining Angela. Each one of them was sitting cross-legged like the rest of the participants, which made me realize that everyone here probably knew what they were doing and what to expect.

Each one of them had an instrument of sorts. There was a big gong, a couple of strange-looking bowls in various sizes, some type of hanging chimes like the ones I had pictured were making the noise all over the resort, and there was a bongo, which I thought looked the most fun. I had a sneaking suspicion it wasn't going to be used for loud banging like I'd only ever seen one used.

"De-stress and listen to tuning forks, singing bowls, cello with clarinet, gongs, a twenty-minute raga, and then a winding down with gongs, tuning forks, and Tibetan singing bells." Angela's sweet voice was like its own instrument as she tuned in with her eyes closed.

"Taking a deep breath, inhaling deeply in through your nose..." Angela sucked in a deep breath while at the same time taking some sort of wood mallet and rolling it around the lip of the bowl, letting the instrument sing with a pure tone. "And exhaling with a sigh."

With one eye open, I watched Angela and mimicked her breathing technique before I turned to look at everyone around me doing the exact same thing. Except Aunt Maxi.

She was still trying to situate herself in the muumuu she was wearing. She lifted one thigh up, tugging on the hem before she lifted the other thigh up to tug on that side of the dress.

"It's all bunched up under me," she tried to whisper, but it turned out she was louder than the bowl Angela was playing.

Angela opened her eyes and looked at us.

"Sh," I told Aunt Maxi and nodded to the stage.

"Well, I can't be doing no breathing with it all up under me like that." She huffed and closed her eyes, not paying a bit of attention to the ruckus she was causing.

"I invite you to close your eyes if that feels comfortable for you, taking this moment to relax your bodies, calling all of your energy back to you and coming into sacred space. Bringing your consciousness fully into this present moment and bringing your awareness to the base of your spine." Angela continued to instruct the class without playing the instrument.

I could see Aunt Maxi's forehead wrinkling up as she tried to follow Angela's instructions. "What was that about the spine?" Aunt Maxi asked. "I'm still stuck in the exhaling."

I shook my head for her to stop talking as Angela continued.

"Visualize sending down a root to the base of your spine. A tall strong root like the root of the ancient grandfather redwood tree."

I had to look over at Aunt Maxi and see exactly where in the tree-rooting process she was and tried to keep in my laughter when I saw the look on her face. It was all scrunched up, brows furrowed and head tilted as she looked at Angela.

"I'm not some tree," Aunt Maxi whispered with her chin to her chest.

"Root clean down from the base of your spine through your sacrum and all the way to the very center of the earth, as you feel yourself anchored and planted in your physical body that is connected to the earth, as you allow any areas of tension in your body to just be released."

"That's it." Aunt Maxi stood up. "I'm out."

Aunt Maxi yanked the edge of her yoga mat into the air, allowing it to dangle behind her as she made her way out of the room.

If Angela heard or even saw Aunt Maxi, she didn't let on. She just continued with her class.

"Check to see if there's any adjustments you can make to make yourselves more comfortable in this moment as you surrender your cells to the force of gravity and feel the crown of the top of your head reaching toward the sky and the base of your spine elongating toward the center of the earth. Inhale deeply through your nose and exhale through your mouth, inhaling the mantra 'I am' and exhaling the word 'truth.'" Angela inhaled while saying one mantra and exhaled with the other before she continued with the words, "Sat Nam, Sat Nam."

As she finished, one of the other teachers on stage with her started to play the gongs and let the sound reverberate through the room.

The hour-long class really seemed like two hours to me, and I had never been so glad when Angela told us to go on our way.

"That was so refreshing." Camey had sweat on her upper lip and brow.

"Wow, looks like you really took that rooting business to heart." On our way out, I took a small glass of water in exchange for my yoga mat from the same young lady who'd given us the mats on the way in.

"You didn't give it a shot. I saw you over there looking around and not doing the exercises." Camey downed her water and took mine before I could even take a sip and downed it too. "What?" She gave me a funny look. "You didn't sweat a bit." She looked me up and down. "Did you even do any of it?"

"Sure I did, but I was also too busy looking around to see if we knew anyone who could be the silent partner because Angela said the silent partner was going to be in her class." I stood just outside the door, watching everyone file out. I didn't recognize a soul.

"Maybe it's someone you don't know and that Crissy met in California." Camey had a great point.

"If that's the case, then why would they tell her not to tell me?" I still didn't have that little piece of the puzzle solved.

"Oh, I don't know." Camey pulled out the brochure Crissy had given each one of us and glanced over it. "She might've told them she knew of a lawyer, and the silent partner wanted to use their lawyer and possibly had her sign a confidentiality agreement. It's not uncommon in business."

"Yes. I know that too." It was time I just give it up and resign to the fact that I wasn't going to find out who it was, only when I had this gut feeling, I knew something was off. But I stuck it in the back of my head and peered over at the brochure to see what Camey was looking at. "Where are you going next?"

"I'm going to go take a look at the Chi Nei Tsang massage, where they put some oil all over your belly and massage your internal organs." The sound of that coming out of her mouth made my internal organs hurt.

"I think I might go look at the guest rooms. Crissy said they are amazing," I told her and looked around to see exactly which way I should go.

Camey held the map up in the air and tilted it all sorts of ways until she settled on a position.

"It looks like I'm going that way and you're going that way." She pointed in opposite directions.

"I'll see you back at the juice bar in like an hour?" I asked and noticed it was around four.

"Five o'clock it is," she agreed. "By that time, I'll be all loosey-goosey and ready to go back for some real food."

"You and me both." I laughed and headed out in the direction of the guest rooms.

They appeared to be the farthest away up on the hill, which meant I had some time to call Patrick and check on him.

"How's the spa?" he asked.

"It's crazy. I just took this crazy chanting class. Poor Aunt Maxi. She got up and left after the instructor asked us to root down like a tree." My ears were met with Patrick's laughter. "I'll be leaving here in about an hour. I'm going to get a look at the guest rooms while Camey gets her organs tended to."

"I don't even want to know, but you're going to love the rooms. I didn't want to tell you about them because you just wouldn't believe the view." Patrick would know since he had gone over to do that little bit of extra work Crissy needed as a favor, but that was the extent of it.

He wasn't necessarily really upset she didn't hire him for the job, because he knew it was business. It was me that took it a little too personally, and that was probably why I wanted to know who the silent partner was. I knew Crissy, and she would've had a local do all the work. At least, I wanted to believe that about her.

"I ran by the Bean Hive and grabbed Pepper," he said. "Birdie seems to be doing fine." That was good to hear.

"Well, I'll relieve her at five and then close up. Did you want to come back to the boardwalk to have supper at the Watershed?" I asked. "I don't want to cook. Do you?"

"The Watershed it is. What time are you closing?"

"Let's say seven thirtyish." I didn't want to set a specific time even though there were store hours. I never kicked anyone out for coming in a second before closing, nor did I kick people out if they were in there having coffee and visiting with friends. I worked around them, and if anyone did come in, I offered them what I had left and didn't make anything new while getting the place ready for the next day.

"Sounds good. I'll see you later."

We said our goodbyes, and before I even realized it, I was already at the first building with guest rooms.

"Welcome to the Bee Happy Resort." A woman in a long skirt with bells fastened around her waist and a flowing long-sleeved top greeted me when I stepped into the building. "We believe that personal evolution starts with self-love. This private, all-inclusive luxury healing resort will recharge and rejuvenate your body, mind, and soul! Here on the island, we offer a truly unique and tropical healing for you, married with a daily mediation, healthy cuisine, massage treatments to fit your body type, a wellness consultation, and coaching that will go along with your experience level. You may just want to relax today with a sit by the infinity pool while you wind down from the crazy world you just left, but don't wait too long to tell me what you'd like to enjoy in this paradise of Kentucky so we can start right away on focusing on your personal growth and evolution."

"I'm a local and a friend of Crissy Lane's. She told me to come up here and check out the views of the pier. I own the Bean Hive—" I was about to finish, but she clapped her hands, getting my mouth to stop talking.

"Ah, yes. Roxanne, is it?" the woman asked in a gentle voice, slightly tilting her head to the side.

"It seems like everyone around here knows my name or at least who I am." That made me think the silent partner had already warned them. And there was only one person who I could pinpoint who was smart enough to do this ahead of time: Aunt Maxi.

Was Aunt Maxi Crissy's secret partner? I felt a surge of adrenaline thinking about it because it would all make sense. If Aunt Maxi had even suggested she wanted to invest in something like this, I would've told her not to do it. But then again, her reaction to the chanting class was authentic, and I couldn't imagine she'd invest in something she didn't believe in. Or would she?

"We welcome you." The woman spread her hands out in front of her. "Enjoy the view."

She slipped away as quietly as the bells that jingled upon her exit and left me there, where the views didn't disappoint.

This was even a better view of the boardwalk.

I took in a few long, deep breaths because it was virtually impossible not to feel somewhat relaxed being in nature. During one of my long exhales, Big Bib pulling up to the marina with Tom Foster got my attention.

I couldn't stop myself from smiling when I noticed Tom had gotten off the boat and walked up the boardwalk toward the Bean Hive.

"Maybe I should call Birdie and tell her to be nice to him," I told myself and was a smidge relieved when I watched him take a hard right down the pier, across from the Bean Hive. "Tom Foster, you don't seem like the fishing kind." I made the observation as I watched him walk into the Bait Shop, which was located in the middle of the pier. You had to walk through the little store to get to the other side of the pier.

Shortly after I said that, he walked out the other side, which gave him zero time to even look around or purchase anything. I watched as he approached another person wearing a long brown trench coat with a hood, hands shoved into the pockets.

"What is that about?" I asked myself when I noticed the two appeared to be arguing and watched closely.

As if I were watching a movie, the drama played out before me, and not too long into the drama, I saw the trench-coat wearer pull what looked like a gun from his pocket.

For a second I stood there, stunned. Was this really happening? I questioned what I was seeing. Tom Foster stumbled forward a little before falling to the ground, and I realized there had been no shot.

"Help!" I screamed. "Call 911!" Frantically, I bolted past the lady who had come back out to see what on earth I was yelling about. "Silencer! Someone used a silencer!"

I fumbled with my cell phone as I tried to call Spencer Shepard, the Honey Springs sheriff, to tell him I'd just witnessed a shooting and get an ambulance to the pier. When he didn't answer, I called Gloria Dei.

"Gloria, I'm so glad you answered," I gasped and ran down the path toward the boat dock. "I was just at the Bee Happy Resort."

"I'm dying to get off work so I can get over there. I told Big Bib that—"

"Gloria, stop talking!" I screamed into the phone. "Listen to me." I slowed down to tell her exactly what I'd seen, while in front of me, Big Bib drove the pontoon up to the Bee Happy Resort dock with even more guests.

"I'm sorry. You have to wait," I told a couple of the guests waiting to get a ride back over to Honey Springs. "Listen, I need you to put this thing in high speed and get me across the lake. Someone was shot."

"Shot?" Big Bib looked at me with a confused look.

"Yes. Tom Foster, the man you just dropped off, was shot on the pier. I saw it with my own two eyes." My chest heaved up and down at the thought of wasting any more time to save Tom. "Go!"

I slid my gaze over to the pier by the boat dock in anticipation of what I was going to find once we got across lake. A chill scurried up my legs, leaving a trail of goose bumps and bringing me back to this morning's thought when my feet had hit my cold floor. I had known it was going to be a chilly day—I just didn't know how chilly until now.

CHAPTER EIGHT

"Let me try to understand this." Spencer Shepard, the Honey Springs sheriff, stood in front of me, shielding my view of Tom Foster's body. "You were standing on the balcony of a guest room at the Bee Happy Resort when you watched someone in a trench coat and hood pull a gun out and shoot our victim?"

"Tom Foster." My head bobbled around on my shoulders to try to look past Spencer, but he did a little dance back and forth so I couldn't see. "I know him. Well, sorta know him. He has been to the Bean Hive the past couple of days, and he's a writer for the *Healthy Women's Magazine*. He is..." I swallowed hard. "Was," I corrected myself, "going to do an article on the Bean Hive, though I don't really think he liked my coffee because he called it burnt."

"I'm guessing you didn't like his review of your coffee?" Spencer gave me that look.

"No. I didn't shoot him." I scoffed, rolling my eyes. "I was at the resort, and plenty of people saw me and talked to me, including Big Bib, who drove me back in the boat."

"I'm not saying you killed him." Spencer shook his head and took out his little notebook where he kept notes during his investigations.

One of these days, I just might take that notebook and smack him upside the head because he was only driven by the facts of the case and not the hearsay.

"But there's apparently a lot of people who didn't like him," I said in a hushed whisper so the crowd that was gathering around us didn't hear just in case the killer was standing near.

I'd heard how killers that hadn't been caught often went back to the scene of the crime just to see what was going on. Sick, really, but a reality.

"Who are they?" Spencer asked.

"I don't know, really." I knew this wasn't going to sit well with the sheriff. "I overheard Tom talking to someone in the woods of the resort when Crissy Lane came up to me. Well, not really talking." My thoughts were all over the place. "They were arguing."

My mind was a jumbled mess. Coffee. I knew I needed a coffee to get me all straightened out.

"Crissy Lane and Tom were arguing?" he asked as he stopped writing and looked up at me. "Did he give her a bad review?"

"No. I don't know, but not him and Crissy. Tom and someone else. Crissy interrupted my…" I bit my lip.

"Your eavesdropping?" Shepard's brow cocked.

"Something like that." I sighed and noticed Kevin Roberts, the Honey Springs coroner, had walked past us, pushing the gurney. "What else is going on? Kevin is looking at Tom's body funny."

"Why would you say that?" Spencer acted like this was my first time seeing a murder and doing the professional cop thing.

"Really, Spencer? Are you seriously acting like this?" My lips puckered in annoyance. "I've seen people with gunshots before and helped you out. Why is Kevin so interested in Tom's face?"

I clearly saw Tom get shot in the torso. But something else was going on.

"Fine." Spencer's jaw tightened. "There is something else strange." He shuffled around before he let me know what he was thinking. "He had some foam coming from his mouth."

"Foam?" I questioned. "Like, poison?"

"I've seen it before when people overdose, so I'm not really sure what is going on. And you didn't see a face?" he asked.

"No. There was a person, and I can't even tell you how tall they were because I was so far up looking down." I glanced up at the top of the island, where I could picture myself standing, even though you couldn't see the resort from here due to all the woods. "I watched him take the boat ride over with Big Bib, and when I noticed he was walking on the boardwalk, I wondered if he was going to go into the coffeehouse, which I was actually hoping he wouldn't because I had no idea..."

I stopped my mouth before the thought came out, a rarity.

"No idea what?" he asked with a curious look in his eye.

"I had no idea what blend he would be ordering," I lied.

Honestly, I had no idea what Birdie would've said to him or if they'd gotten into another argument. With her chemistry skills, had Birdie taken the ultimate revenge out on Tom, and someone else did too?

Then it occurred to me. The person who shot him couldn't've come off the island because I'd not seen anyone leave with him. I didn't see the person who shot him until I noticed he'd walked out on the pier.

But there was one thing for sure that I did know. Birdie and Tom had had words. I didn't know her, but I did know she had a past of turning her smarts into bad behavior. Would a young high school girl really be able to kill someone?

"Did he come in this morning to get some coffee?" Spencer asked.

"He did." I nodded.

"And did you poison him?" he asked.

I laughed and looked at him.

"Oh. You're serious." I blinked at him a few times to see if his facial expression had changed, but he was not joking. "Of course I didn't."

"Then you won't mind if we test your roastery for some samples?" He phrased it as a question, but it wasn't meant that way.

"No. I don't mind, but there's no reason to even think he was poisoned at the coffee shop, is there?" I gulped, recalling what Loretta had said about Birdie. "I saw him drinking a water at the resort long after he was at the coffee shop. Maybe they poisoned him."

"Why on earth would someone poison him?" Spencer asked.

"Why on earth would I poison him?" I shook my head, trying to clear it of my theory that Birdie could very well be the one who poisoned Tom.

"I'm going to have Kevin put a rush on why Tom was foaming at the mouth, so I'm just letting you know that if someone poisoned his coffee from the Bean Hive, I will find out."

"No doubt you will." My chest heaved up and down. My nerves were shot, and I needed my coffee.

"Which way did the shooter leave the boardwalk?" he asked.

"I have no idea. After I saw the shot, I immediately called you. Then when you didn't answer, I called Gloria and ran down the path to get Big Bib to bring me here." I closed my eyes and shook my head. "I didn't even think about watching what the shooter did after that. I was just hoping Tom was alive."

"I better get over there. As always, call me if you remember anything." Spencer turned and walked over to the body, where all the deputies and Kevin were, leaving me standing by myself.

Slowly, I turned around and looked at the Bean Hive.

Birdie was standing in the window. She caught my eye and quickly disappeared.

CHAPTER NINE

"Roxy!"

I turned and looked down the boardwalk at Camey, who was flailing her arms in the air.

"What on earth?" she hollered as we both walked to meet each other in the middle of the boardwalk.

"What is wrong with your neck?" My eyes focused on the circular red spots along the sides of her neck.

"I was in a cupping session when I heard someone say something about a murder." She ran her hand along the side of her neck.

"Cupping?" I asked.

"Yes. It's this crazy form of holistic massage where they use these small glass cups as suction devices on your skin to disperse and break up stagnation and congestion by drawing up congested blood and energy." She waved her hands in the air. "What is going on?"

"Do you have time for some coffee?" I asked and gestured toward the Bean Hive.

"Do I?" She snorted. "Let me guess—you found the body."

"Don't I always?" I asked even though we both knew the answer to that question.

It was like I'd become the dead-body magnet around Honey Springs over the past few years. So when Spencer was giving me the runaround about the body, he knew I had some experience.

"Tom Foster is dead." I quickly told her about how I'd seen the murder happen, only that it might not just have been the shot that killed him. "He was foaming at the mouth like he'd been poisoned," I said when I hung up my light jacket on the coatrack and noticed Birdie's reaction.

She wasn't looking at me, but she was busying herself with the coffeepots behind the counter. She'd stopped as if she were taking in what I was telling Camey. She blinked a few times, and her deep gulps didn't go unnoticed.

"Spencer had the nerve to ask me if I had slipped poison into Tom's coffee this morning since Tom did say he thought my beans were burnt. Like we would know anything about poison." I looked at Birdie again. "Right, Birdie?"

"Yeah. Right." She wiped her hands down her apron and excused herself into the kitchen.

"What was that about?" Camey asked, bringing her mug up to her lips and taking a sip.

"That was planting a seed." I left it at that while Camey and I watched Kevin Roberts put Tom's body in the body bag.

The buzz about the dead body found on the pier quickly spread, and soon, the coffee shop was filled with locals trying to figure out what was going on. I hated to admit it, but when a rumor circulated in Honey Springs, the Bean Hive was like a magnet for gossip. There was never a better time to go to a coffee shop.

Camey had to get back to the Cocoon Hotel. Mom had to go back to her real estate office downtown because it was rental season in Honey Springs. She had a few clients who were renting their cabins out for the early spring, and she needed to meet them. It was up to me and Birdie to work the line of customers and get the orders out.

The gossip was flowing as fast as I could walk around and top off customers' coffees. Over the years, I'd learned that the best thing to do was to keep silent and to listen to the gossip. Not all the gossip was true, but there was always a little bit of truth in all gossip. It was just the way it was.

Working alongside Birdie made me keep a closer eye on her. She was as cool as a cucumber, and if she really did have a hand in Tom's murder, that hand was steady as she handed each customer their order.

I'd yet to have a moment to ask her what the fight was about.

"Do you think you can stay until we close?" I asked her, realizing I had totally forgotten to call Patrick to let him know that our date to the Watershed was off when I saw him walking past the window to the door.

"I'd rather be here than at Grandma's or in jail," she grumbled.

"Hey," I greeted Patrick. "Did you hear about Tom Foster?"

"Hear? It's all over the news." He looked around the coffee shop. "I'm guessing our date is off?"

"Grab an apron." I gestured to the coat-tree at the end of the counter, my way of telling him that he needed to pitch in. "Can I help you?" I asked the next customer in line and tried not to laugh as I watched Patrick fight with the coat-tree as he tried to wrangle the apron off the hook, causing it to teeter on its legs before he caught it in time, saving my purse and Birdie's purse from spilling out all over the ground.

"How long have y'all been married?" Birdie seemed to be as amused as I was.

"A couple of blissful years." I tried to stop my smile from seeing him in the apron, but I couldn't.

"You look very happy." Birdie sighed. "Your kids will be very lucky to have happy parents like you."

"I'm sure your parents are happy." I could sense a little tension from her.

"Far from it. Why do you think I try not to be home?" She looked up from the slow brew maker. "I'm sure they sent me here because they are probably getting a divorce and didn't want me around to hear them fight. Which is no different than what I'm used to."

"I'm sorry you've had to be in the middle of all of that." My heart ached. Not that my parents had gotten divorced, but I understood tension.

My mom didn't like Honey Springs or even Aunt Maxi when I was a child. She always protested when my dad would tell her he was bringing me here. She was always welcome to come, but she refused.

"Listen." I leaned my hip up against the counter after she gave the last customer their coffee. "I know and you know that you didn't kill anyone." I had to give her the benefit of the doubt. "But I do need to know what you and Tom were arguing about just in case someone other than my husband overheard you."

"He started in on how my generation is rude and how we could take a lesson or two from a manners book or something. I rolled my eyes and wasn't going to say anything, and the other man—"

I interrupted. "Other man? What man?"

There had been another man in here, and Patrick had left that out.

"Yeah. The dead guy and the other man had a few words about some sort of write-up in a magazine. It was kinda comical, because I think the dead guy thought I was the other man's age." She got a funny grin on her face. "People always think I'm older than I really am."

"Did you get the other guy's name?" I whispered, "If they were fighting, he could be the killer."

"He was the same guy that came in early this morning." She shrugged and planted a big grin on her face to wait on the next customer.

Was she talking about Casper? As in Angela and Casper?

I stood there deep in thought and recalled how the two of them did turn away from Tom when he came in. It was obvious they didn't want Tom to see them, but then just a little while later, I did see Tom and Angela on the boardwalk. Come to think of it, I'd not seen Casper since he was in here.

How odd.

"Roxanne." I'd been so deep in replaying the day's earlier events that I'd not even noticed Aunt Maxi had come into the coffee shop. "Roxanne."

"Hey. I'm super busy. I'll be right back." I grabbed a latte from Birdie and swiveled my way around the counter to give it to a customer who was sitting next to the fire. "Excuse me, excuse me," I repeated over and over while I weaved in and out of the crowd.

It was hard not to hear the murmurs of murder and the possibilities that were flying out of people's mouths.

"Sorry for your wait." I gave the customer her hot latte with the special heart drawn with creamer that appeared on top.

On my way back, I noticed Aunt Maxi had moved from the counter. There was a woman with her who appeared to be around my mom's age. Her wavy red hair was pulled back in a ponytail, with little wisps of hair falling around her face.

Big pearl studs were in her earlobes, and a matching strand hung around her neck. She wore a fitted red jacket with a belt that cinched her waist and a pair of black riding leggings, the kind with the little brown patches on the knees, tucked into a pair of knee-high riding boots. To complete the outfit, she had on a pair of gloves.

Whether she wore them to compliment her outfit or to ward off the chill that now hung in the air from the murder that'd taken place, she looked very stylish.

"I need you to come back here with us." Aunt Maxi took me by the arm and dragged me right along with the woman through the swinging door, where she swung me into the kitchen. "This is Robin Foster. Her husband is the man that was killed."

"I'm so sorry." My heart instantly hurt as I began to recognize the agony on her face. Her eyes were set back, with red tinting the white and lingering tears holding her eyelashes together. "Is there anything I can do? Coffee perhaps? Something to eat?"

"That's the best you can offer?" Aunt Maxi's voice rose an octave.

I glanced at her, then it hit me like a ton of bricks. Not that I wasn't already doing what she'd obviously come here to get me to do, which was to find out what really happened to Tom Foster, but the fact that she'd brought his wife here made me wonder if it was to settle the legal side of things.

"There's nothing you can do to make me feel better. He's not coming back. I keep thinking about your coffee shop and how he was so sweet this morning when he brought me a nice cup of coffee and one of your strawberry-and-cream donuts." She gave a little snort. "We had even talked about how your donuts were the most delicious combination we'd ever eaten. And we've been a lot of places with his work. But this week, here, was my special trip, and for him to have..." Her voice fell off as she teared up again.

"It's okay, honey." Aunt Maxi patted her back but gave me the stink eye overtop of Robin's head. "Roxy will help you."

"Yes. I have more of those donuts." I pitched a hard look at Aunt Maxi.

"In the legal department, dear." Aunt Maxi raised her chin, setting it in the air, and looked down her nose at me. "I told Robin that you'd be the legal representation between Sheriff Shepard and the investigation, because she's not leaving Honey Springs until the killer is found."

"I see." I curled in my lips and took a deep breath, wondering exactly how I was going to let Robin down gently. "I'm sure Mrs. Foster has legal representation at home."

"You are right, but I feel like I need someone here. Someone who knows the law enforcement and area like your aunt said you did." Robin blinked a few times, wiping away the tears that'd fallen down her face.

"I can't promise anything, but I'm more than happy to listen to how things transpired on your end today." I needed all the details.

"Okay." She folded her hands in her lap. "While I was going to the Bee Happy Resort for all the treatments I'd signed up for, he was going to do some research at the library. We'd agreed that after my cupping and colonics, I would meet him back in town for some lunch." Her face softened as her memory of the event took place. "If you know anything about colonics, there was no way I was going to be able to really eat lunch, but he loved to find little out-of-the-way places to eat when we traveled so he could write about them in *Healthy Women's Magazine*. He has… er, had," she corrected herself, "planned on writing up an article about Honey Springs since we were here."

"That's so nice." Aunt Maxi was all involved in Robin's story, but being a lawyer, I always found the other side of the story to be more intriguing, and with Tom dead, someone else had a different story to tell altogether.

"When he didn't meet me for lunch, I thought it was odd. I even called his cell phone several times, and it just went to voicemail. Instead of waiting around, I headed back to the cottage and found all of his things he needed for research there."

"What do you mean?" I asked.

"His briefcase, his notebooks, all of his notes on Honey Springs. Everything. He always carried his briefcase."

"I'm not the right person to be telling this to. I'm flattered my Aunt Maxi here has given me such a glowing introduction, but honestly, I think you need to tell the sheriff all of this information." It was my way of letting her down easily and telling her no.

"I understand, and he has asked me several questions like I'm a suspect. I was telling your aunt about how I was treated, and that's when she said that I should have a buffer of sorts. A local lawyer to go between us in case they do think I killed him."

"I don't know what the sheriff is thinking about your husband's case, but I do know they always look to the spouse in a homicide as the first suspect." By the look on her face, I could tell my words didn't sit well with her and truly only dug me deeper into the hole I was trying to claw out of.

Aunt Maxi gave me another one of her stern looks.

"I will give you all of his documents and a list of who might've wanted to kill him, but I do have my own suspicions of who it is." Her words tugged on that curious side of me.

"Who?" I asked.

"Angela Paul. She's an instructor for this week's events at the Bee Happy Resort. She's not going to stay here to work or live, but she's a special guest of the opening retreat." Robin had just confirmed something I'd already had a hunch about.

"Angela the inhale-exhale queen." Aunt Maxi was yammering on as if I didn't know who Angela was. "That root-down-like-a-tree-root babbling Angela. Whoever heard of such a thing," Aunt Maxi muttered under her breath.

"Well, to give her credit, the technique does work," Robin noted and sucked in a deep breath like Angela had instructed during the class. "I mean, I am a mess, but on the inside, I am calm because I can breathe properly and I can see the situation for what it is, and clearly, she has killed my husband."

"Okay." I was probably going to regret my next move, but what the heck. I reached underneath the workstation and got a wipe-off board to write down what she had to say. When the time came, I'd combine all my information on one board, but for now, I needed to have all of Robin's details on a board of her own. "Tell me what you think you know."

In reality, what she thought she knew and the actual truth were a lot different. It was up to me, the lawyer, to figure out where that truth was and what it had to do with Tom's murder.

Aunt Maxi jumped up from her stool and worked her way over to the slow-drip coffee maker. Both of us knew that in a time like this, we needed a good strong cup of coffee. Plus, I really did believe my coffee brought out the truth in people's conversations. And if Robin was going to give me some insight into why she believed Angela killed her husband, I needed all the facts.

"All right, honey," Aunt Maxi assured Robin. "You've got Roxanne's attention. So you sit here and you tell her everything like you told me while I make us some coffee."

"Let's start off with the reason you feel like Angela killed your husband." I put the end of a dry-erase marker between my teeth and jerked off the cap while I adjusted the board so I could write on it.

"They were having an affair up until six months ago."

"Okay. That's a good reason for you to have killed him, but why her?" My mouth dried. I glanced over at the slow-drip and suddenly wished it wasn't so slow.

"He assured me it was over. When I noticed she was on the guest list of celebrity speakers for the Bee Happy Resort, I couldn't help but think he gave me the trip because it was his way of seeing her." She slipped the gloves off of her hands as though she'd made the decision she was going to stay a while. She placed them neatly, one on top of the other, on the workstation. "You see, I'm not a fool. But our marriage has been going strong for the last six months since I caught them. Also, during this time, Angela had been trying to contact him on his old phone. I had him get a new phone, and I secretly kept his old phone, which I told the sheriff. When I went to get the old phone to show the sheriff the evidence of her stalking Tom over the last few months, the phone was gone."

"You had the phone here, but now it's gone?" I wanted to make sure I was understanding everything accurately.

"Yes." She nodded.

Aunt Maxi had gotten the freshly made coffee and put the mug in front of Robin. She went back over to the slow-drip to make another one. The steam from the kettle curled up in the air as Aunt Maxi poured hot water over the grinds to let the coffee beans drip into perfection.

"Are you sure your husband didn't take it?" I asked.

"He has no idea I still have it. Like I said, he travels all over for work, so when I insisted on getting him a new phone to save our marriage so he'd not have contact with her, he was fine with it. He was very happy about it. Only I couldn't give up the phone, and he doesn't pay the bills, so he never knew I never turned off the phone or cancelled the line." She picked up the coffee and took a sip, so I took the time to catch up on writing down what she was saying. "I continued to see text messages from her, missed phone calls. It was disgusting, but I knew then from her begging him to talk to her that my husband was true to his word. 'Call me,' she'd beg. 'I need to hear your voice,' she'd say."

"Yep. I bet she did it." Aunt Maxi brought over my cup of freshly brewed coffee before she went back over to make hers.

I couldn't imagine how Robin felt being in a town where she didn't know a soul and thought it was a little getaway, only to find out that her husband's adulteress was here too.

"Are you sure he didn't know she was going to be here? Maybe he did and he needed to tell her face-to-face that he had to end it with her." I was about to tell her how I'd seen them together this morning but decided it might be best just to go to Spencer with this information instead.

I mean, I was agreeing to be her lawyer. I could go to him on her behalf.

"Of course I'm sure. If I only had that darn phone." She took some uneasy breaths as though she were on the verge of crying. "I think she somehow got my phone."

"When would that have happened?" I asked and knew I needed to get a timeline of her whereabouts. "But before we even talk about that, I need to know exactly where you were all day."

"Why me? Are you accusing me too?" She drew back, offended by my request.

"No, but if I don't establish your alibi, Spencer will spend too much time trying to figure it out while the real killer is on the loose." It was simply a tactic that was used in the legal world that would help clear her as a suspect, which she'd already said she felt like Spencer had positioned her as.

"I told you. I got up this morning and had your donuts with Tom. He told me he was going to the library to do the research." She began to tell me again what she'd already told me, but I stopped her.

"I understand what he was doing. I need to know what you were doing." I had to redirect her.

"I got ready and walked from the cottage to the marina, where I was to catch the ferry over to the spa." That made sense since downtown was a short walk from here. The weather, though a tad bit nippy, still was pleasant enough for a walk. "I had appointments set in stone months ago, from when Tom met Crissy in California. He had called me, so happy about meeting her during a conference that he insisted I get signed up that day. He talked about how bright the young woman was and how successful her resort was going to be, not to mention the impact it would have on the economy here. That's when I insisted he come with me so he could do an article on it."

I could tell that I was going to have to continually bring her back to the present, but I also knew she had to grieve.

"Anyways." She blinked herself back to what I'd asked. "After my appointments, I came back on the ferry to meet Tom at the Watershed. When he didn't show up, I walked back to the cottage, thinking he thought I was to meet him there. I thought he was there when I walked in because all of his research materials were there with his briefcase. Then there was a knock at the door." She gave a few sniffles before she broke into a meltdown.

"Now, now." Aunt Maxi embraced her, cuddling the mourning wife close to her chest.

"I think this is probably enough for me to start asking some questions around." I could feel the stress coming off of her. "You're in shock, and I understand you must feel a lot of pressure right now. Honestly, the best thing for you to do is to rest and let me see what I can find out."

I would revisit all of this with her after a little time had passed. In my experience, when someone was in shock, they couldn't remember all the fine details that were truly where the answers were hidden. Their mind was so jumbled with the situation that they would forget, and memories would come back to them when they least expected it. So she needed time. That was something I could give her.

"I do have one question that could be important." I watched as she uncurled from Aunt Maxi's embrace. "Did you see or talk to anyone who could give you a solid alibi?"

"Just the appointments I had." She shook her head. "I didn't talk to anyone on my walk back to the cottage."

"I can ask Crissy for a list of her appointments and talk to Big Bib about the ferry ride over. I'll be able to establish your timeline of events and your husband's to show where you were in correlation to the time of his death." A solid timeline would be good for us to establish so that I could cut Spencer off at the path.

"I guess I better go back to the cottage." She looked at Aunt Maxi and dragged her gloves off the work station. "I think I need to lay down."

As she snugged the gloves over each finger, I said, "One more question. Do you own a brown trench coat with a hood on it?"

"No," she confirmed.

"What about Tom?" I asked.

"No." The edges of her eyes dipped. "Can we go now?"

"Yes." Aunt Maxi nodded then looked at me. "Now, you get out there and get some answers. Root down like a big oak tree," she teased as she led Robin out of the kitchen.

I took a moment to sip on my coffee and look over the notes I'd taken on the whiteboard. Unfortunately, I had more questions than answers on the board. I wanted to know where that phone was and just how I was going to get my hands on it.

If Robin was correct and Angela took it, maybe it was in her room at the Cocoon Hotel. There was no way Camey Montgomery was going to let me waltz in there and take a look-see around, so I knew it was up to me to figure out how to get in there.

Birdie popped her head through swinging kitchen door. "Roxy, I just saw your aunt leave. But I sure could use a little help out here."

"Sure." I left the whiteboard there and hurried out behind her to take my spot at the counter. "You take the orders, and I'll bag them."

It was a nice little system we had going. She was quick to take the orders and the money while I knew exactly where everything was located in the displays, so I didn't have to think too hard as I boxed up their orders.

"Thank you so much." I reached over the display case and handed a customer a bag of bagels. "Please come back to see us."

The bell over the door dinged. I looked past the customer's shoulder and noticed Crissy Lane with a scowl on her face standing in the doorway. The look on her face wasn't the thing that caught my breath—it was the brown trench coat with a hood that stopped my gaze dead in its tracks.

CHAPTER TEN

"We need to talk." Crissy pointed her finger at me and dragged it through the air across the coffee shop to a table in the corner before she turned on the toes of her tennis shoes and headed that way.

I watched the hem of the brown trench coat flapping behind her as she took her seat and drummed her fingers on the café table.

"Do you think you're okay for a second?" I asked Birdie since the rush had died down a little.

"I'm good." Of course she was. I watched her grab the rag from the sink behind the counter and wipe down the tops of the display cases where we put some of the customers' pickup orders.

I walked over to the case with the quiches in them and opened it up while grabbing a couple of plates and forks.

"I'll be right over there." I took a quiche out and cut two nice-size pieces to plate. Along with the quiches, I got two of our biggest mugs and filled them to the brim with coffee before putting all of it on a tray so I could carry it over to the table.

There was one thing I knew and that was how a lot of problems could be solved over a simple cup of coffee and a nice piece of quiche.

And there was a big problem—that coat Crissy was wearing.

"So you think that you can keep me quiet with just food?" Crissy questioned after I sat the tray on the table and took a seat across from her. "Trying to keep our mouths stuffed so you can't hear what I have to say?" she asked.

I could see in her eyes that it did look good to her.

"No. I think that you and I have something to talk about and that food brings us together. Plus, I care about you and your well-being." And the fact that this could be her last supper before she headed to jail, but I shook the notion from my head.

"I'll go first. I don't understand why you can't just be happy for me." She picked up the fork and sent it down into the quiche, picking up a nice big piece to stuff in her mouth.

"What do you mean, Crissy?" I always took pleasure in the faces my customers made when they appeared to be enjoying something I'd created with my own hands. No matter how mad she looked to be at me for a reason I didn't know, she still was enjoying the quiche. "I don't understand what you're talking about and why you're upset with me."

I'd learned it was always good to let the other person talk so that while they hooted and hollered about whatever it was that they were fussing about, I was able to formulate exactly what I wanted to say, so I put the ball in her court, so to speak.

"I'm talking about how someone said that the lady at the coffee shop was screaming that someone was murdered at the resort, and now, everyone is trying to escape the resort. There is a line from the boat dock through the Bee Farm and around the island to the Bee Happy Resort because you said someone was murdered," she said through a mouthful of food. "If they aren't in line, then they are in the office, asking for their money back. Do you understand what this is going to do to me? This is gonna put me under, and if Tom Foster gets ahold of this information, he will crucify me."

"Wait." I stopped her because she'd referred to Tom Foster in the present. "You don't know about Tom, do you?"

"Oh, I know that one of his reviews will take me under before I even get above." She bent down and took a few sips out of the full mug before it looked like she could pick it up without spilling any.

"Tom Foster was murdered." The words spilled out like the coffee that just spilled out of her mug.

She put the mug down and grabbed for a few napkins from the center of the table.

"What?" Her eyes narrowed and her mouth gaped open before the color left her face. "Are you saying that there was really a murder, and it was Tom?"

"Yes. And"—I planted my elbows on the edge of the table and leaned over to whisper—"I saw it with my own eyes when I took your advice to enjoy the view of the boardwalk from the guest rooms at your resort." I took a deep breath and eased back into my chair to let the information sink into her brain. "I watched Tom leave the island with Big Bib. I took in the views as I watched him walk along the boardwalk where he walked down the pier before the Bait Shop."

Crissy's eyes grew bigger and rounder as I continued to tell the story. Her shoulders leaned forward.

"I watched him approach someone in a brown trench coat with a hood just like the one you have on. That person had their hands in their pockets. They were visibly arguing when the person pulled a gun out of their pocket and shot him."

Crissy gasped. She brought her hand to her mouth. By the looks of it, she didn't know what had happened.

"I-I..." She grappled for words.

She put down her fork and curled her arms around her waist. "I think I'm going to be sick." She rocked back and forth in the chair.

"Take a sip of coffee." I pointed to her mug. "Coffee always helps," I told her.

Well, at least it always helped me. Her hands were shaking, and the coffee teetered to and fro in the mug as she carefully brought it up to her lips. I let her focus on what the hot substance was doing to her insides as she closed her eyes and set it back on the table.

"Oh no. This is not good." Her eyes popped open. "This is even worse than my business going under. This means that..." She buried her head in her hands. "Oh my gosh. I'll never be able to recoup from this."

"I don't understand," I questioned. "Never recoup because you had something to do with this?" I couldn't take my eyes off of her coat.

"Are you accusing me of killing Tom Foster, Roxanne Bloom?" Her head tilted and her eyes narrowed. There was a little hatred spewing from her.

"I'm saying I saw with my own two eyes someone in that exact trench coat shoot Tom Foster." It was a fact, and there was no need to sugarcoat it. "I've already told Spencer Shephard what I saw."

"There are hundreds of people who have this coat." She tugged it a little tighter to her chest, exposing the Bee Happy Resort logo—a sunrise, only with the sun in the shape of a bee's hive. "We sell them on the website. I have told my guests that the weather in Kentucky between the winter and spring season is unpredictable and offer these coats at a discounted price."

"Do you keep a record of who purchased them?" I knew deep down that Crissy didn't kill anyone. "If you do, I'd like to see who so we can find out who really did kill Tom Foster."

"Oh my goodness, you are you already looking into this murder." She reached over the table and gently touched my hand. "What am I going to do?"

"I need that list. Tom Foster's wife has hired me to be her lawyer while she is in town. She said she's not leaving until the killer is brought to justice, and she thinks Angela Paul is the killer." I knew Crissy had to have thought highly of Angela if Angela had been one of the main reasons she'd opened the resort.

"There is no way Angela killed anyone." Crissy leaned back, crossed one leg over the other, and bounced her foot in the air.

"There is a way. She and Tom had an affair that was apparently cut off by Tom six months ago. If a woman scorned isn't enough motive, then I don't know what is." I took the last bite of my quiche and pushed the plate away from me.

"That's ridiculous. If anyone had motive to kill Tom, it would be Casper. I mean, after all, Tom did write that article in *Healthy Women's Magazine* about Casper's consulting business and how it made more businesses go under than thrive."

"No wonder Casper turned from him this morning," I said about my observation. "Angela and Casper came into the coffee shop this morning. Tom came in after them, and when they noticed it was him, they turned away from him like they didn't want him to recognize them. And he didn't notice them."

"Wait." Crissy's head jerked up. "They came in here for what?"

"Coffee and something to eat." Suddenly, it occurred to me what they said about the kombucha.

"They had caffeine?" she cried out. "They aren't supposed to have anything but clean foods, and not coffee."

"I don't know anything about that." Sometimes, it was just best to keep things to yourself, and this just so happened to be one of those times. Crissy already looked fragile from the news about Tom. I could see in her eyes that she put Angela on a pedestal, though I still believed Angela might have had the best motive to kill Tom.

"Tom did tell me that I should not hire Casper as my consultant. Angela said that Casper would be fine, and I went with what Angela had told me. Casper and Tom have been at each other since Tom printed that write-up in the magazine about Casper's business ethics. Tom even claimed Casper's $100,000 rate wasn't a good return on investment, but Angela assured me it was. Not that her $80,000 fee is anything to sneeze at." Crissy gnawed on her lip. "Tom has literally put a stop to anyone wanting a consult with Casper. At least that's what Casper and Angela told me."

"Why would you go against such a loud voice who obviously has clout in the industry you're in?" It seemed like a good question to ask her.

"I have a lot on the line. I had to get it started off the ground correctly or it would take years for me to pay my investor back, and don't ask me about my investor." She glared. "We have bigger fish to fry instead of gossiping about my silent partner, who will remain silent even in this scandal. And we have to figure this out before the silent partner finds out that someone who came to the resort did this." She tapped the jacket, referring to the killer wearing the same coat. "There is one thing in this business that I've learned."

"What is that?" I was curious.

"All you have is your reputation. If someone claims to be a master in chanting, cupping, or whatever and they don't deliver, then they are done." She let out a long sigh. "I'll go belly-up." She buried her head again. "I'll email you that list."

"Good. Get it to me as soon as possible." I knew the killer had to be on there. The coat was the key to solving this murder.

It was the exact same thing I'd heard from Angela's lips and also what I'd overheard Tom say to whoever was on the phone with him when he was hiding in the woods at the Bee Happy Resort.

The bell over the door dinged, and I looked over my shoulder to see who it was.

It was Spencer Shepard, with Angela Paul tailing him. He stopped and looked around the coffee shop until our eyes locked. He bolted over to my table. He looked between me and Crissy.

Crissy scooted around in her seat. I could only imagine she was thinking he was there for her.

"Can I talk to you in private?" he asked me.

"Sure." I was a bit surprised because I thought he was there for Crissy. "Excuse me."

"I'm leaving," she mouthed to me with her hand up over her lips, hiding them from anyone else's eyes.

I got up and gestured for them to follow me. Birdie had stopped making a latte and watched the three of us walk back into the kitchen, giving us the privacy Spencer had requested.

I stopped at the workstation and turned around, leaned against it, and crossed my arms.

"How can I help you?" I asked and ignored Angela. I had a few choice words for her about her involvement in what was going on in my little town.

"It's been brought to my attention that you had had some run-ins with our victim." He rested his hands on his utility belt.

"Oh, is that right?" I snorted. "I'm assuming that she told you that. Is that right, Angela?"

"Yes. I'm sorry. I had to tell him what I knew, and what I know is that Tom said that your coffee was burnt, and you said that he was going to crucify you." She just told a bold-faced lie. "All of us in the business know that when Tom Foster says that he's going to crucify someone, that means your business is going to go under if he prints that article."

"Bravo." I clapped in a smart-alecky way. "First off, I won't let you lie, because you are the one who said he was going to crucify me. Needless to say, I stand by my coffee, and Tom Foster is nobody in the coffee world, so no one will care what his opinion is of my coffee." I adjusted my stance to become a little taller. "It is you who had a reason to kill Mr. Foster, as I understand from his wife, Robin Foster, that he had an affair with you and called it off about six months ago."

Angela's jaw dropped. She started to dance back and forth on her feet as her fists clenched.

"I'm guessing you didn't let our little town's sheriff know about that, did you?" I shot back at her. "In fact, I'm Robin Foster's lawyer while she's in town to see that the killer is brought to justice, so I'd love to get a statement from you."

"All right, ladies." Spencer stepped in. "I can see that we need to take this down to the department. Let's go."

Spencer led the way out of the kitchen.

"Birdie, I'll be back in an hour or so," I said as I untied my apron and went to grab my coat and purse off the coat-tree.

"You might be here longer than that." Angela twisted around and tripped over the coat-tree as she tried to maneuver around me.

The coat-tree began to topple over, and I went to grab it, but it was too late. My purse flung across the coffee shop, and Birdie's coat fell on the floor along with her purse, which dumped out all its contents, including a bag of what appeared to be mushrooms.

I gasped, shifting my eyes up to Birdie.

CHAPTER ELEVEN

"How could you do this, Rox-anne Bloom?" Loretta's Southern accent was always much deeper when she was in distress.

Not only could everyone hear her before she burst into the Honey Springs Sheriff's Department, but the stomping of her feet told me a big-sized Low-retta hissy fit was about to go down for all to see.

"How could you let this happen to a minor?" Loretta had laser focus on me where I was sitting in a chair in front of Spencer Shepard's desk. "And you." She shook her finger at Spencer. "You outta be ashamed of yourself. Your mama is going to get an earful when I see her at the Southern Women's Club tomorrow."

"Tomorrow?" I questioned since I'd yet to hear about the meeting. After all, I held up to my end of the deal Loretta and I had made about giving Birdie a job.

"Uh." She shifted her weight and gaze back to me. "If you think after this little stunt that you're going to become a Southern Women's Club cardholding member, you've lost your marbles."

"Mrs. Bebe." Spencer was trying to be polite. It was the Southern way to be, and the poor man had to do his job, though I, too, felt he was off base with Birdie. "Please, let me do my job, and I'll turn her over to you after we finish processing her fingerprints."

"You touch one little fingernail on my granddaughter, and I'll have your badge the next election. I'd vote for Maxine Bloom before I'd vote you in again." Loretta picked up the nameplate on Spencer's desk that proudly displayed his name, as if we didn't know it was his desk or he needed help remembering where his desk was located. I guess I never understood nameplates. "This is going right in the trash with your reputation for accusing a minor of murder."

Angela Paul, who was sitting next to me in the other chair, took the liberty to open her mouth. "I'm sorry, but you do know that the poisonous mushrooms were in her purse? And she did serve him a coffee last night after they had an argument."

I gulped. I closed my eyes and knew she'd just unleashed a Southern bear.

"I don't know who you are or whose DNA recombined to make you, but you're dang lucky we are in a poo-leece station, because if he wasn't here, I'd rip you open and eat your insides, then I'd regurgitate them up and feed them to my granddaughter." I put my hand over my mouth to keep from laughing and watched as Angela's face turned to horror as Loretta kept tearing her a new one.

"Mrs. Bebe." Spencer stood up.

"Oh, I'll get to you in a minute." She shushed him up real quick. "Now, back to you." Loretta dragged her finger to point directly at me. "Out of all the places in Honey Springs, I trusted you with Birdie. I thought you were going to help her, and by "help," I didn't mean for you to get her put in jail. Aeee-rested!"

"Loretta." Gloria Dei had snuck up behind us and gently touched her friend on the arm. "Why don't I take you back to see Birdie."

"Gloria, she's seventeen years old." Loretta jerked her arm out from under Gloria's touch.

"Loretta, this is not going to help Birdie." Gloria spoke calmly to her. "You coming in here and getting upset and acting like you're acting. Now." Gloria pushed her shoulders back. "You need to get yourself together. We don't need Birdie any more upset than she already is."

Loretta turned her emotions on a dime. She frowned, sniffed, and reached inside her purse to retrieve a tissue and dab her eyes. Even though I didn't agree with how Loretta was handling the situation, my heart did break for her at the thought of how she must feel as the one person her son had trusted with his own daughter.

Gloria took Loretta by the elbow and gestured for them to step aside. She took a hard gulp, lifted her chin in a very prideful Southern-woman way, and took the first step, which was all she needed to go with Gloria.

"Can I go talk to her for a second?" I asked Spencer for permission since he had me there to sort out whatever Angela Paul had cooked up in her own head and to answer the questions she'd fed him. "You can ask her whatever you need to while I'm gone. I have nothing to hide, and whatever she says, I'm sure I've got a reason to dispute why she thinks I killed Tom."

Angela had her arms crossed and her cheeks sucked in as she tried not to pay me any attention. Gloria and Loretta were headed back to the one holding cell in the department when I stopped them in the hallway.

"Can I talk to Loretta for a minute?" I asked Gloria, who looked at Loretta for confirmation. "Thanks. It'll only take a second. I know you want to see Birdie, but I assure you she's okay. I talked with her about all of this, and I told her I'd talk to you."

"I'm not sure if I want to hear what you have to say." Loretta was really good at letting her pride get in the way, and both of us knew that today was not the day for that.

"I know you're upset with me. I don't blame you. If this was my daughter or granddaughter, I'd be upset too. I've got a solution." Though she didn't ask me what my solution was, I could see a little spark of hope flicker in her eyes. "The problem is that Tom Foster was poisoned with a destroying angel mushroom. As citizens of Honey Springs, you and I both know the mushroom grows on the island near the Bee Farm and also near the Bee Happy Resort." I watched her intently as I continued to tell her my plan, so I knew she was following along and not just staring at me.

"Well, Birdie was seen on the island the other morning, and with her chemistry background, it really does look like she went over there to get the mushrooms. But"—I put my hand up when I noticed Loretta was about to interrupt—"that doesn't make her a murderer. What makes it look bad is that she had a fight with Tom the night before he died. The mushrooms were in her purse."

Loretta blinked several times quickly. Her lashes drew shadows down her cheeks as she tried to register what I was saying.

"Oh dear me." She drew her jeweled fingers up to her lips. "What does this mean?"

"It means that not only did she have motive, since he really did insult her in front of Patrick, which does make a teenager pretty mad, but worse, one of the murder weapons was in her purse. How did it get there?" I knew it wasn't a question I necessarily wanted her to answer, but it was a question that needed to be discovered if Birdie wasn't going to be a suspect. "I can't be her lawyer since I am already looking into it for Tom's wife, Robin."

"Yes, you can. We are family, Roxanne Bloom. If you've learned one thing since you've been here, you know that our community is a family, and during times like these, we have to rely on our family." She was right about the community coming together during rough times.

It was one of the reasons I loved living in Honey Springs. It was a tight-knit community that pulled together when someone needed it. It didn't matter if you were ill, having money issues, needed an ear, had death in the family, or apparently were a murder suspect. Every time, the citizens of Honey Springs pulled through for each other.

"Technically, I can't by law—" I started to say before she interrupted me.

"By law, we aren't blood-related either, but we are town-related. Southern small town, if I need to refresh your memory, and we took you in. Now." She sucked in a deep breath. "I expect you to use whatever means necessary to find out how those mushrooms made it into my Birdie's bag. I will tell you this. She was at the Bee Farm because I needed some honey for my sweet honey corn bread for the Southern Women's Club meeting tomorrow. I called Kayla and asked her if she could get some ready for Birdie to pick up before she came to your coffee shop for a job interview. In fact, I also called Big Bib. So you can check with them about Birdie's reason for going over there."

"I do remember Kayla mentioning Birdie was there, and she said Birdie didn't even get out of Big Bib's pontoon." Surely that would give Spencer some other reasons to look into someone else who was actually staying on the island. "Other than her coming to work, has she ever done anything else?"

"No. She stays in her room or on her phone all the time. We did go to the boutique to get her some new school clothes so she can start, but I was with her the entire time." Loretta was going to do everything to make her happy. "Roxanne, I wasn't the best mother to Elliott." Loretta gulped. "I did what I thought was best. I sent him off to one of the finest boarding schools to get the best education. We were one of the biggest donors. I made sure I was in the finest clubs and not only locally but nationally as well so that I made contacts all over in case Elliott ever needed anything."

"You did the best you could." I knew this was Loretta's big moment to make things right with Elliot, and it sure did look like she was messing up. My thoughts traveled back to when she said we were a community and how during hard times, we stuck together. Well, this seemed to be her hard time.

"I'm going to go in and talk to her. I'll do everything I can to solve this murder for the best outcomes for everyone." I knew I wasn't going to be able to promise her anything, but words seemed to comfort her for the moment.

She nodded.

The room—or cell, as they referred to it at the station—was no more than just a box with a conference table and some old beat-up chairs that I'm sure they'd gotten from donations. It wasn't like some big jail cells that you'd see on crime television shows.

Birdie's head popped up from the table when she heard the click of the door.

"Roxy, what on earth is going on?" Her eyes were red around the edges, and she had big blotches on her face. "I didn't kill that man. And I have no idea where those mushrooms came from."

"Remember how I told you I was a lawyer?" I asked and pulled out the chair next to her. I bent over and gave her a hug because I could tell she needed it.

"Yes. I remember." She sniffled and dragged the sleeve of her shirt underneath her nose.

"I'm going to ask you some questions, and I need you to be truthful with me, or I'm not going to be able to help get you out of here." I didn't need to tell her that I wasn't her lawyer. She was a kid, and at this point, I was just a friend helping another friend out with my knowledge.

She nodded.

"You have to tell me the truth." I lowered my chin and gave her a hard look so she'd take me seriously. "I know you took the boat ride over to meet Kayla Noro at the Bee Farm to pick up the honey for your grandma. According to Kayla, you didn't get out of the boat. Have you gone back to the Bee Farm since or even gone back to the island?"

"No. Are you kidding? Loretta Bebe is better than any security system. If I as much as shift on the couch, she asks me what I'm doing. Every move I make is seen by her." Birdie's eyes didn't shift, her face didn't contort, and she didn't move uneasily in her chair—all different types of body language I had gotten good at reading to see if people were telling the truth.

Birdie was telling the truth.

"What was your fight with Tom about?" I asked her. "I need details. Words exchanged and so on."

"He told me the coffee was burnt after I gave him his order. I got offended because I messed up. I'd poured him old coffee from the old pot, and when I picked up the cup of coffee, I realized it was cold and put it in the microwave to heat, which molecularly we both know does make coffee taste burnt and stale. So when he did take the drink and told me that it was old and started to make a note on his little notepad, I got nervous since he was tying the problem to you and the coffeehouse when it was my fault. That's when I told him that he didn't know what he was talking about and you had the best roastery, and I started churning out chemistry terms."

She started talking fast, which told me she was getting all worked up again.

"Okay." I put my hand on her hands. "I want you to stop talking because you're getting all worked up, and I need you to be clearheaded. I want you to take a deep inhale through your nose." I started to recall Angela's, of all people's, breathing technique so I could get Birdie to think clearly. "Long exhale out your mouth."

Birdie nodded and did it. We did it together three times before I could see the skin around her eyes relax.

"What did Tom say when you told him all that chemistry stuff?" I asked.

"He said I was smart but that I needed to spend time in the chemistry lab instead of a coffee shop. That's when your husband put the kitten down and came over to tell me who he was." She shook her head. "I was embarrassed but thought we were good since there was only one other person in the coffee shop."

"There was the other guy in the coffee shop too." I remembered her telling me about someone who she described as Casper.

"There were actually two. One I'd forgotten about," Birdie said. "Now that I have to remember everything, there was another guy there."

"Do you know who the guy was?" I asked.

"No. I tried to make some chitchat with him, but he insisted on telling me not to worry about that old man, meaning Mr. Foster. He said the old man probably liked coffee from a chain and didn't appreciate the finer roasted blends. He was nice." She shrugged.

"Did he say he lived in town?" I asked.

"No. He did ask about the kitten. Before your husband came in, he was playing with the kitten and holding him a lot. Then when Mr. Foster came in, he put the kitten back and sat on the couch to drink his coffee." She shook her head.

"This man, what did he do after he told you not to worry about Mr. Foster? Did he stay around the coffee shop? Did my husband see him?" I asked.

"He left me a twenty-dollar tip and left." Her jaw dropped. "Do you think he is the killer?"

"Anything is possible. Especially if he overheard you fighting with Tom. What if he came back and put the mushrooms in your purse? He knew there was a fight, and he could easily set you up. Did you see him again in the Bean Hive?" I asked.

"No. And I would've recognized him from his strange voice. I even asked him where he was from. He said New York City, and I remember because I dream of going there one day. Plus, he's scared to death of dogs, so when he came in, he asked about the kitten and dog beds. He said when he was a kid in New York, dogs ran the streets, and one bit him. He had to get stitches." She frowned. "I'll never get to New York now if I'm in jail for a murder I didn't commit."

I didn't tell her, but there were two murderers on the loose, and unfortunately, I did believe Birdie had been set up to take the fall.

CHAPTER TWELVE

I'd made it out of the room without Spencer coming to find me, and I had a few answers to at least start with, and when I walked back to where all the officers' desks were located, I noticed everyone was gone but Spencer. Loretta had gone into the room after me to talk to Birdie, so we were alone.

He looked at me and tapped the eraser-end of his pencil on the desk.

"Where is everyone?" I asked.

"I sent everyone away but you." Spencer's deep-green eyes held some questions. His hard jaw was set just below the curls of his sandy-blond hair that hung down by his ears.

No wonder he didn't come looking for me. He was waiting for me. Like prey, my eyes narrowed as I tried to read the room.

"I guess now that Crissy is not cutting hair at the Honey Comb, you've let your hair grow." Nervously, I laughed, and he didn't crack a grin. "Bad timing."

"What did Birdie say?" His roller chair groaned as he put the pencil down, and he clasped his hands together as he leaned back in the chair, bringing them to rest on his broad chest.

"I guess I should've asked you to see her first, but I saw the opportunity and took it." I smiled and sat down since I knew he wasn't going to just let me walk out without giving me some grief about it, though he technically couldn't keep me here.

"You and I both know that you're going to keep digging until you can get that girl out of trouble even though you've already taken the case for Robin Foster. It's the girl and your connection to her that'll drive you to do it." He pushed himself upright again. "That's when I'm smart enough to say to myself, 'Spencer, Roxanne Bloom just isn't disciplined enough to keep her nose out of it, so why go through the hassle of telling her to stop snooping when you can use her kinda like a hound dog?'"

"Spencer Shepard, is that your gentlemanly way of asking me to help you? I know you're having a hard time believing that I just might be right and Birdie Bebe is innocent." I could feel the edges of my lips starting to curl. "Or is it that she is young, and if you do get it wrong, your job will be on the line?"

Even though Spencer was the law, it was an elected position.

"You and I both know that if you make one wrong move in this job, you won't *have* a job." I did like to remind him of how it was the citizens that he was wrongfully accusing who gave him the shiny five-pointed-star badge on his collar.

"Are you going to take my offer or not?" He wasn't about to go toe-to-toe with me.

"I didn't hear an offer." I tilted my head to the side like I was confused when I knew all the cards were in my hands. When he didn't budge, I continued, "Fine. What if Angela actually picked the mushrooms because she's working over there on the island because all these holistic-type people forage for mushrooms and all sorts of crazy things to use in their diets? All that green juicing and stuff." I stuck my tongue out and crinkled up my face. "They know all about mushrooms, so don't let her little 'I'm so fit and pious' act ruin you. And we know she had the affair with Tom." I pointed back and forth between myself and him. "We know from past crimes that a scorned woman is deadly."

He sighed, dragging his feet from their laid-out position to plant the soles of his shoes on the floor, becoming a little more attentive to what I was saying.

"I saw her and Tom the morning of his death. I'm not so sure they didn't see each other the night before. She set it all up. She and Tom could've been talking, and he told her my coffee was burnt, and she knew it would be a good way to kill him. If he had coffee from my place, it was the last thing he drank. He got a stomachache and diarrhea, all the symptoms of the poison, and was left to continue being seen at the coffee shop, letting the argument with the seventeen-year-old, hot-headed teenager run the gossip of the small town, placing Birdie as the killer." My eyes narrowed as I told the story I'd made up in my head of what had happened, or even just one possibility of what had happened, which was how all of my clients' stories started out until we hit on something factual to help them. "She came into the coffee shop and slipped the mushroom bag into Birdie's." My mouth dried.

Slowly, my eyes moved from the top of Spencer's desk and drew up to his eyes.

"She knocked over the coat-tree," both of us said in unison.

"She did it on purpose. She put the mushrooms in Birdie's bag when it tumbled to the ground. She tried to pick up the purse so fast, she slipped it in there." Spencer had now made a connection that gave Birdie the slightest bit of hope and gave him the tiniest bit of doubt in his "Birdie was the killer" theory, which gave me an opportunity to take, which I did.

"Which means, you don't have sufficient evidence to keep Birdie here, and she can leave." I smacked the table, leaned back in my chair, and smiled.

"And I let Angela go." He opened up the file and thumbed through it. "I need to call her and tell her that I have a few more questions and not to leave town."

"I think she's still teaching, because I believe Crissy still plans to keep the retreat open even with Tom's murder. I mean, I would if I were her, because he wasn't killed on her property." My voice filled the dead air between me and Spencer.

"Then who shot him?" Spencer asked.

"Let's solve one murder at a time." I just knew that Angela had done something and, possibly, so had one of the two men that Birdie had mentioned, but I kept that close to my cuff. I could've told Spencer about them, but there was no real threat, and I wasn't sure how I would even find out who these men were.

"I'm not done. I will go to the resort and follow up on some leads that I'm hoping to get from Tom's notes. Robin said I could look over his notes from his articles, and Crissy will let me look at her registration to see if the notes match anyone he's written articles about. That'll at least give us some more suspects."

"I was hoping to shorten the list, not expand it." Spencer really did act as if he thought this was going to be buttoned up in a few hours.

"By the way"—I'd almost forgotten—"did you get Tom's cell phone?"

"He didn't have a cell on him or a wallet. We do have his record subpoenaed, so I'm hoping to get those back soon." His voice turned sharp. "Why do you ask?"

"According to his wife, he had a different cell before, when she caught him and Angela texting back and forth. I overheard him talking to someone on the phone, and Tom was very threatening to them." It was starting to feel like an endless list of people that he'd made mad and had great motive to kill the man.

"He mentioned how he could ruin their reputation, which Angela also said he could do, as did Crissy." I gnawed on the idea that whoever was on the other end of the phone was the shooter. Then I went there. "What if the second killer was the person on the other end of the phone? They were setting up a meeting or something?"

"I'll see if I can get a rush on the phone records." He jotted something down in his notes.

"Crissy is beside herself over it."

"And..." I was going to tell him to get the other phone from Robin so he could see exactly how involved Angela was with the victim, but I got a vibe from him that I had to point out. "Are you and Crissy...?" I asked and smiled, knowing they'd make a great couple.

"My personal life is none of your business." He made it quite clear that was off-limits.

"Then you know who the secret partner is, don't you?" I looked at him. "What if the secret partner is the killer? I mean, the secret partner has access to the trench coat I saw the killer had on, and maybe Tom was going to write a bad article about the retreat, which would make the retreat unsuccessful."

He hesitated, which told me I'd planted the seed, and it would fester there until he couldn't stand it any longer, when he'd look into the secret partner. "I'm not going to even talk to you about this."

"No stone left unturned. You have to look at every person, and that means the money trail." I held up two fingers. "Scorned woman. Money. Two of the biggest motives for murder."

CHAPTER THIRTEEN

It wasn't like I was going to let Patrick Cane off the hook, because I know it was his big mouth that told Spencer Shepard about the fight between Tom and Birdie. Plus, I had to find out about the other customer in the coffee shop.

The cabin was glowing when I pulled up. Smoke billowed out of the chimney, and the smell of wood filled the air. A feeling of gratitude filled me when I saw Patrick in the window, knowing he was nothing like Tom Foster.

I couldn't imagine what Robin was going through knowing the man she loved had been cheating on her and wondering if he still was, being it was what had gotten him killed.

There was a sense of calm that fell over me as I opened the door.

"Welcome home." Patrick got up from the couch and walked over to help me with my coat. He bent down to give me a kiss on the lips. "I made us a fire. We better enjoy it while we can because soon it'll be too hot for one."

I had two pups vying for attention. Sassy was knocking Pepper with her tail that was a nubbin but longer than Pepper's. Pepper growled and tapped his way to my other side.

"There's enough for everyone." I spoke in baby language to them, giving them some good rubs before I looked up at Patrick. "The fire feels so good." I stood up and looked around at what we'd created. "Thank you for being such a wonderful husband."

"What's going on in that little head of yours?" He had an inquisitive look in his eyes. "Tom Foster?"

"Yeah." I shrugged. "I talked to his wife, and honestly, he wasn't a good person. Though I don't think anyone deserves to be murdered. It's the fact that he just wasn't nice to anyone and loved writing terrible reviews to get the name he has. I mean." I shook my head. "Couldn't he have been a little nicer and offered suggestions to the people? What made him God?"

"Honey, these are all questions you're never going to get answers to, but if I know you—and I do—I know that you are going to do whatever you need to do to find out the answers." He placed each of his hands on one of my shoulders and turned me around. "Which is why I got takeout from the Watershed, since we couldn't go on our date, and I went by the library. Joanne Stone pulled some of the old *Healthy Women's Magazine*s. They might be old, but they do have some of his reviews in them, and let's just say that every one of the people he talked about had good motive to kill the man."

"Looks like my work is cut out for me." I looked at the stack next to the to-go box from the restaurant.

"You go sit and love on the dogs while I get your supper warmed up and a tall glass of wine." His words were music to my ears.

"Thank you." I kissed him one more time before I took the opportunity to love on the babies some more. "I can't believe you told Spencer everything."

"He asked, and he is the law, so we have nothing to hide." Patrick had taken the food out of the box and put it on a plate to warm in the microwave.

"I know, but I wish you'd told me about it." I eased down on the couch and melted into the fluffy cushions. It felt so good to be home. I slipped my shoes off and propped them up on the coffee table. The warmth from the fire warmed them quickly. "I was like a deer in headlights when he told me what he knew."

"Are you upset?" He walked over and put my food on the coffee table so he could go back and get our wine.

"No. I just really want to help out Birdie, and even though I don't think she killed Tom, the evidence isn't that great." I sat up on the edge of the couch and took the wine glass from him.

"I'm sure you'll help her somehow." He took a stack of magazines under his arm and carried them over and put them on the table. "I think this will drag on if they do a good job at going through all the reviews he did. I don't think I saw even one that was good."

"Looks like I'll have to go over them tomorrow." I looked at the plate, and I was almost too tired to eat. "Right now, I think I'll just enjoy this glass of wine, snuggled up to you."

It was a perfect night to have stayed in. While I let Patrick pamper me with a lot of hugs and kisses, Sassy found a warm spot near the fireplace, and Pepper lay right up against me until we all decided to move the snooze-fest to bed.

As much as I wanted to sleep all night, when I woke up around three, and I mean fully awoke, I didn't bother trying to force myself to lay there when I knew I wasn't going to be able to stop the hamster wheel in my head.

Patrick didn't move when I sat on the edge of the bed and slipped my feet into my slippers. I grabbed my robe and put it on as I left the bedroom. Pepper soon joined me next to the fire, where there was still an orange glow from what remained of the last pieces of wood we'd put in.

I dragged the *Healthy Women's Magazine*s from the coffee table along with a blanket and curled the blanket around me. There was an inward need to cocoon myself from the reviews I was about to read that were written by Tom. Boy, was I naive about just how mean Tom could be. Honestly, I was beginning to wonder if I needed to bring justice to the man's death at all because after reading the few reviews we had right here, there were no redeeming qualities about him.

Angela Paul was right about one thing. The man crucified everyone he came into contact with.

CHAPTER FOURTEEN

There was no way I was going to go back to sleep. I was so disturbed by his mean-spirited words about people and their livelihoods that I had to regroup with a hot shower and pot of coffee before Pepper and I headed to work.

"First off, we need to get the coffee shop open," I told Pepper when we walked down the boardwalk toward the Bean Hive. "Then I need to go to the library to see Joanne about Tom Foster going there and if she saw him."

I put the key into the door and unlocked it. I flipped the lights on and locked the door behind us.

"Hello, kitty." I greeted the little black furball and gave it little slow blinks so it knew I was friendly. "Are you hungry?" Pepper danced around. "Not you. You're always hungry." I laughed. "I was talking about kitty."

I sighed and headed back to the industrial coffeepots, flipping them on as I went down the line on my way to get Pepper's and the kitten's kibble.

After I got them settled and the stoves turned on, Aunt Maxi was already at the door.

"Any news?" she asked and swept past me before turning around to give me a hug. She headed straight to the coffee, where she did fix us both one.

"About what?" I didn't know exactly what she meant or who the news could be about. There was so much going on that she could've been talking about anything.

"I hear Spencer let Birdie go and that they have no idea who killed Tom Foster." Aunt Maxi took a couple of sips of coffee, letting go of a deep sigh. "This is good stuff, right here." She put the two cups of coffee on the small café table closest to the counter, where I sat down with her.

I loved spending time with her, and the timing was perfect, before we opened with no one else around.

"Thank you." I gestured to the coffee. I loved her so much. She'd always been so kind and good to me. I only could think of Birdie and hoped that Loretta would be the same for Birdie.

There was a banging on the door.

Aunt Maxi and I both jumped, neither of us expecting anyone until Birdie showed up at nine.

"Lordy bee, is that old Bunny Bowowski?" Aunt Maxi asked when we noticed there was some sort of hat on top of the person's head but it was still too dark out to see the face.

"Nah." I pushed the idea away. "But it sure does look like her."

Aunt Maxi and I didn't move from the chairs as our heads bobbed back and forth as we tried to get a better view of the person.

"Are y'all gonna let me in or not?" It was Bunny. "I left my key at home in my other pocketbook."

"That old codger. What is she doing here?" Aunt Maxi snarled. She patted the table as I was getting up to go let Bunny in. "I reckon I'll let her in. You sit right there." She rolled her eyes, sighed, and got up.

Bunny continued to jiggle the door handle with one hand and bang on it with the other.

"Keep your britches on, Bunny Bowowski. I'm comin'!" Aunt Maxi yelled at her.

If I knew Aunt Maxi—and I did—I swear she took the long way around and even patted kitty before she got to the door.

"You're a devil," Bunny spat at Aunt Maxi. "Leavin' me standing out there with a killer on the loose. Why, Maxine Bloom, you're nuttier than a fruit cake."

"Aw, go on. I was teasing you, Bunny. Why can't you ever take a joke?" Aunt

Maxi was no more joking with Bunny than Tom Foster's killer was having a little disagreement with him. "You don't look so good."

"I could say the same thing about you." Bunny shoved past Aunt Maxi. "If you're here, I guess I have to tell you too."

"What's wrong?" My goodness. My heart couldn't take much more. I got up to help Bunny with her coat and purse while she took care of taking her pillbox hat off her head.

"Me and Floyd are kaput." Sprinkles of spit sprayed out of her mouth.

"That's nasty. We aren't flowers that need to be watered." Aunt Maxi ran her hand down her arms like Bunny had spit on her, which she hadn't.

"I guess my news makes you happy, Maxine." Bunny took her coat and purse from me. "You can have him. You can have any man in Honey Springs you want because I am done with men." She made her way over to the coatrack and hung up her things.

"You outta be. You're nearly one hundred." Aunt Maxi continued to poke poor ole Bunny.

"Stop it. Can't you see she's heartbroken?" I told Aunt Maxi when Bunny had gone back into the kitchen to do her normal routine for when she worked mornings.

"That means Floyd is back on the market." Aunt Maxi's eyes lit up.

"Don't even think of it," I warned her. "He obviously did something to Bunny that wasn't good, so you better just stay away from him. Besides, I need everyone to keep the peace." I drank the last little bit of my coffee. "We need peace around here more than ever."

Aunt Maxi pulled her lips together when Bunny came back through the kitchen door with some trays full of tasty treats to put in the bakery counter.

"I hear we've had some scuffling around here. Mae Bell Donovan called me five times about the murder." She talked and worked her way down the line, putting the pastries on the various trays and rearranging them to look pleasing to customers' eyes. "By the look of the wipe-off board, I reckon you've gone and stuck your nose in it. Another reason why I figured on coming on back."

The industrial coffeepots beeped done. I went over and removed them and replaced them to start another batch. Normally, I had at least three on hand of each brew since coffee went fast. Today, I was going to make at least four each since I knew people would be coming in about the murder and getting the scoop.

"What happened between you and Floyd?" I asked and noticed Aunt Maxi had stopped refilling the napkins in the middle of each table to take a listen.

"You really want to know?" Bunny slid the door shut on the display case and turned around to get herself a cup of the freshly brewed coffee.

"Of course we do. How else are we going to pray for him?" Aunt Maxi questioned when Bunny and I both knew that she meant gossip.

When any of their friends said they were going to pray for someone, they were going to talk about them. Plain and simple.

"It was a hot mess. I guess I'm just old fashioned. We got back from supper with his family, and it was all good. I excused myself to go to bed because I wanted to finish reading our book from book club, and he was naked as a jaybird in my bedroom."

Aunt Maxi busted out laughing.

"What is so funny?" Bunny drew her hand up to her chest. "You might be some loosey-goosey but I'm not. And it's just something I can't untell."

By "untell," she meant in Southern it was something she just couldn't unsee.

"No." Aunt Maxi was crying she was laughing so hard. She waved her hand in the air, practically doubled over. "Just the thought of Floyd being, well, in his glory, makes me laugh."

"It horrified me. I'm not looking to take care of some man in my golden years. I was looking for companionship, and Floyd is not that."

"It's better you found out now," I told her to make her feel somewhat better, though I probably didn't.

"What?" Aunt Maxi asked. "You didn't want to play pig in a poke?" She could hardly get it out from her cackling.

"Maxine Bloom, you are plum awful, and I'm not gonna stand here and listen to this." Bunny shuffled back into the kitchen. "Besides, I wanted to come back for Crissy's opening weekend. From the pictures on the website, it looks like it's a lot of fun."

"You be nice to her," I instructed Aunt Maxi. "Bunny is a good woman. Floyd is a nice man. He's just a man, that's all."

"That is so funny. I can't wait to tell the ladies at the Southern Women's Club about this." She shook her head. "Which reminds me, can you bring some of the leftover pastries from breakfast to the library? I'm in charge of desserts, and I counted on you donating some."

"Of course you did." I snickered. "About the Southern Women's Club..." I quickly told her the deal I'd made with Loretta and to bring up my membership because if I knew Loretta—and I did—then I was going to have to keep on her to make good on her promise to me. "Speaking of promises, now that Bunny is here, I can go see all the people I promised Spencer I'd see today. I'll grab the coffees and donuts for the Cocoon Hotel so I can drop them off on my way since I parked on that side of the boardwalk."

Aunt Maxi pulled her coat back on and excused herself to the bathroom, where I knew she'd be fluffing up her hair.

"I'm sorry you had a difficult trip." I wanted Bunny to know that I cared for her and her feelings. I grabbed a couple of bags and put a few donuts in each to put in my purse like I did every time I left the coffeehouse. I never knew when I'd run into someone, and I never liked to be empty-handed.

"You got lucky with the second one." She wagged a finger at me. "Let me tell you that there's no way I'm going back out there on the market. Bunny Bowowski is going to be single as I walk through those pearly gates."

Bunny's way of telling me how she was going to stay single until she died made me cackle.

"I wouldn't close the door so soon. You are a catch." I got my jacket on and flipped Pepper a treat. "Here is the information on the kitten. Birdie will be in around nine, and she can tell you all about the sweet feline."

"No problem here." She handed me the box of sweets she'd gotten together for the Cocoon Hotel. "I'm looking forward to getting to know her better. Do you know her hours?"

I placed my purse strap across my body and, with each hand, grabbed a handle of the pot.

"She'll start school here next week. Hopefully, she'll step into the afternoon role if we can just be sure that she didn't poison anyone." It wasn't like she was completely off the hook as a suspect. I had all the intention today to figure out how to get any and all evidence that pointed to her out of the way so she didn't go to jail. "Which means I've got to get these down to the Cocoon so I can make all the stops I need before I come back here this afternoon." I nodded to Pepper. "Are you good with him? If not, I can call Patrick to pick him up."

If I'd known Bunny was going to be there, I'd have left Pepper home. I'd planned on working this morning with him there then taking him back after Birdie and I finished the lunch crowd.

"You kidding?" she asked. "I love that little feller."

"I'll be back in a couple of hours to grab the coffee, and if you don't mind, take that marble tea cake out of the freezer so I can take it to the Southern Women's Club." I knew every one of those women were going to love a marble tea cake. If they were anything like men, I knew if I could just get my food in front of them, I'd have their hearts.

CHAPTER FIFTEEN

The sunrise was spectacular over Lake Honey Springs, and if you'd not heard what had happened on the boardwalk, you'd think this was an amazing place to be. Not that the murder was just a random killing. I didn't believe that, and with all the evidence, there were too many suspects for me to be able to narrow down exactly which one was the real killer using just my sleuthing skills.

My mind was occupied with the difference between me and Spencer. While he did look at the hardcore evidence, I honestly knew how to manipulate it and carefully place it for pointing fingers at someone else.

In this case, with Birdie as Spencer's main focus for the poisoning, I hoped I'd made a good strong case for him to take a solid look at Angela Paul. Not only did I believe she had a very good motive as a scorned ex-girlfriend in an affair that Tom Foster himself had put an end to six months ago, but I couldn't help but wonder if he was going to write a review on her. It was something I needed to explore when I went over to the Airbnb Aunt Maxi had rented to Tom and his wife, Robin.

I shifted my gaze and thoughts down to the marina when I heard some rattling coming from the docks. I still had to make my way to see Big Bib since I'd yet to find out from him what he meant when he commented on how I must've been who Angela and Casper were talking about.

With a little giddyup in my step, I moved to get these hospitality treats to Camey so I could get my amateur-sleuthing hat on and get life in Honey Springs back to normal. As the day's list of visits I needed to make rolled through my busy mind, I didn't even notice the flurry of people when I walked into the Cocoon Hotel at such an early hour.

"There you are." Camey had rushed in the room. Haphazardly, I put the industrial coffee carafes up on the credenza so she could place them the way she wanted, but she just shoved them back a little and took the box of pastries from me, popping open the box for the taking.

"You didn't display them." I made the comment with a tilted head, furrowed brows, and my finger pointing at them. "What's going on around here?" All the people milling around suddenly dawned on me.

"That's what I was going to tell you." She snuggled closer and whispered, "Spencer Shepard is upstairs right now. He had a search warrant for Angela Paul's room, and he's been up there for like an hour."

"You're kidding me," I gasped.

I knew she wasn't kidding. My excitement combined with the notion that what I had presented to him at the station last night must've taken root and festered.

Without even hearing her response, I busted through the group that had gathered for some coffee and headed out the door and up the stairs to where the rooms were located. It didn't take much to figure out Angela Paul's room was on the left, number three.

The deputies gathered outside of the room told me.

"Ahem." I put my hands behind my back, slowed my speed, and walked past, craning my neck to see if I could see anything through the cracked door.

Just as my luck would have it, as soon as I took a step, the door opened, and Spencer was guiding Angela out in handcuffs.

"Take this to get fingerprinted." Spencer had yet to see it was me when he passed off an evidence bag with a cell phone in it to one of the deputies.

"Is that Tom's?" I questioned.

Spencer shifted his eyes to me. "Roxy, what are you doing here?"

"Help me. I didn't kill anyone. You have to help me," Angela pleaded with me as Spencer walked her past me. "I don't know where the phone came from. Someone planted it in my room."

"Let's go. You can call a lawyer when we get down to the station." Spencer didn't leave a second for me to even comment back, and I stood there, watching as they walked down the steps past Camey Montgomery and a slew of onlookers before he took her out the door.

CHAPTER SIXTEEN

"Gloria." I had called Gloria Dei on the phone when I realized the deputies were still combing Angela's room for evidence. "What on earth happened?"

"I reckon Spencer got to thinking about what you said. I came in early this morning and noticed he'd made an entire new clue board just on her. He also got some cell phone records back with her number on there."

"I'll call you later," I mouthed to Camey on my way out and tried to listen to what Gloria was saying.

"He said that some of the records showed that Angela hadn't been as truthful as she had told him, and when he saw she'd been talking to Tom, Spencer wanted some answers and called in a warrant to the judge, who decided to grant it to him about two hours ago. Tom had a photo of him and Angela on his phone from that night along with a text. Both of them had a cup of coffee in their hands. Spencer thinks this was when she slipped the deadly mushrooms in."

"I guess that's when he found Tom's cell phone." I couldn't believe it. "I guess this means Birdie is free and Robin Foster will head home."

"I reckon. Listen, he's coming in now with her. I'll call you back. Before I go, I wanted you to know that his wife said something about a review being run in this week's magazine that he'd gotten in before deadline. I'm not sure if it was anything about the Bean Hive, but I do know that it was an article about the town." Gloria sounded like she knew more than she was letting on.

"Maybe I'll go pay Robin a visit before she leaves and see if she knew anything about it."

That's when I decided to get in my car as planned and go see Robin. I already had a few extra treats in my bag since I never went without in case I ran into someone, so why not give Robin a few?

Downtown was still sleeping, and I couldn't help but think I was probably going to just drive past the cottage, which was just one street behind the main street, to see that Robin wasn't up yet.

As her lawyer, I had a duty to let her know someone had been brought into custody, and I could only imagine the look on her face when I told her it was Angela Paul.

"That's the best news!" She did in fact break down in tears after I woke her up. "I can't believe it. Do you have time for me to make a pot of coffee? I know it's not as tasty as your coffee, but it's the best I've got to offer."

She had on one of those fancy pajama pant suits with a matching robe and a pair of slippers.

"Sure. And I brought some donuts." I opened my purse and pulled out one of the bags I'd brought from the Bean Hive.

"Get in here." A sigh of relief descended upon her, and I could feel the tension leaving her body. "Now what happens?"

I followed her into the small cottage that I knew well since Aunt Maxi owned it. On a few occasions, I would help her clean it after guests would leave if I had the extra time. Even though she insisted she didn't need my help, she did, just as I'd always needed hers.

"Oh. You've already got your bags packed." I noticed when we walked into the small kitchen, where there were a couple of bags next to the door.

"Yes. I've got an Uber coming this afternoon to drive me to the airport." She ran a hand over the plane tickets on the table. "I've got an extra one if you want to get away to California. I'm not sure I can even cancel it. Tom made all the arrangements."

"I'm so sorry." I didn't really know what to say, but I did know how to make store-bought coffee not so bitter. "You enjoy a donut, and I'll make the coffee."

I knew my way around the kitchen and the process of making the coffee, adding a little pinch of salt to help with the bitter taste store blends naturally had. "Spencer just took Angela in," I said, "and he will put a rush on the phone."

I turned back to see a shocked look on her face. "She has the phone?" She blinked a few times, stunned.

"Yes. I talked to Spencer last night and told him my thoughts about Angela's motives along with how she slipped the poisonous mushrooms in my employee's purse when she knocked over the coat-tree, which she actually did on purpose." I had replayed that scene in my head over and over. "I don't know where we stand on the shooter. But we will take it one weapon at a time."

"I can't believe it. I told my children last night, and they wanted to come here to be with me, but I told them I was going to come on home." She picked up one of the airplane tickets with her free hand. "I guess I can just get it switched. If not, I'm sure there are a lot of hotels around the airport."

"There are." I knew Lexington, where the Bluegrass Airport was located, well since I was from there. "I'm sure you can get your flight changed if you go to the airlines, and if not, call me. I have a lot of great places you can tour while you are in Lexington."

"I'll take that phone number." She put the ticket back on the table and wiped a tear that'd fallen from her eye. "I just hope I can get home to see my family. Our daughter is expecting her third baby."

"Oh. That's wonderful." I took a couple of cups from the cabinet and filled them with the freshly brewed coffee. I walked them over to the table and allowed her to continue talking.

"Do you have any children?" she asked and dragged the mug to herself.

"No. But I'm feeling the expectations from my Aunt Maxi and my mom." I laughed and took a sip so I could swallow my own words that made me nervous to think about. "I'm a great dog mom. I'm not sure if I'd be a decent mom to a human. It's a lot of responsibility."

"You know, Tom was building his career during our children's lives, but when he came home, he was such a great dad." She sucked in a couple of sad sighs before she sniffled. "I can't even..."

"You don't need to right now." I didn't really know what she was going to say, maybe something like move on or think about her future without Tom, so I tried to give her permission to not even worry about anything. "I think you've got the right to just be and not try to figure it all out now."

"You know, you give much more to this community than coffee." She smiled. "You have a knack for listening and giving great advice. I think you're going to be a fantastic mom when you're ready."

"Goodness." I took another drink and listened to her talk about her children and grandchildren with pride on her face. She got lost in the stories, and for a few minutes, at least, she seemed to have a moment where she forgot her current situation.

"I've taken up more of your time than I meant to, but before I leave, I wanted to know if you knew Tom had sent in his new review for *Healthy Women's Magazine*." She looked at me with a furrowed brow. I continued, "The sheriff's department told me they'd gotten word that he had gotten his article written in time for deadline, and it's about Honey Springs. From what I understand—"

It was her turn to interrupt me.

"You hear that he's a little harsh in his reviews." She smiled. "That's made his opinions and reviews so popular and made many try to do their best."

I'd never looked at her husband's voice in the way that she presented it.

"But I assure you that he was charmed by this little town. When he left your coffee shop the first night we were here, he came back and told me he'd found a little gem, though there was a cat." She smiled at the memory. "If there's anything, it might be in his briefcase."

"Now that Angela is in custody, I guess you can use me to continue to look into who might've shot him." I guess she was thinking Angela had shot and poisoned Tom, because she looked at me funny. "You think there's two killers?"

"I don't know. I haven't really thought too much about two, just one and..." Her voice trailed off. "Maybe I need to stay in town." She glanced over at the briefcase next to the luggage.

"Why don't you touch base with Spencer, and I'll take the briefcase to continue looking into other possible suspects. There's no doubt in my mind Angela had her part in this, but I don't think she could pull a trigger."

"And there's a difference? He's dead." Robin's chest started to move up and down a lot faster.

"I know, I know, but someone like Angela couldn't hurt a person when actually looking them in the face. I don't believe her soulful life would allow that, but if she slipped a little poison into his coffee, then she wouldn't have to watch him die." I knew it was a visual none of us wanted to face, but Robin needed to be reminded of the reality that there was another person out there.

At least in my mind.

"I'd love for you to be my eyes and ears. Please, take the briefcase." She gestured her flat hand out to it.

"I really want to bring the killers to justice. No matter what your husband said or wrote about anyone, he didn't deserve to die." I couldn't wait to get my hands on the briefcase and see the contents.

"I don't know if he had finished the article on Honey Springs, but you will find all of his contacts from the magazine in his briefcase as well." Her eyes were dipped, as were the corners of her mouth. She patted her hair. "I guess I better get ready. My driver will be here soon."

I got up and walked over to the counter where Aunt Maxi kept a notebook for guests to sign and ripped a piece out. I used the pen to scribble my name and home phone number. Even though she had my cell number, I wasn't tethered to it like most people, so I also gave her the coffeehouse phone number.

"Here's all my contact information in case you can't get me on my cell. I'm not sure if you'll remember any more details, threats, or people you think might've come to Honey Springs to do this, but sometimes our minds are tricky and stop some of our tragic memories." Our fingers touched when I handed her the piece of paper.

"Thank you. You have been so helpful." She sucked in a deep breath, got up, and walked over to the briefcase, where she handed it off to me.

CHAPTER SEVENTEEN

My drive to really solve Tom's murder was honestly fueled by the fact that Birdie Bebe had been named a suspect since she and Tom had their public argument, the fact she had a very volatile past, and the hard evidence that the poisonous mushrooms that were found in Tom's system were in her purse, though they were now believed to have been planted by Angela Paul.

The fact remained that the case wasn't over until the killer who pulled the trigger on the gun was brought to justice. Even though the new evidence about Angela was brought to life, no matter how much Spencer tried to get her to confess, there wasn't real evidence other than phone bills and the photos of Tom and her together that Gloria had mentioned.

Without the confession from her, the state wouldn't have a case because there was reasonable doubt. I didn't know for sure if she'd planted the mushrooms in Birdie's bag, but as a lawyer in her defense, I knew I had to plant that seed in Spencer's head.

"Hey, Gloria." I had her on my car speakerphone. "I was thinking about Angela and the whole Tom Foster murder. Maybe Angela isn't the killer. I know she looks guilty with the phone found on her and all, but maybe someone planted it in her room like someone planted the mushrooms in Birdie Bebe's bag."

"I don't want to hear it." Gloria knew me well enough that calling her back to discuss something that seemed to be solved wasn't a good call. "Right now, Spencer is calm and working through the evidence of the case. So why don't you let him do that until you decide why Angela isn't the killer. The final autopsy came in."

"Really? Is there something in there that we didn't know?" I asked.

"The mushrooms in Tom's system weren't enough to kill him. Just enough to make him feel sick, maybe keeping him from the resort for a while," she told me.

"Then Angela wouldn't get charged with murder, just an intent to harm," I noted out loud to myself. "Which makes me come to the conclusion that I was right about her not having the nerve to hurt someone to their face, which means we might be starting at ground zero."

"She could've given him a few mushrooms to make him sick, but she insists she's innocent. It also means the gunshot was what killed him, and Spencer is really focusing on that right now until Angela's lawyer gets into town."

"She called a lawyer?" I asked.

"From what I understand, Crissy Lane called her one." Gloria got my mind shifted from Tom's case to the Bee Happy Resort.

"Do you know who?" I was a little taken aback since I thought Crissy would think of me—not that I was practicing for anyone other than family and friends and the occasional favor like with Robin Foster, but all the other times, Crissy had no issues sending someone to me.

Or maybe it was Crissy's silent partner's lawyer, and if that was the case, I wanted to know who that was.

"I have no idea, but I'll be sure to let you know when I do. I've got to go." She hung up the phone just as I put the car in park at the boardwalk.

I couldn't help but glance over at the island while walking across the boardwalk toward the Bean Hive and wonder who on the island had the motive to pull that trigger.

"Where have you been?" Bunny Bowowski had the items for the Southern Women's Club luncheon all packed up and ready to go. "I was thinkin' you forgot, and I got all nervous thinkin' I was going to have to deee-liver this stuff myself. And I don't want to have any questions regarding me and Floyd. It's no one's business, and I don't want to have to be rude to people."

"Thank you for doing all this." I touched the bags and the box of coffee. "But when I went down to the Cocoon this morning, Spencer was there arresting Angela Paul."

"Really?" Birdie asked from behind the counter, her voice an octave higher than usual. There was relief on her face.

"Yep." I sucked in a deep breath and bent down to pick up Pepper so I could give him some good hugs and kisses. "He found Tom's phone in her hotel room."

"Does that mean…?" Birdie didn't finish her sentence like she was unsure that she should.

"It means that you aren't a suspect right now. But you could be again. Not that I think you will be, but I can never read Spencer Shepard's mind when it comes to these things." I looked around the coffeehouse.

The breakfast crowd had settled down, and I was sure the citizens who loved to gossip had moved on down toward the Buzz In and Out Diner, where they'd continue their gossip over greasy bacon and eggs along with some deeply buttered bread.

"Come on back here, and I'll tell y'all about it." I gestured for them to follow me into the kitchen, where I knew no one was trying to listen in on our conversation.

I took the wipe-off board and went down the list of why Angela could be charged for intent to harm but not murder before I wiped off the whiteboard since we'd be starting over from scratch.

"What are you doing?" Bunny gave me a hard look.

"There's one thing that I do know, and if we find a gun and someone who is over at the Bee Happy Resort who can't give a good alibi, then we have the person who delivered Tom's final blow." I looked between the two. "And I think I will find my answer in Tom's briefcase, which Robin Foster has given me."

"How are you doing to do that?" Birdie seemed very interested.

"He had been doing some research at the library, and he was also working on some new articles for the magazine. When I drop off the Southern Women's Club items, I am going to see if Joanne can pull some of the old magazines and compare the list of attendees who purchased a coat with the list of people Tom has reviewed."

"Oh. And no matter whether the review was good or bad, you'll be able to ask them about their relationship with Tom and if they have an alibi." Birdie nodded as it all clicked in her head.

"You're pretty good at this." I smiled and recognized there was more to this young lady than met the eye.

"Here's a little secret that my grandmother probably doesn't want anyone to know because she wants all of y'all to believe she's working around her house, her garden, getting menus together, and whatever else in her head a Southern woman does. In reality, she sits on the couch with a bowl of ice cream every night and watches those old crime shows." As Birdie told the story of how it really was in Loretta's fancy house, it played in my head like a comical movie, and I couldn't help but laugh.

"She'd sooner die than tell us that." Bunny giggled like we had some big deep secret.

"Yep, she would." Birdie looked back at the kitchen door when we heard the bell ding. "I better get out there."

"And you better get to the library." Bunny practically shoved me out the kitchen door into the coffee shop. "Me and Birdie have got this. You go out there and make our town safe."

"Yes, ma'am," I said with a stern voice and grabbed the bags of goodies before I made my way across the coffee shop.

I stopped once I got to the door and said hello to the kitten, who was coming out of her shell a little more, but her eyes were still nice and big, full of uncertainty. Pepper was fast asleep in his bed next to the counter. The noon sun was starting to warm the entire boardwalk, which meant we no longer needed the fire to ward off the chill.

It was shaping up to be a perfect afternoon with the best temperatures to ride a bike. It was too bad I didn't have mine.

I continued to keep my face up to the sunshine as I walked along the boardwalk back to my car with my hands full of goodies for the club. There was no doubt in my mind the women would love them, but would they listen to Aunt Maxi about me joining or my little agreement with Loretta?

I snickered at the thought of using how Loretta sat on the couch with a big bowl of ice cream every night as ammunition since she always tried to convince people she ate healthily and never anything with sugar, but I'd never betray Birdie's trust.

Then it dawned on me how I might just be able to help Birdie by letting her talk out what she'd like the next step in her life to be. My thoughts were all over the place, but once I got into the car, it was like autopilot, right back to downtown, where I ended up snagging a parking spot right in front of the library.

"There you are." Aunt Maxi had on a crazy-looking ankle-length tie-dye skirt with a long white T-shirt and a long-sleeved crocheted cardigan that was orange and hung loosely around her. "What's that?" She gestured to Tom Foster's briefcase I'd stuck up under my arm so I could carry it all in.

"I told you I'd be here. I'm right on time. It's Tom Foster's briefcase. I'm too lazy to make two trips out to the car." I shrugged and followed her into the library. "Is Joanne here today?"

"She is at the circulation desk, but I'll take those." Aunt Maxi reached for the bags.

"I thought I'd take them in and have a few words with the ladies about me joining." I really wanted to make this happen. "Just think how I can cater their other fancy luncheons. It's a win for everyone."

"I'll let you come in at the end. We are discussing old business." She pish poshed me, which sent me on alert that she didn't want me in there.

"Fine." I pushed the bags and coffee box into her arms. "I've got other things to attend to. Like solving a murder."

"I'll keep my ears peeled for anything." She smiled, wiggled her brows, and turned to go into the conference room.

Sometimes, pushing on Aunt Maxi about things was worth it, and at other times, it was not. In this case, it would have been if I didn't have more important things on my mind, like Tom Foster and what was in the briefcase. I headed on back to the circulation desk where Joanne was sitting with a couple of the other library employees.

"Good afternoon, Roxy." She greeted me with a smile. "What's going on?"

"I had to bring some treats to the Southern Women's Club, and I wanted to see if I could get a few more of the old *Healthy Women's Magazine*s with Tom Foster's reviews. I'm helping Spencer out with some leads."

"Yeah. Of course." Her eyes grew big, and she got up from the chair behind the desk. "Did Patrick give you the ones I pulled for him?"

"He did, and I honestly couldn't believe them. Tom really doesn't sugarcoat a thing, and I can't help but wonder if whoever shot him was a victim of one of the criticisms." I didn't bother going into detail as we headed in the direction of the nonfiction and magazine area.

"The ones older than a month are kept in the back. You can help yourself to any desk, and I'll find you."

"I'm going to go jump on a computer. I'm going to check my email." I pointed the briefcase over to the media center, where there were computers for the public to use, and headed on over that way.

It was nice not to have a computer at my home. I did have the coffeehouse laptop but rarely used it. If I did, it was generally to pull up substitutes for ingredients for the baked items if I was low on something, but that's about it. I wasn't on social media and didn't have time to be, so there was really no sense in keeping a computer around all the time.

Plus, I was able to use the computer here for free, and it was nice to be able to chat with Joanne when I could because we didn't see each other often, and she didn't make it down to the boardwalk on a regular basis.

With a few short keystrokes, I logged into my email, where I was happy to see Crissy had sent me an attachment with the list of attendees of the retreat who had purchased a coat. I hit the print button, and the printer below the computer came to life.

"I heard Spencer made an arrest at the Cocoon." Joanne put the stack of magazines next to the computer. "I swear. Everyone is out for revenge for something. You really have to watch every move you make nowadays, don't you?"

"Yes. It's awful." I put my hand on top of the magazines. "Thank you."

"You're very welcome. Let me know what else I can do." She smiled.

"You can tell me if you saw Tom when he was in here the day he died." I knew from book club that Joanne didn't go to the opening of the Bee Happy Resort because she had to work, and Robin confirmed to me that he was here that day doing research.

"I did see him, and I told Spencer that there was another man that'd come in to talk to him."

"Really? How do you know?" I asked.

"The other guy came in looking for him, and I pointed him back to the desks, where Tom was writing away."

Two things she mentioned turned on my "hm" meter. First, I wanted to know who the guy was, and secondly, what on earth was Tom writing? A review?

"Do you think you'd recognize the guy if I pulled him up?" I knew the Bee Happy Resort had been posting all the new photos on the website, so I quickly pulled it up on the computer so we could click through the gallery.

Joanne bent over my shoulder and watched as I took a little time with each photo so she could get a good look.

"Go back." She used her finger to motion me to click the mouse to return to the previous photo.

"He looks familiar, but I can't say for certain." She moved her face closer to the screen. "Can you blow it up? Make it bigger?"

I doubled clicked it, but it really didn't do much, but I did recognize him.

Casper.

"If it's the person I think it is, his name is Casper." I mentally searched for a last name, but I never recalled if I'd even known it. "He and Angela came into the coffee shop the morning Tom was murdered." I turned around my chair to look at her. "When he and Angela saw Tom, he turned from Tom so Tom didn't see him."

I gasped.

"What?" Joanne asked me as though she wasn't sure if she wanted to know.

"He is Crissy Lane's consultant, and his fee is crazy expensive." I gave a hard swallow as goose bumps crawled along my arms. "Tom had given him a bad review, but Crissy decided to go ahead and give him a chance."

"Which means he has a motive and that same coat." Joanne finished my thought. "When this Casper left, that's when Tom tore up what he was writing."

"Was he writing on a tablet or notebook?" I asked in hopes I'd find it in the briefcase. "Or on a computer? Because we could go to that computer and take a look at the history," I suggested.

"He was writing on a paper pad, and he had something like that with him." She pointed to the briefcase.

"This is his." I picked it up from the floor and unzipped it. I looked inside and pulled out a notebook and a few file folders.

"That looks like the notebook." She nodded when she saw the simple spiral notebook. "I had to tell them to lower their voices as their conversation escalated."

"Escalated as in an argument?" I needed her to be a lot clearer.

"You could say it was loud whispers. After the man left, Tom seemed very flustered and ripped up whatever he had written down." She shifted her gaze back to the notebook. "The reason why I know he ripped up the pages is because I was with another person when I heard him rip it off the spirals then in two."

I looked into the briefcase to see if there were any ripped-up pages, but there was nothing. I looked around, trying to put myself in his shoes. Then it hit me when I noticed every single workstation in the library had a small trash can.

"What do you do with the trash?" I asked.

"The cleaning crew empties them every night and then puts everything in the dumpster out back." She folded her arms and swayed a little with narrowed eyes. "The trash comes once a week, and that would be tomorrow." Her brows rose.

"Thank you!" I jumped up and threw all the things in the briefcase and darted out of the library.

CHAPTER EIGHTEEN

There was little to nothing I wouldn't do to scratch that desire to figure out what had happened to Tom Foster. I recognized that dumpster diving was about as low as one could get but thought a dumpster full of library papers or whatever was thrown away in there had to be better than any other dumpster around.

Boy, was I wrong.

It became apparent that everyone thought this dumpster was a public one after I had to move a beat-up chair and bags of fast-food trash to even get to what looked like the same garbage-bag liners used in the library trashcans.

A long sigh escaped me as I tore into each bag and carefully looked at the contents, making sure I kept my balance on the bags below me that were holding me up in the nasty dumpster. In fear of catching something weird and to keep the stench away, I pulled the neck of my shirt up over my nose and continued to rip open each trash bag until I found some ripped-up sheets of paper.

"Aha!" I yelled, very proud of myself. I quickly tied up the bag and flung it out of the top of the dumpster.

"Are you okay in there?" I heard Spencer call from outside.

I jerked my head up, and my eyes were in perfect line with the edge of the dumpster.

"Roxy?" he questioned.

"Yep." I clawed my way back up to the top of the pile of trash and tossed bags out of my way as I went. "Want to give me a hand?"

"Sure." He shook his head and laughed, sticking his hand out to help hoist me up and then placing his hands on my hips to make sure I didn't fall flat on my face when I threw one leg over then my other one. "Do I even want to know what you were doing?"

My phone buzzed from my back pocket. I put a finger out for Spencer to hold on, and when I pulled out my phone, the voucher Crissy had given me for a massage fell out of my back pocket. It'd been so dark this morning when I got dressed, I must've put on the same jeans I had worn to book club.

Oh well.

Spencer bent down to pick up the voucher while I looked to see who was calling. It was Patrick, so I sent him to voicemail because I wanted to talk to Spencer then call Patrick back when I had a little more privacy and time to talk.

"Thank you." I took the voucher from him and stuck it back in my pocket.

"Okay. What were you looking for in there?" His eyes moved past my shoulders.

I didn't waste any time telling him how I had asked Joanne about Tom being there. "And I forgot the list I printed off." I planted my palm on my forehead when I realized I'd left Crissy's list on the printer.

"Then I'll take the bag and go in there to get the list." Spencer burst my bubble.

"You can't steal my thunder," I teased with a little bit of an aw-shucks feeling inside. I was really wanting to do all the digging in and checking out who was possibly another suspect. "Fine."

I held out the garbage bag when I thought he was going to grab it from me, but instead, he pulled a piece of scrap paper out of my hair that'd gotten stuck in one of my curls. Then he took the bag.

"Why don't you go use that voucher and relax," he suggested. "I will let you know if anyone raises a red flag."

"Fine. But if you need me to look into anyone while I'm over there, call me." I held my hand up to my ear like a telephone.

His eyes grew, his head tilted back, and he nodded as he took in a deep breath as if he were just entertaining me with an agreement that was probably not going to happen before he turned to head back around to the front of the library.

"By the way, I am still going to represent Robin while the investigation is ongoing." I'd almost forgotten to tell him. "And that means that I am able to see all the information, including all the stuff I just gave you from me risking my life by crawling into a nasty dumpster."

"Get a massage," he called over his shoulder without stopping, shaking the bag in the air.

I gave up and headed in the direction of the car.

"Spencer!" I hollered as he went into the library. "Casper might've killed him," I muttered under my breath when he didn't hear me and figured I'd just see exactly what Casper knew myself when I got my massage.

CHAPTER NINETEEN

"Do you really think he did it?" Birdie was sitting on the stool that was up against the workstation, with the kitten in her lap.

I didn't tell her that the kitten wasn't allowed in here, because I wasn't cooking and I wanted to talk to her about her school and what Loretta had really thought I was going to try to do.

To give the poor gal some direction.

"You know, I wouldn't be going over all of this with you if you'd not been a suspect," I told her. "You are a teenager and should be doing teenager things, not trying to solve a crime."

"I love solving crimes. I always get the killer on *Monk*. Grandma never gets it right, even when they show the crime before Monk even gets involved." She laughed.

It was really nice to see her laugh and smile. I was glad I'd gone back to the coffee shop to make my appointment for the massage. It was worth it just to sit here with Birdie and get to know her better.

"I don't know, but I think I might ask Grandma if I can have this kitten." She rubbed the kitten's back. "She is such a loud purrer."

"She?" I asked since we really didn't know what gender it was.

"Yeah. Today, Regina Fowler came in." She was referring to the local veterinarian. "She knew it right off."

"Did the kitten let her look?" I asked since the kitten had been so shy and none of us had wanted to upset the baby's world any more than it already was.

"Regina didn't care. She just picked her up and flipped her right on over." Birdie was sweet. She had a very caring heart under her exterior, and I could see that she loved animals.

"Have you thought about working at the Pet Palace? Not that I'm trying to get rid of you because you are by far my best employee, outside of Bunny," I said for good measure in case Bunny walked through the door any second.

"I like Ms. Bunny. She's really nice. And I love how she says my grandma's name." Birdie laughed again. "I don't know. I like it here. Especially when we do this kind of stuff."

She pointed to the wipe-off board, where I'd started to write down the reasons I felt Casper might be the shooter.

"I've been thinking about the whole lawyer gig." Birdie adjusted herself on the stool, and the kitten didn't even open its eyes. "What if I wanted to be a lawyer or some sort of forensic scientist? I mean, I think I would be good at both."

"There's no doubt in my mind that you will be able to do anything you want. You're very smart." I put the cap back on the dry-erase marker and set it on the workstation as I got up. "I'd love to explore that option with you more, but for now, I need a massage."

"Fancy," Birdie teased. Her face stilled. "I'm sorry I brought the kitten in here."

"Oh yeah?" She'd caught me off guard.

"I wanted to see if you'd say anything because I know the cat shouldn't be in here, but you didn't." She stood up and cradled the cat. "Why?"

"I don't know." I put my arm around her and smiled. We walked over to the door. "I think you want people around here to think you're somebody you're not. All we want to do is love you and help you succeed in whatever you want to do. And your grandmamaw is the same."

"Grandmamaw, huh?" Birdie questioned in a tone that told me she was going to start calling Loretta by the name Loretta wanted to be called.

"Loretta might be a bit of a pill to swallow sometimes, but she's done more good for Honey Springs than most people around here. So if she does do her crosswords, laze around at night, and watch TV or even have a little ice cream, she deserves it." We pushed through the kitchen door.

"Thanks, Roxy." Birdie went ahead and walked across the coffee shop to put the kitten back on the cat tree before she headed toward the bathroom.

"What was that thank-you for?" Bunny asked.

"I think you're really going to enjoy Birdie." I gave Bunny a hug and grabbed my purse. "You think you'll be okay while I go get my massage?" I rolled my head around my shoulders and acted all loosey-goosey.

"We was fine before. Get on out of here." Bunny dragged the hand towel from over top of her shoulder and flung one end at me.

"Come on, Pepper." I took the leash off the coatrack and decided on a whim to take him with me. He loved going over on the boat, and if he wasn't allowed to go in the massage room with me, I could leave him at the Bee Farm with Kayla.

Pepper needed a good walk and to go potty. He'd been so good over the last few days with me and my nose stuck in the investigation that I almost felt bad for him. Patrick always told me that I humanized the dogs too much, but I didn't care. He was probably right, and it was all right with me.

Pepper danced around my feet with the anticipation of the leash getting hooked on his collar. He loved going for walks, and a lot of the time, I didn't put him on a leash, but with the traffic that'd picked up with all the people on the boardwalk who were nosey about the murder and new tourists in town who were going to the resort, it was just too much for me to trust him to stay by my side. He loved everyone, and some people just didn't like it when a dog would run up to them.

"You want to go for a boat ride?" I asked Pepper in a baby voice, and we headed out of the coffee shop.

Big Bib's pontoon was almost full.

"Room for one and a half more?" I picked up Pepper.

"I've got room for him any day." Big Bib pointed at me. "But you're questionable." He grinned up under that big burly beard of his. "Get on in here."

I took my seat on the back couch of the pontoon near Big Bib, and Pepper sat in my lap.

"What's going on with that man's murder?" he asked from the helm of the boat.

"Do you remember that couple I asked you about, when you mentioned to me and Camey that I must've been the one they were talking about?" I helped jog his memory.

He kept one hand on the wheel of the boat and the other hand on the gearshift as he easily and steadily pushed it up to make the boat go faster.

"I think they did it. I'm not sure if they planned it together, but I think she poisoned him just enough to make him sick and not able to go to the events so he couldn't write a bad review for her class, because he apparently had broken off an affair that they were having, about six months earlier." It all sounded so sad when I told him. "Senseless, really." I sighed.

"That's terrible." Big had settled the boat into a steady speed and took a seat in the captain's chair. "What about the man?"

"Casper. He actually had motive. A big motive. He'd been victim to Tom's reviews already and come to find out Tom advised Crissy not to use Casper as a consultant. So I'm sure when you picked him up to bring him back here, you had no idea he had a gun in the pocket of that brown coat." I looked around at the people sitting in the boat and started to wonder what they had covered up in their jackets and purses.

"I never brought him back until later that night after the murder." Big Bib started to slow the boat down and waved at the person standing on the island's pier who would grab the edge of the boat once Big Bib put it in neutral so it could easily glide in to a smooth stop.

"He didn't come—" I paused. "Did you see anyone with that brown overcoat on that day before the shooting?"

"Yeah. I talked to some guy with a New York accent. He had on the coat. When I asked him what type of work he did for Crissy, he just said he was there as a customer." He slid the gearshift to the middle and let the boat idle.

"You said New York accent?" I questioned, recalling Birdie saying a man from New York had come into the coffee shop.

I gulped and patted around for my phone.

"What's that look on your face?" Big Bib asked.

"Nothing. I just forgot my phone." I smiled. "No big deal. See you soon."

"Why don't you leave Pepper with me?" he asked. "He loves the boat. Plus, the chicks like him."

"You are a bachelor." I looked at Pepper. He'd jumped into Big Bib's chair and appeared to have settled in.

"Look at him. He wants to stay. What are you going to be, like an hour?" he asked.

"If that long." I noodled over whether I should just take the boat ride back over to Honey Springs and call Spencer to let him know he should be looking for someone who had registered from New York.

Then I saw Crissy Lane standing near the dock and greeting each guest with one of the green juice thingies.

"You be good," I said.

"He is always good," Bib commented.

"I meant you." I laughed and jumped off the boat.

"How are you?" I asked Crissy when it was my turn to get my juice.

"Ugh," she groaned. "I guess it hasn't been as bad as I thought. Angela's class being cancelled was a little touch-and-go since a lot of people had signed up for her. Since she is here in Kentucky, a lot of her followers from all over the East Coast came to see her."

"Do you know if anyone, a man, specifically from New York, is here?" I asked.

"A lot of men from New York are here." Crissy handed the tray off to one of her employees. "I don't know. Maybe I'm not cut out to be a business owner. It's a lot of stress."

"I think you'll be just fine once we can get the killer in custody." I could tell by the look on her face that she'd not heard in full Spencer's new theory about Angela.

"I think I need more than a juice." She gestured for me to head up the hill toward the pool bar. "I have beverages that are a little more adult up there. I don't know how these people can live on this juicing stuff." She made a face, sticking out her tongue. "Yuck."

I laughed. The Crissy I knew was right here with me, and I loved it.

"Maybe you can own and run it, just not be the client. You don't have to be," I suggested.

"I guess." She and I walked up the trail.

I let the silence hang between us because I could tell she was having a difficult time processing her place in this venture. I also wondered if her silent partner had been the one with the big idea after she'd come back from her experience and had talked her into recreating what she had felt.

I could feel her starting to get upset.

"You know, you don't have to be one of these people. You only need to sell the experience."

"What do you mean?" she asked, and we sat down at the pool bar, where Pierre hurried right over.

"Ladies." His French accent was so charming. It was so different from the country accent we heard around these parts. "I'll be right back to serve you. I've got to take these cocktails to the cupping spa."

"They aren't cocktails," Crissy whispered to me like she thought I really did think they were. "But I've got a bottle of bourbon hidden behind the counter."

She started to get up, but I put my hand on her forearm.

"I'll make it. You sit and relax." I for sure was going to miss my massage appointment, but I figured Crissy needed me more than I needed the massage.

"What is going on? Just tell me." She laid her head on the bar.

Without even asking her where she hid the bourbon, I just took two of those fancy flutes since there weren't any different glasses and sat them on the bar before I went opening and closing cabinets to find the spirit.

"I think Angela poisoned Tom so he couldn't come here, but it wasn't enough poison to kill him. It was just enough to make him sick to his stomach so he didn't have any information to critique her for in his article." It was pretty much that simple. "And the killer, I believe, is..."

I bent down and looked into one of the bottom cabinets.

"Who? You believe it's who?" she asked.

I blinked a few times when I saw there was a brown overcoat rolled up on the cabinet shelf. I pulled it out and held it up in the air. As it unrolled, a passport and a gun with a silencer fell to the ground.

"What the heck?" Crissy rolled up on her forearms and looked over the bar at me.

"Pierre," I gasped after I picked up the passport and opened it up to his photo. "Alex Flatley."

"Crap." The voice caused me to jump.

"Pierre, do you know where Crissy's bourbon went?" I asked, throwing my arm behind me in hopes he didn't realize I had his passport that told me he was not Pierre from France but Alex Flatley from New York.

"Not sure." His accent had gone from charming to bold and loud. "But I do know that this little agreement must end." He gestured between the three of us and held out his hand. "I'll take my passport back and that little thing." He extended his leg and put his foot on the gun, sweeping it over to himself.

"What on earth is going on?" Crissy looked at him. "Pierre?"

"Honestly, me being Pierre from France is like you being Zen Crissy Lane. Honey, there's nothing Zen going on in there." He circled his finger around her head.

Her mouth dropped, then she clamped it shut when Alex picked up the gun and stuck it in my side.

"You head on over there with her. And we will need to figure out what we are going to do about this." He was snide.

I closed my eyes and sucked in a deep breath, wincing at the pain of the silencer digging into my ribs.

"I have no problem with you killing Tom." I wanted to get us out of this crazy situation. "Tom was a jerk, and the world will be so much better without him."

"What did he ever do to you?" Crissy decided to open up that big mouth of hers.

"Now is not the time to not be Zen, Crissy." I snapped at her. "Deep breathing."

"She could never be like Angela." Alex snickered. "You have no idea what Tom did to me."

"Maybe it can be our little secret," I suggested and walked back into the pool's mechanical room with the aid of the gun.

"The sound of these machines will help muffle whoever squeals when I kill the first one of you, but you won't cry for long, because I have to kill you both." He shoved Crissy next to me and removed the gun from my ribs, taking a couple of steps back.

"Listen, we don't care. We just want Crissy's resort to take off, and with Tom dead, we know he won't write a bad review about her." I was pulling out all the stops. "Besides, Angela is in custody, and they think she did the poisoning while Casper did the shooting."

There was someone outside of the mechanical room calling for Pierre.

"I knew this Podunk sheriff wouldn't figure it out." He peeked out the door with the gun on us. "In here!" he hollered to whoever it was looking for him.

"Are you ready?" Robin Foster walked in, and when the light from the outside filtered into the mechanical room, she stopped dead in her tracks. "Oh. Her."

"Robin?" I questioned. "What are you doing?"

"I'm finishing off what I came to Honey Springs to do. After I poisoned Tom with the mushrooms Pierre gave me, which ended up not killing the jerk, I made sure it was all planned out. Angela not being able to let him go and calling him was a perfect setup. I wanted to let him go. Only I am the one with all the money, and if we were to divorce, then he'd have gotten half of my fortune, and well, Alex and I have expensive tastes."

"So when you didn't succeed with the poison, you shot him?" I asked.

"Alex thought he could reason with Tom, so he had Tom come up here to talk, but Tom had already caught on to the fact that Pierre was my friend." She used the word "friend" loosely. "And when you came up here that morning, you kinda ruined it. Tom left the island, and well, as you can see"—she reached up and pulled a wig from Alex's head—"Alex was just Alex on his way over to the island, where he finished off the job."

Arf, arf! Pepper bolted through the door and headed straight over to me.

The door hit Alex in the back, making him jerk forward and drop the gun.

Crissy scurried across the floor to grab it and turn the gun on them.

"Thank goodness." I grabbed Pepper and nuzzled him. "Alex is scared of dogs."

CHAPTER TWENTY

"This coffee shop is in a lovely building, and it has a rustic/retro feel to it. The decor is very nice, they have a great selection of drinks/food, and the staff are very friendly. The young teenager who worked there already had a very clear understanding of the chemical makeup of the perfect coffee bean. When I challenged her on the flavor of the few-hours-old coffee, I could see in her eyes that she realized she'd given me the wrong coffee from the older carafe, but she was bound and determined to keep the reputation of the Bean Hive alive and well.

"The determination in this little town of Honey Springs, Kentucky, is one that will make sure not only the little cozy coffee shop survives but that the Bee Happy Resort makes a mark in the holistic community as a top resort to unwind, relax, and just smell the fresh country air."

The eruption of cheers from the locals who had gathered at the Bean Hive to hear the last review written by Tom Foster in the *Healthy Women's Magazine* was much welcomed.

There was no mention about Tom's murder and how his wife and Alex had conspired to kill him. Or the fact those two would be locked up for the rest of their lives for what they did.

Before I cut the review out of the magazine, I looked at the photo they had in there of Tom. It was of his family including his grandchildren. My heart hurt for them. Losing both parents for very different reasons.

"A round of coffee for everyone!" I yelled since giving away things always made me feel so much better.

Bunny and Birdie eyeballed me with glaring looks.

"Get to work," I said in a chipper voice and pointed to all the freshly brewed carafes. "One for each of you," I told them and gestured for them to take around to each customer for their refill.

"That's great. Congratulations!" Kirk, my ex-husband, walked up to the counter after I'd gotten everyone a round of coffee on the house. "It's a win-win for all."

Patrick took a step forward. I put my hand on him so he didn't do something that would cause him to go to jail.

"He's not worth it." I gave Patrick a hard look telling him not to start anything with Kirk, who'd not been the best husband. "If it weren't for him, we wouldn't be together."

I tried to look for the positive in the situation. It was true. If Kirk hadn't been the jerk he was, then I would've never left our loveless marriage or law firm to move to Honey Springs, where Patrick and I reconnected.

"What are you doing here?" Aunt Maxi shoved past me and Patrick to get her hands on Kirk. "I thought we ran you out of town a year or so ago when you last showed your face around these parts." She snarled. "I outta kick you in the you-know-where, all the way to the border."

"No. No." Crissy Lane rushed up to the counter. "Don't touch him."

She glanced up at Kirk, but he didn't give her a chance to continue.

"I'm Crissy's silent partner, so I'm thinking you better get used to seeing me around here. I've invested a lot of money in Honey Springs." He snorted. "In fact, I'm hoping to get a seat on the town council." He looked at Aunt Maxi. "It seems to me there's been a lot of crime around here the past few years, and we could use some fresh voices on the council."

"Are you trying to say that you are going to try to beat me?" Aunt Maxi had been voted onto the town council every year she'd run. "You can try, but no one has ever beaten me in an election."

"I'm not no one." Kirk turned around and left us standing inside the Bean Hive with our mouths dropped to the ground.

THE END

If you enjoyed reading this book as much as I enjoyed writing it then be sure to return to the Amazon page and leave a review.

Go to Tonyakappes.com for a full reading order of my novels and while there join my newsletter. You can also find links to Facebook, Instagram and Goodreads.

Keep reading for a sneak peek of the next book in the series. Spoonful of Murder is now available to purchase on Amazon.

But wait! Before you flip on through to the yummy recipes, I wanted to answer a question I get from so many readers. Readers want to know if any part of my fictional characters imitate my real life.

I've got a story for y'all. A real story.

Whooo hooo!! I'm so glad we are a week out from last Coffee Chat with Tonya and happy to report the poison ivy is almost gone! But y'all, we got more issues than Time magazine up in our family.

When y'all ask me if my real life ever creeps into books, well...grab your coffee because here is a prime example!

My sweet mom's birthday was over the weekend. Now, I'd already decided me and Rowena was going to stay there for a couple of extra days.

On her birthday, Sunday, Tracy and David were there too, and we were talking about what else...poison ivy! I was telling them how I can't stand not shaving my legs. Mom and Tracy told me they don't shave daily, and I might've curled my nose a smidgen. And apparently it didn't go unnoticed.

I went inside the house to start cooking breakfast for everyone, Mom went up to her room to get her bathing suit on, and Tracy was with me. All the men were already outside on the porch.

The awfulest crash came from upstairs, and my sister tore out of that kitchen like a bat out of hell, and I kept flipping the bacon. My mom had fallen...shaving her legs!

Great. Now it's my fault.

Her wrist was a little stiff, but she kept saying she was fine. We had a great day. We celebrated her birthday, swam, and had cake. When it came time for everyone to leave but me and Ro, I told Mom that she should probably go get an x-ray because her wrist was a little swollen.

After a lot of coaxing, she agreed, and I put my shoes on and told Tracy, David, and Eddy to go on home and we'd call them.

My mama looked me square in the face and said, "You're going with that top knot on your head?"

I said, "Yes."

She sat back down in the chair and said, "I'm not going with you lookin' like that."

"Are you serious?" I asked.

"Yes. I'm dead serious. I'm not going with you looking like that. What if we see someone?" She was serious, y'all!

She protested against my hair!

Now...this is exactly like the southern mamas I write about! I looked at Eddy, and he was laughing. Tracy and David were laughing, and I said, "I can't wait until I tell my coffee chat people about this."

As you can see in the above photo, the before and after photo.

Yep...we went, and she broke her wrist! Can you believe that? We were a tad bit shocked, and I'll probably be staying a few extra days (which will give us even more to talk about over coffee next week).

Oh...we didn't see anyone we knew, so I could've worn my top knot! As I'm writing this, you can bet your bottom dollar my hair is pulled up in my top knot!

Okay, so y'all might be asking why I'm putting this little story in the back of my book. Well, that's a darn tootin' good question.

This is exactly what you can expect when you sign up for my newsletter. There's always something going on in my life that I have to chat with y'all about each Tuesday on Coffee Chat with Tonya. Go to Tonyakappes.com and click on subscribe in the upper right corner to join.

Chapter One of Book Ten
Spoonful of Murder

Even after three years, it never got any easier to hear my alarm go off at four o'clock in the morning. A chill seeped through the small hole at my feet where Pepper, my schnauzer, stuck his nose out from underneath the covers.

"Can't you go in late?" My bedmate, Patrick, rolled over and tugged me into his arms. He snuggled his nose in my neck. "It's cold and snowy."

When Patrick broke the silence of the night, Pepper and Sassy jumped off the bed.

"That's the best time to be open." I gave him a quick kiss before I rolled to the edge of the bed, where I slipped my feet into my cozy slippers. "I'll stoke the fire."

Patrick was already snoring before I could slip my thick robe on over my pajamas and leave our bedroom in our small cabin.

"Okay. Okay." At the door, the tippy-tap of Sassy and Pepper's toenails clicked on the old hardwood floors.

I flipped on the light in the family room to greet the black standard poodle and grey schnauzer, Patrick's children and mine.

They bolted out the door and bounced off the porch into the deep snow. I shook my head and went to get a towel out of the laundry room so I could brush off their paws when they came back in.

They were taking their sweet time, giving me the opportunity to stoke the embers and put some more logs in the woodburning stove. The cabin was small, and the wood burner was the perfect solution to keep the chill out and heat the house quickly. We rarely had to use the gas heat.

"I'm coming."

The dogs scratched at the door.

"Are y'all hungry?"

Both of them were so well trained, they knew to stop on the towel I'd laid in front of the door so I could brush the snow off their furry feet and keep it from balling up.

The inside of the cabin was one big room with a combination kitchen and dining room. The bathroom and laundry room were located in the back, on the far right. A set of stairs led up to one big room we considered our bedroom.

"Good night, Sass." I called for her before she darted back up the stairs to go back to bed with her dad. "Just me and you."

Pepper stayed at my heels as we headed into the kitchen area, where I grabbed a quick scoop of Pepper's kibble to hold him over while I got ready for work. He would get his real breakfast there.

It was our routine, except for Sundays. Like Pepper, the Bean Hive Coffeehouse was my baby, and it was open six days a week. On Sunday after church, I spent most of the afternoon at the Bean Hive, making treats like muffins, casseroles, quiche, cookies, and really anything that I wanted to serve with the coffee.

Plus I'd been really working hard on creating my own coffee with my new roastery equipment. Creating some new Christmas blends had been a lot of fun, and I was excited to serve those this morning. The snow was going to bring in a lot of customers.

Some people might think the opposite, but residents of Honey Springs, Kentucky, loved to get together and gossip—um... talk over coffee.

Let's be clear. When someone consumed something as delicious as coffee, it warmed the body, invigorated the mind, and made one feel good. The Bean Hive created a fun atmosphere for locals to come together and enjoy a cup of coffee while catching up on the day's news, and even the tourists had found their spot there too.

They came in after a day of shopping at the boardwalk's local small businesses next to the coffeehouse to take a load off their feet and enjoy a delicious cup of coffee with a sweet treat. They also took advantage of looking at my corkboard, where the month's local activities were posted.

The board was filled with fun things for the Christmas season. I was looking forward to two events—the Christmas Pawrade, featuring a parade downtown for fur babies, and the Holiday Progressive Dinner, which was a fundraiser for Pet Palace, our local SPCA.

The progressive dinner was new this year, and I was excited about it. Anything I could do for the local animals, I was all over it.

"Slow down," I called to Pepper. He was scarfing down the kibble like it was his last meal. "I'll be back."

I talked to my four-legged companion like he understood me. Most times, I felt like he did.

If I stopped to listen, I could hear Patrick's light snoring. I smiled and flipped on the light in the laundry room, where I kept my uniform for work.

It would inevitably get coffee sloshed on it or food where I'd haphazardly swipe my hands down me, missing the apron I also wore. But it was nice to have a few long-sleeved shirts with the Bean Hive logo on them so I didn't have to think too hard about what to wear.

"You ready?"

Pepper was curled up on his bed in front of the potbelly but perked right up when he heard me get my keys off the hook that hung next to the door.

I took one good look around the cabin before I left, checking that everything was in order and nothing could set the cabin on fire, like the wood-burning stove.

A fire had happened here once. Luckily, I wasn't home, but with my world—Patrick and Sassy—inside, double checking had become part of my morning routine, since they did sleep in a little longer.

"Let's get your sweater on."

Pepper loved his little winter wear. The drive to the boardwalk wasn't too far from here, but the car would be cold, and I just couldn't bear seeing him shiver.

Based on the way he stood there waiting patiently, wagging his tail, he, too, was excited to be warm and toasty.

"There you go." The smile was stuck on my face at the sheer sight of my sweet fur baby. He'd been such a joy and companion.

The moon hung high in the sky, shining the perfect spotlight to our car. It had snowed about two feet over the past couple of days, which I loved. The snow fell at a nice steady pace that allowed just enough snow to cover the grass, trees, and tops of buildings while letting the snowplows keep the streets from getting covered and icy.

This was exactly what Honey Springs needed.

A white Christmas.

"How about some festive tunes?" I asked Pepper, who was already nestled in the passenger seat with his doggy seatbelt clipped. He sat there like a human child, staring out the window.

I flipped the radio on to our local station, which played twenty-four-seven Christmas music this time of year. Just hearing Bing sing "Rudolph" had my fingers drumming and toes tapping, creating a joy that was truly so intense that I knew it was going to be a really great day.

Even though I'd taken the curvy road from the cabin along the banks of Lake Honey Springs, I got through hearing only "Rudolph" and the hippopotamus song, the one in which the kid asked for a hippo for Christmas, before we pulled into the parking lot for the boardwalk.

Lake Honey Springs was really what brought tourists to Honey Springs. People loved to boat, fish, and rent cabins along the area, which made for great business on the boardwalk. That was where the Bean Hive Coffeehouse was located.

My dream job of owning a coffee shop came to life after I'd gotten a divorce from my college sweetheart, who turned out to be a sweetheart to many, and returned to where I'd known comfort and solace as a child.

Right into the arms of my aunt, Maxine Bloom, known around here as Maxi. Honey Springs was also where I'd gotten to visit with Patrick Cane, now my husband, when we were kids. Let's just say that we had feelings for each other from the first day I laid eyes on the scrawny kid.

Fast forward to now. We were happily married, I rented the Bean Hive Coffeehouse space from Aunt Maxi, and my ex, Kirk, was out of our life until recently.

Let's just say he was a new citizen of Honey Springs, and discussing him would require me to indulge in a lot of coffee. I'd yet to have my normal servings.

"Okay. What do you say we get our day started?" I unclipped my seat belt and then Pepper's, grabbed my bag from the back seat, and opened the door.

Pepper delighted so much in the snow. I stood on the bottom step of the stairs that led up to the boardwalk and watched him shove his nose into the snow and come up with a snowball mustache.

"Come on," I called out to him and headed up the steps.

The carriage lights along the boardwalk had twinkling lights roped around the base. The dowel rods had a light-up wreath hanging down. Even the railing of the boardwalk was covered in garland and red bows every few feet.

The Beautification Committee had really gone out of their way to make the boardwalk a new tourist destination for holiday travelers. The annual Christmas Pawrade had become super popular. In this fun little Christmas event, locals dressed up their animals, and we marched around the downtown park.

Since we started it, Christmas in Honey Springs had grown bigger and bigger. The townspeople had added a tree-lighting ceremony, Santa, and vendor booths, just to name a few.

This year, a progressive dinner was added to the list, only it was a little different than the typical progressive dinner held at people's homes. Not only was this progressive dinner meant to raise money, but it was a cool way for local businesses to showcase their shops. During the winter months, the lack of tourism made lean times for small businesses like mine and the other shops on the boardwalk.

Of course I was hosting the after-dinner coffee and desserts in my shop's honor. Aunt Maxi had been the one to really get the dinner together.

The first stop would be for cocktails down at the Watershed Restaurant, located on the lake. The appetizers were taking place at All About the Details, the shop next door to mine. The dinner portion would be hosted at Wild and Whimsy Antiques, though the food was coming from the In and Out Diner. After that, it would be my turn to provide everyone with the best coffee in Kentucky. Or at least in Honey Springs.

Today my agenda was to make as many of the desserts as possible so we only had to pull them out of the refrigerator, flip on the industrial coffee pots, and enjoy the winding down of the evening's festivities.

It didn't take long for Pepper to catch up to me and dart right on past. He knew exactly where to go and wait for me.

"You're so good." I got the coffeeshop keys out of my bag and unlocked the door.

I ran my hand up along the inside wall and felt for the light switch. The inside came to life.

A few café tables dotted the café's interior, as did two long window tables that had stools butted up to them on each side of the front door. The front of the café was a perfect spot to sit, enjoy the beautiful Lake Honey Springs, and sip on your favorite beverage.

Today would be especially gorgeous, thanks to the view of all the fresh snow lying on top of the frozen lake. This was my favorite spot in the coffeehouse, but today I was sure my spot would be glued behind the counter, making all the warm drinks for customers.

On my way back to the kitchen to get the ovens started, I knew Pepper would be ready for something to eat. Since he wasn't allowed to go into the food prep area because of health department regulations, I got a scoop of his kibble and tossed it into his bowl. He could get his belly full, lie down in his doggy bed, and take a nap while I got the coffeehouse ready for the day.

There were so many things to do. Flipping on all the industrial coffee makers was the priority. I walked behind the L-shaped counter and flipped the coffee makers on one by one before I finally walked through the swinging kitchen doors.

I loved the kitchen so much. The big workstation in the middle was perfect! I could mix, stir, add, cut, or do whatever I needed to do to get all the food made. The kitchen had a huge walk-in freezer, a big refrigerator, several shelving units that held all the dry ingredients, and a big pantry I used to store many of the bags of coffee beans I'd ordered from all over the world.

Now that I had my own roastery attached to the kitchen, I made a point of adding roasting fresh beans to my Sunday ritual.

"Yoooo-hoooo!" I heard my one and only employee call from the coffeehouse just as I turned on the ovens.

Soon the door swung open, and there stood Bunny Bowowski. Her little brown coat had great big buttons up the front, and her pillbox hat matched it perfectly. Her brown pocketbook hung from the crease of her arm and swung back and forth.

"You're here early." I was delighted to see her. Bunny was a regular at the coffeehouse when I first opened. Since she'd long been retired, she decided to help me out, which was how she became an employee.

"Floyd said he'd bring me, since he is heading out of town to visit some family this morning." She pulled the bobby pins from her short grey hair and took off the hat. With her mouth, she pulled the pins apart and slipped them on the lacy part of her hat.

"You didn't want to go?" I asked.

"Heavens no." She peeled off her coat and folded it over her arm. "If I did that, Floyd would think I wanted more than companionship. At my age, there's no way I want to take care of a man in the"—her head wobbled from side to side as she came up with a number—"ten years."

"You're going to be alive longer than ten years." I laughed and slipped the muffin tin in the oven. "I'd never figure you to be in your seventies. Ever."

"I attribute that to lots of coffee that keeps me active." She wiggled her brows. "I'll go get the rest of the duties done. I bet we're busy today. Everyone is looking forward to the progressive dinner tonight."

She left me alone in the kitchen. With Bunny being early, it would be a good time for me to get the coffee and treats down to the Cocoon Inn.

Every day, Camey Montgomery, owner of the inn, served Bean Hive Coffeehouse coffee and a breakfast-type item in the Inn's hospitality room. Sometimes if I was running a little behind on getting them to her, she'd send up her husband, Walker Peavler.

Not today. I hurried over to the workstation and grabbed three industrial coffee pots with the cantilever push arm from the shelf underneath.

"How do you think Maxine is going to take the news that All About the Details won't be able to host the appetizers?" Bunny's question caught me off guard.

"What?" I asked and stopped to see her face. "Why isn't Babette doing the appetizers?"

Babette Cliff was the owner of All About the Details. Her store was really an events venue with spectacular views of Lake Honey Springs and the little island across it.

"Fell on ice." Bunny tsked. "I told her just the other day how she needed to invest in some good snow boots to walk from the parking lot because she was going to fall in those heels." Bunny tapped her temple. "I should be reading people's fortunes. The very next day, she slipped on some black ice, and down she went."

Bunny clapped her hands together then slid them apart like one hand was the pavement and the other was Babette slipping on it.

"Broke an ankle." Bunny shook her head and headed behind the bar, where a few of the industrial pots had beeped.

I grabbed a couple of the carafes, set them aside, and replaced them with the ones for the hospitality room at the hotel.

"I think she's going to have a meltdown." Bunny gave a sly smile like she was going to love seeing Aunt Maxi in a little pickle. She walked over, got one carafe from the counter at a time, and took them over to the coffee bar.

"Who?" I asked, not sure if she was talking about Babette.

"Maxine Bloom." Bunny's smile told me she would personally love to see Aunt Maxi squirm, since they weren't the best of friends. She made her way to the end of the counter to the coffee bar.

On each side of the counter was a drink stand. One was a coffee bar with six industrial thermoses containing different blends of my specialty coffees as well as one filled with a decaffeinated blend, even though I never clearly understood the concept of decaffeinated coffee. When I first opened, Aunt Maxi made sure I understood some people drank only the unleaded stuff.

The coffee bar had everything you needed to take a coffee with you, even an honor system that let you pay and go. Honestly, I never truly took the time to see if the honor system worked. In my head and heart, I liked to believe everyone was kind and honest.

"I guess I could do the appetizers then come back for coffee." It was a mere suggestion. The last thing I wanted to do was come up with appetizers today and make sure the coffee beans I'd roasted for the special occasion were perfect.

Out of the corner of my eye, I saw Bunny tidying up everything as she went along.

During her shift, she took pride in making sure everything looked nice and presentable. *This is just like your home. You need to keep it tidy and clean,* she'd told me one time. I've never forgotten those words either.

While Bunny did the straightening and I waited for the coffee to brew for the hotel, I decided to change out the menus.

Instead of investing in a fancy menu or even menu boards that attached to the wall, I'd bought four large chalkboards that hung down from the ceiling over the L-shaped glass countertop.

The first chalkboard menu hung over the pie counter and listed the pies and cookies and their prices. The second menu hung over the tortes and quiches. The third menu, over where the L-shaped counter bent, listed the breakfast casseroles and drinks. Above the other counter, the chalkboard listed lunch options, including soups, as well as catering information.

"I better get rid of these soups if I'm going to make some mini-soup bowls for appetizers. It'll be a good night for them." I swiped the eraser across the chalk board, taking the harvest soup off the menu.

Bunny had moved on to the tea bar to get it ready for the breakfast crowd.

On the opposite end of the counter from the coffee bar stood the tea bar, which offered a nice selection of gourmet, loose-leaf, and cold teas. I'd even gotten a few antique teapots from the Wild and Whimsy Antique Shop, which happened to be the first shop on the boardwalk. If a customer came in and wanted a pot of hot tea, I could fix it for them, or they could fix their own to their taste.

I heard a knock on the window. From the outline of the silhouette, I knew exactly who was trying to wave me over.

Loretta Bebe.

"What on earth is she doing here at this hour?" Bunny glanced back.

"I don't know." I walked over to the door and decided to just flip the sign to Open. If people were milling about, I reckoned I better serve them. "I sure hope Birdie is okay."

"Get in here," I said to Loretta in a gleeful voice, but I knew something was going on to warrant a visit at this time of the morning. "You're gonna get frostbite."

"Are you kidding?" I heard Bunny mutter to herself, only it wasn't so quiet. "She's too mean to get frostbitten."

"Is Birdie okay?" I asked about Loretta's granddaughter, who had been working for me since she moved in with Loretta.

"Oh yes." Loretta kept tilting her head out the door.

"Are you waiting for someone?" I asked and looked out.

"Yes. My new helper dropped me off at the steps and is parking the car. I don't think she's ever been here, love her heart, and I told you were located in the middle of the boardwalk."

"She'll find us," I assured her and shut the door, since it was so cold out. "What's going on?"

"I heard, and I'm here." She tugged on each fingertip of her glove, gracefully slipping her hands out of each one. "I'm here to let you know that I'll be taking over," Loretta said in her slow southern drawl, not making it sound as bad as my gut told me it was.

"Taking over what?" Bunny's interest got piqued.

"The appetizer part of the progressive dinner." She sounded as nonchalant as though the decision was hers to make. "Now, before you two start in on me" —she slapped her gloves in one hand—"I know I wouldn't make no fundraiser about any animals. It's just me, but I like to give money back into our community."

"The animals are part of our community." I walked over to the coffee bar and plucked one of the stacked paper cups to fill for Loretta.

When you were the barista of a coffeehouse and had regular customers, you could make their orders in your sleep. Loretta liked her coffee with two light creamers, one vanilla creamer, and two packs of sugar.

"I am not here to argue with you, Roxanne." Loretta batted her fake lashes a few times before she took the cup from me. Instead of saying, "Thank you for fixing this amazing cup of coffee for me," she continued, "What's done is done. The fundraiser is set, and I've come to just turn the other cheek. This year." She let me know in her own subtle way that she would make sure to intervene for next year. "All under the bridge. What we have to deal with is the here and now, and right now I'm stepping up to the plate to offer my services."

The fundraiser was Aunt Maxi's, and if Aunt Maxi was here, there'd be no way in H-E-double-hockey-sticks that she'd let Loretta participate.

"Before you poo-poo the idea"—the bangles of her wrist jingled and jangled when she held up her finger to stop me from talking—"I'm going to give you my idea. Now..." She moved past me to walk deeper into the coffeehouse. "I've decided to host it at the Cocoon Hotel. I've already gotten confirmation with Camey Montgomery to use the appetizers. The only difference is that I'll be providing the appetizers instead of Babette."

"I'm gonna need to take some Tums tonight," Bunny murmured on her way past me back to the coffee bar. There, she cleaned up the leftover sprinkles of sugar that'd found their way out of their packet when I opened them to stir into Loretta's coffee.

The bell over the door dinged. A frazzled, snow-covered young woman walked in.

"Good." Loretta called to her. "You found it. Lana, Roxy, Roxy, Lana." Loretta waved a finger in introduction between us.

"Let me get you a coffee, Lana," I said to her when I noticed her shivering jawline.

When I reached for another cup, Bunny smacked my hands away.

"I'll fix it," she snapped, knowing full well that I'd make another mess she'd feel like she had to clean up.

Poor Bunny spent most of her shift cleaning up after people. I just let her do what made her happy.

"Lana, take off that coat and go stand in front of the fireplace. I'm sure Roxy is about to start one." Loretta had a way of giving orders indirectly. "I'll be right back."

Loretta excused herself to the bathroom.

"Lana, what do you like in your coffee, dear?" Bunny asked Lana.

"How did Loretta take hers?" she asked.

"Don't you mind Low-retta," Bunny said, her voice deepening on the end syllable of Loretta's name.

Loretta Bebe was somewhat hard to deal with in the community. She was a little forward and, well, bossy. She never bothered me any, but she did bother a lot of people. If it weren't for Loretta's volunteering, things would probably take a lot longer to get done around Honey Springs. She was not only the president of the Southern Women's Club but also a big member of the local church, which put you right on top of the society list, even though she did exaggerate about her year-round suntan.

Loretta claimed she was part Cherokee, and, well, that could have been true, since the Cherokee people were indigenous to Honey Springs, but it didn't coincide with her using Lisa Stalh's tanning bed a few times a week to keep her skin's pigment. And if you asked Loretta about it, she'd get all torn up. So we just brushed the subject underneath the rug like most secrets around here.

Funny thing I'd found out since I moved to Honey Springs—those really dark secrets were like dust bunnies. They found their way into the light when they lurked too long in the shadows.

"Black is good." Lana offered a sweet smile.

"Let me get a fire started." I had Lana move away from the front of the fireplace so I could throw in a starter log. "Pepper is excited." I laughed when he ran over and got into his dog bed.

"He's cute." She smiled.

"How long have you worked for Loretta?" I started some chitchat while the flame took.

Bunny walked behind the counter and tried to secretly write a text message on her phone. She wasn't foolin' me any. I'd bet she was texting Mae Belle Donovan, her partner in crime.

"A few weeks. She keeps me on my toes." Lana rubbed her hands together. "I'm there to cook and clean up a bit. She's so busy with all her volunteer work, and now she's offered to make the cheese balls."

She abruptly stopped talking when the handle of the bathroom door jiggled as if Loretta couldn't get it open.

"I bet she has." Bunny's flat voice and ticked-up brow made Lana smile even bigger. "What are y'all doing out so early?" Bunny handed Lana a cup of coffee.

"She put a call in to the owners down at the Wild and Whimsy about a piece missing from the Christmas china she'd bought from them. They told her they found it in another box and were holding it for her." Lana sipped on the coffee and took a seat on the hearth, giving me just enough space to lay a few of the seasoned pieces of firewood on the starter log.

"Where's my cup?" Loretta had joined us again, this time without her coat. She tapped her maroon fingernail on her big-faced watch. "I'm expected at Wild and Whimsy when they open, so we need to make this a quick chat."

"We are chatting?" I asked and glanced up at Bunny, who was pointing to where Loretta had set her cup down previously.

Bunny snarled and rolled her eyes.

"I know that your aunt is going to be all sort of, well, let's just be honest, shall we?" Loretta eased down on the edge of one of the couches, crossing her legs at the ankles like a good southern woman would sit.

"Nothing but around here," I said, giving the fire a little stoke with the poker.

"You and I both know Maxine has her opinions of me, and that's all fine and dandy, but she's going to have to put those out of her way for the good of the community. We need someone to take over the appetizers, and I've stepped up to the plate."

"Did Maxine ask you to do anything for the progressive dinner?" Bunny asked a question we all knew the answers to.

Loretta's shoulders peeled down from her ears, her head tilted and her face flat when she looked at Bunny.

"Maybe she wants you to enjoy it," Bunny suggested. All of us in the room, including Lana, knew the truth. Again, we were sweeping it under the rug, so to speak.

Here was the strange part. Bunny seemed to be taking up for Aunt Maxi, which told me she didn't want Loretta to do the appetizers either. I snickered.

"Anyways, I just wanted you to know that I've once again saved the event." Loretta was also good at taking credit where it wasn't hers to take. Her quirks were very entertaining to me. Not so much to Aunt Maxi.

"I guess I'm not sure where our visit this early comes in?" I asked.

"Honestly, Roxy." Loretta uncrossed her ankles and sighed, carefully putting the mug on the coffee table in front of her. "I'm going to need you to back me up because I'm sure when Maxine Bloom hears that I've had to save her once again, she'll be a little perturbed."

"And you think I can calm her down if she is? Then you don't know her too well." I snickered, knowing Aunt Maxi would fume once she got word, and trust me, she was going to get word before the sun popped up in about an hour and a half.

The faint sound of a ding caused Pepper to lift his head.

"The ovens are preheated. I've got to get some items cooked before we really open." It was my way of excusing myself.

"We have to get going anyways. Beverly is going to meet us down there so I can get that platter for one of my famous cheese balls." Loretta stood up. "Lana."

"Thanks for the coffee and the warm fire. I'll be back." Lana helped Loretta with her coat.

"I hope you do." I felt sorry for Lana. She was at Loretta's mercy.

Bunny and I walked them over to the door.

"From what I hear, Loretta can't keep a helper. How long do you think that girl will last?" Bunny asked.

"Maybe Lana will last. She's got a little gumption. I do know one thing." I watched out the door as Loretta and Lana hurried down the boardwalk. "Aunt Maxi sure is going to be mad."

"Mmm-hmmm, she sure is. And I thought this was going to be a good day." Bunny sighed, breathing into her coffee mug before she took a sip.

Unfortunately, Bunny was right. I could feel the chill in my bones.

Spoonful of Murder is now available to purchase on Amazon.

RECIPES FROM THE BEAN HIVE

Coffee Tip
Strawberry and Cream Donuts

Coffee Tip

No one likes bitter coffee. No one makes coffee the same either. Even if you buy the best coffee maker, some store bought coffees come with a bitter taste.

I have the solution! A pinch of salt. That's it. How simple?

All you have to do is a pinch of salt to the coffee carafe or even just the grounds to get the best tasting coffee!

Enjoy~

Roxy Bloom

Strawberry and Cream Donuts

Ingredients for the Dough

- 2 envelopes active dry yeast
- ¼ cup warm water
- 1/3 cup shortening
- 1/2 cup white sugar
- 2 large eggs
- 1 3/4 cups warm milk
- 1 tsp. salt
- 5 cups all-purpose flour
- 1 quart vegetable oil for frying ~ yes, these are fried but sooooo good!

Ingredients for the Glaze

- 1/3 cup butter
- 1 1/2 tsp. vanilla
- 2 cups powdered sugar
- 1/4 cup warm milk

Directions

1. Sprinkle yeast over warm water and let it sit for about five minutes. It's done when it's foamy.
2. Pour the mixture in a large mixing bowl and add shortening, sugar, eggs & milk.
3. Mix together until incorporated.
4. Add the salt and 2 cups of flour and mix for 3 mins on a low speed.
5. Slowly add the remaining 3 cups of flour at ½ a cup at a time while you mix.
6. When dough no longer sticks to the bowl it's done.

7. Transfer the dough to a clean floured surface then knead the dough for about 5-6 mins until it becomes smooth and stretchy.
8. Grease a bowl and put the dough in it. You will need to cover it with a towel or plastic wrap, then put it in a warm place so the dough will rise. It needs to double the size and no finger indents when you touch it.
9. Roll the dough out on your floured surface to about 1/2" thick.
10. Use a floured donut cutter to cut the donuts.
11. You will need to cover them again with a towel because they will need to double in size again.
12. This is a good time to go ahead and make the glaze.
13. Mix ¼ cup strawberry jam ¼ cup heavy whipping cream in a saucepan and put on medium heat.
14. Mix in the vanilla extract & powdered sugar until it's nice and smooth.
15. Turn off the heat and mix until the icing is thin but not watery. Pour into a measuring cup and set aside.
16. In a deep-fryer or large cast iron skillet, heat oil to 350 degrees F.
17. CAREFULLY place 3-4 donuts in the hot oil at a time using a slotted spoon or spatula.
18. In about 1 minute, the donuts will begin to brown, turn them over and let them brown another minute on the bottom turn them
19. Remove them from the hot oil, and drain on cooling rack.
20. While still hot, dip donuts into glaze. Place back on rack to drain extra glaze. Or you can drizzle the glaze over top of them.

Enjoy!

Frothy Foul Play Book Club Discussion Questions

This instalment is centered around the new holistic spa opening on the island called Bee Happy Resort owned by Chrissy Lane.

Have you ever gone to a Holistic spa? Or even on a Holistic retreat?

Loretta's granddaughter Birdie comes to stay, and Roxy gets roped into hiring her, but she seems like a natural. I personally loved the interaction between Roxy and Birdie.

what were your thoughts about Birdie, and do you think she will be a good addition to the Bean Hive family?

There seemed to be a bit or confusion as to where Tom Foster and his wife were staying while in town. Roxy thought they were staying at the Cocoon Hotel, but Aunt Maxi reveals they are staying at her Air B&B.

What were your thoughts?

Aunt Maxi suddenly arrives at the Bean Hive with Tom's wife Robin. Once she becomes Robin's legal council, accusations start flying!

The spouse is always a suspect, but now several come to light. When test results show Tom was also poisoned, Birdie becomes a suspect.

Did you think Birdie had anything to do with his poisoning?

When Roxy takes coffee and treats to the Cocoon, she finds Sheriff Spencer Shepherd arresting Angela with the missing cell phone in her possession. Angela denies she took his phone and that someone was framing he.

Did you believe her?

Not only was there one killer but TWO! I had my suspicions about one of them but not the other.

Were you caught off guard like I was?

I love how Roxy brought everyone together at the end of the story. Now the finale of the book!!!

When we found out who Chrissy has as a silent partner in Bee Happy Resort... Did your jaw drop when you found out like mine did?

What was one of your favorite parts of this book?

BOOKS BY TONYA
SOUTHERN HOSPITALITY WITH A SMIDGEN OF HOMICIDE

Camper & Criminals Cozy Mystery Series

All is good in the camper-hood until a dead body shows up in the woods.

BEACHES, BUNGALOWS, AND BURGLARIES
DESERTS, DRIVING, & DERELICTS
FORESTS, FISHING, & FORGERY
CHRISTMAS, CRIMINALS, AND CAMPERS
MOTORHOMES, MAPS, & MURDER
CANYONS, CARAVANS, & CADAVERS
HITCHES, HIDEOUTS, & HOMICIDES
ASSAILANTS, ASPHALT & ALIBIS
VALLEYS, VEHICLES & VICTIMS
SUNSETS, SABBATICAL AND SCANDAL
TENTS, TRAILS AND TURMOIL
KICKBACKS, KAYAKS, AND KIDNAPPING
GEAR, GRILLS & GUNS
EGGNOG, EXTORTION, AND EVERGREEN
ROPES, RIDDLES, & ROBBERIES
PADDLERS, PROMISES & POISON
INSECTS, IVY, & INVESTIGATIONS
OUTDOORS, OARS, & OATH
WILDLIFE, WARRANTS, & WEAPONS
BLOSSOMS, BBQ, & BLACKMAIL
LANTERNS, LAKES, & LARCENY
JACKETS, JACK-O-LANTERN, & JUSTICE
SANTA, SUNRISES, & SUSPICIONS
VISTAS, VICES, & VALENTINES
ADVENTURE, ABDUCTION, & ARREST
RANGERS, RVS, & REVENGE
CAMPFIRES, COURAGE & CONVICTS

TRAPPING, TURKEY & THANKSGIVING
GIFTS, GLAMPING & GLOCKS
ZONING, ZEALOTS, & ZIPLINES
HAMMOCKS, HANDGUNS, & HEARSAY
QUESTIONS, QUARRELS, & QUANDARY
WITNESS, WOODS, & WEDDING
ELVES, EVERGREENS, & EVIDENCE
MOONLIGHT, MARSHMALLOWS, & MANSLAUGHTER
BONFIRE, BACKPACKS, & BRAWLS

Killer Coffee Cozy Mystery Series

Welcome to the Bean Hive Coffee Shop where the gossip is just as hot as the coffee.

SCENE OF THE GRIND
MOCHA AND MURDER
FRESHLY GROUND MURDER
COLD BLOODED BREW
DECAFFEINATED SCANDAL
A KILLER LATTE
HOLIDAY ROAST MORTEM
DEAD TO THE LAST DROP
A CHARMING BLEND NOVELLA (CROSSOVER WITH MAGICAL CURES MYSTERY)
FROTHY FOUL PLAY
SPOONFUL OF MURDER
BARISTA BUMP-OFF
CAPPUCCINO CRIMINAL
MACCHIATO MURDER

Holiday Cozy Mystery Series

CELEBRATE GOOD CRIMES!

FOUR LEAF FELONY

MOTHER'S DAY MURDER
A HALLOWEEN HOMICIDE
NEW YEAR NUISANCE
CHOCOLATE BUNNY BETRAYAL
FOURTH OF JULY FORGERY
SANTA CLAUSE SURPRISE
APRIL FOOL'S ALIBI

Kenni Lowry Mystery Series

Mysteries so delicious it'll make your mouth water and leave you hankerin' for more.

FIXIN' TO DIE
SOUTHERN FRIED
AX TO GRIND
SIX FEET UNDER
DEAD AS A DOORNAIL
TANGLED UP IN TINSEL
DIGGIN' UP DIRT
BLOWIN' UP A MURDER
HEAVENS TO BRIBERY

Magical Cures Mystery Series

Welcome to Whispering Falls where magic and mystery collide.

A CHARMING CRIME
A CHARMING CURE
A CHARMING POTION (novella)
A CHARMING WISH
A CHARMING SPELL
A CHARMING MAGIC
A CHARMING SECRET
A CHARMING CHRISTMAS (novella)

A CHARMING FATALITY
A CHARMING DEATH (novella)
A CHARMING GHOST
A CHARMING HEX
A CHARMING VOODOO
A CHARMING CORPSE
A CHARMING MISFORTUNE
A CHARMING BLEND (CROSSOVER WITH A KILLER COFFEE COZY)
A CHARMING DECEPTION

Mail Carrier Cozy Mystery Series

Welcome to Sugar Creek Gap where more than the mail is being delivered.

STAMPED OUT
ADDRESS FOR MURDER
ALL SHE WROTE
RETURN TO SENDER
FIRST CLASS KILLER
POST MORTEM
DEADLY DELIVERY
RED LETTER SLAY

About Tonya

Tonya has written over 100 novels, all of which have graced numerous bestseller lists, including the USA Today. *Best known for stories charged with emotion and humor and filled with flawed characters, her novels have garnered reader praise and glowing critical reviews. She lives with her husband and a very spoiled rescue cat named Ro. Tonya grew up in the small southern Kentucky town of Nicholasville. Now that her four boys are grown men, Tonya writes full-time in her camper she calls her SHAMPER (she-camper).*

Learn more about her be sure to check out her website tonyakappes.com. Find her on Facebook, Twitter, BookBub, and Instagram

Sign up to receive her newsletter, where you'll get free books, exclusive bonus content, and news of her releases and sales.

If you liked this book, please take a few minutes to leave a review now! Authors (Tonya included) really appreciate this, and it helps draw more readers to books they might like. Thanks!

Cover artist: Mariah Sinclair: The Cover Vault

Made in the USA
Las Vegas, NV
25 September 2024

95680231R00272